OVID

METAMORPHOSES

BOOK VIII

OVID

METAMORPHOSES

BOOK VIII

EDITED WITH AN INTRODUCTION
AND COMMENTARY
BY
A. S. HOLLIS
FELLOW OF KEBLE COLLEGE
OXFORD

OXFORD
AT THE CLARENDON PRESS

Oxford University Press, Walton Street, Oxford OX2 6DP

Oxford New York Toronto
Delhi Bombay Calcutta Madras Karachi
Kuala Lumpur Singapore Hong Kong Tokyo
Nairobi Dar es Salaam Cape Town
Melbourne Auckland Madrid

and associated companies in
Berlin Ibadan

Oxford is a trade mark of Oxford University Press

Published in the United States by
Oxford University Press Inc., New York

British Library Cataloguing in Publication Data
Data available

Library of Congress Cataloging in Publication Data
Data available
ISBN 0-19-814460-1

5 7 9 10 8 6

Printed in Hong Kong

PREFACE

THIS edition grew out of an Oxford B.Phil. thesis, covering nearly half the book, which was presented in 1964. Since then I have filled in the missing parts while rewriting and expanding my earlier work, for three years at St. Andrews and then back in Oxford.

My thanks are due first to Mr. R. G. M. Nisbet, who supervised the B.Phil. and has continued to offer help and encouragement. I owe an equal debt to Professor Gordon Williams for reading the whole commentary in its first draft and suggesting many fresh lines of thought. Dr. M. Winterbottom gave valuable advice on matters of presentation; some of my other obligations are noted in their place. My wife accepted with good grace the task of typing the manuscript; and finally I must pay tribute to the vigilant proof-readers of the Clarendon Press.

The work has been shaped primarily for undergraduates, but I hope that it will also interest professional scholars. With the latter in mind I have added quite a full *index locorum*, which may help, for example, those studying the links between Hellenistic and Roman poetry.

A. S. HOLLIS

Keble College, Oxford
October 1969

Addition to Preface

Reprinting of this book has allowed brief additional bibliography and notes (pp. 159–60). It has not, however, been possible to alter the Introduction or Commentary so as to take proper account of reviews (e.g. by Kenney in *CR* NS 22 [1972], 214–16), suggestions kindly sent to me by colleagues, or important works published since 1970 (e.g. Bömer's Commentary, and Lyne's edition of the *Ciris*).

Keble College, Oxford   A.S.H.
February 1983

CONTENTS

LIST OF PLATES

INTRODUCTION

Composition of the Metamorphoses

OVID seems to have been working on his *Metamorphoses* from
the turn of the era, when he was in his mid-forties. By that time
he had exhausted his vein of love-poetry. The *Amores* had been
followed by the *Heroides*, and three mock-didactic poems,
Medicamina Faciei Femineae, *Ars Amatoria*, and *Remedia
Amoris*; then he had treated the rather limited material from
every possible angle. So, in spite of his brilliant success, Ovid
would naturally wish to attempt something bigger.

We can trace several earlier gestures towards more serious
poetry. These must be taken with a pinch of salt; no one should
argue from *Amores* i. 1. 1–2 or ii. 1. 11–12 that Ovid had even
tried to write a *Gigantomachia*. But his words at the conclusion
of the *Amores* 'pulsanda est magnis area maior equis' (iii. 15.
18) may be meant sincerely, though they were for the moment
fruitless. And the hope to write tragedy (*Am.* iii. 1. 69–70) need
not be thought vain; we know the high reputation of Ovid's
Medea.

After deciding to compose a large-scale hexameter work, the
poet still had various alternatives. Troy or Thebes were con-
ventional epic subjects, though at this date it required a Virgil's
genius to bring them to life. The old Roman tradition was to
write either *Annales* or poems on individual wars—the latter
were not so out-dated; for instance, the defeat of Sextus
Pompey had evoked a *Bellum Siculum* from Cornelius Severus.
But all these possibilities were alien to the nature and talent of
our poet. His final choice, which should earn our gratitude, had
been prefigured by the charming mythological diversions in the
Ars Amatoria.

During the years from (*circa*) A.D. 1 Ovid was engaged on
both the *Metamorphoses* and the *Fasti*. Then in A.D. 8 came

the great catastrophe of his life and banishment to Tomis in
Rumania. Ovid tells us himself about the state of the *Meta-
morphoses* at this time (*Tristia* i. 7. 13 ff.):

> carmina mutatas hominum dicentia formas
>   infelix domini quod fuga rupit opus.
> haec ego discedens, sicut bene multa meorum,
>   ipse mea posui maestus in igne manu. . . .
> (21)   vel quod eram Musas, ut crimina nostra, perosus,
>   vel quod adhuc crescens et rude carmen erat.
> quae quoniam non sunt penitus sublata, sed exstant
>   (pluribus exemplis scripta fuisse reor),
> nunc precor ut vivant, et non ignava legentem
>   otia delectent admoneantque mei.

To burn the manuscript was a somewhat melodramatic gesture;
so Plato had burnt a tragedy with the words "Ἥφαιστε πρόμολ'
ὧδε· Πλάτων νύ τι σεῖο χατίζει (parodying *Iliad* xviii. 392), and
Virgil's example in forbidding publication of the *Aeneid* was
evident. Perhaps Ovid knew that copies had been made. He
continues (27–30):

> nec tamen illa legi poterunt patienter ab ullo,
>   nesciet his summam siquis abesse manum.
> ablatum mediis opus est incudibus illud,
>   defuit et scriptis ultima lima meis.

This claim is understandable; no doubt Ovid would have liked
time for a final revision. But any changes could hardly have
been extensive. Some scholars detect a loss of quality in the
last few books, but, if allowed, this may as well be due to
flagging interest as to a lack of polish.

Double Recension

One notorious problem is particularly relevant to bk. viii. In
several places the MSS. seem to offer alternative versions;
should one of them always be deleted, or could they sometimes
both be genuinely Ovidian? It has been argued that Ovid
revised the *Metamorphoses* in exile. But that seems unlikely;

the famous lines on Actaeon (iii. 141–2) arise naturally from their context, even if the poet used similar language and the same mythological example for his own case (*Tristia* ii. 105 ff., cf. *Tristia* iii. 5. 49 ff.). Also the praise of Tiberius (xv. 836–7) could well have been written before A.D. 8. Certainly the passages where our MSS. give alternative versions have no relevance to Ovid's exile.

It may be thought suspicious that some second versions in the MSS. are demonstrably spurious (see on lines 696–8)—also that more than half the instances occur in this most celebrated eighth book. But in certain cases, notably at 596 ff. of our book, the longer version appearing in the so-called 'deteriores' is eminently Ovidian, and even superior to the shorter one. This question cannot be settled definitely. At most we may hold that in specific places neither version can be rejected on grounds of style, and I agree with such a position, adopted by many modern scholars. A possible cause of the doublets is that the 'several copies' made at Rome (*Tristia* i. 7. 24 above) should have varied, as representing different stages of the author's rough draft.

The Nature of the Poem

(a) 'Carmen Perpetuum'

In his invocation of the gods (i. 3–4) Ovid prays to write a 'perpetuum . . . carmen' from the beginning of the world to his own time:

> . . . primaque ab origine mundi
> ad mea *perpetuum* deducite tempora *carmen.*

This technical term is no doubt connected with Callimachus' ἄεισμα διηνεκές in the celebrated *Aetia*-prologue (fr. 1. 3 Pfeiffer). Now the epithets διηνεκές and 'perpetuum' do not specify the exact kind of continuity involved, whether thematic or temporal; that must be gleaned from the context. Callimachus meant a long 'cyclic' epic, as against his own preference for short epics ('epyllia') such as the *Hecale*, hardly more than

a thousand lines long,[1] or stories linked together (the *Aetia*).
But Ovid appears by 'perpetuum carmen' to denote a narrative
unbroken in time from the beginning to his own day, rather
than any unity of theme, or any artificial unity gained through
linking episodes. Horace throws more light upon the term (*Odes*
i. 7. 5–6):

> sunt quibus unum opus est intactae Palladis urbem
> carmine perpetuo celebrare . . .

There were Hellenistic poems which probably dealt with
individual states from the earliest times, e.g. the *Mopsopia* of
Euphorion (about Attica, and perhaps in Horace's mind, cf. fr.
34 Powell), or the *Thessalica* of Rhianus (cf. fr. 25 Powell). We
know little about these works, but they could have been partial
ancestors of the *Metamorphoses*. Such poems may have gained
popularity after Callimachus, so accounting for the shift of
meaning from the *Aetia*-prologue's ἄεισμα διηνεκές to 'carmen
perpetuum' in Horace and Ovid.

(b) The Linking of Stories

Yet of course there is no simple progress in time through the
Metamorphoses. To give the poem any coherence at all was
a severe problem, and the devices with which Ovid joins epi-
sodes are legion. Sometimes these are brilliant, at others the
invention wears a little thin; so there is justification both for
the bare tolerance of Quintilian (4. 1. 77), speaking of those
who seek applause by clever transitions, '. . . ut Ovidius
lascivire in Metamorphosesin solet, quem tamen excusare
necessitas potest, res diversissimas in speciem unius corporis
colligentem', and for the greater enthusiasm of a writer in
1560:[2]

> Hys tales do ioyne in suche a goodly wyse
> That one doth hange upon anothers ende.

---

[1] An unpublished Oxyrhynchus Papyrus shows that Eratosthenes'
Hermes contained between 600 and 700 lines.

[2] From the *Moralization* of the anonymous *The Fable of Ovid treating
of Narcissus*, cf. C. S. Lewis, *English Literature in the Sixteenth Century*
(Oxford, 1954), p. 250.

Ovid owes a general debt here to Callimachus' *Aetia*, in which bks. i–ii had their stories linked together. But we cannot say whether Callimachus expended such hair-raising ingenuity on his transitions; fr. 178 Pfeiffer (with which L. P. Wilkinson compares *Met.* vii. 670 ff.) contains a most elaborate introduction to an Ician tale, but there is no clue how this may have been linked with the preceding aetion. A closer parallel with neoteric poetry can, however, be drawn; one regular feature of the 'epyllion' was a subsidiary myth woven cleverly into the main narrative, and some episodes in the *Metamorphoses* exhibit this structure, notably the Io-story in bk. i.

(c) The Metamorphoses and Epic

A question may be raised whether the *Metamorphoses* should be considered an epic. We should realize first of all that the genesis of the poem was somewhat different. As Professor Sullivan remarks, it sprang rather from a Hellenistic substitute for epic; one could not call, e.g., the *Heteroeumena* of Nicander (see later paragraphs) an epic. There was no doubt a vast difference between Nicander and Ovid, but, in my opinion, the term 'epic' says little about the *Metamorphoses*, and may cause more misunderstanding than enlightenment. Certainly the work is composed on a grand scale; some episodes are of traditionally heroic subject-matter, though Ovid either will not or cannot sustain the heroic manner for long. A factor on which Professor Brooks Otis lays much stress is continuity of narrative (*Ovid as an Epic Poet*, e.g., pp. 64–5); this indeed distinguishes the *Metamorphoses* from epyllion, and, to a lesser extent, from elegiac style, but is hardly enough alone to produce an epic quality. We may also grant a wide use of Virgilian language and conventions—the latter often twisted in an idiosyncratic way, as Brooks Otis well illustrates.

Yet stylistic features which are uniform throughout the poem, so making it 'epic', tend to vanish into thin air. Richard Heinze's comparison of the Persephone-legend in the *Fasti* (iv. 417–620) and *Metamorphoses* (v. 341–661) is famous (*Ovids elegische Erzählung* [1919], reprinted in *Vom Geist des Römertums* [1960], pp. 308–403), and his distinctions (e.g. concerning the treatment of the gods) have some validity. But who could establish a difference in style between the Daedalus-myth in the *A.A.* (ii. 21–96) and *Met.* (viii. 183–235)? And Ovid's touch is equally light in other sections of the *Metamorphoses*.

Far more striking than any uniformity of tone is the extraordinary variety of styles within this poem. We find severely 'epic' portions such as the Calydonian Boar-hunt, a tragic ἀγών between Ajax and Odysseus, Euripidean monologues, some philosophy with a faint Lucretian tinge, and one pleasant parody of Theocritus; almost every type of poetry had left a mark on Ovid's receptive mind. Obviously some styles and themes were more congenial than others, and better suited to his own talent; often we feel that he is wearing a mask, and all his cleverness does not carry conviction. But he succeeded remarkably in exhibiting the πολυείδεια of the great Alexandrian Callimachus (see fr. 203 Pf. and Diegesis) in a single work and metre. And yet this poem is not just a fragmented series of episodes. There is a definite unity, given by the author's personality, which obtrudes time and time again with perhaps a particularly sharp visual detail, a comment on the action, some piece of cleverness, or a witty observation of human (and divine) foibles. Ovid may lack the astringency of Callimachus, but his mixture of simplicity and sophistication can still be most attractive. It is unlikely that the regaining of any lost work would rob the *Metamorphoses* of its unique character. Single features can be paralleled, but scope, variety, and richness all place Ovid's poem in a class by itself. No wonder, then, if it will not fit easily into conventional literary categories.

(d) Architectonic Schemes

The bewildering variety of stories which tumble over each other has naturally brought efforts at systematization. One may mark off chronological divisions, or form sections round a hero (e.g. Cadmus, Theseus, Heracles) or a state (Thebes,

Troy, Rome). The results are helpful, but not very startling—
any attempt to progress beyond the most general divisions
usually ends in confusion. More ambitious and challenging is
the scheme of Brooks Otis (*Ovid as an Epic Poet*, pp. 84–5). He
is concerned with motifs and style rather than with chronology
or genealogy, and claims to detect a development of motifs
through four sections entitled The Divine Comedy (bks. i–ii), The
Avenging Gods (bks. iii–vi. 400), The Pathos of Love (bks. vi.
401–xi), and Rome and the Deified Ruler (bks. xii–xv). In my
opinion Brooks Otis does not quite establish the four sections,
and so the implied development is weakened. Occasionally, too,
he becomes over-subtle; but much in his discussion of parallel
and contrasted motifs seems both new and valuable. Even an
observant reader might well miss such larger links, but it is
a mistake to think that the *Metamorphoses* can reveal nothing
to deeper consideration.

Transformation

Changes of shape figure prominently in the primitive religion
and fable of many cultures (see Stith Thompson, *Motif Index of
Folk-Literature*, s.v. Transformation). Why this should have
been so is a question outside my province. But it is possible
that gods who change into animals may originally have been
identified with those animals. And one can see how the shape
of a rock or tree, the cry and behaviour of animals or birds,
might seem so nearly human as to suggest a tale of meta-
morphosis. At any rate, transformations are found in Greek
poetry from the earliest times; in Homer the gods change into
particular men and women, or even birds, and transform both
human beings and inanimate objects. Such transformation is
quite as common in the *Iliad* as in the *Odyssey*, though the
latter includes characters like Proteus and Circe who more
obviously have links with folk-tale.

A considerable part in the crystallizing of Greek mythology
was played by the poetry ascribed to Hesiod, and there too

metamorphosis was common. One example is the gift of
Poseidon by which Periclymenus could assume any shape (fr.
33a. 14–17 Merkelbach–West):

> ἄλλοτε μὲν γὰρ ἐν ὀρνίθεσσι φάνεσκεν
> αἰετός, ἄλλοτε δ' αὖ γινέσκετο, θαῦμα ἰδέσθαι,
> μύρμηξ, ἄλλοτε δ' αὖτε μελισσέων ἀγλαὰ φῦλα,
> ἄλλοτε δεινὸς ὄφις καὶ ἀμείλιχος.

Mestra, the versatile daughter of Erysicthon whom we meet
in this book of the *Metamorphoses*, already appeared in the
Hesiodic *Catalogue of Women* (frs. 43–5 M.–W.), and Ovid
almost certainly used the Hesiodic account (see on 738 ff.).

At a later date two important developments occur, first the
collection of tales with metamorphoses, and secondly an inter-
est in the actual mechanism of change. The latter may be due
to the rationalistic attitude deriving from the sophists and
Euripides, as L. P. Wilkinson accepts (*Ovid Recalled*, p. 160).
Noteworthy is Euripides, fr. 930 N². , surely describing Cadmus
as he changes into a snake:

> οἴμοι, δράκων μου γίγνεται τὸ ἥμισυ·
> τέκνον, περιπλάκηθι τῷ λοιπῷ πατρί.

This fragment perhaps came from a satyric play, and the
technique of interrupting the metamorphosis when still in-
complete prefigures Ovid; indeed Ovid is clearly influenced by
Euripides at *Met.* iv. 583–5:

> 'accede, o coniunx, accede miserrima', dixit,
> 'dumque aliquid superest de me, me tange, manumque
> accipe, dum manus est, dum non totum occupat anguis.'

Observe particularly how 'dumque aliquid superest de me'
picks up τῷ λοιπῷ. From Sophocles' *Inachus*, almost certainly
a satyric play, comes *P.Oxy.* 2369, fr. 1, col. 2 (cf. fr. 279 Pear-
son), where the poet graphically describes Io turning into
a cow. The effect is no doubt meant to be humorous; again one
is reminded of Ovid (compare Io's reverse transformation at
Met. i. 738–42).

So even in the fifth century we can find descriptions of gradual or incomplete metamorphosis. They became commoner during the Hellenistic age, the locus classicus being Apollonius' picture of Jason sowing the dragon's teeth, and slaying the armed men as they arose in their different stages of development (*Arg.* iii. 1381–98, cf. *Met.* iii. 106–10 of Cadmus). Lucretius (ii. 702–3) was obviously familiar with such poetic transformations in mentioning among impossibilities 'et altos / interdum ramos egigni corpore vivo' (cf. Baucis and Philemon, *Met.* viii. 714 ff.), and Horace's fantasy of himself turning into a swan (*Odes* ii. 20. 9–12) shows clear Hellenistic influence. Wilkinson also gives examples of incomplete metamorphosis from Hellenistic-inspired painting (*Ovid Recalled*, p. 160). At least in Lucian's time Daphne was a favourite subject: τοιαύτην παρ' ἡμῖν τὴν Δάφνην γράφουσιν ἄρτι τοῦ Ἀπόλλωνος καταλαμβάνοντος ἀποδενδρουμένην (*Vera Historia* i. 8, cf. *Met.* i. 555–6).

Interest in detailed metamorphosis may be considered a somewhat jaded taste, but it goes with the greater psychological awareness of Hellenistic writers. Herman Fränkel, whose approach is perhaps most fruitful here, says: 'The theme gave ample scope for displaying the phenomena of insecure and fleeting identity, of a self divided in itself or spilling over into another self' (*Ovid, a Poet between Two Worlds*, p. 99).

Collections of tales involving metamorphosis seem to begin in the third century B.C. One of the earliest may have been the Ὀρνιθογονία of Boeus or Boeo (cf. Powell, *Collectanea Alexandrina*, pp. 24–5), a poem in at least two books which dealt with the transformation of human beings into birds. The author is a shadowy figure, sometimes appearing as Boeus, sometimes as Boeo; the work's apparent preoccupation with augury may indicate that it was attributed to the legendary Pythian priestess Boeo. But the date of composition was no doubt Hellenistic; the early third century has been suggested, though no proof is possible. Another specialist work was the surviving collection of *Catasterismi*, or transformations into stars, ascribed to the polymath Eratosthenes (*c.* 275–194 B.C.). These stories were the mythological reflection of contemporary interest in astronomy.

The first collection of all kinds of metamorphoses was probably the *Heteroeumena* by Nicander of Colophon, who flourished *c.* 135 B.C. in the Attalid kingdom. This was a hexameter poem in either four or five books. As with the 'Ορνιθογονία, almost our only information on the work comes from the paraphrases of Antoninus Liberalis (? second century A.D.) and these suggest that Nicander concentrated on *surviving* cults, landmarks, customs, etc., together with the stories that explained them, thus following the *Aetia* of Callimachus. One would have liked more information concerning the *Metamorphoses* of Parthenius of Nicaea in Bithynia, who came to Rome as a prisoner of war, and influenced many Latin neoteric poets, even teaching Virgil Greek, according to tradition. But unfortunately only one story is attested for Parthenius' *Metamorphoses*, that of Scylla daughter of Nisus. Finally there is a Theodorus, whom Ovid once followed according to a Virgil scholiast ([Probus] on *Georgics* i. 399); little else is known about him.[1] My section on Ovid's use of sources tries to discover the quality of earlier poetic collections, and their likely influence on Ovid. We should remember that, besides these compilations, metamorphosis was a favourite theme of much neoteric poetry; almost all the known epyllia of Latin neoteric poets treated legends with prominent metamorphoses.

Transformation in Ovid

This background only partially explains why Ovid chose to write his *magnum opus* within the framework of transformation. Of course gifted artists often seem content to observe the conventions of their day, while in fact enlarging them. But still there must have been something in metamorphosis which particularly appealed to Ovid. In the first place our poet had a vivid imagination, and a penchant for pure fantasy, so that he would gladly be free from the restriction of what was physically

[1] His *Metamorphoses* was apparently in prose.

possible. There is in the last book a more important idea which
we may easily underestimate through distaste for the patriotic
finale. When expounding his principle of universal change,
Pythagoras cites the rise and fall of states, saying of Rome
(xv. 431–5)

> nunc quoque Dardaniam fama est consurgere Romam,
> Appenninigenae quae proxima Thybridis undis
> mole sub ingenti rerum fundamina ponit.
> haec igitur formam crescendo mutat, et olim
> immensi caput orbis erit.

The metamorphosis of Rome into the world's capital must have
been an idea basic to Ovid's conception, even though most of
the work is written in a very different spirit.

Transformations in the *Metamorphoses* are nearly always
from the human state; exceptions, such as the story of Pyg-
malion, are thus all the more notable. The change may be
a punishment, an act of pity, or even an honour as conferring
a kind of immortality. Of course divine intervention is neces-
sary, but in some most interesting cases this is minimized, and
the change seems a logical outcome of the state to which
human beings have reduced themselves (cf. Brooks Otis, *Ovid
as an Epic Poet*, p. 214). Tereus, Procne, and Philomela have
already sunk to animal status before they are changed; the
ferocity of Hecuba is already that of a dog. Niobe's trans-
formation produces a notable tableau—she sits amid her dead
children, petrified by grief (vi. 301–5):

> orba resedit
> exanimes inter natos natasque virumque,
> deriguitque malis. nullos movet aura capillos,
> in vultu color est sine sanguine, lumina maestis
> stant immota genis; nihil est in imagine vivum.

This deeper conception of metamorphosis may well be due to
Ovid himself.

In his description of the change Ovid follows and refines
Hellenistic models. We find the same clinical detail; the effect

sometimes is humorous, sometimes grotesque, sometimes night-
marish, as with the transformation of Scylla into a sea-monster
(xiv. 60–5):

> cum sua foedari latrantibus **inguina monstris**
> aspicit. ac primo credens non **corporis illas**
> esse sui partes, refugitque abigitque timetque
> ora proterva canum; sed quos fugit attrahit una,
> et corpus quaerens femorum crurumque pedumque
> Cerbereos rictus pro partibus invenit illis.

One feature in Ovid's handling of people changed into
animals deserves a mention. Although their body may be
transformed, often it is stressed that their mind remains
human. As so often, we can find a precedent in Homer, who
says of Circe's victims (*Od.* x. 239–40): οἱ δὲ συῶν μὲν ἔχον
κεφαλὰς φωνήν τε τρίχας τε / καὶ δέμας, αὐτὰρ νοῦς ἦν ἔμπεδος ὡς
τὸ πάρος περ. But Ovid goes much further; e.g. with Actaeon
(iii. 198–203):

> fugit Autonoeius heros
> et se tam celerem cursu miratur in ipso.
> ut vero vultus et cornua vidit in unda,
> 'me miserum!' dicturus erat, vox nulla secuta est:
> ingemuit, vox illa fuit; lacrimaeque per ora
> non sua fluxerunt. mens tantum pristina mansit.

and with Io (i. 635–8):

> illa etiam supplex Argo cum bracchia vellet
> tendere, non habuit quae bracchia tenderet Argo;
> et conata queri mugitus edidit ore
> pertimuitque sonos propriaque exterrita voce est.

We can with probability carry this technique back to neo-
teric models. Consider the treatment of Io at Propertius ii. 33.
7–12:

> tu certe Iovis occultis in amoribus, Io,
>   sensisti multas quid sit inire vias,
> cum te iussit habere puellam cornua Iuno
>   et pecoris duro perdere verba sono.
> a quotiens quernis laesisti frondibus ora
>   mandisti et stabulis arbuta pasta tuis!

Here the style is very similar; Io, though transformed, is spoken of partly in human terms, so that what is natural for a cow becomes incongruous and grotesque for her. Ovid, *Heroides* 14. 85–108 is another passage in the same vein, and a final witness to the tradition lies in *Amores* i. 3. 21:

> carmine nomen habent *exterrita cornibus* Io . . .

The similarity in tone of these passages may well be explained by derivation from a single source, the *Io* of Catullus' friend Calvus. We know that Ovid used Calvus for the *Metamorphoses* account, and a stray surviving line (fr. 9 Morel)

> a virgo infelix, herbis pasceris amaris

shows not only the typical neoteric blend of sentiment and irony, but also juxtaposition of Io's two natures to produce an incongruous effect much as in Propertius (above).

This manner of depicting transformed human beings may also have been found in Hellenistic poetry. The late epic poet Nonnus writes of Actaeon μύθους μὲν προέηκεν ἐχέφρονας, ἀντὶ δὲ φωνῆς / ἀνδρομέης κελάδησεν ἀσημάντου θρόος ἠχοῦς (*Dionysiaca* v. 368–9); it is not clear, however, whether he is using a Hellenistic source, or Ovid (cf. *Met.* iii. 229–31).

Ovid's Use of Sources[1]

Ovid shares with Mozart a seemingly effortless fluency of composition. But in both cases this very fluency can mislead us to overlook the labour involved. And just such a misconception was the theory, now abandoned, that our poet drew his material for the *Metamorphoses* from some prose mythological handbook. Nothing could be further from the truth. Although he may have used a prose source for out-of-the-way stories, it was poetry which stimulated Ovid; his memory must have been phenomenal, and his reading very wide. Also he had that kind

[1] Only a few topics can be treated here. For discussion of each episode's sources, on the whole admirable, see Brooks Otis, *Ovid as an Epic Poet*, Appendix, pp. 346–94.

of genius which is stirred by other men's efforts to create something quite personal to himself. Therefore one of the bitterest features of exile in Tomis was the lack of books to kindle his imagination, 'non hic librorum per quos inviter alarque / copia' (*Tristia* iii. 14. 37–8).

Almost certainly many of the works used by Ovid as source material were no better than mediocre. Even so, our poet did not despise them; indeed he gave them new life beyond their deserts. This may be illustrated by the case of Nicander. Time has been unkind to the Colophonian in preserving his repulsive *Theriaca* and *Alexipharmaca* rather than the *Heteroeumena*, or the *Georgics*, honourably mentioned by Cicero (*De Or.* i. 69). But one cannot believe the *Heteroeumena* to have been very much better. Only one probable fragment of any length has survived, no. 62 Gow–Scholfield, concerning the transformation of Hecuba, a story also treated by Ovid (xiii. 481 ff.):

ἔνθ' Ἑκάβη Κισσηίς, ὅτ' ἐν πυρὶ δέρκετο πάτρην
καὶ πόσιν ἑλκηθεῖσα παρασπαίροντα θυηλαῖς,
εἰς ἅλα ποσσὶν ὄρουσε καὶ ἣν ἠλλάξατο μορφὴν
γρήιον, Ὑρκανίδεσσιν ἐειδομένην σκυλάκεσσιν.

The style is bald and unexciting; nothing is made of the actual metamorphosis, though of course succeeding lines could have amplified it. Also worth quoting are two hexameters (fr. 50 G.–S.) from a tale resembling the better-known Acontius and Cydippe (Callimachus, *Aetia*, bk. iii). The young man Hermochares is about to inscribe on an apple the oath which will bind his beloved:

αὐτίχ' ὅγ' ἢ Σιδόεντος ἠὲ Πλείστου ἀπὸ κήπων
μῆλα ταμὼν χνοάοντα τύπους ἐνεμάσσετο Κάδμου.

Callimachus might have turned in his grave!

The Ὀρνιθογονία of Boeus or Boeo is not likely to have been any more inspiring—we must suspend judgement on the *Metamorphoses* of Parthenius, who perhaps had greater talent. But Ovid not only uses Nicander and Boeus, particularly the former, for subject-matter; he sometimes imitates their conventions (see on lines 251–9), and may even cast a story taken from elsewhere in the mould of one of these authors. By such means Ovid places himself firmly in the tradition of Hellenistic transformation-poetry. But he will never be tied down by any one set of conventions for long. As Georges Lafaye put it (*Les Métamorphoses d'Ovide et leurs modèles grecs*, p. 53), Ovid has read everything, but is too wise to follow his predecessors wherever they lead.

When there already existed a famous and successful poetic treatment of some legend, Ovid feels obliged to strike out in a different direction. Often he will alter the tone of the narrative. Thus Ovid's Erysicthon is written in the high epic style, quite unlike the comedy of manners in Callimachus, *hymn* 6. On the other hand Virgil's Achaemenides episode (*Aen.* iii. 588–683) becomes less brutal, more suave and urbane, at *Met.* xiv. 154–222 (see the comparison of Brooks Otis, op. cit., pp. 73–6), while the Theocritean Polyphemus-lament is almost parodied (*Met.* xiii. 789–869). Alternatively Ovid chooses different aspects of the story to emphasize, passing quickly over those treated in full by his great predecessor. Since Ovid seldom relies on a single source for each episode, there was no lack of material for a varying version. In these cases the results are not always happy. It is a fair guess that Ovid would have liked to handle the Orpheus–Eurydice legend in much the same spirit as Virgil (*Georgics* iv). But he felt forced to write in another style—one that hardly suited him—and so suffers by comparison. Seldom will Ovid compete directly with a Virgil, as in the list of portents which foretell Caesar's death (*Met.* xv. 783–98, cf. *Georgics* i. 466–88).

Language and atmosphere form quite as important a debt to predecessors as the subject-matter. In so chameleon-like a work we must be sensitive to every hint, for a small linguistic imitation may be enough to set the narrative's tone. The following are a few examples of colour borrowed from widely differing poetic styles.

(a) *Ennian Colour*: xv. 30–2,

> candidus Oceano nitidum caput abdiderat Sol
> et caput extulerat densissima sidereum Nox:
> visus adesse idem deus est . . .

Note the consecutive monosyllabic line-endings, the unsubtle epithets 'candidus . . . nitidum', and the rather jejune personification, exactly parallel in 30 and 31. All this amounts to a delicious parody of the Ennian style—though the lightness and speed of movement are Ovid's own. Line 32 contains a more specific echo, of Homer appearing to Ennius in a dream 'visus Homerus adesse poeta' (*Annals* 5 Warmington).[1] The effect is of solemnity, or rather mock-solemnity; Ovid means the episode to be little more than amusing (cf. 45–6). For Ennius and Ovid see further my note to lines 549 ff.

(b) *Accian Colour*: vi. 645–6 (*the cooking of Itys*),

>   pars inde cavis exsultat aenis,
> pars veribus stridunt.

Compare Accius, *Atreus* 187–9 Warmington 'concoquit / partem vapore flammae, veribus in focos / lacerta tribuit' (Bergk's 'verubus in foco / lacerta stridunt' is closer to Ovid). Our poet seems to have used the Thyestean banquet in Accius' *Atreus* for a parallel situation in the myth of Philomela; vi. 665 'seque vocat bustum miserabile nati' clearly recalls *Atreus* 190 W. 'natis sepulcro ipse est parens'. It is of course conceivable that Accius repeated himself in the *Tereus*. But more important is to recognize the Accian spirit here—a ferocious prince and deeds of unspeakable wickedness. Some of the more bloodthirsty characters and episodes in the *Metamorphoses* are strongly Accian. Ovid may also pick up a striking Accian phrase; when Accius, imitating Homer, had called Achilles 'the wall of the Argives' ('moerus Argivum' 561 W.), our poet follows with 'Graium murus Achilles' (xiii. 281).

[1] I quote Old Latin from the Loeb collection as the most helpful and easily accessible to students. The volumes have concordances with Vahlen, Ribbeck, and Marx.

Ennius and Accius are the only archaic Latin poets to have
influenced Ovid extensively; they also appear together among
the immortals at *Amores* I. 15. 19.

(c) *Lucretian Colour*: xv. 88–90 (*Pythagoras on vegetarianism*),

> heu quantum scelus est in viscera viscera condi . . .
> alteriusque animantem animantis vivere leto!

We find here not only a definite echo of the *De Rerum Natura*
v. 993 'viva videns vivo sepeliri viscera busto'. 'Animans' = 'liv-
ing creature' is also a Lucretian favourite; even elision of 'ani-
mant(em)' over the caesura, rare in Ovid, helps the impression.
This earnest didactic tone is just right for the speech of Pytha-
goras. The Creation in *Met.* i also contains Lucretian elements.

(d) *Neoteric Colour*: i. 732 (Io),

> et gemitu et lacrimis et luctisono mugitu.

Ovid's debt to the *Io* of Calvus in this episode cannot be ques-
tioned, but the present line stands out particularly. As well as
a spondaic fifth foot, there is the rare special rhythm caused by
a trisyllabic ending,[1] cf. *Aeneid* xii. 863, [Virgil], *Ciris* 519 'rupi-
bus et scopulis et litoribus desertis'. The compound 'luctisonus'
is of a type which survived in neoteric epyllia as a legacy from
the archaic style, cf. 'clarisonus', 'fluentisonus', and 'rauci-
sonus' in Catullus 64. Generally speaking, neoteric elements do
not stand out in the *Metamorphoses* because they have been
absorbed into Ovid's constant personal style. At a time when
the influence of Alexandria on Rome had all but vanished, our
poet enshrines much that was best in the neoteric tradition.

The Text

No manuscript of the *Metamorphoses* older than the ninth
century[2] has survived. But the growing popularity of Ovid,

[1] Greek proper names, however, are quite common in this position
(see 315 n.).
[2] Two probable ninth-century fragments, Munari, nos. 37 and 270.

which culminated in the twelfth century, produced a vast num-
ber of MSS., thereby offering some compensation. Professor
Munari in his catalogue (*London Univ. Inst. of Class. Stud.
Bulletin*, Supplement no. 4 [1957]) records no fewer than 390.
One consequence of this profusion is that to construct a *stemma
codicum* becomes a hazardous task, or at least it is hard to have
full confidence in the result;[1] the possibilities of contamination
between MSS. or their putative ancestors are almost unlimited.
We may doubt whether all existing MSS. go back to a common
archetype, that is, whether the 'Lactantians' (see below) can be
integrated with the other amorphous group called X by Mag-
nus. Certainly efforts to establish such an archetype have not
been successful hitherto (Brooks Otis, *AJP* lxxxi [1960] 87).

Since the time of Heinsius (Slater, *Towards a Text of the
Metamorphosis of Ovid* [Oxford, 1927], p. 16) editors have
thought it to be a vital question whether or not a manuscript
carries the prose summaries of 'Lactantius' (given by Slater
and by Magnus in his 1914 edition). These 'Narrationes' or
'Argumenta', which occasionally resemble a commentary more
than a summary, derive from an unknown scholar probably in
the fifth or sixth century (see Brooks Otis, *Harvard Stud. Class.
Phil.* xlvii [1936] 131–63), and may first have belonged to
a carefully revised edition of the poem. They occur in three
extant MSS. (M N U), two lost or unplaced ones (J S) and
several fragments, thus forming a family, but not a very close-
knit one. M and N are cousins rather than brothers, and all the
Lactantians where available must be given full consideration as
individuals.

For a long period in the nineteenth and early twentieth cen-
turies M and N were considered much the best MSS., or almost
the only ones worth attending to, with M usually being pre-
ferred. Scholars saw on the one hand a 'pure' tradition (the
'Lactantians', represented by M and N),[2] on the other an

---

[1] See R. T. Bruère, *Harvard Stud. Class. Phil.* l (1939) 122 for a
stemma.

[2] U was only brought back to light by Slater.

'interpolated' tradition (the remaining MSS., grouped together as X by Magnus). Recent years have brought attacks on the pre-eminence of M and N. Although their high quality cannot be disputed, they have faults of their own (e.g. the omission of lines or intrusion of words from a near-by line). The 'X' group (E e F h L P etc.), so widely spread that they can scarcely be called a family, should by no means be despised, even when in conflict with all the Lactantians. Furthermore, apparent truth may be preserved in the most unlikely places. Worthy of attention is the Greek rendering of a Byzantine monk and diplomat Maximus Planudes, who was born in the late thirteenth century. As far as we can see, he did not have a notably good Latin text to work from; yet sometimes he has plausible readings either by himself or with few others (Slater, pp. 20–1). So our touchstone must be the excellence of individual readings—neither the number nor the prejudged value of their manuscript sponsors.

The problem of alternative versions appearing in our MSS. has already been discussed (pp. x–xi). It seems likely that the assumed fifth- or sixth-century annotated edition from which M and N descend rejected the longer versions.[1] These latter, which often seem to represent Ovid's second thoughts, must have survived antiquity without the benefit of a careful edition (Brooks Otis, *AJP* [1960] 88), until they reached our so-called 'deteriores'. So it will be seen that the general merit of MSS. which either carry or lack the longer version can not establish or disprove double recension. Brooks Otis (ibid.) appears to suggest that other variants in the non-Lactantian MSS. may go back to antiquity and even to Ovid himself. This seems to me more doubtful.

Manuscript readings have been taken almost exclusively from Burman (1727), Magnus (1914), and Slater. Professor Munari kindly lent me reports of some minor MSS. at crucial points. In general I quote variants or conjectures only when there is conceivable doubt as to the text, or when the variant is

---

[1] 'Lactantius' appears not to know them.

in some way instructive, e.g. showing a reminiscence or an intrusion. I have not always thought it necessary, nor always been able to provide full coverage of the more important MSS. But, when only a variant is given in the apparatus, the principle is that other more important MSS. agree essentially with the text adopted. I make no claim to contribute to the history of the tradition, and can only hope that the final text does not suffer from my deficiencies here. Many MSS. used by older scholars (particularly Heinsius) remain unidentified, or identification has not been confirmed for the *Metamorphoses*. Professor Munari has made considerable progress in this direction (see his paper in *Ovidiana*, pp. 347–9). Heinsius himself still stands out among the poem's critics; time and time again it is a preference or conjecture of Heinsius which must be considered.

MANUSCRIPTS[1]

E   *Palatinus 1669, Vaticanus.* 12th cent. first half (Slater), or possibly 11th (365).

F   *Marcianus 223, Florentinus.* 11th–12th cent. (177).

J   *S. Iohannis in Viridario, Patavinus.* At present not located; Heinsius' collation reported sparingly by Slater. Included 'Lactantius' (281).

L   *Laurentianus 36. 12, Florentinus.* 11th cent. (Chatelain), or early 12th (Magnus, Bruère). *Primus Mediceus* of Heinsius (131).

M   *Marcianus 225, Florentinus.* 10th cent. (Chatelain), 11th (Magnus), 11th–12th (Slater), 12th (Bruère). 'Lactantius' in text by first hand (178).

N   *Neapolitanus iv. F. 3.* 11th cent. (Riese, Magnus, Ehwald), 12th (Loew, Rand, Slater, Bruère). 'Lactantius' in margin by first hand (206).

P   *Parisinus 8001.* 12th cent. or at latest early 13th. *Berneggerianus* of Heinsius. Heinsius's collation used by Slater (240).

---

[1] Numbers in brackets refer to Munari's catalogue (*London Univ. Inst. of Class. Stud. Bulletin*, Suppl. no. 4, 1957), which gives fuller information.

S   *Spirensis*, now lost[1] (? 11th cent.); included 'Lactantius'.
    Heinsius's collation used by Slater (313).

U   *Urbinas 341*, *Vaticanus*. 11th–12th cent. 'Lactantius' in text
    (370).

ρ   *fragmenta Rhenana*. Late 12th–early 13th cent. Of bk. viii
    they have 1–19, 22–112, 119–42, 150–73, 307–30, 337–422,
    425–53, 456–84. Collated by Magnus (*Philologus* lxxxix [1923]
    159–187) (295).

τ   *Tegernseensis*, now *Monacensis 29. 007*. 12th cent. Of bk. viii
    it has 179–234, 632–87 (321).

υ   *Urbinas 342*, *Vaticanus*. 9th–10th cent. (Stornajolo), 10th
    (Bruère), 11th (Hosius, Slater). Of bk. viii it has 1–104 (371).

a   *Londiniensis, Mus. Britann. King's 26*. 11th cent. (172).

e   *Erfurtanus, Amplonianus prior*. 12th cent. (Merkel, Grau),
    13th (Korn) (81).

g   *Graecensis 1415*. 12th cent. or early 13th (102).

h   *Hauniensis 2008*. 12th cent. or early 13th (112).

s₁ *Laurentianus Strozzianus 121*. Early 12th cent. (141).

s₂ *Laurentianus Strozzianus 120*. Late 12th cent. (140).

x   *Bibl. Armamentarii 1045, Parisinus*. A.D. 1472 (233).

Bruxellensis 2100. 13th cent. *Lovanensis* of Heinsius (61).

Francofurtanus 110. 13th cent. (95).

Genavensis 94. 13th cent. *Genevensis* of Heinsius (96).

Hauniensis 2009. 13th cent. (113).

Heidelbergensis 1661. Late 12th or 13th cent. Probably the *Alter Palatinus* of Heinsius (115).

Laurentianus 36. 10. 13th cent. *Tertius Mediceus* of Heinsius (129).

Laurentianus 36. 14. Late 12th cent. *Quartus Mediceus* of Heinsius (133).

Londiniensis Harl. 2673. 14th cent. (167).

Londiniensis Harl. 2742. 13th cent. (169).

[1] The fragment κ (111), which does not contain bk. viii, belonged
originally to the *Spirensis*.

xxx INTRODUCTION

Oxoniensis Bodl. Auct. F. 4. 22. First half of 13th cent. *Sprotianus* of Heinsius (218).

Parisinus 7993. Second half of 12th cent. (238).

Parisinus 8000. 12th cent. (Bruère) or 13th (239).

Turicensis 413. 12th cent. *Rhenovanus* used by Bach (329).

Vaticanus 1593. 12th cent. *Primus Vaticanus* of Heinsius (334).

Vaticanus Barberinianus 70. 13th cent. *Barberinianus* of Heinsius (349).

Plan.	The Greek translation of Maximus Planudes, from Boissonade (Paris, 1822).
s	A manuscript, or manuscripts, of more recent date.
A	All or the great majority of more important MSS. not otherwise mentioned.
s Heinsius	A reading either adopted or commended by Heinsius from one or more MSS. of relatively recent date.
e.v.l.	*erasa vetere lectione.*

P. OVIDI NASONIS

METAMORPHOSEON

LIBER VIII

IAM nitidum retegente diem noctisque fugante
tempora Lucifero cadit eurus, et umida surgunt
nubila: dant placidi cursum redeuntibus austri
Aeacidis Cephaloque, quibus feliciter acti
ante exspectatum portus tenuere petitos.   5
    Interea Minos Lelegeia litora vastat
praetemptatque sui vires Mavortis in urbe
Alcathoe, quam Nisus habet, cui splendidus ostro
inter honoratos medioque in vertice canos
crinis inhaerebat, magni fiducia regni.   10
    Sexta resurgebant orientis cornua lunae,
et pendebat adhuc belli fortuna, diuque
inter utrumque volat dubiis Victoria pennis.
regia turris erat vocalibus addita muris,
in quibus auratam proles Letoia fertur   15
deposuisse lyram: saxo sonus eius inhaesit.
saepe illuc solita est ascendere filia Nisi
et petere exiguo resonantia saxa lapillo,
tum cum pax esset; bello quoque saepe solebat
spectare ex illa rigidi certamina Martis.   20
iamque mora belli procerum quoque nomina norat
armaque equosque habitusque Cydonaeasque pharetras.

---

4 actis *MN*[1]: usi *'iv veteres' Heinsii*   8 Alcathoi *Heinsius*
9 medioque in *vM*: medio de *EL Plan.*: medio sub *NU*   11 lunae]
Phoebes *unus Med. et unus Ambros.*   13 vagat *M*[1] *unus Med. et unus*
Bonon.   15 Letoia *vM Plan.*: Latoia *eN*: Latonia *Fh*   16 eius
inhaesit *nonnullis suspectum*: haesit in illo *Lovan.*: Eïus haesit *Slater*
19–20 bellum *NP*[1]*U* saepe] turre *N* ex] e(? -que) *U* bellum quoque
turre ... / ... eque illa *Heinsius*

noverat ante alios faciem ducis Europaei,
plus etiam quam nosse sat est. hac iudice Minos,
seu caput abdiderat cristata casside pennis,   25
in galea formosus erat; seu sumpserat aere
fulgentem clipeum, clipeum sumpsisse decebat.
torserat adductis hastilia lenta lacertis:
laudabat virgo iunctam cum viribus artem.
imposito calamo patulos sinuaverat arcus: 30
sic Phoebum sumptis iurabat stare sagittis.
cum vero faciem dempto nudaverat aere
purpureusque albi stratis insignia pictis
terga premebat equi spumantiaque ora regebat,
vix sua, vix sanae virgo Niseia compos   35
mentis erat. felix iaculum quod tangeret ille,
quaeque manu premeret felicia frena vocabat.
impetus est illi, liceat modo, ferre per agmen
virgineos hostile gradus; est impetus illi
turribus e summis in Cnosia mittere corpus   40
castra, vel aeratas hosti recludere portas,
vel siquid Minos aliud velit. utque sedebat
candida Dictaei spectans tentoria regis,
'laeter' ait 'doleamne geri lacrimabile bellum
in dubio est: doleo quod Minos hostis amanti est,   45
sed, nisi bella forent, numquam mihi cognitus esset.
me tamen accepta poterat deponere bellum
obside, me comitem, me pacis pignus haberet.
si quae te peperit talis, pulcherrime regum,
qualis es ipse fuit, merito deus arsit in illa.   50
o ego ter felix, si pennis lapsa per auras
Cnosiaci possem castris insistere regis,
fassaque me flammasque meas, qua dote, rogarem,

---

26 auro *Paris. 8000 Heinsius*   30 impositis calamis *vE*   **33 alti**
Burman   46 numquid *L Heinsius*   47 poterit *Lovan.*
48 habere *Francof. Heinsius*   49 peperit] genuit *E Heinsius*
regum *A Plan.*: rer(? r *ex* g)um *U*: rerum *ex 'decem veteribus' Heinsius*
50 ipse (? -e *ex* -a *U) EU Plan. Heinsius*: ipsa *A*

vellet emi; tantum patrias ne posceret arces!
nam pereant potius sperata cubilia, quam sim   55
proditione potens—quamvis saepe utile vinci
victoris placidi fecit clementia multis.
iusta gerit certe pro nato bella perempto,
et causaque valet causamque tenentibus armis.
   'At, puto, vincemur: qui si manet exitus urbem,   60
cur suus haec illi reseret mea moenia Mavors
et non noster amor? melius sine caede moraque
impensaque sui poterit superare cruoris.
non metuam certe ne quis tua pectora, Minos,
vulneret imprudens (quis enim tam durus, ut in te   65
dirigere immitem non inscius audeat hastam?)
   'Coepta placent, et stat sententia tradere mecum
dotalem patriam finemque imponere bello.
verum velle parum est: aditus custodia servat,
claustraque portarum genitor tenet. hunc ego solum   70
infelix timeo, solus mea vota moratur.
di facerent sine patre forem!—sibi quisque profecto
est deus; ignavis precibus Fortuna repugnat.
altera iamdudum succensa cupidine tanto
perdere gauderet quodcumque obstaret amori.   75
et cur ulla foret me fortior? ire per ignes
et gladios ausim; nec in hoc tamen ignibus ullis
aut gladiis opus est, opus est mihi crine paterno.
ille mihi est auro pretiosior, illa beatam
purpura me votique mei factura potentem.'   80
   Talia dicenti curarum maxima nutrix

   57 multis] victis *tempt. Riese*   58 gerit] facit *Lovan. Burman*
certe *A*: placidus *M¹* (*ex* 57)   59 et causaque *eς*: in causaque *LP*
(*e.v.l. N²U²*) *Heinsius*: e causaque *M*   tenentibus *vFMPS*: tuentibus
v²EU (*e.v.l. N²*)   60 at *Markland*: et *EMNPSU*: ut *M²U²* *Plan.*
qui˙si (?*v*)*E*: quis enim *A*   61 reseret mea] reserabit *Gronov. Prim.*:
reserarit *malit Heinsius*   64 non metuo *N*: nam metuo *EN²U*: quam
metuo *Heinsius*   65 dirus *eς Heinsius*   66 nisi nescius *duo Moreti
Heinsius*   67 secum *M et Vatic. Prim.*   75 prodere *ς*   77 in
hoc] adhuc *N*   79 ille mihi *vELNPU Plan.*: illa mihi *v²M*

nox intervenit, tenebrisque audacia crevit.
prima quies aderat, qua curis fessa diurnis
pectora somnus habet: thalamos taciturna paternos
intrat et (heu facinus!) fatali nata parentem   85
crine suum spoliat, praedaque potita nefanda
fert secum spolium celeris, progressaque porta
per medios hostis (meriti fiducia tanta est!)
pervenit ad regem, quem sic adfata paventem est:
  'Suasit amor facinus: proles ego regia Nisi   90
Scylla tibi trado patriaeque meosque penates.
praemia nulla peto nisi te: cape pignus amoris
purpureum crinem, nec me nunc tradere crinem
sed patrium tibi crede caput!' scelerataque dextra
munera porrexit. Minos porrecta refugit   95
turbatusque novi respondit imagine facti:
'di te summoveant, o nostri infamia saecli,
orbe suo, tellusque tibi pontusque negetur!
certe ego non patiar Iovis incunabula, Creten,
qui meus est orbis, tantum contingere monstrum.'   100
  Dixit, et ut leges captis iustissimus auctor
hostibus imposuit, classis retinacula solvi
iussit, et aeratas impelli remige puppes.
  Scylla freto postquam deductas nare carinas
nec praestare ducem sceleris sibi praemia vidit,   105
consumptis precibus violentam transit in iram,
intendensque manus passis furibunda capillis
'quo fugis', exclamat, 'meritorum auctore relicta,
o patriae praelate meae, praelate parenti?
quo fugis, immitis, cuius victoria nostrum   110
et scelus et meritum est? nec te data munera, nec te

---

85 fatali $h^1LN^2P^2$ (*ex silentio et S*): vitali *vEMNPU*   87 *om.*
vMN, damnat Heinsius   celeris *eLS Priscianus*: sceleris *A* (*quo accepto*
pretium *pro* spolium *Bentley*, pignus *Vollmer*)   90 regia] gloria
v^1M^1 91 patriaeque (ae *ex* o *M*) *vM*: patriamque *N Plan.*: patri-
osque *EPU Heinsius*   98 suo v^2EM^2PU *Plan.*: tuo *vMS*: polus
N: pio *Heinsius*   103 impelli $v^2\varsigma$: impleri *A Plan.*   105 sceleri
sua *Heinsius*   107 passis ELM^2U: fusis $S\rho$: sparsis *e.v.l.* N^2: fossis *M*

noster amor movit, nec quod spes omnis in unum
te mea congesta est? nam quo deserta revertar?
in patriam? superata iacet. sed finge manere:
proditione mea clausa est mihi. patris ad ora?   115
quem tibi donavi? cives odere merentem,
finitimi exemplum metuunt: obstruximus orbem
terrarum, nobis ut Crete sola pateret.
hac quoque si prohibes et nos, ingrate, relinquis,
non genetrix Europa tibi est, sed inhospita Syrtis,   120
Armeniae tigres austroque agitata Charybdis.
nec Iove tu natus, nec mater imagine tauri
capta tua est (generis falsa est ea fabula!): verus   123
qui te progenuit taurus fuit! exige poenas,   125
Nise pater! gaudete malis, modo prodita, nostris
moenia! nam (fateor) merui et sum digna perire.
sed tamen ex illis aliquis, quos impia laesi,
me perimat. cur, qui vicisti crimine nostro,
insequeris crimen? scelus hoc patriaeque patrique est, 130
officium tibi sit! te vere coniuge digna est
quae torvum ligno decepit adultera taurum
discordemque utero fetum tulit. ecquid ad aures
perveniunt mea dicta tuas? an inania venti
verba ferunt idemque tuas, ingrate, carinas?   135
iamiam Pasiphaen non est mirabile taurum
praeposuisse tibi—tu plus feritatis habebas!
   'Me miseram! properare iubet, divolsaque remis
unda sonat, mecumque simul mea terra recedit.

116 qu(a)e *EN²U*   manentem *U¹*   117 metuunt exemplum *ax*
obstruximus *EhLM²N²Ux Plan.*: exponimur *M*: exponimus *NPS*
orbem *A*: orbe *M* (*velut* orbae *interpretatus est Bentley*): exponimur
orbae *von Winterfeld, Magnus*: *alii alia*   119 hanc *hM Plan.*
121 Armeniaeque *hNU*   123 capta *N*: ducta *M*: lusa *EM²U*
generis *M²NU Plan*: genetrix *S*: genitrix *EMU²*   verus *e²ϛ*: verum
aEN: versus *M¹SU*   124 et ferus et captus nullius amore iuvencae
(puellae *Barth*) *del. Merkel*   131 fit *e*   vere *Eρ*: vero *A*
133 dissortemque *Heinsius*   138 iubet *MN¹U*: iuvat *A*   divisa-
que *EPU²*   139 mecumque simul *ENU*: mecum simul ah (ha) *LM*:
mecum simul et *P*

'Nil agis, o frustra meritorum oblite meorum: 140
insequar invitum, puppemque amplexa recurvam
per freta longa trahar!' vix dixerat, insilit undis
consequiturque rates, faciente cupidine vires,
Cnosiacaeque haeret comes invidiosa carinae.

Quam pater ut vidit (nam iam pendebat in auras   145
et modo factus erat fulvis haliaeetus alis),
ibat ut haerentem rostro laceraret adunco.
illa metu puppim dimisit, et aura cadentem
sustinuisse levis, ne tangeret aequora, visa est.
pluma fuit: plumis in avem mutata vocatur   150
Ciris, et a tonso est hoc nomen adepta capillo.

Vota Iovi Minos taurorum corpora centum
solvit, ut egressus ratibus Curetida terram
contigit; et spoliis decorata est regia fixis.

Creverat opprobrium generis, foedumque patebat   155
matris adulterium monstri novitate biformis.
destinat hunc Minos thalamo removere pudorem
multiplicique domo caecisque includere tectis.
Daedalus ingenio fabrae celeberrimus artis
ponit opus turbatque notas et lumina flexu   160
ducit in errorem variarum ambage viarum.
non secus ac liquidis Phrygius Maeandrus in undis
ludit et ambiguo lapsu refluitque fluitque
occurrensque sibi venturas aspicit undas
et nunc ad fontes, nunc ad mare versus apertum   165
incertas exercet aquas: ita Daedalus implet
innumeras errore vias; vixque ipse reverti
ad limen potuit, tanta est fallacia tecti.

142 undas *Med. Tert. et tres alii Heinsius*   145 auras *A* : aura *P*[1] :
auris *S*   147 laniaret *Sprot.*   148 dimisit: pluma *Magnus*
150 ὀλόπτερος δὲ γέγονε (? plumea fit) *Plan.*: spuma ruit plumis *Havet*
152 corpora] sanguine *ELP*[1]*U*   153 ut *ς Heinsius*: et *A Plan.*
Creteida *LP*[2] *Plan.*   157 thalamo *N*: thalamis *N*[2]*U*: thalami
EMP Plan.   160 lumina *FhS*: limina *A Plan.*   flexu *EFLMN*:
flexum *Sς*: flexim *Heinsius*   162 liquidis f(ph)ry(i)gius *aEhUρ*:
liquidus Phrygiis *LM*[2]*N*   in arvis *P*[2] *Plan.*   164 prospicit
Arondel.   166 incertas] et dubias *NS*

Quo postquam geminam tauri iuvenisque figuram
clausit et Actaeo bis pastum sanguine monstrum   170
tertia sors annis domuit repetita novenis,
utque ope virginea nullis iterata priorum
ianua difficilis filo est inventa relecto,
protinus Aegides rapta Minoide Diam
vela dedit, comitemque suam crudelis in illo   175
litore destituit. desertae et multa querenti
amplexus et opem Liber tulit, utque perenni
sidere clara foret, sumptam de fronte coronam
immisit caelo. tenues volat illa per auras,
dumque volat, gemmae nitidos vertuntur in ignes   180
consistuntque loco, specie remanente coronae,
qui medius Nixique genu est Anguemque tenentis.

Daedalus interea Creten longumque perosus
exilium, tactusque loci natalis amore,
clausus erat pelago. 'terras licet' inquit 'et undas   185
obstruat, at caelum certe patet; ibimus illac:
omnia possideat, non possidet aera Minos.'

Dixit, et ignotas animum dimittit in artes
naturamque novat. nam ponit in ordine pennas   189
ut clivo crevisse putes. sic rustica quondam   191
fistula disparibus paulatim surgit avenis.
tum lino medias et ceris alligat imas
atque ita compositas parvo curvamine flectit
ut veras imitetur aves. puer Icarus una   195
stabat et, ignarus sua se tractare pericla,
ore renidenti modo quas vaga moverat aura
captabat plumas, flavam modo pollice ceram

172 nulli S   superata NS   173 relecto *Palat. unus et man. sec.*
Arondel. Dan. Heinsius: relicto *A*   176 deseruit '*quinque veteres*'
Heinsius   180 nitidos] subitos *EU Heinsius*   182 *del. Bentley*
genus *S*   tuentis '*Leidens. et alius*' (*Burman*) *et fortasse Plan.*
184 tractusque *unus Med. Heinsius*   soli *unus Leidens. Heinsius*
190 a minima coeptas, longam (longa *Holland*) breviore sequenti
(sequente *Eτ*) *del. Merkel*   195 imitentur *Moreti Prim. et Quart.*
Med. et alii Heinsius

mollibat, lusuque suo mirabile patris
impediebat opus. postquam manus ultima coepto   200
imposita est, geminas opifex libravit in alas
ipse suum corpus, motaque pependit in aura.

Instruit et natum, 'medio' que 'ut limite curras,
Icare,' ait 'moneo, ne, si demissior ibis,
unda gravet pennas, si celsior, ignis adurat.   205
inter utrumque vola! nec te spectare Booten
aut Helicen iubeo strictumque Orionis ensem:
me duce carpe viam!' pariter praecepta volandi
tradit et ignotas umeris accommodat alas.
inter opus monitusque genae maduere seniles,   210
et patriae tremuere manus. dedit oscula nato
non iterum repetenda suo, pennisque levatus
ante volat comitique timet, velut ales, ab alto
quae teneram prolem produxit in aera nido,
hortaturque sequi, damnosasque erudit artes,   215
et movet ipse suas et nati respicit alas.
hos aliquis tremula dum captat harundine pisces,
aut pastor baculo stivave innixus arator
vidit et obstipuit, quique aethera carpere possent
credidit esse deos. et iam Iunonia laeva   220
parte Samos (fuerant Delosque Parosque relictae),
dextra Lebinthos erat fecundaque melle Calymne,
cum puer audaci coepit gaudere volatu
deseruitque ducem, caelique cupidine tactus
altius egit iter. rapidi vicinia solis   225
mollit odoratas, pennarum vincula, ceras:
tabuerant cerae; nudos quatit ille lacertos
remigioque carens non ullas percipit auras,

---

200 coeptis EM^2U 201 geminis P alis P 206 nec
EU: neu $LMNPS$ 207 strictumve 5 $Burman$ 208 volando
MN^1S 211 cecidere $Haun.$ 2009 218 stivave NU $Plan.$:
stivaque $EMPS$ 221 $distinxit$ $Gierig$ fuerant ex vii $codd.$ $Hein$-
$sius$: fuerat A $Plan.$ 224 tractus M^1S: captus U^1 225 rabidi P
226 adornatas U $Heinsius$ 227 tabuerunt $unus$ $Med.$

oraque caerulea patrium clamantia nomen
excipiuntur aqua, quae nomen traxit ab illo.   230
   At pater infelix, nec iam pater, 'Icare,' dixit,
'Icare,' dixit 'ubi es? qua te regione requiram?'
'Icare' dicebat: pennas aspexit in undis,
devovitque suas artes, corpusque sepulcro
condidit, et tellus a nomine dicta sepulti.   235
   Hunc miseri tumulo ponentem corpora nati
garrula ramosa prospexit ab ilice perdix
et plausit pennis testataque gaudia cantu est,
unica tunc volucris nec visa prioribus annis,
factaque nuper avis, longum tibi, Daedale, crimen.   240
namque huic tradiderat, fatorum ignara, docendam
progeniem germana suam, natalibus actis
bis puerum senis animi ad praecepta capacis.
ille etiam medio spinas in pisce notatas
traxit in exemplum ferroque incidit acuto   245
perpetuos dentes et serrae repperit usum.
primus et ex uno duo ferrea bracchia nodo
vinxit ut, aequali spatio distantibus illis,
altera pars staret, pars altera duceret orbem.
Daedalus invidit, sacraque ex arce Minervae   250
praecipitem misit, lapsum mentitus; at illum
quae favet ingeniis excepit Pallas, avemque
reddidit et medio velavit in aere pennis.
sed vigor ingenii quondam velocis in alas
inque pedes abiit; nomen quod et ante remansit.   255
non tamen haec alte volucris sua corpora tollit,
nec facit in ramis altoque cacumine nidos:
propter humum volitat, ponitque in saepibus ova,
antiquique memor metuit sublimia casus.

231 nec iam] sed nec N   233 conspexit FP   237 ramosa
(clamosa Moreti Prim.) . . . ilice (elice h²) A Plan.: limoso . . . elice
Auctor de dub. nom. (G.L.K. v. 587) Merkel: lamoso . . . elice Hous-
man: ramoso . . . ulice R. G. M. Nisbet   238 cantu] voce EU
242 actis] auctum unus Strozz.   243 pueri e.v.l. P   rapacis (corr.
N²U²) A Plan.   253 plumis ς

Iamque fatigatum tellus Aetnaea tenebat   260
Daedalon, et sumptis pro supplice Cocalus armis
mitis habebatur; iam lamentabile Athenae
pendere desierant Thesea laude tributum.
templa coronantur, bellatricemque Minervam
cum Iove disque vocant aliis, quos sanguine voto   265
muneribusque datis et acerris turis honorant.
Sparserat Argolicas nomen vaga fama per urbes
Theseos, et populi quos dives Achaia cepit
huius opem magnis imploravere periclis.
huius opem Calydon, quamvis Meleagron haberet,   270
sollicita supplex petiit prece: causa petendi
sus erat, infestae famulus vindexque Dianae.
Oenea namque ferunt pleni successibus anni
primitias frugum Cereri, sua vina Lyaeo,
Palladios flavae latices libasse Minervae.   275
coeptus ab agricolis superos pervenit ad omnes
ambitiosus honor: solas sine ture relictas
praeteritae cessasse ferunt Latoidos aras.
tangit et ira deos. 'at non impune feremus,
quaeque inhonoratae, non et dicemur inultae.'   280
inquit, et Olenios ultorem spreta per agros
misit aprum, quanto maiores herbida tauros
non habet Epiros, sed habent Sicula arva minores.
sanguine et igne micant oculi, riget horrida cervix,   284

260 Hennaea P   262 mitis habebatur *nonnullis suspectum*:
mactus habebatur *Merkel*   263 debuerant *Moreti Prim.*: desuerant
glossator L, ex coni. Heinsius   264 iaculatricemque *Lovan.*
266 acerris *LN²ς*: acervis *eFhMNP Plan.*   271 petenti *N*
272 incultae *Langermann*   273 pleni ... anni *EU*: plenis ... annis
LPS: de MN non constat: pleno ... anno *J. S. Reid*   274 frugem
unus Med. et unus Voss. Heinsius   276 Argolicis *FP²*   277 in-
vidiosus *N Heinsius*   278 praeteritae *e Thuan. et sex alii Heinsius*:
praeteritas *A Plan.*   279 at non dicemur inultae *MN*: at non
impune feretis *Bentley*   280 nec nos impune feremus *MN*
281 Olenios *Heinsius* (Olenyos *e²*): implenos *M*: plenos *N¹*: Oenios *FhL*:
Oeneos *S*   284 ardua *Francof.*   285 et saetae similes rigidis
(densis similes *nonnulli Heinsii*) hastilibus horrent *del. Bentley*

stantque velut vallum, velut alta hastilia saetae: 286
fervida cum rauco latos stridore per armos
spuma fluit, dentes aequantur dentibus Indis,
fulmen ab ore venit, frondes afflatibus ardent.
is modo crescentes segetes proculcat in herba,   290
nunc matura metit fleturi vota coloni
et Cererem in spicis intercipit. area frustra
et frustra exspectant promissas horrea messes.
sternuntur gravidi longo cum palmite fetus
bacaque cum ramis semper frondentis olivae.   295
saevit et in pecudes: non has pastorve canisve,
non armenta truces possunt defendere tauri.

Diffugiunt populi nec se nisi moenibus urbis
esse putant tutos, donec Meleagros et una
lecta manus iuvenum coiere cupidine laudis   300
Tyndaridae gemini, spectandus caestibus alter,
alter equo, primaeque ratis molitor Iason
et cum Pirithoo, felix concordia, Theseus
et duo Thestiadae prolesque Aphareia, Lynceus
et velox Idas, et iam non femina Caeneus   305
Leucippusque ferox iaculoque insignis Acastus
Hippothousque Dryasque et cretus Amyntore Phoenix
Actoridaeque pares et missus ab Elide Phyleus.
nec Telamon aberat magnique creator Achillis
cumque Pheretiade et Hyanteo Iolao   310
impiger Eurytion et cursu invictus Echion
Naryciusque Lelex Panopeusque Hyleusque feroxque
Hippasus et primis etiamnum Nestor in annis,
et quos Hippocoon antiquis misit Amyclis,

286 *in margine man. al.* EMNSU   vel ut alta *Burman*   289 arent
Heinsius   290 vix modo crescenti *Rhen.*, *ex coni. Heinsius*
291 nec matura ꜱ *Heinsius*   298 se nisi *M*: sese in *ELM*²: magnis
N   300 caluere *EN*²*U Plan.*   301 spectandus *NU*: spectatus
P: spectantes *M*¹: praestantes *EL*   305. 306 *hoc ordine F*ꜱ: 306.
305 *A Plan.*   311 et cursu] cursuque *EU*   312 Panopeusque
L: Panopeus *A*   313 in armis *N*² *Vatic. Prim. Cantabrig. et multi
alii Heinsius*

Penelopaeque socer cum Parrhasio Ancaeo   315
Ampycidesque sagax et adhuc a coniuge tutus
Oeclides nemorisque decus Tegeaea Lycaei:
rasilis huic summam mordebat fibula vestem,
crinis erat simplex, nodum collectus in unum;
ex umero pendens resonabat eburnea laevo   320
telorum custos, arcum quoque laeva tenebat;
talis erat cultu, facies quam dicere vere
virgineam in puero, puerilem in virgine possis.
hanc pariter vidit, pariter Calydonius heros
optavit, renuente deo, flammasque latentes   325
hausit et 'o felix, si quem dignabitur' inquit
'ista virum!' nec plura sinit tempusque pudorque
dicere: maius opus magni certaminis urget.
  Silva frequens trabibus, quam nulla ceciderat aetas,
incipit a plano devexaque prospicit arva;   330
quo postquam venere viri, pars retia tendunt,
vincula pars adimunt canibus, pars pressa sequuntur
signa pedum cupiuntque suum reperire periclum.
concava vallis erat, quo se demittere rivi
adsuerant pluvialis aquae: tenet ima lacunae   335
lenta salix ulvaeque leves iuncique palustres
viminaque et longa parvae sub harundine cannae.
hinc aper excitus medios violentus in hostes
fertur ut excussis elisi nubibus ignes.
sternitur incursu nemus, et propulsa fragorem   340
silva dat. exclamant iuvenes praetentaque forti
tela tenent dextra lato vibrantia ferro.

---

post 317 venit At(h)alantis (S)c(h)oeni pulcherrima virgo *in textu hMP*
in margine N^2 318 summam] primam *NU*   322 cultus *Thuan.*
et complures alii Heinsius   323 posses *Lp*   334 qua ς de-
mittere $E\varsigma$: dimittere *A*   337 longa parvae *PU Vatic. Prim. et tres*
alii Heinsius: long(a)e parva *A Plan.*   339 excussis elisus . . . ignis
aELP: excussus elisis (collisis *Tiliobroga*) . . . ignis $S\varsigma$ *Ciofanus*
340–402 *om. MN*; *in margine* M^2 (*tribus manibus* 340–56, 357–70, 371–
402); *folio postea inserto* N^2 341 praetentaque $N^2\varsigma$: protentaque *A*
342 venabula *Sprot.*

ille ruit spargitque canes, ut quisque furenti
obstat, et obliquo latrantes dissipat ictu.
Cuspis Echionio primum contorta lacerto 345
vana fuit truncoque dedit leve vulnus acerno;
proxima, si nimiis mittentis viribus usa
non foret, in tergo visa est haesura petito:
longius it; auctor teli Pagasaeus Iason.
'Phoebe,' ait Ampycides, 'si te coluique coloque, 350
da mihi quod petitur certo contingere telo!'
qua potuit, precibus deus annuit: ictus ab illo est,
sed sine vulnere, aper; ferrum Diana volanti
abstulerat iaculo: lignum sine acumine venit.
Ira feri mota est, nec fulmine lenius arsit: 355
emicat ex oculis, spirat quoque pectore flamma,
utque volat moles adducto concita nervo,
cum petit aut muros aut plenas milite turres,
in iuvenes certo sic impete vulnificus sus
fertur, et Hippalmon Pelagonaque, dextra tuentes 360
cornua, prosternit; socii rapuere iacentes.
at non letiferos effugit Enaesimus ictus,
Hippocoonte satus: trepidantem et terga parantem
vertere succiso liquerunt poplite nervi.
Forsitan et Pylius citra Troiana perisset 365
tempora, sed sumpto posita conamine ab hasta
arboris insiluit, quae stabat proxima, ramis
despexitque, loco tutus, quem fugerat hostem.
dentibus ille ferox in querno stipite tritis
imminet exitio, fidensque recentibus armis 370
Eurytidae magni rostro femur hausit adunco.

343 ruenti *unus Bonon. Heinsius* 356 lux micat *ç Heinsius*: fax
micat *Schepper* spiratque e *ç Jahn* flamma *h¹FM²*: flammas *A Plan.*
359 certo] vasto *unus Leidens. et Sixian. Burman* 360 Hippalmon
Riese (hipalmon *U*): (h)ippalamon *FP*: hi(y)palemon *EM²N²*: Eupa-
lamon *Plan. cod. Paris. 2848*: Euphemon *tempt. Slater* 364 suc-
ciduo *Sixian. et Gronov. Tert.* 370 frendensque *varia lectio in Sprot.
Burman* 371 Eurytidae *Merkel²*: Othriadae *Palat. Alter Heinsii*:
Actoridae *quattuor Heinsii*: orithiae *vel similia A*

At gemini, nondum caelestia sidera, fratres,
ambo conspicui, nive candidioribus ambo
vectabantur equis, ambo vibrata per auras
hastarum tremulo quatiebant spicula motu.   375
vulnera fecissent, nisi saetiger inter opacas
nec iaculis isset nec equo loca pervia silvas.
persequitur Telamon, studioque incautus eundi
pronus ab arborea cecidit radice retentus.
    Dum levat hunc Peleus, celerem Tegeaea sagittam   380
imposuit nervo sinuatoque expulit arcu:
fixa sub aure feri summum destrinxit harundo
corpus, et exiguo rubefecit sanguine saetas;
nec tamen illa sui successu laetior ictus
quam Meleagros erat: primus vidisse putatur   385
et primus sociis visum ostendisse cruorem
et 'meritum' dixisse 'feres virtutis honorem.'
erubuere viri seque exhortantur et addunt
cum clamore animos iaciuntque sine ordine tela;
turba nocet iactis, et, quos petit, impedit ictus.   390
    Ecce furens contra sua fata bipennifer Arcas
'discite, femineis quid tela virilia praestent,
o iuvenes, operique meo concedite!' dixit:
'ipsa suis licet hunc Latonia protegat armis,
invita tamen hunc perimet mea dextra Diana.'   395
talia magniloquo tumidus memoraverat ore,
ancipitemque manu tollens utraque securim
institerat digitis primos suspensus in artus.
occupat audentem, quaque est via proxima leto
summa ferus geminos direxit ad inguina dentes.   400
concidit Ancaeus, glomerataque sanguine multo
viscera lapsa fluunt; madefacta est terra cruore.

---

372 sidera] corpora M^2N^2U 375 quatientes *unus Med. et Prior
Twisden. Heinsius*   377 isset nec iaculo nec equis ρ *Sprot.*
382 destringit *Rhenov. Heinsius*   389 iactantque ς *Heinsius*
398 pronos suspensus in artus *Merkel*[2]: pronos suspensus in ictus *Ehwald*
399 audacem *Gronov. Prim. et Arondel. et alii Heinsius*   402 made-
facta est terra cruore M^2ς: madefactaque terra cruore est *EU*: made-
factaque sanguine terra est *FL: de N^2 et P non liquet*

Ibat in adversum proles Ixionis hostem
Pirithous valida quatiens venabula dextra;
cui 'procul' Aegides 'o me mihi carior' inquit   405
'pars animae consiste meae! licet eminus esse
fortibus: Ancaeo nocuit temeraria virtus.'
dixit et aerata torsit grave cuspide cornum;
quo bene librato votique potente futuro,
obstitit aesculea frondosus ab arbore ramus.   410

Misit et Aesonides iaculum, quod casus ab illo
vertit in immeriti fatum latrantis, et inter
ilia coniectum tellure per ilia fixum est.

At manus Oenidae variat, missisque duabus
hasta prior terra, medio stetit altera tergo.   415
nec mora, dum saevit, dum corpora versat in orbem
stridentemque novo spumam cum sanguine fundit,
vulneris auctor adest hostemque irritat ad iram
splendidaque adversos venabula condit in armos.

Gaudia testantur socii clamore secundo   420
victricemque petunt dextrae coniungere dextram,
immanemque ferum multa tellure iacentem
mirantes spectant, neque adhuc contingere tutum
esse putant, sed tela tamen sua quisque cruentat.

ipse pede imposito caput exitiabile pressit   425
atque ita 'sume mei spolium, Nonacria, iuris,'
dixit 'et in partem veniat mea gloria tecum!'
protinus exuvias, rigidis horrentia saetis
terga dat et magnis insignia dentibus ora.
illi laetitiae est cum munere muneris auctor;   430

---

405 *distinxit Burman*   409 quo *EU*² ⟨ *Heinsius*: cui *A*   votoque
*hM*¹   410 (a)esculea *ELU (e.v.l. N²)*: herculea ρ *Sprot.*: abscisa
JMS: obstipa *tempt. Merkel*   412 in immeriti fatum *Cantabrig.*: in
immeritum fatum *Rottendorph.*: et inmentum (immeritum *e.v.l. M²*)
figi(t) *A*   latrantis *EU Cantabrig. et Rottendorph.*: geladanten *e.v.l. N²*:
de M non liquet, de P siletur   vertit in immeriti fatum Celadontis *post*
Heinsium Ehwald: vertit in immeritam figi Geladantin *Heinsius*
419 adversis venabula condidit armis *N*   421 dextram coniungere
dextrae ⟨   430 laetitiae *Eh*: laetitia *A*

invidere alii, totoque erat agmine murmur.
e quibus ingenti tendentes bracchia voce
'pone age nec titulos intercipe, femina, nostros,'
Thestiadae clamant, 'nec te fiducia formae
decipiat, ne sit longe tibi captus amore   435
auctor!' et huic adimunt munus, ius muneris illi.

Non tulit, et tumida frendens Mavortius ira
'discite, raptores alieni' dixit 'honoris,
facta minis quantum distent!' hausitque nefando
pectora Plexippi, nil tale timentia, ferro.   440
Toxea, quid faciat dubium pariterque volentem
ulcisci fratrem fraternaque fata timentem,
haud patitur dubitare diu calidumque priori
caede recalfecit consorti sanguine telum.

Dona deum templis nato victore ferebat,   445
cum videt exstinctos fratres Althaea referri.
quae plangore dato maestis clamoribus urbem
implet et auratis mutavit vestibus atras;
at simul est auctor necis editus, excidit omnis
luctus et a lacrimis in poenae versus amorem est.   450

Stipes erat, quem, cum partus enixa iaceret
Thestias, in flammam triplices posuere sorores;
staminaque impresso fatalia pollice nentes
'tempora' dixerunt 'eadem lignoque tibique,
o modo nate, damus.' quo postquam carmine dicto   455
excessere deae, flagrantem mater ab igne
eripuit ramum sparsitque liquentibus undis.
ille diu fuerat penetralibus abditus imis
servatusque tuos, iuvenis, servaverat annos.
protulit hunc genetrix taedasque et fragmina poni   460
imperat et positis inimicos admovet ignes.

435 *sic Plan. et ex corr.* M   nec *E*: neu *L*   longo tibi (tibi longo
E) *A*   decipiat longeque tuo sit *unus Palat. et Moreti fragm. Heinsius*
443 prioris *ENU*   447 ululatibus *Moreti Prim. et octo alii Heinsius*
448 auratas . . . atris ρ *Lovan. et Sprot. Heinsius*   452 flamma *duo
Medd.*   453 fatali *M¹N¹S¹*   455 quae *M*   457 ramum]
torrem *ς Heinsius*   460 et] in *ς Heinsius*

tum, conata quater flammis imponere ramum,
coepta quater tenuit. pugnat materque sororque,
et diversa trahunt unum duo nomina pectus.
saepe metu sceleris pallebant ora futuri,   465
saepe suum fervens oculis dabat ira ruborem.
et modo nescio quid similis crudele minanti
vultus erat, modo quem misereri credere posses;
cumque ferus lacrimas animi siccaverat ardor,
inveniebantur lacrimae tamen, utque carina,   470
quam ventus ventoque rapit contrarius aestus,
vim geminam sentit paretque incerta duobus,
Thestias haud aliter dubiis affectibus errat
inque vices ponit positamque resuscitat iram.

  Incipit esse tamen melior germana parente,   475
et, consanguineas ut sanguine leniat umbras,
impietate pia est. nam postquam pestifer ignis
convaluit, 'rogus iste cremet mea viscera!' dixit.
utque manu dira lignum fatale tenebat,
ante sepulcrales infelix adstitit aras   480
'poenarum' que 'deae triplices, furialibus,' inquit
'Eumenides, sacris vultus advertite vestros!
ulciscor facioque nefas: mors morte pianda est,
in scelus addendum scelus est, in funera funus:
per coacervatos pereat domus impia luctus!   485
an felix Oeneus nato victore fruetur,
Thestius orbus erit? melius lugebitis ambo.
vos modo, fraterni manes animaeque recentes,
officium sentite meum magnoque paratas
accipite inferias, uteri mala pignora nostri!   490
  'Ei mihi! quo rapior? fratres, ignoscite matri!

  463 pugnat *EMU*: pugnant *Nς Heinsius*   464 et] in *unus
Moreti Heinsius*   466 colorem *EU*: calorem *e*: furorem *duo Heinsii*
468 qui *M*   credere posses] posset amato *M*: posse videres *S*
474 perque *ELPU*   478 concaluit *ς*   479 manu lignum dextra
Sprot.   486 fruatur *Arondel.*: feratur *Gronov.*: feretur *unus Moreti*
487 erat *Arondel. et Rottendorph.*: eat *Heinsius*

deficiunt ad coepta manus: meruisse fatemur
illum cur pereat, mortis mihi displicet auctor.

'Ergo impune feret, vivusque et victor et ipso
successu tumidus regnum Calydonis habebit,   495
vos cinis exiguus gelidaeque iacebitis umbrae?
haud equidem patiar: pereat sceleratus et ille,
spemque patris regnumque trahat patriaeque ruinam!

'Mens ubi materna est? ubi sunt pia iura parentum,
et quos sustinui bis mensum quinque labores?   500
'O utinam primis arsisses ignibus infans
idque ego passa forem! vixisti munere nostro;
nunc merito moriere tuo. cape praemia facti,
bisque datam, primum partu, mox stipite rapto,
redde animam; vel me fraternis adde sepulcris!   505
'Et cupio et nequeo: quid agam? modo vulnera fratrum
ante oculos mihi sunt et tantae caedis imago,
nunc animum pietas maternaque nomina frangunt.

'Me miseram! male vincetis, sed vincite, fratres,
dummodo quae dedero vobis solacia vosque   510
ipsa sequar!' dixit, dextraque aversa trementi
funereum torrem medios coniecit in ignes.
aut dedit aut visus gemitus est ille dedisse
stipes, et invitis correptus ab ignibus arsit.

Inscius atque absens flamma Meleagros ab illa   515
uritur et caecis torreri viscera sentit
ignibus; at magnos superat virtute dolores.
quod tamen ignavo cadat et sine sanguine leto
maeret, et Ancaei felicia vulnera dicit;
grandaevumque patrem fratresque piasque sorores   520
cum gemitu, sociamque tori vocat ore supremo—
forsitan et matrem. crescunt ignisque dolorque,

497 ille] una *malit Heinsius*   498 regnique *Haun. 2009 Heinsius*
499 sunt] nunc *ϛ Burman*   iura] vota *EhU*   500 bis *hic MN Pri-
scianus, ante* quinque *A*   mensum *eMNPU² Priscianus*: menses *EU*
513 ipse *Bentley*   514 ut *e Merkel*   515 ab] in *ϛ Heinsius*
517 at *E Heinsius*: ac *A*   518 sine vulnere *EU*   519 funera
Senat.

languescuntque iterum; simul est exstinctus uterque,
inque leves abiit paulatim spiritus auras
paulatim cana prunam velante favilla. 525

Alta iacet Calydon: lugent iuvenesque senesque,
vulgusque proceresque gemunt, scissaeque capillos
planguntur matres Calydonides Eueninae.
pulvere canitiem genitor vultusque seniles
foedat humi fusus, spatiosumque increpat aevum. 530
nam de matre manus diri sibi conscia facti
exegit poenas acto per viscera ferro.
non mihi si centum deus ora sonantia linguis
ingeniumque capax totumque Helicona dedisset,
tristia persequerer miserarum dicta sororum. 535
immemores decoris liventia pectora tundunt,
dumque manet corpus, corpus refoventque foventque,
oscula dant ipsi, posito dant oscula lecto.
post cinerem, cineres haustos ad pectora pressant,
adfusaeque iacent tumulo, signataque saxo 540
nomina complexae lacrimas in nomina fundunt.
quas Parthaoniae tandem Latonia clade
exsatiata domus, praeter Gorgenque nurumque
nobilis Alcmenae, natis in corpore pennis
adlevat et longas per bracchia porrigit alas, 545
corneaque ora facit, versasque per aera mittit.

Interea Theseus, sociati parte laboris
functus, Erectheas Tritonidos ibat ad arces.
clausit iter fecitque moras Achelous eunti
imbre tumens. 'succede meis,' ait 'inclite, tectis, 550

525 om. EU¹ Plan., del. Heinsius   527 vulgusque] et vulgus L
scissosque N   528 planguntur F: plangunt (addito hunc MP, se
EU) A: plangebant S   Eueninae Heinsius (Euveninae S): Oeneus
atque P, peiora fere A   plangunt ora simul matres Calydonides.
Oeneus N² (post rasuras)   533 linguae M¹N¹P   535 prose-
querer NU²   dicta NU² Plan. Heinsius: vota EMU: voce Merkel²
537 corpus²] tangunt N   539 post cineres cineres N   pressant
EFhL: versant MNU   540–1 signataque saxa / nomine ς Heinsius
541 in nomine ς Heinsius

Cecropida, nec te committe rapacibus undis:
ferre trabes solidas obliquaque volvere magno
murmure saxa solent. vidi contermina ripae
cum gregibus stabula alta trahi; nec fortibus illic
profuit armentis nec equis velocibus esse.   555
multa quoque hic torrens nivibus de monte solutis
corpora turbineo iuvenalia culmine mersit.
tutior est requies, solito dum flumina currant
limite, dum tenues capiat suus alveus undas.'

Adnuit Aegides, 'utor,' que 'Acheloe, domoque   560
consilioque tuo' respondit, et usus utroque est.
pumice multicavo nec levibus atria tophis
structa subit; molli tellus erat umida musco,
summa lacunabant alterno murice conchae.
iamque duas lucis partes Hyperione menso   565
discubuere toris Theseus comitesque laborum:
hac Ixionides, illa Troezenius heros
parte Lelex, raris iam sparsus tempora canis,
quosque alios parili fuerat dignatus honore
amnis Acarnanum, laetissimus hospite tanto.   570
protinus appositas nudae vestigia nymphae
instruxere epulis mensas, dapibusque remotis
in gemma posuere merum. tum maximus heros
aequora prospiciens oculis subiecta 'quis' inquit
'ille locus?' (digitoque ostendit) 'et insula nomen   575
quod gerit illa doce—quamquam non una videtur.'

    Amnis ad haec 'non est' inquit 'quod cernitis unum:
quinque iacent terrae; spatium discrimina fallit.

551 Cecropida *LMP*: Cecropide *ENU*   553 contraria *M*¹*S*
557 culmine h*LMNP*: vertice *ESU*: flumine *Heinsius*   559 capiat
ς *Heinsius*: capiet *e*: captat *A*   560 utarque (? *E*) ς *Plan.*
564 lacus nabant *ELM*²*U*¹   567 Troezenius ς *Plan.*: Trozenius *A*
568 pariis *E*: parvis *FU*   sparsus iam *F*   569 alii *MNU*
572 epulis mensas *EU Plan.*: epulas mensis (mensa *N*) *MNS*
573 gemmam *U*   576 gerat *E*   gerit illa? doce! *distinxit Münster*
577 cernitis *MU*²: cernimus *ELNU Plan.*   578 spatii . . . fallunt
EU: spatii discrimine fallunt *U*² *Heinsius*

quoque minus spretae factum mirere Dianae,
naides hae fuerant. quae cum bis quinque iuvencos   580
mactassent, rurisque deos ad sacra vocassent,
immemores nostri festas duxere choreas.
intumui, quantusque feror cum plurimus umquam
tantus eram, pariterque animis immanis et undis
a silvis silvas et ab arvis arva revelli,   585
cumque loco nymphas, memores tum denique nostri,
in freta provolvi. fluctus nosterque marisque
continuam diduxit humum, partesque resolvit
in totidem mediis quot cernis Echinadas undis.
ut tamen ipse vides, procul, en procul, una recessit   590
insula, grata mihi (Perimelen navita dicit).
huic ego virgineum dilectae nomen ademi,
quod pater Hippodamas aegre tulit, inque profundum
propulit e scopulo periturae corpora natae.
excepi, nantemque ferens "o proxima mundi   595
regna vagae" dixi "sortite, tridentifer, undae,
in quo desinimus quot sacri currimus amnes,
huc ades atque audi placidus, Neptune, precantem.
huic ego, quam porto, nocui: si mitis et aequus,
si pater Hippodamas, aut si minus impius esset,   600
debuit illius misereri, ignoscere nobis.   600b
cui quoniam tellus clausa est feritate paterna,   601a
[adfer opem, mersaeque, precor, feritate paterna]   601
da, Neptune, locum—vel sit locus ipsa licebit:

---

585 revelli *LMNP*: revulsi (?*E*)*M*[2]*N*[2]*U*   588 partesque *Harl.*
2742 et Moreti fragm.: pariterque *A*   resolvit *Quart. Med. et man. sec.*
Rottendorph.: revellit *A*   591 Perimeden *malit Magnus*   594 pro-
tulit *N Sprot.*   pariturae *unus Leidens. et Rhenov. Heinsius*
595 mundi *LMNS*[1]*U*: terrae *aEU*[2]: mundo *Heinsius*: caelo *edd. vett.*
597–601[a] *om. aELMNSU; habent in textu ehPs*[1]*s*[2]*, in rasura F*[2]*, in*
margine E[2]*N*[2]*; damnat Magnus, def. Enk*   597 in quem decidii-
mus *unus Moreti*: in quem deferimur *Paris. 7993 Heinsius*: in quem
defluimus *Paris. unus*   quot *Burman*: quo *A*   598 *del. Hein-*
sius   599 sis mitis *eF*[2] *Lovan.*   601[a] quondam *A, corr. Bothe*
601, 602 *om. N*

hunc quoque complectar!" movit caput aequoreus rex,
concussitque suis omnes adsensibus undas.
extimuit nymphe, nabat tamen; ipse natantis   605
pectora tangebam trepido salientia motu.
dumque ea contrecto, totum durescere sensi
corpus, et inducta condi praecordia terra.'
[dum loquor, amplexa est artus nova terra natantis,
et gravis increvit mutatis insula membris.]   610

   Amnis ab his tacuit. factum mirabile cunctos
moverat: irridet credentes, utque deorum
spretor erat mentisque ferox, Ixione natus
'ficta refers, nimiumque putas, Acheloe, potentes
esse deos' dixit, 'si dant adimuntque figuras.'   615

   Obstipuere omnes nec talia dicta probarunt,
ante omnesque Lelex, animo maturus et aevo,
sic ait: 'immensa est finemque potentia caeli
non habet, et quidquid superi voluere peractum est.
quoque minus dubites, tiliae contermina quercus   620
collibus est Phrygiis modico circumdata muro.
ipse locum vidi; nam me Pelopeia Pittheus
misit in arva, suo quondam regnata parenti.

   'Haud procul hinc stagnum est, tellus habitabilis olim,
nunc celebres mergis fulicisque palustribus undae.   625
Iuppiter huc specie mortali cumque parente
venit Atlantiades positis caducifer alis.
mille domos adiere locum requiemque petentes,
mille domos clausere serae. tamen una recepit
parva quidem, stipulis et canna tecta palustri,   630

603–608 om. aEFLMNS; habent eodem modo qui supra (597–601ᵃ)
adhibentur testes; damnat Magnus, def. Enk   603 hunc ehς: hanc A:
tunc Heinsius: sic Burman   complector N²   607 tactum Sixian.
608 inducta . . . terra E²N²ς: inductis . . . terris A   609 natantis
Nς: natantes A   611 fatum Heinsius   615 qui dent adimant-
que Heinsius   616 obstrepuere unus Med. Burman   618 'vis'
ait Burman: 'dis' ait olim Heinsius   619 paratum unus Ciofani
620 tiliae e.v.l. L²M²N²U²: vel nunc E: de me P¹   621 modico
eF²ς: medio A Plan.   625 statio . . . uda (ὑγρὸν ἐνδιαίτημα) Plan.
630 stipulisque et Capoferreus   texta post Priceum Heinsius

sed pia Baucis anus parilique aetate Philemon
illa sunt annis iuncti iuvenalibus, illa
consenuere casa, paupertatemque fatendo
effecere levem nec iniqua mente ferendo.
nec refert dominos illic famulosne requiras:⁣ 635
tota domus duo sunt, idem parentque iubentque.

'Ergo ubi caelicolae parvos tetigere penates
summissoque humiles intrarunt vertice postes,
membra senex posito iussit relevare sedili,
quo superiniecit textum rude sedula Baucis 640
inque foco tepidum cinerem dimovit et ignes
suscitat hesternos foliisque et cortice sicco
nutrit et ad flammas anima producit anili;
multifidasque faces ramaliaque arida tecto
detulit et minuit parvoque admovit aeno, 645
quodque suus coniunx riguo collegerat horto
truncat holus foliis. furca levat ille bicorni
sordida terga suis nigro pendentia tigno,
servatoque diu resecat de tergore partem
exiguam, sectamque domat ferventibus undis. 650

'Interea medias fallunt sermonibus horas
sentirique moram prohibent. erat alveus illic
fagineus, curva clavo suspensus ab ansa:
is tepidis impletur aquis artusque fovendos
accipit. in medio torus est de mollibus ulvis 655ᵃ

631 sed pia: Baucis *distinxit Ehwald* 633 fatendo *EMSU Plan.*:
favendo *N*: ferendo *LP* 634 ferendo *M¹SU*: ferendam *EFNP
Plan.* 637 parvos *LNU² Plan.*: paucos *EMS*: parcos *man. sec.
Rottendorph.* 640 cui *Madvig* 641 inque] inde *E*: eque
Heinsius 647 ille *A Plan.*: ill(-e *e.v.l.*) *N²*: illa *M¹ ex suis Ciofa-
nus* 650 eximiam *Polle* 652–655ᵃ *sic fere EeFhLPSs₁s₂U Plan.*;
in margine M²N²; damnat Magnus, def. Enk 652 sentirique
EM²N²Ps₁s₂U: et sentire *FLS Plan.* 653 curva *var. lect. in Bar-
berin.*: dura *A Plan.*: curta *vel* vara *tempt. Heinsius* 654 trepidis *r*
655ᵃ–656ᵃ accipit. inde torum sternunt de mollibus ulvis / impositum
lecto *tempt. Heinsius* *inter* 655ᵃ *et* 656ᵃ *habent hunc versum (cf.* 655) *eS
aliquot* ς: concutiuntque (*vel* conficiuntque *vel* consternuntque) torum
de molli fluminis ulva

impositus lecto sponda pedibusque salignis: 656ᵃ
[concutiuntque torum de molli fluminis ulva   655
impositum lecto sponda pedibusque salignis:]   656
vestibus hunc velant, quas non nisi tempore festo
sternere consuerant, sed et haec vilisque vetusque
vestis erat, lecto non indignanda saligno.
accubuere dei. mensam succincta tremensque   660
ponit anus, mensae sed erat pes tertius impar;
testa parem fecit, quae postquam subdita clivum
sustulit, aequatam mentae tersere virentes.
ponitur hic bicolor sincerae baca Minervae
conditaque in liquida corna autumnalia faece,   665
intibaque et radix et lactis massa coacti
ovaque non acri leviter versata favilla,
omnia fictilibus. post haec caelatus eodem
sistitur argento crater fabricataque fago
pocula, qua cava sunt, flaventibus illita ceris.   670
parva mora est, epulasque foci misere calentes,
nec longae rursus referuntur vina senectae
dantque locum mensis paulum seducta secundis.
hic nux, hic mixta est rugosis carica palmis,
prunaque et in patulis redolentia mala canistris   675
et de purpureis collectae vitibus uvae.
candidus in medio favus est; super omnia vultus
accessere boni, nec iners pauperque voluntas.
'Interea totiens haustum cratera repleri
sponte sua per seque vident succrescere vina: 680
attoniti novitate pavent manibusque supinis
concipiunt Baucisque preces timidusque Philemon
et veniam dapibus nullisque paratibus orant.

656ᵃ impositus (-us *in rasura* U) *FLM²PU*: impositis (-is *e.v.l. N²s₁*)
aEN²s₁s₂: imposito *S*   655 *habent MN (virgula del. M²)*; *om. A*
concutiuntque *M* : conficiuntque *N*   656 *vide ad* 656ᵃ   impositum
videtur fuisse in MN (Magnus)   663 menta . . . virenti *e²*
extersere *aENU*   668–9 eadem | . . . argilla (argilla *Palat. unus*)
Dan. Heinsius   670 quae *aLM¹PU*   675 olentia *LS*: volentia
(v *supra lineam*) *M*: halantia *vel* ridentia *Heinsius*   679 quotiens *ς*
Heinsius   683 *om. M¹N¹*

unicus anser erat, minimae custodia villae;
quem dis hospitibus domini mactare parabant.   685
ille celer penna tardos aetate fatigat
eluditque diu, tandemque est visus ad ipsos
confugisse deos. superi vetuere necari
"di" que "sumus, meritasque luet vicinia poenas
impia" dixerunt; "vobis immunibus huius   690
esse mali dabitur. modo vestra relinquite tecta
ac nostros comitate gradus, et in ardua montis
[ite simul!" parent ambo, baculisque levati]   693
ite simul!" parent, et dis praeeuntibus ambo   693ª
membra levant baculis, tardique senilibus annis   693ᵇ
nituntur longo vestigia ponere clivo.

'Tantum aberant summo quantum semel ire sagitta   695
missa potest: flexere oculos et mersa palude
cetera prospiciunt, tantum sua tecta manere.
dumque ea mirantur, dum deflent fata suorum,
illa vetus, dominis etiam casa parva duobus,
vertitur in templum: furcas subiere columnae,   700
stramina flavescunt, aurataque tecta videntur
caelataeque fores, adopertaque marmore tellus.
talia tum placido Saturnius edidit ore:
"dicite, iuste senex et femina coniuge iusto
digna, quid optetis!" cum Baucide pauca locutus   705

693 *habent MS; om. A Plan.; N¹ eras.*   *levati S: levatis M*
693ª, 693ᵇ *sic (e.v.l. N²) A Plan.; in margine M²S²; damnat Magnus, def.*
Enk   695 *semel ire] finire N*   696 *ad hunc versum in margine e²*
(696ª) *missa potest flexere oculos et inhospita tecta* / (697ᵇ) *mersa*
vident quaeruntque ubi sint pia culmina villae   697 *'mira hinc*
varietas' (Magnus) velut: (697ª) *mersa (cuncta Vollgraff) vident quae-*
runtque suae pia culmina villae / (698ª) *sola loco stabant (stabat*
Bersm.) dum deflent fata suorum (quae dis fuit hospita magnis Berol.)
697ª *et* 698ª *'primo, ni fallor, versui* 699 *in margine ab eadem, quae add.*
693ª *et* 693ᵇ, *manu adscripta in M, fluxerunt inde in F et multos 5'*
(Magnus); damnant Magnus, Enk   699 *plena Burman*   701 *aura-*
taque tecta videntur ae Plan.: adopertaque marmore tellus hMNS
702 *adopertaque marmore tellus ae Plan.: aurataque tecta videntur*
hMNS   *post* 702 *iteratum habent v.* 682 *aeU Plan.*   703 *cum*
EU: dum N

iudicium superis aperit commune Philemon:
"esse sacerdotes delubraque vestra tueri
poscimus, et, quoniam concordes egimus annos,
auferat hora duos eadem, nec coniugis unquam
busta meae videam, neu sim tumulandus ab illa."   710

'Vota fides sequitur: templi tutela fuere
donec vita data est; annis aevoque soluti
ante gradus sacros cum starent forte, locique
narrarent casus, frondere Philemona Baucis,
Baucida conspexit senior frondere Philemon.   715
iamque super geminos crescente cacumine vultus
mutua, dum licuit, reddebant dicta "vale"-que
"o coniunx" dixere simul, simul abdita texit
ora frutex. ostendit adhuc Thÿneius illic
incola de gemino vicinos corpore truncos.   720

'Haec mihi non vani (neque erat cur fallere vellent)
narravere senes; equidem pendentia vidi
serta super ramos, ponensque recentia dixi
"cura deum di sint, et qui coluere colantur." '

Desierat, cunctosque et res et moverat auctor,   725
Thesea praecipue; quem facta audire volentem
mira deum innixus cubito Calydonius amnis
talibus alloquitur: 'sunt, o fortissime, quorum
forma semel mota est et in hoc renovamine mansit,
sunt quibus in plures ius est transire figuras,   730
ut tibi, complexi terram maris incola, Proteu.
nam modo te iuvenem, modo te videre leonem,
nunc violentus aper, nunc, quem tetigisse timerent,
anguis eras, modo te faciebant cornua taurum;
saepe lapis poteras, arbor quoque saepe videri,   735

---

710 tumulatus *EU*   714 narrassent *FL*: inciperent *N*: navarent
deinde curas) *Merkel*[2] *p. xxvii*   716 gelidos *Iunian. Burman*
718 addita *L*: obdita *Heinsius*   719 Thyneius *Ehwald* (thineius
EFLMN): thimeius *P*: Tyaneius *ς*: Tyrieius *Polle*: *alii alia*
720 gemina . . . arbore *EN*[2]*U*   724 di sint] dii sint *M*: di sunt *N*
colantur *hMN*: coluntur *FL*   cura pii dis sunt . . . coluntur *Heinsius*
730 transisse F

interdum, faciem liquidarum imitatus aquarum,
flumen eras, interdum undis contrarius ignis.
 'Nec minus Autolyci coniunx, Erysicthone nata,
iuris habet. pater huius erat qui numina divum
sperneret et nullos aris adoleret odores.   740
ille etiam Cereale nemus violasse securi
dicitur et lucos ferro temerasse vetustos.
stabat in his ingens annoso robore quercus,
una nemus; vittae mediam memoresque tabellae
sertaque cingebant, voti argumenta potentum.   745
saepe sub hac dryades festas duxere choreas,
saepe etiam manibus nexis ex ordine trunci
circuiere modum, mensuraque roboris ulnas
quinque ter implebat. nec non et cetera tantum
silva sub hac, silva quantum fuit herba sub omni. 750
 'Non tamen idcirco ferrum Dryopeius illa
abstinuit, famulosque iubet succidere sacrum
robur, et, ut iussos cunctari vidit, ab uno
edidit haec rapta sceleratus verba securi:
"non dilecta deae solum, sed et ipsa licebit   755
sit dea, iam tanget frondente cacumine terram."
 'Dixit, et, obliquos dum telum librat in ictus,
contremuit gemitumque dedit Deoia quercus:
et pariter frondes, pariter pallescere glandes
coepere, ac longi pallorem ducere rami.   760
cuius ut in trunco fecit manus impia vulnus,
haud aliter fluxit discusso cortice sanguis,
quam solet, ante aras ingens ubi victima taurus
concidit, abrupta cruor e cervice profundi.

740 odores *MN*: honores *EPU*[1] *Plan.*   745 potentum *Heinsius*:
potentis *A*   749 tantum *EM*[2]*NU*: tanto *MPS*   750 silva[2]
Heinsius: omnis *A*   quantum *EM*[2]*NU*: quanto *MPS*   sub illa
hς   751 Dry(i)opeius *A Plan.*: Triopeius (T *ex corr. man. rec. U*)
U Rhenov.   illa *FhL*: ab illa *A*   757 telum dum *EU*   758 Deoia
Vivianus: deoida *vel similia A*: decidua *S*[1]   762 cortice sanguis
(*e.v.l. U*[2]) *e*[2] *Lond. Harl. 2673 et multi ς*: sanguine cortex *EMNPS*:
discussus sanguine cortex *Med. Quart. Heinsius et ex coni. Magnus*

'Obstipuere omnes, aliquisque ex omnibus audet   765
deterrere nefas saevamque inhibere bipennem.
aspicit hunc "mentis" que "piae cape praemia!" dixit
Thessalus, inque virum convertit ab arbore ferrum,
detruncatque caput repetitaque robora caedit,
redditus e medio sonus est cum robore talis: 770
"nympha sub hoc ego sum Cereri gratissima ligno,
quae tibi factorum poenas instare tuorum
vaticinor moriens, nostri solacia leti."
'Persequitur scelus ille suum, labefactaque tandem
ictibus innumeris adductaque funibus arbor   —   775
corruit, et multam prostravit pondere silvam.
attonitae dryades damno nemorumque suoque,
omnes germanae, Cererem cum vestibus atris
maerentes adeunt, poenamque Erysicthonis orant.
annuit his capitisque sui pulcherrima motu   780
concussit gravidis oneratos messibus agros,
moliturque genus poenae miserabile, si non
ille suis esset nulli miserabilis actis,
pestifera lacerare fame. quae quatinus ipsi
non adeunda deae est (neque enim Cereremque Famemque   785
fata coire sinunt) montani numinis unam
talibus agrestem compellat oreada dictis:
'"Est locus extremis Scythiae glacialis in oris,
triste solum, sterilis, sine fruge, sine arbore tellus;
Frigus iners illic habitant Pallorque Tremorque   790
et ieiuna Fames. ea se in praecordia condat
sacrilegi scelerata iube. nec copia rerum
vincat eam, superetque meas certamine vires.
neve viae spatium te terreat, accipe currus,
accipe quos frenis alte moderere dracones!"   795
'Et dedit. illa dato subvecta per aera curru

770 redditus *Mς*: editus *ENUς Heinsius*   e medio . . . cum *gN²*
Lovan. et alii ς: et medio . . . de *MS*   778 et nece germanae *Bar-*
berin. et Senat. et ex coni. Zielinski   784 quatinus *A*: quatenus *FLς*
790 habitat *ς*   792 ne *MP*

devenit in Scythiam, rigidique cacumine montis
(Caucason appellant) serpentum colla levavit,
quaesitamque Famem lapidoso vidit in agro
unguibus et raras vellentem dentibus herbas.   800
hirtus erat crinis, cava lumina, pallor in ore,
labra incana situ, scabrae rubigine fauces,
dura cutis, per quam spectari viscera possent;
ossa sub incurvis exstabant arida lumbis,
ventris erat pro ventre locus, pendere putares   805
pectus, et a spinae tantummodo crate teneri.
auxerat articulos macies, genuumque tumebat
orbis, et immodico prodibant tubere tali.
hanc procul ut vidit (neque enim est accedere iuxta
ausa), refert mandata deae, paulumque morata,   810
quamquam aberat longe, quamquam modo venerat illuc,
visa tamen sensisse famem est, retroque dracones
egit in Haemoniam versis sublimis habenis.

'Dicta Fames Cereris, quamvis contraria semper
illius est operi, peragit, perque aera vento   815
ad iussam delata domum est et protinus intrat
sacrilegi thalamos, altoque sopore solutum
(noctis enim tempus) geminis amplectitur ulnis
seque viro inspirat, faucesque et pectus et ora
afflat, et in vacuis spargit ieiunia venis;   820
functaque mandato fecundum deserit orbem
inque domos inopes adsueta revertitur antra.

'Lenis adhuc somnus placidis Erysicthona pennis
mulcebat: petit ille dapes sub imagine somni,
oraque vana movet, dentemque in dente fatigat   825

797 cacumina *MNP Plan.*   800 raras *M² unus Bonon. Heinsius*:
raris *A Plan.*   802 huic cana *M*   scabri . . . dentes *Gronov.
et Gryph.*: livent . . . fauces *Genev.*   803 numerari *Lovan.*
805–7 pendere . . . macies *om. M¹N¹, del. Merkel*   807 rigebat
Arondel. et duo alii Heinsius   815 vento *eFLM*: vecta *hN*
816–17 et . . . thalamos *om. M¹N¹S*   818 enim *EMU*: eum *N*: erat
ehP alis *N²U*   820 spargit *Vatic. Prim. et alii Heinsii Plan.*:
peragit *A*   822 antra *MNU²*: arva *A Plan. Heinsius*

exercetque cibo delusum guttur inani
proque epulis tenues nequiquam devorat auras.
ut vero est expulsa quies, furit ardor edendi
perque avidas fauces incensaque viscera regnat.
nec mora, quod pontus, quod terra, quod educat aer,   830
poscit et appositis queritur ieiunia mensis,
inque epulis epulas quaerit; quodque urbibus esse
quodque satis poterat populo, non sufficit uni,
plusque cupit quo plura suam demittit in alvum.
utque fretum recipit de tota flumina terra   835
nec satiatur aquis peregrinosque ebibit amnes,
utque rapax ignis non umquam alimenta recusat
innumerasque faces cremat, et, quo copia maior
est data, plura petit, turbaque voracior ipsa est:
sic epulas omnes Erysicthonis ora profani   840
accipiunt poscuntque simul; cibus omnis in illo
causa cibi est, semperque locus fit inanis edendo.
   'Iamque fame patrias altique voragine ventris
attenuarat opes, sed inattenuata manebat
tum quoque dira fames, implacataeque vigebat   845
flamma gulae. tandem, demisso in viscera censu,
filia restabat, non illo digna parente.
hanc quoque vendit inops: dominum generosa recusat,
et vicina suas tendens super aequora palmas
"eripe me domino qui raptae praemia nobis   850
virginitatis habes" ait—haec Neptunus habebat—
qui prece non spreta, quamvis modo visa sequenti
esset ero, formamque novat vultumque virilem
induit et cultus piscem capientibus aptos.
hanc dominus spectans "o qui pendentia parvo   855

---

826 desuetum M unus Bonon.   829 incensaque Heinsius: im-
mensaque A   834 capit ς   836 saturatur U   838 faces
NSU: trabes M   843 altique ENU: altaque Mς   844 maneb
N²U   845 tum] tu NU   852 modo M²P: ea (e.v.l. N²) ELU:
non M   854 cultus 'veteres' Naugerii unus Med. et unus Palat.
Dan. Heinsius: vultus A   piscem LMNP: pisces EU Plan.

aera cibo celas, moderator harundinis," inquit
"sic mare compositum, sic sit tibi piscis in unda
credulus et nullos, nisi fixus, sentiat hamos:
quae modo cum vili turbatis veste capillis
litore in hoc steterat (nam stantem in litore vidi)   860
dic ubi sit! neque enim vestigia longius exstant."
illa dei munus bene cedere sensit, et, a se
se quaeri gaudens, his est resecuta rogantem:
"quisquis es, ignoscas; in nullam lumina partem
gurgite ab hoc flexi studioque operatus inhaesi,   865
quoque minus dubites, sic has deus aequoris artes
adiuvet ut nemo iamdudum litore in isto,
me tamen excepto, nec femina constitit ulla."
    'Credidit et verso dominus pede pressit harenam,
elususque abiit: illi sua reddita forma est.   870
    'Ast ubi habere suam transformia corpora sensit,
saepe pater dominis Dryopeida tradit, at illa
nunc equa, nunc ales, modo bos, modo cervus abibat
praebebatque avido non iusta alimenta parenti.
vis tamen illa mali postquam consumpserat omnem   875
materiam, dederatque gravi nova pabula morbo,
ipse suos artus lacero divellere morsu
coepit et infelix minuendo corpus alebat.
    'Quid moror externis? etiam mihi nempe novandi est
corporis, o iuvenis, numero finita potestas.   880
nam modo qui nunc sum videor, modo flector in anguem,
armenti modo dux vires in cornua sumo—
cornua, dum potui! nunc pars caret altera telo
frontis, ut ipse vides.' gemitus sunt verba secuti.

---

    858 nullos *E*: nullus *MNPU*   865 operatus *Med. Tert. et Thuan.*
Heinsius, ἐργαζόμενος *Plan.*: (h)oneratus *A*   871 suam] satam *Bothe*
872 Dry(i)opeida *A Plan.*: Triopeida *cod. Menardi teste Heinsio*: Trio-
paeam *unus Heinsii*   873 cerva redibat *Zielinski*   876 deerant-
que *Burman* (dederantque *Lovan.*)   877 lacerans *cum Planude*
Postgate   879 nempe *Polle*: saepe *A*   881 qui] quod *e²ς*
883 potui *Mς*: sumpsi *M²NPU*

COMMENTARY

1–151. Scylla

The Development of the Legend

We can trace the story of Scylla, daughter of Nisus, back no further than Aeschylus (*Choephoroe* 612–22). There she is quoted as an example of pitiless cruelty in women; bribed, like Eriphyle, with a golden necklace, she cuts off her father's fateful lock of hair, and so kills him. The legend surely cried out for treatment in a tragedy, and Ovid, *Tristia* ii. 393–4 suggests that this was done:

> impia nec tragicos tetigisset Scylla cothurnos
> ni patrium crinem desecuisset amor.

But we have no clue what play Ovid had in mind. Sophocles wrote a *Minos*, but this most probably described the king's death in Sicily (fr. 407 Pearson, perhaps an alternative name for his *Camici*, see on 260–1). If the Ovidian reference can be trusted, Scylla's love for Minos has already supplanted mere greed, the Aeschylean motive for her parricide. Such a plot would certainly appeal to a follower of Euripides, and the general opinion is that this tragedy was post-Euripidean, but not necessarily Hellenistic.

Our next encounter with Scylla is in the third century B.C. She receives a mention in the *Hecale* of Callimachus (fr. 288 Pfeiffer), which points to this story's canonical form:

> Σκύλλα γυνὴ κατακᾶσα καὶ οὐ ψύθος οὔνομ' ἔχουσα
> πορφυρέην ἤμησε κρέκα.

Nisus here has his crimson lock, and Scylla is called 'whore' no doubt because she fell in love with her enemy Minos, and offered herself to him. It is also possible that Callimachus wrote more fully of her in his *Aetia*. In the miserable remnants of fr. 113 which have survived the proper name Κεῖρις can be restored twice; also οἰωνός. So we have some evidence that in the *Aetia* Scylla was transformed into a bird, as against the simpler and perhaps older opinion that she was drowned for her wickedness (Apollodorus iii. 15. 8, Pausanias ii. 34. 7). Pfeiffer suggests that this story may have occurred in *Aetia*, bk. i; see his notes on fr. 113 and fr. 31 for the mystifying problem of placing.

PLATE I

SCYLLA

Scylla with the lock. Wall-painting now in the Vatican Library

The transformation of Scylla was definitely related by the Bithynian poet Parthenius of Nicaea (fr. 20 Martini, our only certain reference to his own *Metamorphoses*). Parthenius himself is a most intriguing figure, captured in war-time and brought to Rome, a friend of Cornelius Gallus and perhaps also of Virgil, and a vital connecting link between the old Alexandrians and the new Roman poets. W. Ehlers (*Museum Helveticum* xi [1954] 65–88) attacks the traditional view that Parthenius was a main source for the pseudo-Virgilian *Ciris*, but his arguments do not seem decisive to me—the possibility remains, though unprovable. No doubt the *Ciris*-poet could find other Hellenistic models besides Parthenius and Callimachus. Some have thought that the paraphrase of Dionysius (*De Avibus* ii. 14) may go back to the *Ornithogonia* of Boeus or Boeo (see Introduction p. xxi and on 236–59) and it is significant that Nonnus, who is much influenced by Alexandrian models, chooses to write a piece on Scylla (*Dionysiaca* xxv. 148 ff.). Tibullus (i. 4. 63) at least suggests that this legend was a common subject for poetry.

The date and authorship of the *Ciris* have excited much *odium philologicum* since the romantic but rash theory of Franz Skutsch that the author was Cornelius Gallus. Stylistically the poem could well be dated about 45 B.C., but the number of undoubted Virgilian lines or phrases which are definitely less appropriate in the *Ciris* must place it after 19 B.C., at least in its present form. R. Helm (*Hermes* lxxii [1937] 78–103) makes a good statement of the orthodox position nowadays; unlike Helm, though, I believe that the poet is clearly pretending to be Virgil. Whether the *Ciris* is also later than Ovid's Scylla or not remains a thorny problem. The usual opinion now is that Ovid wrote first; this may well be right, but is hardly supported by a comparison of the two accounts. Slight indications tend the other way. For several times Ovid seemingly alludes to a version of the story as in the *Ciris*, and is not quite consistent with his own version (see on 10, 114, 128–30); or he writes in a way only fully intelligible to those who knew a more detailed account (145–6). But in such cases Ovid and the *Ciris*-poet could have some common source, whether or not Parthenius, and the language of the *Ciris* has points of contact with other parts of Ovid's work, not only this episode in the *Metamorphoses*. See R. Thomason in *CP* xviii (1923) 239 ff., 334 ff., xix (1924) 147 ff., for a linguistic study, although some of his examples are unintelligent, and his conclusion not compelling. On matters relating to Ovid and the *Ciris* see also the paragraphs below, and notes to lines 8–9, 10, 14–17, 18, 35, 43, 65–6, 81–3, 95–6, 101–2, 128–30, 142, 145–6, 147, 151. Brooks Otis makes a good stylistic comparison of the two treatments (*Ovid as an Epic Poet*, pp. 62–5); an oddity is noted on 145–6.

34 COMMENTARY

Variations in the Story

The *Ciris* gives a principal part to Scylla's nurse, as on a wall-painting from Pompeii (Plate II, cf. 95–6 n.), and in many similar stories. Some writers make Nisus' lock golden instead of crimson (Tzetzes on Lycophron 650, scholiast on Euripides, *Hippolytus* 1200) like the lock of Pterelaus (cf. Euphorion quoted below). Usually Scylla is bound to Minos' ship and dragged through the water (Euripides scholiast ibid., Parthenius fr. 20, Propertius iii. 19. 26, *Ciris* 390, cf. Ovid, line 142). Intriguing is the statement of Hyginus (*fab.* 198) that she became a fish (also Servius on *Aen.* vi. 286, cf. *Ciris* 485), the more so because Hyginus' language suggests that he is also drawing on Ovid (cf. 99–100 n., 140–4 n.) and perhaps the *Ciris*. There was indeed a fish called the κίρρις (e.g. Oppian, *Halieutica* i. 129).

Parallel Legends

In essence, the story of Scylla is just a Megarian version of a very common folk-tale. A city is being besieged; then a woman, often the king's daughter, falls in love with her country's enemy whom she has seen from the walls, and opens the gates to him on the understanding that he will marry her. We have at least eight closely parallel tales from all over the Graeco-Roman world, and others with partial resemblances; on the type generally see Krappe, *Rheinisches Museum* lxxviii (1929) 249 ff., and Udo Hetzner, *Andromeda und Tarpeia* (*Beiträge zur klassischen Philologie*, Heft 8, 1963) 54 ff. Sometimes the context is a would-be historical one from relatively recent times, such as the fall of Sardis to Cyrus (Parthenius, *Narr. Amat.* 22), or a siege of Ephesus by the Gauls under Brennus ([Plutarch], *Parall. Min.* 15). The most surprising example is that of Moses and Tharbis, daughter of the king of Ethiopia (Josephus, *A.J.* ii. 238–53). This story was perhaps invented by the Jewish colony in Alexandria to explain Moses' Ethiopian wife at Numbers 12: 1. A fascinating fusion of the two cultures; be it noted that Moses alone keeps his promise to marry the girl!

One such legend appeared in the Epic Cycle (see Pausanias i. 2. 1), but it is significant that many of them were treated by Hellenistic poets, such as Apollonius Rhodius (fr. 12 Powell) and Hermesianax (frs. 5 and 6 Powell), who liked out-of-the-way tales with romantic colouring. Several examples are known from the love-stories of Parthenius, which he collected for his friend Cornelius Gallus; Propertius iv. 4 handles a Roman myth (Tarpeia) very much in the Hellenistic manner.

The closest parallel to Scylla is the legend of Comaetho, daughter of Pterelaus, and Amphitryon (Apollodorus ii. 4. 7), which also

COMMENTARY 35

contained a magic lock; this receives a passing mention in the *Thrax* of Euphorion (D. L. Page, Loeb *Greek Literary Papyri* [Poetry], p. 498, lines 31–2):

> ἔκ τε τρίχα χρυσέην κόρσης ὤλοψε Κομαιθὼ
> πατρὸς ἑοῦ, ὡς [θ]ὴρ ἄταφος τάφος εἶο πέλοιτο.

Ovid knew Pterelaus' fate, and compared it to that of Nisus (*Ibis* 361–2).

But there are other types of story to which Ovid owes a great deal. The last speech of Scylla (108 ff.) is very reminiscent of the laments and reproaches of an Ariadne abandoned on Naxos, a Medea, or even a Dido. Perhaps, against all surviving authors, Ovid makes Minos sail straight back to Crete, leaving Scylla behind, so that she can deliver this highly Euripidean monologue while he vanishes into the distance.

Ovid's Treatment

There were several possible ways of handling this episode which Ovid has firmly rejected. He does not try to portray Scylla's passion for Minos as Apollonius described the love of Medea for Jason. Nor is he using the epyllion-technique of the *Ciris*, with its concentration on moments of especial pathos. Instead we have a piece which, in spite of a brief flirtation with Homer, is light-hearted, rhetorical, and, at least in Scylla's last speech, has more than a touch of parody about it. It is interesting to compare the characterization in Ovid and in the *Ciris*. Minos is almost a monster in the *Ciris*, while Ovid suppresses anything to the king's discredit (see 101–2 n.). But more important is the contrast between the two Scyllas. In both accounts the action is seen mainly through the girl's eyes, though, while the *Ciris*' long speeches serve to arrest the narrative, in Ovid there is a steady forward movement. Ovid's Scylla has a hard brilliance, but the poet makes little attempt at realistic psychology. The way she gradually changes her position from firm refusal to complete surrender is extremely clever, but hardly credible. On the other hand, in the *Ciris* Scylla is altogether more human, with her doubts and hesitations, and so makes the story come more alive. But it must be realized that Ovid is intentionally not probing very deep; he is not trying to write in the neoteric style and failing. One may object to this superficiality, but, within his terms of reference, Ovid attacks the piece with the utmost *élan*, and by comparing his Scylla with, for instance, Baucis and Philemon and with Erysicthon, one can see what variety of styles and moods he has encompassed in the *Metamorphoses*.

1–5. In book vii Ovid has described Minos' preparations for war against Athens (456 ff.) in revenge for the murder of his son Androgeos, killed out of jealousy for his athletic successes by Athenian and Megarian conspirators (so, e.g., Servius on *Aen.* vi. 14). Most of the states approached by Minos for help complied, but Aegina, ruled by Aeacus, pleaded special ties with Athens (485–6) and instead sent a force to her assistance led by Telamon and Peleus, sons of Aeacus (864–5). Accompanied by the Athenian envoy Cephalus, the party has set sail for Attica.

1–2. At least by the time of Seneca (*Ep.* 122. 11–14, *Ludus,* ch. 2) inflated descriptions of dawn from would-be epic poets were ten a penny. Like Virgil, Ovid is regularly short and unpretentious. Yet there is a certain artistry in the two parallel clauses with corresponding interwoven word-order.

1. retegente : 'unveiling', as if by drawing aside a curtain. Alternatively the world itself is revealed, 'iam rebus luce retectis' (*Aen.* ix. 461, cf. iv. 119, v. 65).

2. cadit eurus: the east wind, which had previously delayed departure from Aegina (vii. 664), would be unfavourable for a voyage north-eastwards to Athens, the south wind favourable. For a sense-break after a trochee in the fourth foot cf. 148, 561, and, for example, *Aen.* v. 167.

6. Lelegeia litora: cf. vii. 443. According to Pausanias (i. 39. 6), Lelex came from Egypt to rule over Megara; after him the people were called Leleges. Memories of this race persisted widely, e.g. in Ceos (Callimachus *Aetia,* fr. 75. 62) and in Locris (312 n.).

7. praetemptatque: his main objective is Athens, though Ovid never tells us specifically of the Athenian war (cf. 102 n.).

    Mavortis: the old epic form (cf. 437). Similarly in Greek, Ἄρης can mean 'warfare'.

    in urbe : basically 'in the case of' or 'over', cf. 50 'arsit in illa'.

8. Alcathoe : Alcathous usually appears as a son of Pelops (e.g. Theognis 1. 773–4); one of the citadels at Megara was called after him (Pausanias i. 42. 1).

    The consensus of MSS. in favour of the Greek form used as an ablative should be respected, cf. vii. 443 'tutus ad Alcathoen'. Ovid is very fond of Greek forms in proper names, e.g. 'in Hyperborea Pallene' (xv. 356) and 'Temesesque metalla' (xv. 707). Heinsius's 'Alcathoi' is irreproachable, cf. *A.A.* ii. 421 'Alcathoi qui mittitur urbe Pelasga', but unnecessary.

8–9. That Nisus had a single bright-coloured magic lock, not ruled out by Aeschylus (*Choephoroe* 619), appears from Callimachus (fr. 288) and later writers (Tibullus i. 4. 63, *Ciris* 120 ff.). Colour terms are notoriously hard to pin down, but I would imagine the lock as scarlet rather than purple (cf. *Ciris* 122 'roseus').

9. **honoratos . . . canos**: to be taken together—the dislocated word-order perhaps reflects the sense. Of all the Latin poets, Ovid is the most sensitive to bright colours and their contrasts (cf. 33–4). He inherited and enlarged this bequest of the Hellenistic poets to their Roman neoteric followers (e.g. Catullus 64. 308–9). But the particular contrast of red and white appears in Latin poetry as far back as Ennius (*Ann.* 352 Warmington), 'et simul erubuit ceu lacte et purpura mixta'.

10. **magni fiducia regni**: Nisus had been told by an oracle either that his life (e.g. Apollodorus iii. 15. 8) or that his kingdom depended on this lock. The *Ciris* speaks only of the loss of his kingdom (123–5, cf. 330, 419, 428), as Nonnus, *Dionysiaca* xxv. 164 βόστρυχον ἀμήσασα πολισσούχοιο καρήνου, and leaves vague the cause of Nisus' death (523). But it emerges that in Ovid both life and kingdom are involved (85 and particularly 94, cf. 115–16 n.); thus Ovid is less consistent than the *Ciris*-poet. Propertius (iii. 19. 21 ff.) can be taken to mean that Nisus survived the fall of Megara (28). In Hyginus *fab.* 242 Nisus commits suicide after losing the lock.

11. For such descriptions of passing time cf. Virgil, *Aeneid* iii. 645, Propertius ii. 20. 21–2.

13. With two lesser MSS. M originally had 'vagat', which is remarkable, but seems too much of an archaism for Ovid—for this form see Bailey on Lucretius iii. 628. Representations of winged Victory in art are very common, see Daremberg and Saglio, s.v. *Victoria*.

14–17. **regia turris erat . . . illuc**: the most usual pattern in an epic-style ecphrasis (see 788 n.). Part of the walls of Megara were said to have been built by Phoebus and Alcathous together (Pausanias i. 42. 2, cf. Theognis 1. 773–4). Thus *Ciris* 105–9 'stat Megara Alcathoi quondam murata labore, / Alcathoi Phoebique, deus namque adfuit illi: / unde etiam citharae voces imitatus acutas / saepe lapis recrepat Cyllenia murmura pulsus / et veterem sonitu Phoebi testatur honorem.'

This echoing stone was a famous tourist attraction at Megara, and no doubt visitors amused themselves in the same way as Scylla here; ἦν δὲ τύχῃ βαλών τις ψηφῖδι, κατὰ ταὐτὰ οὗτός τε ἤχησε καὶ κιθάρα κρουσθεῖσα (Pausanias i. 42. 2), cf. an anonymous epigram in the *Greek Anthology*, Planudean appendix, no. 279. Also the lyre appears on some Megarian coins.

15. **proles Letoia**: the epithet instead of genitive is here probably in imitation of Homeric phrases like Τελαμώνιος υἱός, Καπανήιος υἱός, etc.

16. **eius** has been suspected, on the ground that parts of 'is' are rare in poetry after Lucretius; the genitive does not occur elsewhere in the hexameters of Virgil or Ovid. It appears five times

in Augustan elegiacs (Tibullus i. 6. 25, Propertius iv. 2. 35, iv. 6. 67, *Tristia* iii. 4. 27, *ex Ponto* iv. 15. 6, cf. Platnauer, *Latin Elegiac Verse*, Appendix A), but elegiacs admit a wider range of language than do hexameters.

The recentiores offer 'haesit in illo'. Slater proposed to read 'Eïus haesit' (*CR* xxxix [1925] 160–1), comparing H.H., *Delian Apollo* 120 ἦιε Φοῖβε. But we want the reference to Phoebus' lyre which 'eius' gives, and 'inhaesit' is just the right word, cf. vii. 447 'scopulis nomen Scironis inhaeret.' In this book we find also 'is' (290, 654), 'ea' fem. (123, 791), 'eam' (793), 'id' (502), 'ea' neut. (607, 698)—admittedly a larger harvest than usual, but scholars may have been unnecessarily squeamish over 'is'.

18. This picture of a childish, unsophisticated Scylla is interestingly paralleled by the unlucky ball-game at *Ciris* 149 ff.

19. tum cum pax esset: though he has none of Homer's pathos, Ovid is thinking of the stone troughs by the gates of Troy where the women used to wash their clothes τὸ πρὶν ἐπ' εἰρήνης, πρὶν ἐλθεῖν υἷας Ἀχαιῶν (*Il.* xxii. 153 ff., cf. ix. 403). Virgil has a similar touch at *Aen.* ii. 455–7, contrasting peace with the horrors of war. Here as elsewhere, Ovid's phrase fills the same part of the line as his epic pattern, cf. on 26–7, 30, 381, 399, 402, 427, 695–6.

20 ff. In *Il.* iii. 121–244 Helen points out all the Greek heroes to Priam from the walls of Troy as they watch the armies fighting in the plain below. Thereafter τειχοσκοπία becomes one of the most distinctive themes of epic war-poetry. A fine fifth- or sixth-century picture of women watching from the walls of Troy is reproduced as the frontispiece of Austin's *Aeneid* ii.

τειχοσκοπία is also a vital feature of stories of our type; e.g. Pisidice and Achilles (Parthenius, *Narr. Amat.* 21, cf. Ap. Rh., fr. 12) θεασαμένην ἀπὸ τοῦ τείχους τὸν Ἀχιλλέα ἐρασθῆναι αὐτοῦ.

20. rigidi certamina Martis: a grandiose phrase, probably of a traditional cast, cf. Lucretius i. 475 'saevi certamina belli', Horace, *Odes* iv. 14. 17 'certamine Martio', *Aen.* xii. 73 'duri certamina Martis'.

22. The rhythm of this line, lacking a fourth-foot caesura, strongly suggests a Greek hexameter with repeated τε. This repeated '-que', very rare in prose, is high epic derived from Homer's τε . . . τε via Ennius; see Austin on *Aen.* iv. 83.

Cydonaeasque pharetras: Cydonia was on the north coast of Crete; the Cydones are mentioned as one of the island's five peoples in *Od.* xix. 176. Even when the context does not demand it, archery epithets are usually Cretan, because of all the Greeks Cretans were the archers *par excellence*, Ἕλλησιν ὅτι μὴ Κρησὶν οὐκ ἐπιχώριον ὂν τοξεύειν (Pausanias i. 23. 4).

23. ducis Europaei: son of Europa. A spondaic fifth foot, men-

tioned by Cicero (*ad Att.* vii. 2. 1) as an affectation of the
Hellenistic-inspired 'novi poetae' of his day, is used with fair
frequency by Ovid in the *Metamorphoses*, nearly always, as
here, for a Greek proper name; cf. 315, 528.

24 ff. 'Whatever she does, whatever she wears, my beloved is
beautiful in my eyes.' The best example in Latin love-poetry of
this common theme is in the elegy on Sulpicia, *Corpus Tibul-
lianum* iii. 8 (iv. 2) 7–12:

> illam quidquid agit, quoquo vestigia movit,
> componit furtim subsequiturque decor.
> seu solvit crines, fusis decet esse capillis,
> seu compsit, comptis est veneranda comis.
> urit, seu Tyria voluit procedere palla,
> urit, seu nivea candida veste venit.

Compare *Heroides* 4. 79–84, *A.A.* ii. 297 ff., Propertius ii. 1.
5–16, and in Greek Paulus Silentiarius, *A.P.* v. 260. A feature of
this pattern is the elegant picking-up of words from the 'seu'-
clauses in each main clause (particularly 26–7 here). Note also
the varied construction, 'seu' (25) . . . 'seu' (26), plain pluperfect
(28–30), 'cum' (32).

Ovid adapts this scheme to his epic-style narrative in a typi-
cally resourceful way; he combines it with arming formulas
taken in part straight from the *Iliad*. Much of his piquant
humour depends on recognition of the Homeric parallels. This
mingling of epic and love-poetry is very noticeable until line 44,
at which point Homer gives way to Euripides.

25. cristata casside pennis: Homeric fighters usually wear a plume
of horse-hair (κυνέην . . . ἵππουριν). To adorn one's helmet with
feathers was an Italian custom (Polybius vi. 23. 12), originally
Samnite (cf. E. T. Salmon, *Samnium and the Samnites* [C.U.P.,
1967], pp. 108–9). So Ovid may have drawn this detail from
early Latin epic.

26–7. seu sumpserat aere / fulgentem clipeum: cf. *Il.* xiv. 9–11
ὣς εἰπὼν σάκος εἷλε . . . / χαλκῷ παμφαῖνον. Although the formula
occurs only this once, phrases like χαλκὸς ἔλαμπε (xiii. 245) are
common enough in the *Iliad*. So there is no need to consider
'auro', approved by Heinsius, even though in the *Ilias Latina*
(311–12) a bronze-shining helmet may turn to gold—'abstrahit
auro / fulgentem galeam'. This apparent echo might suggest
that the variant is an ancient one.

28–9. The javelin, both in war and in athletics, was thrown with
a thong (*amentum*), into the loop of which one inserted the first
or first two fingers, cf. xii. 321–3 'inserit amento digitos . . . nec
plura moratus / in iuvenem torsit iaculum'. The thong was

usually wound several times round the shaft, and, when released
'spun' the javelin, thus giving increased accuracy, penetration,
and probably distance as well (see Gardiner, *JHS* xxvii [1907]
251, H. A. Harris, *Greek Athletes and Athletics*, pp. 92–7). Hence
'torquere', the normal word for throwing such a weapon (also
345, 408).

28. **adductis . . . lacertis** : with the upper arm drawn back towards
the body (cf. *Aeneid* xi. 561). Ovid seems to have in mind a posi-
tion of taking aim, when the right arm is bent back at the elbow,
and the javelin itself points straight ahead, or a little down-
wards, its centre of gravity almost on a level with the thrower's
ear (Gardiner, art. cit., p. 260, fig. 6 and plate 18). Alternatively
the phrase might mean 'with tensed muscles', but 'with arm
drawn back behind his head' will not do.

30. This line perhaps alludes to two Homeric phrases.
    imposito calamo : cf. *Il.* viii. 324 θῆκε δ' ἐπὶ νευρῇ, more clearly
    imitated at 381.
    patulos sinuaverat arcus: perhaps modelled on *Iliad* v. 97
    ἐπιταίνετο καμπύλα τόξα.

31. Ovid may have a statue in mind. Apollo the archer god is some-
times represented in art with a bow in his right hand, as on some
imperial coins of Apollonia (British Museum Catalogue, *Thessaly*,
pl. 13. 6).

32. When Hector takes off his helmet so as not to frighten his baby
son Astyanax, the *Ilias Latina* (570) writes 'utque caput iuvenis
posito detexerat aere', probably remembering our line.

33–4. **purpureusque albi stratis insignia pictis / terga premebat
equi** : Minos is wearing his royal cloak, cf. *ex Ponto* ii. 8. 50; for
the contrast of colours, here threefold, see 9 n. The Homeric
hero is hardly to be found on horseback, preferring to fight from
his chariot, but riding became quite respectable in later epic.

35. **sua** : 'her proper self'.
    virgo Niseia : cf. *Ciris* 390 'Niseia virgo', *Aen.* ii. 403 'Priameia
    virgo'.

36–7. The lover might even pray to turn into something close to his
beloved—the wind which caresses her, the rose which she wears
(*A.P.* v. 83 and 84, cf. *Amores* ii. 15). In Nonnus, *Dionysiaca* xv.
258 ff. the shepherd Hymnus longs first to turn into one of
Nicaea's hunting-weapons, and then adds (264–6):

> παρθένε, κουφίζεις βέλος ὄλβιον, ὑμέτεροι δὲ
> ῞Υμνου μηλονόμοιο μακάρτεροί εἰσιν ὀιστοί
> ὅττι τεῶν ψαύουσιν ἐρωτοτόκων παλαμάων.

These lines are very close to ours. Perhaps they both have
a common source (cf. 688 n.), though in general it is hard to
believe that Nonnus had not read Ovid.

38. impetus est illi: a favourite Ovidian phrase, corresponding to the middle of ἵημι in Greek epic.

40. Cnosia rather than *G*nosia is the preferable form (see Housman, *CQ* xxii [1928] 7–8). Ovid likes to ring the changes on his geographical epithets (cf. on 280, 317, 751). Here he offers also 'Cydonaeasque pharetras' (22) and 'Dictaei regis' (43), hardly meaning more than 'Cretan' in each case.

43. candida Dictaei spectans tentoria regis: in the *Ciris* Scylla also watches the enemy camp-fires by night (176). The name 'Dicte' is usually referred to the mountain range in east central Crete, but perhaps strictly denoted a hill near Palaikastro in the extreme eastern corner of the island (Bosanquet, *BSA* xl [1939–40] 62).

This line offers a rare Ovidian example of a favourite neoteric shape—two nouns, two epithets, and a present participle. Compare, for example, Catullus 64. 59 'irrita ventosae linquens promissa procellae', Cicero, *Aratea*, fr. 33. 88 Buescu 'igniferum mulcens tremibundis aethera pinnis', *Ciris* 3 'Cecropius suavis exspirans hortulus auras', *Met.* i. 716.

44–80. *Scylla's first speech*

There is no real personal conflict here. The girl's only struggle is to fit argument to her already existing desire (cf. 39–41). Whether or not the war is to be regretted (44–6), marriage with Minos would be an honourable way to end it—but she will on no account betray the city (54–5). Yet Minos' cause is just, his army powerful; if Megara must be captured in any case, better at once, so as to save bloodshed on both sides (56–63).

By line 63 Scylla has convinced herself that it is practically her duty to betray Megara. There is just one person whom she has overlooked—Nisus. But by now her mind is made up; she passes over the parricide with a string of proverbial commonplaces, and thinks only of obtaining her desire (72–80).

44. lacrimabile bellum (also *Aen.* vii. 604) is treated as a set formula, δακρυόεις πόλεμος at *Il.* xvii. 512 etc. At the same time Ovid suggests that it would be unnatural for her to rejoice at the war.

47–8. Scylla does not yet dare mention marriage; she thinks of herself first as a hostage, then, more boldly, as a companion and a pledge of peace—'pignus', a word often used of close family ties, cf. 490 n., which turns her thoughts to marriage.

47. poterat: the imperfect implies a tentative but hopeful suggestion, to the speaker still very much a live possibility, cf. i. 679 'quisquis es, hoc poteras mecum considere saxo', Virgil, *Ecl.* 1. 79.

49. pulcherrime regum: 'pulcherrime rerum', favoured by Heinsius with some manuscript support, would be excellent as a colloquial form of address (*Heroides* 4. 125, *A.A.* i. 213, cf.

Horace, *Sat.* i. 9. 4 'dulcissime rerum'), but it does not occur elsewhere in the *Metamorphoses*, and seems too informal here.

50. ipse with Heinsius I have preferred to 'ipsa', though the latter has better authority. Scylla concentrates all her thoughts upon Minos.

arsit in illa: cf. 7 n. 'Ardeo' can also take a direct accusative or plain ablative, but the present construction appears with a wide variety of verbs and phrases meaning to love, e.g. iv. 234–5, vii. 21–2, xiv. 770–1, *Amores* iii. 6. 25–6.

51. o ego ter felix: cf. *Od.* v. 306 τρισμάκαρες Δαναοὶ καὶ τετράκις, Callimachus, fr. 178. 32–3 τρίσμακαρ . . . / ναυτιλίης εἰ νῆυν ἔχεις βίον, *Aen.* i. 94. A desire to take wings, whether to arrive where one wishes or to escape an unpleasant situation, is particularly common in tragedy, e.g. Sophocles, *O.C.* 1081 ff., fr. 476 Pearson, Euripides, *Hipp.* 732 ff., *Ion* 796. The lover besieging Amaryllis' cave in Theocritus 3. 12 prays αἴθε γενοίμαν / ἁ βομβεῦσα μέλισσα, καὶ ἐς τεὸν ἄντρον ἱκοίμαν. Of course there is dramatic irony here; Scylla will indeed get wings, but then she will be less than thrice happy.

For hiatus with 'o ego' cf. Tibullus ii. 3. 5 and ii. 4. 7.

53. In Homer the suitor pays a bride-price for his wife. To give a dowry was the classical practice, projected back into the heroic age also, e.g. by Euripides, *Hipp.* 627–9. Ovidian anachronism is so common (cf. 103 n.) that I doubt whether he can be trying to show Scylla's shamelessness by reversing the norm.

fassaque me: cf. iii. 2 (Zeus in disguise) 'se confessus erat'.

54. emi: a crude word, which Scylla would hardly use herself. This is the poet's device for showing us the flaw in her scheme; Minos the Just (cf. 101–2 n.) is not to be bought.

56. proditione potens: 'proditio', also at 115, is generally a prose word, making only rare appearances in poetry (cf. Austin on *Aen.* ii. 83). There is an echo of Virgil's 'seditione potens' (*Aen.* xi. 340).

quamvis saepe utile vinci: 'but all the same . . .' Scylla begins to waver and launches into the first of a long series of commonplaces (see on 69 ff.); for this one cf. Claudian, *IV Cons. Hon.* 116 'profuit hoc vincente capi', Rutilius Namatianus i. 64 'profuit iniustis te dominante capi', and a remark of Augustus to Cinna 'hodie tam felix et tam dives es ut victo victores invideant' (Seneca, *De Clem.* i. 9. 8). Rome prided herself on clemency to defeated foes—'parcere subiectis'.

58. nato: Androgeos (see on 1–5).

59. tenentibus: better attested, this should be preferred to the more picturesque 'tuentibus', as a technical term, to uphold a case with success, cf. xiii. 190. She conveniently forgets that Megara's forces are equally powerful and have resisted Minos so far.

60. At, puto, vincemur: I have adopted Markland's conjecture,

'At, puto' need not always be ironical, cf. xi. 425. Here it marks the beginning of a new argument, and Scylla's point of decision. 58–9 have convinced her that defeat is inevitable; now she goes on to draw the conclusion.

Magnus printed a comma at the end of 59, then 'et, puto, vincemur', following the manuscript preponderance. But to tack this vital link on to the end of a long sentence is feeble, and 'et' could easily have been influenced by the first word of 59. Older editors, with some manuscript support, started a new sentence and read 'ut puto, vincemur'. Sense is excellent, but 'ut puto' occurs only once in Ovid (*Fasti* iii. 493) and even there the variant 'at, puto' may be right.

qui si manet exitus urbem: so E, perhaps *v*, and older editors. This reading fits the argument perfectly; if Megara must eventually be captured in any case, better to betray it at once. Magnus read 'quis enim manet exitus urbem: / cur . . .', when 'exitus' must mean 'way of escape'. But 'manet' suggests 'outcome', as at ix. 726 'quis me manet exitus'. Also 61 starts abruptly with Magnus's text.

64. non metuam: future, 'I shall not then have to fear'. The whole emphasis is on 'imprudens' (65), which is qualified by 65–6. 'Durus', 'hard-hearted', fits the amatory context much better than 'dirus' in 65; cf. 'immitem' (66).

65–6. This kind of parenthesis, involving a rhetorical question, is frequent in the *Ciris*, and may be typically neoteric; cf. Virgil, *Ecl.* 2. 68 'me tamen urit amor, quis enim modus adsit amori?'

67. M with one lesser manuscript reads 'secum', and this line might be taken as part of a brief comment by the poet; 'coepta placent' runs slightly more easily thus (cf. the parallel ix. 517). But then Scylla's point of resumption is not clear—perhaps 'aditus' (69)?—so it is better to read 'mecum' and preserve direct speech throughout.

68. dotalem patriam: cf. Propertius iv. 4. 56, Seneca, *Medea* 488–9 'tibi patria cessit, tibi pater, frater, pudor, / hac dote nupsi.'

69 ff. In her efforts to justify the murder which she contemplates, Scylla slides from one proverb to another, as if to minimize her personal responsibility. This is almost Ovid's only attempt at realistic psychology, and a notable one.

70. claustraque portarum genitor tenet: to ensure the defeat of Megara, it will be enough to cut off her father's magic lock (cf. 10 n.). But Scylla also has to make her way out of the city to Minos, and reveal that she is his benefactor.

72. di facerent sine patre forem!: one could take this as just an abstract prayer to be ἀπάτωρ in some miraculous way, but Scylla immediately brings it down to earth. Donatus (on Terence, *Adelphi* 521) cites as typical of comedy the young man

in Naevius who wished his parents out of the way, 'deos quaeso
ut adimant et patrem et matrem meos!' (105 Warmington).

72–3. sibi quisque profecto / est deus: and therefore she must get
rid of Nisus for herself. Compare Euripides, fr. 1018 ὁ νοῦς γὰρ
ἡμῶν ἐστιν ἐν ἑκάστῳ θεός, *Aen.* ix. 185 'sua cuique deus fit dira
cupido', *Panegyr. Lat.* xii. 4. 2 (Mynors) 'sua enim cuique pru-
dentia deus est.'

73. ignavis precibus Fortuna repugnat: 'fortes Fortuna adiuvat'
(Terence, *Phormio* 203, with a play on words), an immensely
common saying in both Latin and Greek. See Otto, *Sprichwörter
der Römer*, s.v. *deus* 12 and *fortuna* 9.

76–7. ire per ignes / et gladios ausim: a proverb for someone who
would endure absolutely anything to gain his end, e.g. from the
New Comedy poet Posidippus (fr. 1. 10 Kock) διὰ τῶν μαχαιρῶν
τοῦ πυρός τ᾽ ἐλήλυθεν, cf. Otto, s.v. *ignis* 6.

77. ausim: an old aorist optative form, surviving as a present
subjunctive; cf. Fordyce on Catullus 66. 18.

79. auro pretiosior: again a common proverb, cf. Otto, s.v. *aurum*.

81–3. Night comes and Scylla nerves herself for the task
The situation, sketched here only in outline, resembles that at
the beginning of *Il.* ii and x; all the world is asleep except for
one. In Homer Zeus and Agamemnon are brooding over the war,
and Silius keeps the military context with some success (*Punica*
vii. 282 ff.). But in post-Homeric epic this picture is often applied
to the anguish of lovers. Medea lies awake πολλὰ γὰρ Αἰσονίδαο πόθῳ
μελεδήματ᾽ ἔγειρεν (Ap. Rh. iii. 752); so does Dido (*Aen.* iv. 522 ff.—
see Pease *ad loc.*, though he misunderstands our passage), but
Ovid is not concerned here to describe the girl's heart-searchings,
as Apollonius does so well, followed by the *Ciris* (206 ff.); that
treatment is reserved for another neoteric heroine, Myrrha (x.
368 ff.). The crime itself is also passed over very quickly, and no
play is made with Scylla's night journey past the Megarian guards
and through the enemy lines to Minos. Instead, Ovid hastens to
his own chosen climax, the last speech of Scylla.

81. curarum maxima nutrix: 'the greatest nourisher of love-pangs'.
Probably a general statement, not referring only to Scylla;
compare Nonnus, *Dionysiaca* xxxiii. 264–5 ἐν γὰρ ὀμίχλῃ / θερμό-
τεροι γεγάασιν ἀεὶ σπινθῆρες ἐρώτων.

83. prima quies: also *Aen.* ii. 268. In epic poetry the night is di-
vided into three parts (see Bühler on Moschus, *Europa* 2).

85. fatali is supported by Hyginus (*fab.* 198), and probably by
'Lactantius', who summarizes here 'crinem . . . quo fata patriae
continebantur'; cf. μόρσιμος in the paraphrase from Parthenius
(fr. 20 Martini). But 'vitali', which has better manuscript
authority, produces a more pathetic collocation of words, and is

PLATE II

Scylla before Minos. Wall-painting from Pompeii

certainly not to be rejected as inconsistent with the story. With either word, Nisus must lose his life as well as his throne (cf. 10 n.). There is very little to choose between the two variants.

87. This line is omitted by *v*MN, and was deleted by Heinsius and Merkel. With some hesitation I retain it in the form given by Priscian (v. 16). It must be realized that Priscian's quotation does not necessarily authenticate the line, since one would expect any interpolations already to have been made by the fifth century, and other references show that the grammarian had an unsatisfactory text of the *Metamorphoses* (Slater, *Prolegomena*, p. 41 n. 4).

The Ovidian manuscripts here favour 'sceleris'. But the alliteration would then become excessive, and, although our poet likes to pick up a word recently used in the manner 'spoliat' (86)–'spolium' (87), the dependent genitive 'sceleris' would weaken the force of this device. One might feel inclined to adopt Bentley's conjecture 'pretium'.

The line with 'celeris' avoids these objections. There remains a slight redundancy with 'spolium' as well as 'praeda . . . nefanda' (86), but this is by no means intolerable.

89. paventem: Minos' attitude throughout is one of horror—more, I think, at the parricide than at the city's betrayal. He has made no previous bargain with Scylla, as in most versions of the story, but shrinks from even the slightest contact with her—see further on 101–2.

91. Scylla: the first mention of her name, when she proudly names herself. This accords with the epic tradition of periphrasis rather than personal name (cf. 317, 738), but it also has considerable effect.

95–6. scelerataque dextra / munera porrexit. Minos porrecta refugit: a wall-painting from Pompeii (Plate II) illustrates just this scene; the only discordant note for Ovid is that beside Scylla stands her old nurse, who plays a principal part in the *Ciris*, but not in this account. So this painting is interesting, for it shows Minos' character to be as in Ovid (cf. on 101–2), while portraying the nurse who appears in the *Ciris*, but not in Ovid. One would like to know whether Ovid has some such picture in mind, whether both Ovid and this picture go back to a literary source, or whether Ovid himself can have influenced the pictorial tradition.

To pick up a verb with its past participle as 'porrexit'–'porrecta' is a frequent Ovidian trick; for an early example cf. Sisenna (praetor 78 B.C.), *Historiae*, fr. 27 Peter 'Romanos impetu suo protelant, protelatos persecuntur.'

97–8. di te summoveant . . . / orbe suo: 'orbis' = sphere of influence (cf. 100), perhaps derived from meaning the orbit of

a heavenly body. One is reminded of Theseus' outburst on dis-
covering the apparent villainy of Hippolytus (Eur. *Hipp.* 940–
2); to make our world habitable for decent people θεοῖσι προσβαλεῖν
χθονὶ / ἄλλην δεήσει γαῖαν, ἢ χωρήσεται / τοὺς μὴ δικαίους καὶ κακοὺς
πεφυκότας.

98. tellusque tibi pontusque negetur: a particularly fearful curse—
sometimes directed at tomb-robbers (R. Lattimore, *Themes in
Greek and Latin Epitaphs*, § 22). It is fulfilled in quite an unex-
pected way when Scylla's element becomes the air. The tradi-
tional punishment for a parricide was to be sewn up in a sack,
together with a dog, a snake, a monkey, and a cock, which were
thought to symbolize the qualities of such a person, and then to
be thrown into the sea. Enlarging on this theme, Cicero (*Pro Sex.
Roscio* 71–2) uses language perhaps echoed here: 'ita moriuntur
ut eorum ossa terra non tangat, ita iactantur fluctibus ut nun-
quam adluantur, ita postremo eiciuntur ut ne ad saxa quidem
mortui conquiescant.'

99–100. Here Hyginus (*fab.* 198) betrays his affiliations: 'ille
negavit Creten sanctissimam tantum scelus recepturam.'

99. incunabula: literally swaddling-clothes. For the metaphor
compare a line quoted by Cicero (*ad Att.* ii. 15. 3) 'in montis
patrios et ad incunabula nostra', perhaps from Ennius, cf.
Aeneid iii. 105. Hesiod says that Zeus was born in Crete, and
nurtured in a cave on the Aegean Mountain near Lyctos, now
Lyttos, in the east-central part of the island. For various
modern attempts to identify Hesiod's cave see West on *Theo-
gony* 477–84.

101–2. Cf. Propertius iii. 19. 27–8 'non tamen immerito Minos sedet
arbiter Orci, / victor erat quamvis, aequus in hoste fuit.' Minos
was a great law-giver in Crete, and after his death thought of as
one of the judges in Hades. But some denied this identification
of the judge with our Minos, and we find a wide divergence in
the king's characterization. Attic tragedians, perhaps taking
a hint from *Od.* xi. 322 Μίνωος ὀλοόφρονος (see Stanford on *Od.*
i. 52 for this epithet), regularly portrayed Minos as ἄγριόν τινα
καὶ χαλεπὸν καὶ ἄδικον ([Plato], *Minos* 318 d, cf. Plutarch, *Theseus*
16). In the *Ciris* too he is almost a monster. But Ovid de-
liberately suppresses anything to the king's discredit. Minos
wages a just war (58); contrast *Ciris* 112–15, where he is trying
to recapture the fugitive Polyidus. He breaks no promise to
marry Scylla (contrast *Ciris* 414–15). He treats Megara with
fairness (contrast *Ciris* 53, 191, 423), and, finally, he does not
drag Scylla behind his ship, which would show unnecessary
cruelty. Ovid's rejection of the dragging forces on him a rather
absurd alternative (142–4), but we have at least two other wit-
nesses to this favourable view of Minos. One is the Propertian

poem iii. 19 (lines 27–8 quoted above), where, however, Scylla is dragged behind the king's ship, and also Nisus may survive; our second witness is the Pompeian wall-painting (plate II, see on 95–6). It is clear that many subtly different versions of this story were current in antiquity, most of them now lost to us.

101. auctor: i.e. legum. The imposition of terms is made to sound like the forming of a constitution—all to Minos' credit.

102. hostibus: probably meant to include the Athenians (cf. 7 n.).

103. aeratas: a typical anachronism (cf. 53 n.); metal protection for the bows of ships was not introduced until Hellenistic times. Similarly *Aen.* x. 223 'aeratae . . . prorae', and often.

  impelli (cf. *Heroides* 3. 153) is more vigorous and straightforward than 'impleri', although not nearly so well attested.

  remige: for the collective cf. 358 'milite' and note.

104–44. We are told nothing further of the Athenian war; the poet almost suggests that Scylla's parricide drove Minos straight back in horror from Megara to Crete. Here, for Ovid, is the heart of the episode. While the king prepares to sail, Scylla follows him down to the shore, and opens the flood-gates of rhetoric, hurling at his head all the laments and reproaches of Ariadne, Medea, and Dido. Where can she go? Back to Megara? The city lies in ruins. But let us resurrect it with an orator's wand. Still of no avail—the traitor would never be received. Crete is the only hope. Is Minos going to cut her off even from there? Then he is born of no human stock, but of the wild beasts themselves. This last thought is expanded with the aid of some unfortunate incidents in the king's family history. Meanwhile, however, the Cretan ships are disappearing further and further into the distance. With a last desperate effort Scylla plunges into the water, and, remarkably enough, manages to catch up the fleet and attach herself to Minos' ship.

  If we take this passage too seriously, it will seem forced and artificial. But once we realize that Ovid is not competing with Euripides, Catullus, or Virgil, but writing in a much lighter vein, then we can enjoy his high spirits, and in particular the clever way he varies conventional themes from his distinguished predecessors.

109. o patriae praelate meae, praelate parenti: repetition of a corresponding word in lines of this metrical pattern is found quite frequently, e.g. *Amores* i. 13. 9 'quo properas, ingrata viris, ingrata puellis?', Tibullus ii. 1. 17 'di patrii, purgamus agros, purgamus agrestes.'

111–12. Cf. *Aen.* iv. 307–8 'nec te noster amor, nec te data dextera quondam, / nec moritura tenet crudeli funere Dido?'

112 ff. She finds herself in a predicament similar to that of Medea and Ariadne. Scylla has killed her father, and has no hope from

anyone except Minos. Medea had at least connived at the mur-
der of her brother Absyrtus (Ap. Rh. iv. 410 ff.), while Ariadne,
by helping Theseus out of the labyrinth, participated in the
death of the Minotaur, her 'brother' (Catullus 64. 181). With the
present passage compare first of all Euripides, *Medea* 502–5:

> νῦν ποῖ τράπωμαι; πότερα πρὸς πατρὸς δόμους,
> οὓς σοὶ προδοῦσα καὶ πάτραν ἀφικόμην;
> ἢ πρὸς ταλαίνας Πελιάδας; καλῶς γ' ἂν οὖν
> δέξαιντό μ' οἴκοις ὧν πατέρα κατέκτανον.

Cf. also Ap. Rh. iv. 378 ff., Ennius, *Medea* 284–5 W., Catullus
64. 177 ff., *Aen.* iv. 534 ff., Seneca, *Medea* 451 ff. We should
remember that Ovid too wrote a successful tragedy in his youth
on Medea.

Here poetry and rhetoric come very close to each other, as is
shown by part of a speech of Gaius Gracchus, delivered in 133
B.C. after the murder of his brother Tiberius (Cicero, *De Oratore*
iii. 214): 'quo me miser conferam? quo vertam? in Capito-
liumne? at fratris sanguine redundat. an domum? matremne
ut miseram lamentantem videam et abiectam?' For further
passages in the same style, compare Cicero, *Pro Murena* 88–9,
Sallust, *Jugurtha* 14. 17.

114. superata iacet. sed finge manere: equally rhetorical is the way
she momentarily concedes a point only to demolish it in the next
line. Compare an extract from the great orator L. Licinius
Crassus (140–91 B.C.) given by Cicero (*De Or.* ii. 225–6): '... quid
te agere, cui rei, cui gloriae, cui virtuti studere? patrimonione
augendo? at id non est nobilitatis. sed fac esse; nihil superest;
libidines totum dissupaverunt.' Observe how similar the run of
that passage is to ours. Cf. also Euripides, *Med.* 386 ff., where
Medea pictures her children as already killed (καὶ δὴ τεθνᾶσι) and
reviews the resulting situation.

Ovid's words here, in particular 'manere', suggest a more
violent treatment of Megara, as for instance at *Ciris* 53 and
191 'direpta crudeliter urbe' than do 101–2. The poet seems to
allude to a version of the story which he has not in fact adopted.
Perhaps he wrote this last speech before the earlier parts of the
episode, and would have removed the discrepancy had he been
able to revise his work (cf. *Tristia* i. 7. 13 ff.). Or it may be that
the commoner form of the story exerts an unconscious pull over
him. See also on 128–30.

115–16. patris ad ora? / quem tibi donavi?: Nisus is now dead, as
Scylla herself has told Minos (94). So her suggestion is purely
rhetorical, as is the address to Nisus in 125–6. For the punctu-
ation here, with a second question mark after the relative clause,
see Fordyce on Catullus 64. 180.

117–18. obstruximus orbem / terrarum: the most logical and pointed reading, with excellent manuscript support. The active tense stresses that Scylla herself has caused this situation. As Medea says to Jason (Seneca, *Med.* 458), 'quascumque aperui tibi vias, clausi mihi.' Scylla has committed herself so far that Crete is now her only hope. For 'obstruximus' cf. also 185–6 below.

118. pateret: the change of sequence from perfect indicative to imperfect subjunctive may seem harsh. But one finds similar phenomena when the intention described was a past one (cf. Fordyce on Catullus 101. 3). Also a factor in the more remote imperfect subjunctive is surely Scylla's fear that she will not now be granted refuge in Crete.

120–1. The figure goes right back to Homer, *Il.* xvi. 33–5, where Patroclus is reproaching Achilles for his indifference to the sufferings of the Greeks:

> νηλεές, οὐκ ἄρα σοί γε πατὴρ ἦν ἱππότα Πηλεύς,
> οὐδὲ Θέτις μήτηρ· γλαυκὴ δέ σε τίκτε θάλασσα
> πέτραι τ' ἠλίβατοι.

Cf. Catullus 60. 1 with Fordyce ad loc., and 64. 154–6, *Aen.* iv. 366–7, *Heroides* 10. 131–2.

120. inhospita Syrtis: this line-ending is borrowed from *Aen.* iv. 41; 'inhospitus' is a Virgilian coinage. The name 'Syrtis' applied to quicksands off the north coast of Africa, the Syrtis Major lying west of Cyrenaica, and the Syrtis Minor east of Byzacena; for a vivid description of the area see Ap. Rh. iv. 1228 ff.

121. Armeniae tigres: a picturesque epithet, also at, for example, Virgil, *Ecl.* 5. 29. Pliny says 'tigrim Hyrcani et Indi ferunt' (*N.H.* viii. 66). The tiger was a very rare visitor to Greece and Italy. Seleucus I sent one as a present to the Athenians (Athenaeus xiii. 590 a), very likely an Indian beast, and perhaps the first of its kind to be seen in Greece (Jennison, *Animals for Show and Pleasure in Ancient Rome*, p. 24). Augustus also was presented with a tiger by Indian ambassadors at Samos in the winter of 20–19 B.C. (Dio liv. 9. 8), but the first to reach Rome was a tame animal exhibited in a cage at the dedication of the theatre of Marcellus in 11 B.C. (Pliny, *N.H.* viii. 65).

Charybdis: when mentioning this mythical whirlpool, taken to be on the Sicilian side of the straits of Messana, one would normally include her accomplice, the sea-monster Scylla, as at Catullus 64. 156. Ovid avoids the latter, no doubt, because of the coincidence of names. Other writers sometimes confused the sea-monster with the daughter of Nisus (Virgil, *Ecl.* 6. 75, Propertius iv. 4. 40); even Ovid does this elsewhere (*A.A.* i.

331–2, *Fasti* iv. 500). The *Ciris* argues vehemently and at length against such an identification (54 ff.).

122 ff. In her comparison of Minos' heartlessness to that of a wild beast Scylla makes use of two incidents in the history of the Cretan royal family. Europa was said to have been carried by Zeus in the form of a bull from Phoenicia to Crete, where she became the mother of Minos, Sarpedon, and Rhadamanthys (cf. ii. 836 ff., Frazer on Apollodorus iii. 1. 1). Secondly, Minos' queen Pasiphae became enamoured of a bull, and thereby bore the Minotaur (cf. 131–3). This is very much the technique of a declamation; the speaker has to produce ingenious arguments in even the most improbable and fantastic situations.

122. imagine tauri: the *false* likeness of a bull.

123. ea: emphatic.

124. I have deleted this line, following Merkel; its thought is odd and irrelevant to the argument. The interpolator was perhaps thinking confusedly more of Pasiphae than of Europa. Barth's 'puellae' would be a slight improvement (i.e. the love of Zeus for Europa), but still of little relevance. Without 124 the passage runs very nicely, with great emphasis on 'verus' (123).

126. Nise pater: see on 115–16.

128–30. sed tamen ex illis aliquis, quos impia laesi, / me perimat. cur, qui vicisti crimine nostro, / insequeris crimen?: Scylla can reasonably complain thus in the *Ciris* (421–7):

> verum istaec, Minos, illos scelerata putavi,
> si nostra ante aliqui nudasset foedera casus,
> facturos, quorum direptis moenibus urbis
> o ego crudelis flamma delubra petivi.
> te vero victore prius vel sidera cursus
> mutatura suos quam te mihi talia captae
> facturum metui.

But here nobody is killing her, least of all Minos. This may be good psychology—Scylla feels that she is punished by Minos when he sails away without her. But I suspect influence of the usual version in which Minos drags Scylla through the sea as a punishment (cf. 142 n., and introduction to the episode). See also 114 n.

131. vere is given only by E and ρ. The weight of manuscript authority favours 'vero', which Magnus kept, explaining 'Pasiphae digna est, cuius verus coniunx (qui nunc, quamquam diceris, non es) sis tu, non ille taurus, qui nunc est.' This may speak for itself! vii. 742 hardly defends 'vero' here; if one must descend to technicalities, the bull is never 'coniunx', only 'adulter'.

132. Daedalus was said to have made for Pasiphae a wooden cow

on wheels, hollowed out inside, and sewn up in the hide of a real
cow. This contraption was set down in a meadow where the bull
used to graze (Apollodorus iii. 1. 4).

133. discordemque: cf. Columella vi. 36. 2 (of the birth of mules)
'discordantem utero suo . . . stirpem'. The Minotaur is 'mon-
strum biforme' (156, cf. *Aen.* vi. 25) thought to have had the
head of a bull, but otherwise to have been human (Apollo-
dorus iii. 1. 4). Plutarch quotes from Euripides σύμμικτον εἶδος
κἀποφώλιον βρέφος and ταύρου μέμικται καὶ βροτοῦ διπλῇ φύσει (*Theseus*
15, cf. *P.Oxy.* 2461, fr. 1. 12 for the form of the second line). The
play is Euripides' *Cretans*, not his *Theseus*; see also 155 n.

134–5. A well-known figure for broken promises (Catullus 64. 142),
vain reproaches (ibid. 164), or the like. It goes back to *Odyssey*
viii. 408–9 ἔπος δ᾽ εἴ πέρ τι βέβακται | δεινόν, ἄφαρ τὸ φέροιεν ἀναρπάξασαι
ἄελλαι. But Ovid's version amounts to a parody, because the
metaphorical wind which bears away Scylla's laments is also the
literal wind carrying Minos' fleet; cf. *Heroides* 2. 25 and 7. 8.

137. tu plus feritatis habebas: a rhetorical triumph. The imperfect
corresponds to ἄρα with the imperfect in Greek.

138. iubet : 'he gives the order to make haste'; more vigorous than
the variant 'iuvat', which perhaps arose simply through failure
to understand the text.

138–9. divolsaque remis / unda sonat: observe that Ovid concen-
trates on the sound rather than the usual visual effect of whiten-
ing foam.

139. mecumque simul mea terra recedit: we switch suddenly to
Minos' point of view. For this convention by which the land is
said to move rather than the ships cf. *Aen.* iii. 72 'terraeque
urbesque recedunt', Lucan v. 457 'movitque Ceraunia nautis',
Valerius Flaccus iv. 645 'adversosque vident discedere montes'.

140–4. The manner in which Scylla catches Minos up is somewhat
absurd, but Ovid is softening the usual version in which the girl
is dragged behind the Cretan's ship (see introduction to the
episode and 101–2 n.). Hyginus (*fab.* 198) perhaps agrees with
Ovid at this point—if so, probably from Ovid—but his text is
corrupt.

140. Nil agis : colloquial, 'you are doing no good'.

142. per freta longa trahar : Ovid's verb alludes to the canonical
form of this legend, cf. *Ciris* 390 'per mare caeruleum trahitur
Niseia virgo.' Parthenius' fanciful etymology (fr. 20) derived
the name of the Saronic gulf from the fact that Scylla was
dragged (σύρω) over it.

144. comes invidiosa : notice how completely Ovid has reversed the
normal story.

145–51. Both Nisus and Scylla are transformed into birds, im-
placably hostile to each other. Dionysius, *De Avibus* ii. 14, says

that Scylla earned the hatred of all other birds as well (μισεῖται δὲ παρὰ πάντων ὀρνέων). His account may possibly be based on the Ὀρνιθογονία of Boeo or Boeus (cf. on 236–59), and the idea that a person's wickedness could be punished after transformation by the hostility of other birds seems to have been a favourite one of Hellenistic poets. Compare ii. 595 and xi. 24–5 concerning the owl, perhaps deriving from Callimachus' *Hecale* (cf. Pfeiffer on fr. 326). Euphorion too in his *Thrax* described how Harpalyce (Parthenius, *Narr. Amat.* 13) was transformed into a bird called the chalcis, ἑτέροισιν ἀπεχθομένην ὄρνισιν (*P.S.I.* 1390, fr. A. 14).

145–6. In the fuller treatment of the *Ciris*, Nisus is recalled from the dead by Jupiter for his piety (523–8):

> cum pater exstinctus caeca sub nocte lateret,
> illi pro pietate sua . . .
> reddidit optatam mutato corpore vitam
> fecitque in terris haliaeetos ales ut esset.

Except that the *Ciris* has left vague the cause of Nisus' death (e.g. he could have been killed in the fighting when Megara fell), the two accounts are not at variance. For transformation after death in the *Metamorphoses* cf. xi. 736 ff. (Ceyx). Ovid avoids unnecessary detail, and gives no obvious motive for the transformations, although he nearly always does so. He must have expected readers to know a more detailed account, conceivably Parthenius. Of course Ovid's rejection of the dragging cuts out the *Ciris* motive (481 ff.) for Scylla's transformation; thus we are left in doubt whether she is punished, pitied, or even honoured (cf. *Ciris* 205). I cannot follow Professor Brooks Otis's statement that the end is a quite logical outcome of Scylla's changing psychological situation (*Ovid as an Epic Poet*, p. 65).

The sea-eagle, ἁλιάετος or ἁλιαίετος (both forms occur), is usually taken to be an osprey (Pandion haliaetus). Royds (*The Beasts, Birds and Bees of Virgil*, p. 48) says that this is impossible for Nisus, since the osprey is exclusively a fish-hawk—cf., however, Hyginus, *fab.* 198, where Scylla herself is turned into a fish. He writes 'the name had better be taken as a generic term for the larger falconidae, especially those that habitually take their prey on the wing, striking it down with the powerful hindclaw'.

There has been much argument about the identity of the Ciris itself, but without general agreement, in spite of a detailed description in the epyllion (496 ff.). The wisest words, I think, are those of D'Arcy Thompson in *CQ* xix (1925) 155. He points out that the name Ciris has left no trace in Modern Greek or in any Italian dialect. This suggests strongly that the word was never vernacular, that it never was a name used in popular

speech to signify a familiar species of bird. Although the attacks
of large falconidae on smaller birds are real enough, the Ciris
itself, I am afraid, belongs only to poets and mythographers.

145. pendebat in auras: the accusative, which I retain with over-
whelming manuscript support, is an idiosyncrasy of our poet,
and suggests that Nisus has just launched himself upon the air;
compare 201 and contrast 202. Similar is vii. 379 'factus olor
niveis pendebat in aera pennis', although there the accusative
has less support.

147. On the enmity between the two cf. *Ciris* 536–7 'sic inter sese
tristis haliaeetos iras / et ciris memori servant ad saecula fato.'

150. pluma fuit: sc. 'quae sustinebat illam'. There is no need to
question either this phrase or 'plumis'.

151. tonso: i.e. from the Greek κείρειν, cf. *Ciris* 488 'esset ut in terris
facti de nomine ciris'.

152–82. Having launched Minos safely on his way back to Crete,
Ovid must tread with the utmost delicacy over the story of the
Minotaur and Ariadne, as far as the introduction of Daedalus
and Icarus (183). Above all, he has to avoid the maze of variant
versions contained in the Cretan saga, and this he does by re-
cording the bare minimum of facts necessary for the movement of
his own narrative. Theseus must be taken to Crete so as to pro-
vide a connection with Daedalus and Icarus, but Ovid is hardly
interested in the hero's adventures for their own sake. Ariadne's
desertion with her rescue by Dionysus was an obvious plum,
even having a ready-made metamorphosis attached (179–82).
But all of this is treated in the most perfunctory way. Part of
the explanation is undoubtedly that the famous set-piece of
Ariadne 'deserted and much complaining' (176) would be tedious
after the very similar laments of Scylla. But Ovid's real inten-
tion is to build a bridge to Daedalus and Icarus, for there he had
a story well suited to his own particular poetic genius.

152. Vota . . . taurorum corpora centum: it is both simplest and
best to take 'vota' as a noun, with 'taurorum corpora centum'
in apposition. One might hazard a guess that the originator
of the variant 'sanguine' took 'vota' as a participle, but was
displeased with the collocation 'vota . . . corpora . . . solvit',
though this brachylogy is tolerable. Perhaps also 'sanguine' was
suggested by line 265.

The periphrasis comes from old Tragedy and Epic, cf. Ennius,
Ann. 97–8 W. 'ter quattuor corpora sancta / avium', but it
adds something here by stressing the physical aspect, as at *Aen.*
ii. 18 'delecta virum . . . corpora' (the Greeks crammed into
the Wooden Horse) and *Aen.* vi. 22 'corpora natorum' (fodder
for the Minotaur).

153. Curetida terram: Crete, from the Κουρῆτες, who were said to have drowned the cries of the infant Zeus with their war-dance, and so to have saved him from his father Cronos. The sacrifice is offered immediately on landing, cf. *Aeneid* iii. 21 'in litore'.

154. spoliis decorata est regia fixis: such was the Roman custom, attributed here to the Cretans, as to the Trojans at *Aen.* ii. 504.

155. opprobrium generis: 'the disgrace of the family', i.e. the Minotaur, abstract for concrete as 'pudorem' (157). Libanius, *Decl.* 1, ch. 177 (vol. v, ed. Foerster), mentions as a typical tragic situation τὸν Μίνω δεινὰ πάσχοντα ἐπὶ τῆς σκηνῆς καὶ τὴν οἰκίαν αὐτοῦ διὰ τοῦ τῆς Πασιφάης ἔρωτος ἐν αἰσχύνῃ γεγενημένην. One such play was the *Cretans* of Euripides (cf. Page, *Greek Literary Papyri* [Poetry], pp. 70–6), which Ovid may have in mind here (see also 133 n.). *P.Oxy.* 2461 gives us what is possibly a dialogue between Minos and the chorus of the *Cretans*, describing the Minotaur in detail.

157 ff. Ovid makes Daedalus build the labyrinth on the order of Minos to house the Minotaur; nothing is said of the fate of Pasiphae. In other authors the details varied considerably. Minos commands Pasiphae to be imprisoned with her (?) nurse (Euripides, Page, op. cit., p. 76); alternatively Daedalus is Pasiphae's accomplice, and builds the labyrinth to conceal her shame. When the scandal is discovered, he himself is thrown into prison, to be rescued by the queen (Hyginus, *fab.* 40). In Ovid (185–7) Daedalus is obviously being held under constraint, but we are not told the reason for this.

158 ff. *The labyrinth.* Homer speaks only of a dancing-floor which Daedalus made for Ariadne in Cnossos χορὸν . . . ποτ᾽ ἐνὶ Κνωσῷ εὐρείῃ / Δαίδαλος ἤσκησεν καλλιπλοκάμῳ Ἀριάδνῃ (*Il.* xviii. 590–2). A. B. Cook (*Zeus*, vol. i, pp. 473 ff.) discusses the myth of the labyrinth in detail. He doubts whether it originated in the windings of the palace at Cnossos; classical representations point backwards to a time when the labyrinth was depicted not as a palace, but as a meander or swastika-pattern (p. 476). The latter motif, already familiar to the Cnossians of the Bronze Age (p. 477), was perhaps a stylized representation of the revolving sun (p. 478, cf. p. 489 n. 4). Readers may also like to follow the intriguing speculations of W. F. J. Knight (*Cumaean Gates*, ch. 8).

158. multiplicique domo caecisque includere tectis: one of the few Ovidian hexameters which could have been written by Virgil. Lines of this kind, in which the second half does little more than amplify the first, are a bequest of Virgil to his successors; cf., for instance, *Aen.* iii. 605, vi. 165, x. 82, xi. 894. See also on 343–4.

159. Daedalus, son of Eupalamus, the type of the skilful craftsman, was thought to have been an Athenian who was exiled to

Crete (cf. 184) for the murder of his nephew Perdix (236 ff.); for
the legend see Hyginus, *fab.* 39.

It is clear from Pausanias that people all over the Greek world
had attributed to Daedalus works, especially wooden statues,
which were sufficiently archaic, but yet seemed to show a spark
of genius, Δαίδαλος δὲ ὁπόσα εἰργάσατο, ἀτοπώτερα μέν ἐστιν ἐς τὴν
ὄψιν, ἐπιπρέπει δὲ ὅμως τι καὶ ἔνθεον τούτοις (ii. 4. 5). Pausanias him-
self is a little patronizing about such craftsmanship (viii. 16. 3).

160. notas : the marks which might have helped wanderers to get
their bearings in the labyrinth, cf. *Aen.* v. 590 'signa sequendi'.

162. liquidis Phrygius Maeandrus in undis: Seneca (*Ep.* 104. 15) calls
the river Maeander 'poetarum omnium exercitatio et ludus' (cf.
also Propertius ii. 34. 35–6, Silius vii. 139), but he was not above
trying his own hand at it, 'qualis incertis vagus / Maeander un-
dis ludit et cedit sibi, / instatque dubius litus an fontem petat'
(*Hercules Furens* 683 ff.). There is a clear imitation of Ovid
which supports the text printed; the River-god is pictured as
playing in his stream. As for quality, Ovid here is a class ahead
of other competitors.

163. Notice the alliteration of the liquid *l* in this line.

refluitque fluitque: the natural order may be reversed for
metrical convenience, cf. 537 'refoventque foventque'.

166. incertas exercet aquas: a fine phrase, 'he plies his doubtful
stream'.

167–8. vixque ipse reverti / ad limen potuit: a very Ovidian touch.

169–71. The terms agreed between Minos and the Athenians had
bound the latter to send seven young men and seven girls to
Crete once every nine years (cf. 262–3). Theseus offered himself
voluntarily at the third drawing of lots (so Plutarch, *Theseus* 17).
If the first consignment is imagined as leaving soon after the end
of the war, Theseus would by now be in his middle thirties.

169. geminam tauri iuvenisque figuram: cf. Euripides' ταύρου μέμι-
κται καὶ βροτοῦ διπλῇ φύσει, discussed on 133.

170. Actaeo: 'Attic', a favourite epithet of Ovid's, following the
famous first line of Callimachus' *Hecale*, Ἀκταίη τις ἔναιεν Ἐρεχθέος
ἔν ποτε γουνῷ (fr. 230), cf. also Virgil, *Ecl.* 2. 24 and *Georgics* iv. 463.

172 ff. So familiar a subject is Ariadne on Naxos, abandoned by
Theseus and rescued by Bacchus, that one can hardly remember
how different the oldest version was. In *Odyssey* xi. 321–5
Ariadne seems to have been married to Dionysus, and to have
left him for Theseus; then she was killed on the island of Dia
(174 n.) by Artemis through the god's witness. Hesiod, *Theogony*
947–9, first makes Ariadne the perpetual consort of Dionysus.
For discussion of the whole myth, with illustrations from vase-
painting, see T. B. L. Webster. *Greece & Rome* xiii (1966) 22–31.

172–3. Ariadne's thread enabled Theseus to find his way back out

of the labyrinth after killing the Minotaur, cf. Catullus 64. 113–
15 'errabunda regens tenui vestigia filo, / ne labyrintheis e flexi-
bus egredientem / tecti frustraretur inobservabilis error.'
173. relecto: 'wound up'. For the variant 'relicto' cf. Horace, *Odes*
i. 34. 5, where 'relectos' seems far superior.
174. Minoide: cf. Callimachus, fr. 110. 59 νύμφης Μινωίδος, and
Pfeiffer *ad loc.*
    In Homer Dia is the island where Artemis kills Ariadne (*Od.*
xi. 325), later identified with Naxos: ἐν Δίῃ· τὸ γὰρ ἔσκε παλαίτερον
οὔνομα Νάξῳ (Call., fr. 601 = *P.Ant.* 114, fr. 2 (b) 4).
175. crudelis: the motives attributed to Theseus for abandoning
Ariadne range from pure forgetfulness to another love (pseudo-
Hesiod, fr. 298 Merkelbach–West), or fear of the social disgrace
which a foreign wife would bring, 'cogitans si Ariadnen in
patriam portasset, sibi opprobrium futurum' (Hyginus, *fab.* 43).
Ovid wisely is satisfied with a conventional epithet.
176. desertae et multa querenti: cf. *Heroides* 10. This was one of the
most famous poetic situations—'quis non periurae doluit men-
dacia puppis / desertam vacuo Minoida litore questus?' ([Vir-
gil], *Aetna* 21–2)—perhaps already so in Hellenistic times (see
Fordyce on Catullus 64. 139 and 160). But a full description of
Ariadne's laments would be tedious so soon after those of Scylla,
and therefore Ovid passes on. He had related Ariadne's rescue
by Bacchus with the utmost high spirits at *A.A.* i. 527 ff.
177–82. 'Catasterism' is a favourite type of metamorphosis in Hel-
lenistic poetry. This was the mythological reflection of increased
interest in astronomy, exemplified by such as Aratus and the
poet–scientist Eratosthenes. It is not clear how much is original
of the surviving prose Eratosthenic *Catasterismi.*
    The transformation of Ariadne's crown apparently occurred in
the *Cretica* ascribed to Epimenides (Diels–Kranz 3 B 25); per-
haps also in a tragedy (see *P.Oxy.* 2452, fr. 2), whether this was
the *Theseus* of Sophocles or of Euripides (cf. Webster, *Greece &
Rome* xiii [1966] 27). Later we have Aratus, *Phaenomena* 71–2
αὐτοῦ κἀκεῖνος Στέφανος τὸν ἀγαυὸς ἔθηκεν / σῆμ' ἔμεναι Διόνυσος ἀποιχο-
μένης Ἀριάδνης, and Ap. Rh. iii. 1002–4.
178 ff. The metamorphosis is attractive, though leaving much to
the reader's imagination. As they speed across the heavens in
the god's tiger-drawn chariot (*A.A.* i. 550), Liber takes the
crown off Ariadne's brow, and sends it spinning through the air
like a catherine-wheel. This crown, earlier just a wreath, was
made by Hephaestus ἐκ χρυσοῦ πυρώδους καὶ λίθων Ἰνδικῶν ([Erat.],
Catast. 5 Olivieri), and given to the princess by Aphrodite. In
a rarer version of the legend Ariadne herself, not merely the
crown, is set in the sky.
179. tenues: offering no resistance.

182. qui medius Nixique genu est Anguemque tenentis: Ovid places the Crown between the Serpent-holder (Ophiuchus) and the kneeling figure Engonasin, usually identified with Heracles (Avienus, *Aratea* 169 ff.). But it lies rather between Engonasin and Bootes. Intriguing, then, is the variant 'Anguemque tuentis', 'him that gazes at the Snake' (held by Ophiuchus), ascribed to 'Leidensis atque alius' (Burman) and perhaps read by Planudes (μεταξὺ τοῦ 'Εγγόνασιν καὶ τοῦ Βοώτου). The idea of constellations gazing at one another is common (e.g. Cicero, *Aratea* fr. 23. 2 Buescu), and Bootes might be imagined with his head turned towards the Snake (e.g. Buescu, Cic. *Aratea*, pl. 4, or the Loeb Aratus star-map), though one expects him to face the Great Bear (Wain), Βοώτης / Ἄρκτον ἀποσκοπέων in an astronomical fragment (*P.Oxy.* 2258. 8–9, see Pfeiffer's *Callimachus*, vol. 2, pp. 115–16). But Ovid would hardly *name* Bootes in such a riddling way. So this variant seems just an extraordinarily clever attempt to save the author's credit, possibly introduced by a man with a star-map.

The line cannot well be deleted (Bentley) as in astronomical poetry a new constellation should be fixed by reference to existing ones, e.g. Aratus, *Phaen.* 134–6, Cic. *Arat.*, fr. 33. 45–6 'haec (the Lyre) genus ad levum Nixi delapsa resedit / atque inter flexum genus et caput Alitis haesit', cf. Catullus 66. 65–6, Virgil, *Georgics* i. 32–4. Also 'medius' with the genitive is a particularly Ovidian construction. It is interesting that our poet translates the constellations into Latin. The original Greek terms would cause no offence, but he may have felt that, in a work so full of Greek, translation would gain more effect. At the same time he avoids the compound Anguitenens (Cicero, *Aratea*), perhaps thinking it a little old-fashioned.

183–259. For his next episode Ovid abandons Theseus, and takes the reader back to Crete. The flight of Daedalus and Icarus seems to have been neglected by early writers in a way surprising for such an attractive story. We can hardly infer the existence of the fully-developed legend from Homer's mention of the Icarian sea (*Il.* ii. 145). But a black-figure vase fragment discussed and illustrated by Beazley (*JHS* xlvii [1927] 224 ff. and fig. 2) gives us certain contact with the story from a little before 550 B.C. Of the figure inscribed Icarus there remain the lower edge of his short chiton, and both legs with winged boots on the feet. The posture is probably one of flying, rendered as running through the air with both feet off the ground. A small red-figure lekythos of about 470 B.C. perhaps shows Icarus falling into the sea (ibid., p. 231 and fig. 6), while the fitting of his wings appears on a red-figure kotyle from the end of the fifth century (ibid., pp. 226–8 and pl. XXI, 2). The legend also reached Etruria in the fifth century (G. M. A. Hanfmann, *AJA* xxxix [1935] 189 ff.).

The scholiast on *Il.* ii. 145 gives the whole story of Daedalus, up to Minos' death in Sicily, adding ἱστορεῖ Φιλοστέφανος καὶ Καλλίμαχος ἐν Αἰτίοις. The Callimachus reference probably applies just to the murder of Minos (fr. 43. 48–9), or perhaps also to a mention of the Icarian sea (fr. 23. 3), but Philostephanus of Cyrene is a likely enough source for Ovid. He was a pupil of Callimachus (Athenaeus viii. 331 d), and wrote geographical works with a strong admixture of the marvellous (cf. Aulus Gellius, *NA* ix. 4. 3). The Icarian sea (Ovid, line 230) and the island Icaria (235) would give Philostephanus a chance to indulge his master's passion for aetiology. It is possible, even probable, that Ovid had some Alexandrian poetic source as well, but we seem to have lost sight of this completely. He had already written a lively account of Daedalus and Icarus (*A.A.* ii. 21 ff.) which evidently pleased him, since many details and even whole lines are repeated here. And so light is the poet's touch, that one cannot speak of any stylistic difference between his hexameter and elegiac versions. This tale would have special attractions for an Italian audience because of the local legend that Daedalus had landed at Cumae (Servius on *Aen.* vi. 14, from the *Histories* of Sallust), a legend that no doubt explains the popularity of Daedalus and Icarus on Campanian wall-paintings, and on Italic and Roman gems from the third century B.C. (Furtwängler, *Antike Gemmen* iii, pp. 239–40).

The present episode has become very famous, and justly. It is written in the best Hellenistic tradition of homely realism— L. P. Wilkinson compares the Theocritean *Heracliscus*, *Id.* 24— yet here, as often, Ovid outdoes his masters. The delight in simple things, such as the behaviour of a young child, is very much his own. In the description of the flight, Ovid's imagination soars unfettered, and we may forgive him one or two details which have been thought to be in poor taste. Our poet's excellence can be illustrated by a comparison with Silius Italicus (*Punica* xii. 89–103), who clearly models himself on Ovid, but clumsily 'epicizes' the story, e.g. making the very gods tremble at Daedalus' flight (xii. 95, contrast Ovid, 217–20).

185. clausus erat pelago: a reference to Minos' famous thalasso-cracy, thought to have been the first in Greek history.

185–6. terras licet . . . et undas / obstruat: cf. the elder Seneca, *Contr.* i. 6. 6 (from a rhetorical exercise) 'tu ibis ? quo, infelix ? quas petitura regiones ? est enim tibi aliquis locus ? pater tuus nobis maria praeclusit, meus terras.' For 'obstruat' cf. also 117 n.

189. naturamque novat: possibly 'he changes his own nature', as in the parallel line 'sunt mihi naturae iura novanda meae' (*A.A.* ii. 42). But it is attractive to understand the phrase as some older scholars did—'he alters Nature'. One might also take iv. 279 thus, 'naturae iure novato'; cf. *Tristia* v. 10. 9 'in nobis rerum natura novata est'. Then 'novat' would have its sinister undertones, of doing violence to Nature. Horace certainly presented Daedalus' flight as a transgression of man's proper sphere, 'expertus vacuum Daedalus aëra / pennis non homini datis' (*Odes* i. 3. 34–5), and the same thought appears at *A.A.* ii. 38, where Daedalus prays 'da veniam coepto, Iuppiter alte, meo'.

190. [a minima coeptas, longam breviore sequenti]: I have deleted this line with Merkel. One can say that 'longam breviore sequenti' shifts our point of view to the other end of the wing. But the picture of growing is then resumed in 191 'clivo' and 192 'surgit', so that the confusion of images is very awkward. R. Holland's 'longa breviore sequenti', 'with the long one shorter than the following', should please nobody, although one could well take 'breviore sequenti' thus if a better emendation for 'longam' were forthcoming.

[sequenti]: the ablative in -*i* of a true participle can be paralleled from archaic poetry, but would be very doubtful in Ovid, even with euphony as an inducement. On the other hand a feeble line-ending would result from 'sequente' (far less well attested), and so this is another point against the line's authenticity.

191. ut clivo crevisse putes: such is the art of Daedalus, that the feathers seem to have grown naturally (*crevisse*) in order of ascending length (*clivo*). W. C. Summers saw here a comparison to trees 'on a hill-side', but so pictorial an image would be unwelcome immediately before a quite different simile. Mary Innes translates 'so that the edge seemed to slope upwards'—a little nearer the mark, but, if Ovid meant simply that, why did he add 'putes'?

quondam makes the sentence indefinite, as ποτέ in Greek. Compare with this simile Tibullus ii. 5. 31–2 'fistula cui semper decrescit harundinis ordo, / nam calamus cera iungitur usque minor.'

195–200. Ovid depicts Icarus as a much younger boy than do the classical Greek vase-painters (see introduction to this episode). Here he agrees with Hellenistic taste, for interest in quite small children is very marked in both Hellenistic poetry and art (T. B. L. Webster, *Hellenistic Poetry and Art*, ch. 8). This whole description is completely life-like and charming.

198. captabat: 'snatched at'.

199. mollibat: an archaic form of the imperfect, which survives through metrical necessity.

60 COMMENTARY

201–2. The experiment is put to the test. Ovid conveys the anxiety and tension of this moment with the utmost economy. The accusative 'in alas' (much better than the variant 'in alis') describes Daedalus putting all his weight upon the pair of wings (cf. 145 n., 882); 'mota' suggests their violent beating of the air, and 'pependit' his efforts not to lose height.

203–16. Having proved his workmanship, Daedalus fits wings on Icarus too, giving him instructions as he does so. This scene was a popular subject for ancient artists (cf. introduction to the episode).

203–4. Ovid is very fond of this word-pattern, with '-que' inside the direct speech, followed by the latter's resumption, and then a verb of saying. Marouzeau in *Ovidiana*, pp. 104–5, collects examples—there are no fewer than six in our book (also 481, 560, 689, 717, 767).

206. spectare: cf. *Heroides* 18. 151 and 157. Like sailors, they have to plot a course by the stars, but Icarus must leave navigation to his father. The three constellations mentioned were particularly useful to sailors, cf. Aratus, *Phaen.* 37–8, Ap. Rh. iii. 745; for a similar passage compare Musaeus, *Hero and Leander* 213–14 καί μιν (the lamp) ὀπιπεύων, οὐκ ὀψὲ δύοντα Βοώτην, / οὐ θρασὺν Ὠρίωνα καὶ ἄβροχον ὁλκὸν Ἁμάξης, etc.

207. Helicen: the Great Bear or Wain.

strictumque Orionis ensem: described in a way to catch the boy's attention. I once thought that Daedalus was warning his son against star-gazing, on the ground that Orion at least might be dangerous. But this idea is more appropriate to Phaethon (cf. Nonnus, *Dionysiaca* xxxviii. 336 μὴ θρασὺς Ὠρίων σε κατακτείνειε μαχαίρῃ).

211. et patriae tremuere manus: an echo of Virgil's poignant line on Daedalus 'bis patriae cecidere manus' (*Aen.* vi. 33).

212. repetenda: 'to be sought back', as if lent for a while.

213–15. This fine simile appears also at *A.A.* ii. 65–6. It was admired and imitated by Valerius Flaccus, 'qualis adhuc teneros ut primum pallida fetus / mater ab excelso produxit in aethera nido, / hortaturque sequi' (*Argonautica* vii. 375–7).

215. erudit with an accusative of the subject taught is not found before here. As often, a more complicated verb takes over the construction of a simpler one—'doceo'.

216. The whole line has been transferred from *A.A.* ii. 73.

217–20. Ovid's pleasant motif was a traditional one in such a situation. Cicero (*D.N.D.* ii. 89) preserves a fragment of Accius' *Medea* (381–96 W.) in which a shepherd expresses his astonishment at the sight of Argo, the first ship, taking it for some kind of sea-monster; similarly Ap. Rh. iv. 316–18.

217 = *A.A.* ii. 77.

PLATE III

Peter Bruegel, *The Fall of Icarus*. Musée des Beaux-Arts, Brussels

tremula: perhaps proleptic, describing the fisherman's fear and amazement when he saw the couple, or perhaps he is actually catching a fish.

220–1. Iunonia . . . / . . . Samos: the cult of Hera at Samos was celebrated and long-established; cf. Callimachus, frs. 100 and 101 with Pfeiffer's notes, *Aen.* i. 16.

The list of islands varies little from that at *A.A.* ii. 79–82. The pair's destination is ostensibly Athens (cf. 184). But instead they first fly north from Crete towards the Cyclades, and then turn eastwards, apparently heading for Miletus. Daedalus finally arrives in Sicily (260). Of course the Icarian sea, and the island Icaria, south-west of Samos, were fixed points in the story, so that some awkwardness was inevitable.

222. The honey of Calymna is singled out for its excellence by Strabo (x. 489).

224. caelique cupidine tactus: in both a literal and a metaphorical sense. Otto, *Sprichwörter der Römer*, s.v. *caelum* 9–11, gives examples of a proverb meaning to be blissfully happy ('in caelo esse', and the like). But there was also surely a proverb for extravagant ambition, 'to wish for the moon', e.g. Horace, *Odes* i. 3. 38 'caelum ipsum petimus' (? with one eye on the example of the Giants), Virgil, *Georgics* iv. 325 'quid me caelum sperare iubebas?' (Aristaeus, of course, has cause to hope for actual divinity), and in Greek Rhianus, fr. 1. 15 Powell ἀτραπιτὸν τεκμαίρεται Οὐλυμπόνδε. Alcman warned μή τις ἀνθ]ρώπων ἐς ὠρανὸν ποτήσθω (*Parth.* 16).

225. rapidi . . . solis: 'consuming', a common epithet in poetry for fierce heat. Equally common is the variant 'rabidi' (see Shackleton Bailey, *Propertiana*, pp. 203, 317).

226. odoratas, pennarum vincula, ceras: the interlocking word-order, with first an adjective, then the phrase in apposition, and finally the noun, is sometimes said to be typically Hellenistic. Examples are hard to find, though one can mention Hedylus, *A.P.* v. 199. 5 μαλακαί, μαστῶν ἐκδύματα, μίτραι, and Call., fr. 260. 5 ἐμῷ δέ τις Αἰγέι πατρί. It certainly occurs in Virgil, e.g. *Ecl.* 1 57 'raucae, tua cura, palumbes'. Ovid interweaves in apposition more than a dozen times in the *Metamorphoses* (cf. 372, 377), but with less variety than Virgil. He almost always has a similar pattern at the line-ending; 763 gives a rare possible exception. Of later poets Silius, for instance, follows Ovid.

odoratas: proleptic—the smell of the wax is brought out as it melts in the sun.

227. nudos quatit ille lacertos: a flippant phrase, but it must have pleased the poet, since again the whole line is borrowed from the *A.A.* (ii. 89).

228. remigioque carens: interchange of images between sailing and flying is as old as Hesiod (*Op.* 628) and Homer (*Od.* xi. 125). The movement of a bank of oars could well suggest the beating of a bird's wings, e.g. Ap. Rh. ii. 1255, of Prometheus' eagle, ἴσα δ' εὐξέστοις ὠκύπτερα πάλλεν ἐρετμοῖς. Again, the outstretched wings of a soaring bird quite naturally suggest a sail taut in the wind, cf. Aeschylus, *P.V.* 468 λινόπτερα . . . ναυτίλων ὀχήματα, and in Latin the venerable compound 'velivolus' (see Macrobius, *Sat.* vi. 5. 9 ff.).

These two ideas are well brought out by Lucretius vi. 743, of the birds who suddenly drop dead from the fumes of Lake Avernus: 'remigi oblitae pennarum vela remittunt.' And for this reason it was particularly easy to demythologize the legend of Daedalus and Icarus. In Pausanias (ix. 11. 4–5) Daedalus escapes by ship. His innovation is to make sails, hitherto unknown; with these he outstrips Minos' fleet, which has to rely on oars. According to Diodorus (iv. 77. 6) the demise of Icarus was due to a certain carelessness at the point of disembarkation!

229. patrium . . . nomen = the name 'father', and so slightly different from 508. Of course he cries not 'Daedale', but 'pater, o pater' (*A.A.* ii. 91).

229–30. caerulea . . . / . . . aqua: Austin, on *Aen.* ii. 381, discusses the various comments of Servius on 'caeruleus' in Virgil, among them his remark on *Aen.* vii. 198: 'caerulum est viride cum nigro, ut est mare.' He concludes that Servius thought of the colour as primarily black, or blackish, with blue or blue-green shades at times. Ovid writes here 'caerulea . . . aqua', and at *A.A.* ii. 92 'virides . . . aquae'; the two adjectives are more nearly synonymous than we might be tempted to think.

231–3. The structure of these lines, once more repeated from the *A.A.*, is extremely elegant and effective, with repetition of 'Icare' and 'dixit' followed by the longer imperfect 'dicebat', and a pause at the caesura to mark the moment when Daedalus sees the feathers floating on the water.

231. pater . . . nec iam pater: this represents πατὴρ ἀπάτωρ in Greek; for similar phrases see Fordyce on Catullus 64. 83 'funera . . . nec funera'. But undeniably Ovid's play on words dissipates some of the pathos of this moment.

235. tellus: the island Icaria.

236–59. The story of Daedalus and Icarus has contained two aetia, but no metamorphosis. So we must travel backwards in time to the death of Perdix, whom Daedalus is said to have thrown from the Acropolis, jealous of the boy's ingenious inventions (thus Hyginus, *fab.* 39, cf. Cook, *Zeus*, vol. i, pp. 724ff.). Another version gives the name Perdix to the boy's mother, sister of Daedalus, while he himself is called Calos or Talos, seemingly making a con-

PLATE IV

Daedalus and Icarus. Wall-painting from Pompeii

nection with the bronze warden of Crete (Cook, ibid., p. 719). The
Athenians, indeed, showed the grave of Talos or Calos at the foot
of the Acropolis, probably at the spot where he was supposed to
have fallen from the battlements (Pausanias i. 21. 4, cf. Frazer on
Apollodorus iii. 15. 8). But the boy was certainly called Perdix as
early as the time of Sophocles (fr. 323 Pearson, from his *Camici*).

Perdix's invention of the saw (244–6) and the compass (247–9)
might well have been told in a work περὶ εὑρημάτων, e.g. by Philo-
stephanus, such as was popular in the Hellenistic age. But the
actual description of his metamorphosis into a partridge suggests
as a possible source the 'Ορνιθογονία of Boeus or Boeo, a poem in at
least two books which dealt with the transformation of human
beings into birds (see Introduction, p. xxi and Powell, *Collectanea
Alexandrina*, pp. 24–5). For regular features of the Greek poem,
paralleled here, were the intervention of a particular god to trans-
form a human being into a bird of the same name, and the ex-
planation of the bird's most notable habits as due to a character
trait, or accident which befell it, when still in human form (see on
251 ff. and 256 ff.).

Another poet who wrote an *Ornithogonia* (perhaps a translation
or adaptation of the earlier work) was Aemilius Macer, who also
adapted Nicander's *Theriaca* and *Alexipharmaca*. He was an elder
contemporary of Ovid, who admired Macer's poetry and used to
attend his recitations (*Tristia* iv. 10. 43–4):

> saepe suas volucres legit mihi grandior aevo,
> quaeque nocet serpens, quae iuvat herba, Macer.

Possibly Ovid found a mention of Perdix in Aemilius Macer and/
or the Greek 'Ορνιθογονία; equally well he may just be writing this
story in the same style. In any case the episode is of little impor-
tance here, except to provide variety and to justify the presence of
Daedalus and Icarus in a work devoted to transformations.

236–7. This connection, that Perdix saw Daedalus burying his son,
looks like an invention of Ovid. But the red-figure lekythos which
probably shows the fall of Icarus (*JHS* xlvii [1927] 231, fig. 6) also
has a bird, flying straight downwards. Beazley took this purely
as a directional sign, to indicate that the figure is sinking rather
than rising. But H. J. Rose (*JHS* xlviii [1928] 9–10) suggested
ingeniously that the bird might be Perdix. According to another
tradition (Pausanias ix. 11. 5) Icarus was buried by Heracles.
236. corpora nati: this particular poetic plural may surprise, but
was a favourite of our poet's, cf. 256, 416, 594, 871. He had a cer-
tain precedent in Cicero's *Aratea*, e.g. fr. 33. 435 'Orion fugiens
commendat corpora terris.' One might, however, consider that
a special case, with Maas (*Archiv für Lat. Lex.* xii [1902] 537,

second note), as Orion consists of several individual stars. Other arguable earlier examples are Tibullus i. 2. 25ª and i. 8. 52.

237. garrula ramosa prospexit ab ilice perdix: a famous crux; after much hesitation I retain the manuscript reading. The objections commonly made against it are (*a*) that the partridge does not normally perch, and (*b*) that the whole point of the story is thereby destroyed (cf. 256–9). But, although our common partridge seldom perches, Ovid may have some other member of the family in mind. For instance, the red-legged partridge is said to perch, and this is commoner in Italy—probably the 'picta perdix' of Martial iii. 58. 15 according to D'Arcy Thompson (*A Glossary of Greek Birds*, s.v. Πέρδιξ). As to (*b*), in 257 Ovid merely says that the bird does not nest in the topmost branches, 'in ramis altoque cacumine' (hendiadys). A bird talking or watching from a tree is so frequent a poetic motif from Hellenistic times (Call., fr. 194. 61–3 and fr. 260. 52, Ap. Rh. iii. 928–9, Virgil, *Ecl.* 9. 15, Ovid, *Met.* ii. 557) that Ovid may have adopted it almost automatically.

A reading which has won favour of late rests on the reference of a grammarian (Auctor de Dubiis Nominibus, *G.L.K.*, vol. v, p. 587): 'Perdix generis feminini, ut Varro "garrula limoso prospicit elice perdix" .' Undoubtedly the present line is intended; 'Varro' profits from several chunks of Virgil and Ovid, often horribly mutilated. And, although this grammarian is both careless and ignorant where we can check him, he does seem to preserve material not found elsewhere. Hence Merkel printed 'limoso . . . ab elice', 'from a muddy ditch'; Housman's 'lamoso . . . ab elice' (he postulated 'lamosus' = 'marshy' from the noun 'lama') would produce two equally unusual words. For 'elix' is not found in poetry; among prose-writers the plural alone occurs in Columella and perhaps the elder Pliny. Servius, commenting on *Georgics* i. 109 'elicit', describes the noun as archaic and provincial—certainly it would be surprising in Ovid. Apart from the rarity of 'elix', the picture thus produced is not aesthetically very pleasing. The grammarian's 'limoso . . . elice' could merely be due to chance; 'limoso' for 'ramosa' would be no worse than many of his other mistakes, and 'elice' for 'ilice' is an easy slip. A later hand in *h* has apparently altered 'ilice' to 'elice' without touching 'ramosa'. I do not know what one should infer from that.

If emendation is thought necessary, an attractive suggestion is R. G. M. Nisbet's 'ramoso . . . ab ulice'. The ulex (again an extremely rare word) is a shrub resembling rosemary (Pliny, *N.H.* xxxiii. 76, talking of Spain), so that the partridge would be crouching below the ulex for safety. 'Ramosus' could apply to any shrub with a large number of shoots, though it would

not have the same point as with 'ilice'. One would also have to
imagine the bird as emerging from cover at 237 'plausit pennis'.

garrula . . . perdix: the feminine gender is surprising, since, in
spite of our grammarian, 'perdix' is attested as masculine, and
here the sex is important.

prospexit suggests a vantage-point, although, with 'ulice', it
could imply peeping out cautiously; cf. Phaedrus ii. 4. 20 (feles)
'pavorem simulans prospicit toto die'.

238. et plausit pennis: cf. *Aen.* v. 215–16 (a frightened dove)'plau-
sumque exterrita pennis / dat tecto ingentem'. Here of course
the bird signifies triumphant approval.

240. longum tibi, Daedale, crimen: 'a lasting reproach'. Each suc-
cessive generation of partridges would be a constant reminder of
Daedalus' crime. We are not meant to inquire how a second
bird came into existence to continue the species!

243. animi ad praecepta capacis: descriptive genitive, 'of a mind
receptive to instruction'.

244–5. Greek writers usually attributed his inspiration to the jaw-
bone of a snake rather than a fish's backbone (e.g. Apollodorus
iii. 15. 8). For such invention by observing Nature compare
Pliny, *N.H.* vii. 194 'Gellio (*Annales*, fr. 4 Peter) Toxius Caeli
filius lutei aedificii inventor placet, exemplo sumpto ab hirun-
dinum nidis', and Hyginus, *fab.* 277, where Mercury invents
some Greek letters 'ex gruum volatu' (perhaps also from Gellius,
cf. fr. 2 Peter). The style is probably that of a Hellenistic
treatise. For inventors in general see A. Kleingünther, *ΠΡΩΤΟΣ
ΕΥΡΕΤΗΣ*, *Philologus*, Suppl. 26. 1 (1933), and Cook, *Zeus*, vol. i,
pp. 724 ff. for Perdix. Pliny (*N.H.* vii. 198) attributes the saw to
Daedalus; obviously he succeeded in stealing his nephew's idea!

246. perpetuos dentes: 'a continuous row of teeth'.

247–9. 'And he was the first to bind two iron legs from a knot,
so that, while they remained the same distance apart, one leg
should stay fixed and the other describe a circle'. An obscure
remark of Servius on *Aen.* vi. 14 suggests that Perdix was some-
times called Circinus to fit his invention of the compass.

247. nodo: the point where the two legs meet to form a hinge.

250. arce Minervae: the Athenian Acropolis.

251–9. It is in this part of the episode that Ovid seems to reflect
the technique of the Greek 'Ορνιθογονία. There, stress is laid on
a god's intervention to make the metamorphosis, usually in
pity for undeserved suffering; e.g. from the paraphrases Ant.
Lib. 18 Ἀπόλλων δὲ οἰκτείρας . . . ὄρνιθα ἐποίησε τὸν παῖδα, 7 Ζεὺς δὲ καὶ
Ἀπόλλων οἰκτείραντες . . ., 11 Ζεὺς δὲ οἰκτείρας . . . Compare *Met.* xi.
784–6 'Tethys miserata cadentem / molliter excepit, nantemque
per aequora pennis / texit' (the transformation of Aesacus,
a story that bears all the marks of the 'Ορνιθογονία).

Also in the Greek poem human beings regularly keep their names when changed into birds; in Ant. Lib.'s long-winded paraphrase (7) γενομένους ὄρνιθας ἐποίησαν ὀνόματι καλεῖσθαι καθὰ καὶ πρὶν ἢ μεταβαλεῖν αὐτοὺς ὠνομάζοντο, cf. Ant. Lib. 5, here 'nomen quod et ante remansit' (255). The Greek poet perhaps used the word ὁμώνυμος.

It is typical for Ovid to make his bow to a predecessor in the same field—cf. the 'Nicandrean' touch at 719–20—but equally typical that he will not be tied down to any one set of conventions for very long.

255. nomen quod et ante remansit: probably not = 'et nomen remansit quod ante' (cf. 279 n. for a probable dislocation of 'et'). καθὰ καὶ πρὶν ... ὠνομάζοντο in a typical paraphrase from Boeus (above) suggests that Ovid may echo the Greek poet's language very closely here.

256–9. Cf. Ant. Lib. 18 from the 'Ορνιθογονία: Ἀπόλλων δὲ οἰκτείρας ... ὄρνιθα ἐποίησε τὸν παῖδα ἠέροπον, ὃς ἔτι νῦν τίκτει μὲν ὑπὸ (ἐπὶ? Martini) γῆς, ἀεὶ δὲ μελετᾷ πέτεσθαι. The story is different, but the technique of this passage is suggestively similar to that of Ovid.

260–546. *The Calydonian Boar-hunt* (260–444), *Althaea and the Death of Meleager* (445–525), *and the Transformation of his Sisters* (526–46)

This episode dominates the whole book, by both its length and central position; it consists of three parts, connected by the narrative, but each written in quite a different style—the first epic, the second tragic, and the third whimsically Alexandrian. Although Ovid uses Theseus as a link to the boar-hunt, Theseus plays a very minor part in it, and Meleager son of Oeneus becomes the centre of interest.

History of the Meleager-legend

The story of Meleager was one of the most celebrated Greek myths, treated by poets of all ages, from early epic-writers down to Hellenistic times. J. Th. Kakridis, who examines the legend in detail (*Homeric Researches* [Lund, 1949], ch. 1), believes the original form to have been a folk-tale, in which the Fates visit the hero's mother, and say that her baby son will survive as long as a stick which is burning in the fire-place. So the mother hastens to remove the stick from the fire, and hides it in a chest. But when the hero has grown up, one day he kills his mother's brother after a quarrel, whereupon she burns the fateful stick, and so causes her son's death (Kakridis, pp. 13–18; see further on 451–60).

This was perhaps the original timeless story, but it is modified considerably by early Greek epic poets. Many scholars believe in the existence of a pre-Homeric Meleager-poem, known conven-

tionally as the *Meleagris* (see Kakridis, Index, s.v. Meleagris), and
think that this earlier poem was used by Homer in *Il.* ix. 529–99.
There we are told how Oeneus, king of Aetolia (Calydon), failed to
honour Artemis when sacrificing to the other gods. So in anger she
sent a monstrous wild boar to ravage the land, which caused the
utmost distress until Oeneus' son Meleager collected a chosen
band of heroes and eventually killed the animal. This much is
common to all existing forms of the legend; whether a hunt
figured in the folk-tale, we cannot tell.

In the *Iliad* Artemis then arouses dissension over the relics of
the boar between the Aetolians (Calydonians) and the Curetes of
Pleuron, and in the course of the quarrel Meleager apparently kills
a brother of Althaea his own mother (*Il.* ix. 567). Thereupon she
curses him, and a Fury hears her prayer for Meleager's death
(571–2). Incensed by his mother's attitude, Meleager withdraws
from the fight, after which the Aetolians are hard pressed by the
Curetes; only his wife Cleopatra can persuade him to rejoin the
battle and repulse the Curetes. Even so, we must assume that his
mother's curse was eventually fatal to Meleager, as Pausanias
inferred (x. 31. 3). Homer puts the story in the mouth of Phoenix,
when the Greek embassy tries to persuade Achilles to emerge
from his tent, and the parallels between the two situations are
clear. While Meleager sulks the Calydonians are defeated, but they
prevail on his return, although, like Achilles, Meleager is doomed to
eventual death. Later epic tradition took the similarity even further
by neglecting Althaea's curse, and stating that Meleager was
killed by Apollo who helped the Curetes against the Calydonians
(Hesiodic *Catalogue of Women*, fr. 25. 12–13 Merkelbach–West,
and thus the *Minyad* according to Pausanias [x. 31. 3]). Kakridis
(p. 14) calls this version a later adaptation of the tale in the
Iliad and of no particular importance.

Little can be said of Stesichorus' Συοθῆραι (frs. 44–5 Page), even
though that poem may be richer by *P.Oxy.* 2359, apparently part
of a catalogue of hunters (see on 305). But the tragedians show us
further important elements, whether new or not. Phrynichus in
his *Pleuroniae* (*TGF²*, p. 721) is our first authority for the fire-
brand on which Meleager's life depends, but Pausanias, who quotes
the fragment (x. 31. 4), makes it clear that this was not an innova-
tion; it may be the oldest version of all (see above). Bacchylides
(5. 95–154) shows that the fire-brand did not necessarily exclude
the version in which Meleager dies on the battlefield—Nicander
has been abused unjustly for this particular combination.

Sophocles in his *Meleager* probably followed Homer quite
closely, and concentrated on the hero's part in the war between the
Calydonians and the Curetes rather than the boar-hunt (Pearson,
Fragments of Sophocles, vol. ii, p. 66). But he perhaps made an

important contribution to the legend's development, since Sophocles
is our first known authority for the transformation of Meleager's
sisters into birds (Pliny, *N.H.* xxxvii. 40), which provides the
raison d'être of this episode in the *Metamorphoses*.

But the greatest influence on Ovid was undoubtedly the
Meleager of Euripides (see Page, *Greek Literary Papyri* [Poetry],
pp. 154–8 for the plot and a possible new fragment). This was
probably the model for Lucius Accius' tragedy of the same name.
Atalanta had long been reckoned as a participant in the boar-
hunt, e.g. on the François vase, where she is accompanied by
Milanion (the relevant part reproduced at Plate V), but it was
Euripides who made Meleager's love for her play a vital part in the
story (cf. especially fr. 525). The influence of Euripides is most
clear in the soliloquy of Althaea (478–511). Our poet almost cer-
tainly used Accius' *Meleager* as well as the Greek model.

To come down to Hellenistic times, Ovid could have consulted
the *Meleager* of Sosiphanes, a tragedian of the Pleiad (*TGF²*,
p. 819). And, as an illustration of this legend's popularity, we have
a recently discovered elegiac fragment perhaps composed about
300–275 B.C. (Appendix I; see further on 298 ff.). There is no proof
that Ovid used this, but he certainly owes much, at least in form,
to Nicander of Colophon (second century B.C.) who handled the
story in book iii of his *Heteroeumena* (paraphrased by Ant. Lib. 2).
Nicander also used the transformation of Meleager's sisters as
a peg on which to hang the whole episode of the Calydonian Boar-
hunt, although in subject-matter he seems to have been closer to
Homer than to Euripides. Nicander's chief contribution to our
poet was the description of the actual metamorphosis (526–46).

The Calydonian Boar-Hunt in Greek Art

This was also a favourite subject for Attic black-figure vase-
painters, with their love of vigorous and vivid action. We see the
boar itself as a fearsome creature almost as tall as the hunters,
attacked on both sides by spearsmen, while a dog snaps at its
flanks. The heroes may be marked by their names, with Meleager
and probably Peleus prominent in the fray; at the boar's feet lies
a dead man. The artist may even give us a new name among the
hunters, such as Pegaeus (see R. S. Young, *Hesperia* iv [1935] 430–
41, discussing with illustrations a vase from the Athenian Agora,
also my Pl. V [the François vase]).

Ovid's Treatment

The three-fold structure of this episode has been mentioned
above. The boar-hunt itself (260–444) is perhaps the most strictly
epic passage in all the *Metamorphoses*; we are not even spared

PLATE V

The Calydonian Boar-hunt (upper band). From the François Vase

a full-scale catalogue of heroes as a preliminary (298–328). Al-
thaea's soliloquy (478–511) is clearly inspired by Euripides, and
the actual transformation follows an Alexandrian source, un-
doubtedly Nicander. Georges Lafaye had already noticed Ovid's
habit of grafting an Alexandrian-derived metamorphosis on to
material of quite a different character—he cited the case of
Pentheus (bk. iii). The episode shows well Ovid's insistence on
variety of style, and the eclectic way in which he used his sources.
Evaluation of the whole is not easy, as the constituent parts of the
episode seem to me of uneven quality. Ovid is certainly not as
successful in handling diverse material here as he is with Ceyx (xi.
410–748). But his design is a most ambitious one, and plays an
important part in the structure of the book, for this episode, and
particularly the Hunt itself, gives weight and balance to the
whole book. For further comments on individual parts of the epi-
sode see on 298 ff., 329 ff., 445 ff., 478 ff., and 526 ff.

260–1. The usual story was that the Sicilian Cocalus received
Minos hospitably and promised to surrender Daedalus as he was
asked, but then had the king scalded to death by his daughters
in the bath—so Apollodorus, *Epit.* 1. 15, and also, according to
Pearson (vol. ii, pp. 3–4), Sophocles' *Camici*. Ovid seems to
follow a less well known tradition by which Cocalus openly
resists Minos, cf. Silius xiv. 39–41 'duxerat actos / moenibus e
centum non fausta ad proelia Minos / Daedaleam repetens
poenam', and Pausanias vii. 4. 6. Furthermore, at ix. 437 Minos
appears still to be alive.

262–3. By killing the Minotaur Theseus had relieved Athens of hav-
ing to send young men and girls as tribute to Crete (cf. 170–1).

264. templa coronantur: cf. *Aen.* ii. 248–9, after the supposed
departure of the Greeks, 'nos delubra deum miseri, quibus
ultimus esset / ille dies, festa velamus fronde per urbem'.

bellatricemque Minervam: Lamprocles the Athenian in his
martial hymn (cf. Aristophanes, *Clouds* 967) addressed her as
Παλλάδα περσέπολιν δεινὰν θεὸν ἐγρεκύδοιμον (but see Dover on *Clouds*
967 for the problems of restoration).

266. acerris: incense-boxes. The manuscripts offer a choice between
this and 'acervis'. Either would make excellent sense; for
'acervis', stressing abundance, cf. v. 131 and [Tibullus] iii. 12
(iv. 6). 1. But, in spite of the strong support for 'acervis', I have
preferred 'acerris' as the *difficilior lectio*, and so more liable to
corruption; compare xiii. 703 and *Aen.* v. 745 'plena supplex
veneratur acerra'. The 'acerra' was also a regular part of Roman
ritual.

267. vaga fama: half personified, as often in Virgil (fully so at *Aen.*
iv. 173 ff.). Cf. ὄσσα and φήμη in Greek epic.

268. Achaia: Greece quite generally. We seem to catch an echo of the propaganda which would make Theseus a second Heracles (Plutarch, *Thes.* 29. 3), holding that his labours too were performed for the benefit of mankind, to rid the world of monsters and anti-social human beings. There was a proverb οὐκ ἄνευ Θησέως (Plutarch, ibid.). For Ovid, metre necessitates the Homeric genitive 'Theseŏs'.

270. quamvis Meleagron haberet: this line marks the shift of attention from Theseus to Meleager; the former is not singled out for especial honour in the Catalogue (303), and during the boar-hunt he does no more than throw a spear without effect (408–10).

273–4. Cf. Euripides, fr. 516, from the ill-fated prologue to his *Meleager*, Οἰνεύς ποτ᾽ ἐκ γῆς πολύμετρον λαβὼν στάχυν / θύων ἀπαρχάς . . .

pleni successibus anni / primitias frugum: the exact interpretation is not quite clear. Most probably there is a double genitive dependence, the first-fruits of the earth of a year full of blessing. But 'successibus' could be taken temporally—at the happy outcome either of a complete year or of a plenteous year; parallels for 'plenus' absolutely in the latter sense are hard to find, but it is surely possible. Alternatively we might read 'frugem' (*s*) in 274 with a comma after 'primitias', following older editors. But 'primitias frugum' is a phrase that should hardly be disturbed; cf. x. 433, Quint. *Decl.* 13. 19 'primitiae frugum Cereri offeruntur.'

275. libasse: the idea of offering in this verb accounts for all the object nouns in 274–5.

276. coeptus ab agricolis: 'beginning from the gods of the countryside', among whom are reckoned Dionysus and Athena because of their connection with wine and the olive. 'Argolicis' is a nice anagrammatic error.

277. ambitiosus: 'coveted'. This is much the clearest instance of the very rare passive sense; *Tristia* i. 9. 18 and Martial xii. 68. 2 are also quoted.

277–8. solas . . . : cf. *Il.* ix. 535–6 ἄλλοι δὲ θεοὶ δαίνυνθ᾽ ἑκατόμβας / οἴη δ᾽ οὐκ ἔρρεξε Διὸς κούρῃ μεγάλοιο, a common Homeric pattern which Ovid has embroidered considerably.

278. praeteritae: Magnus printed the much better attested 'praeteritas', to be taken closely with 'cessasse'. But after 'solas' and 'relictas' (277) there are too many syllables with -as. The text gives a more artistic arrangement of nouns and adjectives— a consideration that Ovid rated highly.

279. tangit et ira deos: one would like to understand this as = 'tangit ira et deos', and probably should do so. But it might possibly mean that anger (as well as other nobler emotions) touches the gods. We are a long way from Virgil's probing question 'tantaene animis caelestibus irae ?' (*Aen.* i. 11).

at non impune feremus: an odd expression, which seems to be influenced by the colloquial phrase 'impune ferre', as at 494, cf. Cicero, *ad Fam.* xiii. 77. 3 'cum multos libros surripuisset, nec se impune laturum putaret'. There, however, 'ferre' means not to endure but to carry off, i.e. 'get away with'. If a logical explanation of the present phrase is required, perhaps understand 'esse'; 'that it (or he) should go unpunished', cf. xi. 67, and Tacitus, *Ann.* i. 72 'dicta impune erant'.

280 ff. A wild beast as the destructive agent of a god is a familiar motif from Greek mythology, as for instance the Nemean lion, sent by Hera and killed by Heracles.

280–1. inquit et . . . / misit: ἦ καί or φῆ καί followed by a verb of action are regular ways of closing direct speech in Greek epic poetry.

Olenios: 'Aetolian', from the town of Olenus (*Il.* ii. 639, etc.), Calydon forming part of Aetolia. This epithet is used twice elsewhere of the Calydonian Boar, 'Olenii . . . suis' (Statius, *Theb.* ii. 541), 'Olenio . . . apro' (Ausonius, *Ep.* 4. 39). Here the reading was suggested by Heinsius; e² has 'Olenyos'. The manuscripts are in some confusion, though several have an *l* in their reading, offering 'implenos' or the like.

This confusion points towards 'Oenios', printed by Magnus and others. Of course the sense is satisfactory, cf. Sophocles, fr. 401. 1 Pearson συὸς μέγιστον χρῆμ' ἐπ' Οἰνέως γύαις. But why should Ovid write 'Oenius' instead of 'Oeneus', the form at Statius, *Theb.* ii. 469 and Silius xv. 308? The postulated corruption, which may be very old, is paralleled exactly at Statius, *Theb.* i. 402 'Olenius Tydeus', where D has 'Oenius', and Heinsius suggested 'Oeneus'.

'Olenios' is better than a personal adjective here, for it stresses the fact that Oeneus' impiety brought suffering to many others. Also it gives the line a touch of epic distinction, which is lacking with 'Oenios' or 'Oeneos'.

282–3. A strangely involved and clumsy comparison conflating two figures, either of which would be quite normal by itself. One might say that the creature was as big as, or bigger than, a bull —e.g. Call. *hymn* 3. 102, deer μάσσονες ἢ ταῦροι—or that it was larger than those of a country famed for the particular species, as Horace, *Odes* i. 22. 13–14 'quale portentum neque militaris / Daunias latis alit aesculetis'. Ovid's method of handling this comparison leads to a curious anticlimax in 283.

282. quanto: the confusion of thought is paralleled in the syntax. Ovid seems to conflate 'tantum aprum quantum' with 'aprum quo maiorem'.

283. For the bulls of Epirus cf. Pliny, *N.H.* viii. 176, where their excellence is ascribed to the breeding policy of King Pyrrhus.

sed: not really adversative, but intended to emphasize what follows. See Mayor on Juvenal 5. 147 for similar instances. Even so, the anticlimax remains.

284–6. Here is the first example in this book of apparent doublets in the manuscript tradition, which offers, with slight variations:

> 284   sanguine et igne micant oculi, riget horrida cervix,
> 285   et saetae similes rigidis hastilibus horrent
> 286   stantque velut vallum, velut alta hastilia saetae.

Clearly 285 and 286 cannot be allowed to co-exist; the question is whether we should delete one or both of these lines, or whether they might be alternative versions deriving from Ovid himself.

Here I agree with Enk (in *Ovidiana*, p. 332) that 285 must be rejected. The repetition 'riget horrida' (284) 'rigidis . . . horrent' (285) is intolerable, and not saved by the alternation of verb and adjective; the late variants 'ardua' (284) and 'densis' (285) are merely attempts to remedy the defect. On the other hand 286 is probably genuine, in spite of its omission by E M N S U. The likening of the boar's bristles to stakes in a palisaded rampart, a contemporary Roman touch (cf. 357–8), seems too good to be the work of an interpolator. A glance at the François vase (Pl. V) will show what Ovid had in mind.

One should hardly reject both 285 and 286; as Enk says, we need some reference to the boar's bristles. Statius, who often echoes this episode (though his details vary, cf. on 378–80), writes of the boar 'erectus saetis et aduncae fulmine malae' (*Theb.* ii. 470). And the second comparison in 286 was perhaps traditional; Pancrates (a second-century-A.D. Alexandrian poet) says less appropriately of a lion ἡ δ' ἀπὸ νώτου (sc. χαίτη) / φρισσο]μένη θηκτοῖσιν ὁμοίιος ἦεν ἀκωκαῖς (fr. 2. 22–3 Heitsch).

Ovid's whole picture of the boar is an embroidery of stock epic material. Compare *Il.* xiii. 473–4, and particularly [Hesiod], *Shield of Heracles* 389–91:

> ἀφρὸς δὲ περὶ στόμα μαστιχόωντι
> λείβεται, ὄσσε δέ οἱ πυρὶ λαμπετόωντι ἔικτον
> ὀρθὰς δ' ἐν λοφιῇ φρίσσει τρίχας ἀμφί τε δειρήν.

286. velut . . . velut: Burman's division of the second 'velut' to 'vel ut' is considered necessary by Enk. But surely the two comparisons can stand in asyndeton.

288. dentibus Indis: the tusks of an elephant.

289. frondes afflatibus ardent: a reminder of the boar's supernatural origin and mission; cf. the miraculous bulls of Aeetes (vii. 105).

LINES 283-298 73

290-5. It may be no coincidence that the boar attacks, in corn, vine, and olive, the attributes of Ceres, Bacchus, and Athena, who are said to have been honoured first in preference to Artemis (274-5).

290. is: perhaps imitating the Homeric ὅγε, picking up the narrative, e.g. *Il.* ix. 541 quoted on 294-5.

modo: to be coupled with 'nunc' (291)—'first ... then'. Quite pleasing, though, is the variant 'vix modo crescenti . . . / nec matura' (291) approved by Heinsius with slight manuscript support.

in herba: 'in the blade', cf. the proverbial 'adhuc tua messis in herba est' (*Heroides* 17. 263). For the first time we have here a parallel fragment of Accius' *Meleager*: 'fruges prohibet pergrandescere' (428 W.).

291. metit: a fine vivid piece of irony, the sidelong blow of the boar's tusks being compared to a reaper's sickle.

294-5. Cf. *Il.* ix. 541-2 πολλὰ δ' ὅγε προθέλυμνα χαμαὶ βάλε δένδρεα μακρὰ / αὐτῆσιν ῥίζῃσι καὶ αὐτοῖς ἄνθεσι μήλων.

298-328. *The Catalogue of Hunters*

This was one of the most venerable and characteristic features of epic poetry, which also appealed to Alexandrian taste (e.g. the list of Actaeon's dogs at *Epic. Adesp.* 1 Powell, cf. *Met.* iii. 206 ff.). Sonorous proper names have a certain attractiveness even when not highly significant. Ovid introduces a little light relief by showing us some of the great heroes off duty; Jason back from his travels, Nestor still in his youth, Amphiaraus not yet ruined by his covetous wife, and so on.

Probably there was a formal source for Ovid's catalogue, but we cannot say what this may have been. No one version of the participants succeeded in obliterating its rivals; there are certain variations in the three surviving lists (also Apollodorus i. 8. 2, and Hyginus, *fab.* 173), and the vase-painters may give us a name which has been lost to the literary tradition (Pegaeus, cf. R. S. Young, *Hesperia* iv [1935] 439-40). But most of the heroes mentioned here are old hands from the Argo.

We also have the remains of two further lists of hunters—it is impossible to say how detailed they were. The first comes from *P.Oxy.* 2359, and is plausibly assigned to the Συοθῆραι of Stesichorus (fr. 45 Page, see on 305). The second is an elegiac fragment probably of the early third century B.C. (Appendix I). In the latter the catalogue agrees with Ovid as far as it goes, and so does the description of Ancaeus (22-3, cf. below, 391). But these were well-trodden paths, and the two poets could easily have drawn on the same sources independently.

298. populi: as opposed to the selected heroes (300); the plural here as λαοί in Greek.

300. lecta manus iuvenum: Callimachus speaks of ἐπίκλητοι . . . ἀγρευτῆρες (*hymn* 3. 218), cf. of the Argonauts 'Argivi . . . delecti viri' (Ennius, *Medea* 257 W.), 'lecti iuvenes' (Catullus 64. 4).

301. Tyndaridae: Castor and Pollux (372 ff.). For their accomplishments cf. *Il.* iii. 237 Κάστορά θ' ἱππόδαμον καὶ πὺξ ἀγαθὸν Πολυδεύκεα.

spectandus: cf. Horace, *Odes* iv. 14. 17 'spectandus in certamine Martio'. I follow Magnus in preferring this reading, better attested, to the more prosaic 'spectatus'. Less distinguished than either would be 'praestantes', adopted by Riese.

302. For Argo as the first ship of all cf. Catullus 64. 11, 'illa rudem cursu prima imbuit Amphitriten'; see also on 217–20.

303. The friendship of Theseus and Pirithous was no less famous than that between Achilles and Patroclus (see further on 405–6).

304. Thestiadae: Toxeus and Plexippus (440–1), sons of Thestius king of Pleuron. They were brothers of Althaea, and so Meleager's uncles.

proles: used collectively. Both sons of the Messenian Aphareus were Argonauts (Ap. Rh. i. 151 ff.). Idas, according to one account, would be Meleager's father-in-law. Lynceus was more celebrated for his keen eyesight.

305. et iam non femina Caeneus: for this transformation see xii. 189 ff. It is just possible that Stesichorus referred to the former state of Caeneus in a catalogue of hunters (see Lobel on *P.Oxy.* 2359, fr. 1, col. 1, line 7). Virgil presents Caeneus as restored to female sex in the underworld—'iuvenis quondam, nunc femina Caeneus / rursus et in veterem fato revoluta figuram' (*Aen.* vi. 448–9).

306. Leucippus: brother of Aphareus (304 n.).

iaculoque insignis Acastus: in a full-blown epic Catalogue we would expect to be told of the hero's homeland, his father's name, and his equipment. Ovid never gives us all three elements together. Acastus, also an Argonaut (Ap. Rh. i. 224–5), was son of Pelias king of Iolcus in Thessaly.

307. Hippothous: son of the notorious Arcadian bandit Cercyon (cf. vii. 439). Obviously his presence was due to personal merit rather than family connections.

Dryas: a son of Ares, and brother to Tereus.

Phoenix: later tutor to Achilles.

308. Actoridaeque pares: Ovid probably means Eurytus and Cteatus, twin sons of Actor in the *Iliad* (ii. 621, etc.); for curious traditions about them as Siamese twins see Leaf on *Il.* xi. 709, pseudo-Hesiod, frs. 16. 16 ff., 17, and 18 Merkelbach–West. Ap. Rh. knows of Menoetius (i. 69) and Irus (i. 72) as sons of Actor, but presumably not twins, since the son of Irus accompanies

Menoetius to Colchis. Apollodorus (i. 8. 2) makes Eurytion (311) a son of Actor—grandson, says Ap. Rh. (i. 74).

missus: i.e. sent by his father Augeas, a common formula in an epic Catalogue (cf. 314).

nec Telamon aberat: A negative for variety is another convention of the Catalogue, e.g. Ap. Rh. i. 45 οὐδὲ μὲν Ἴφικλος Φυλάκῃ ἔνι δηρὸν ἔλειπτο. Telamon and Peleus were sons of Aeacus (4).

310. One of those Latin hexameters which could be turned into a Greek line with minimal alteration. But it would be rash to assume that Ovid had in fact borrowed this line from a Greek poet. As usual, the two hiatus involve Greek proper names, cf. 315.

Pheretiade: Admetus, son of the Thessalian king Pheres.

Hyanteo Iolao: 'Boeotian' from the Hyantes, former inhabitants of that region. Iolaus was a son of Heracles' brother Iphiclus.

311. Eurytion (cf. 308 n.) and **Echion** son of Hermes were both Argonauts (Ap. Rh. i. 74 and 52).

312. Lelex, senior statesman of the party (617), came from Naryx in Opuntian Locris, but spent his youth in Troezen under the guidance of Pittheus (622–3, cf. 567–8). As to his name (cf. 6 n.), there was a tradition that the Locrians were descended from Leleges; see W. Oldfather, *AJA* xx (1916) 59–61, pseudo-Hesiod, fr. 234. 1 Merkelbach–West.

Panopeus was a son of Phocus, who was killed by his brothers Telamon and Peleus (Ap. Rh. i. 90 ff.). Of **Hyleus** nothing else is known.

313. Hippasus: son of Eurytus. I wonder how many of Ovid's original readers would realize that he was the same person as 'Eurytides', if that is the right reading at 371. Since Hippasus plays no vital part in the story, this point probably did not worry the poet.

primis etiamnum Nestor in annis: an oblique reference to Nestor's perpetual lament in the *Iliad* (vii. 157, xi. 670, xxiii. 629), εἴθ' ὡς ἡβώοιμι βίη τέ μοι ἔμπεδος εἴη / ὡς ὁπότε . . ., etc., etc. Nestor does not appear in the other surviving lists of hunters, but no doubt Ovid had a precedent for his inclusion.

314. For the characteristic formula cf. 308 and, e.g., Ap. Rh. i. 164. One of the sons of Hippocoon was the ill-fated Enaesimus (362); the others were called Alcon and Dexippus or Leucippus.

Amyclis: Amyclae was a town in Laconia, near Sparta.

315. Penelopaeque socer: Laertes, father of Odysseus.

cum Parrhasio Ancaeo: Arcadian Ancaeus, cf. 391. For the spondaic fifth foot see 23 n., and for the hiatus 310 n. This exact rhythm recurs, for example, at *Aen.* i. 617 'quem Dardanio Anchisae', *Aen.* xi. 31 'qui Parrhasio Euandro'.

316. Ampycides: Mopsus the seer.

316–17. Amphiaraus, not yet betrayed by his wife Eriphyle, who, bribed with a golden necklace, persuaded him to take part in the expedition of the Seven against Thebes, although he knew that this would be fatal to him.

317. Tegeaea: 'the Tegean girl', i.e. Atalanta, kept to the last for emphasis and described in much the greatest detail. The epithet, as 'Lycaei' and 'Nonacria' (426) means little more than 'Arcadian', cf. 40 n. As with Mestra (738 n.), Ovid never mentions Atalanta by name in this episode, always using an epic-style periphrasis. After this line several manuscripts clumsily try to write another giving her name and parentage, but there is no chance of the insertion's being genuine.

decus : 'the glory'. Homer often uses κῦδος thus, e.g. in the song of the Sirens μέγα κῦδος Ἀχαιῶν (*Od.* xii. 184), which Cicero translates 'o decus Argolicum' (fr. 29. 1 Morel).

318 ff. Atalanta is pictured as wearing a fibula of polished metal which clasps her dress, probably at the shoulder. As Miss Lorimer explains (*Homer and the Monuments*, p. 337 n. 4), a fibula is essentially nearer to the modern safety-pin than to the brooch.

319. nodum collectus in unum: such was a common practice in both Greece and Rome, cf. *A.A.* iii. 143–6—a Diana hair-style. Perhaps Ovid calls this style 'simplex' in contrast to the more elaborate fashions which were becoming popular under the early Empire (cf. on 668–9).

320. resonabat: cf. *Il.* i. 46 of Apollo ἔκλαγξαν δ᾽ ἄρ᾽ ὀιστοὶ ἐπ᾽ ὤμων, *Aen.* iv. 149 'tela sonant umeris'.

320–1. eburnea . . . / telorum custos: the phrase corresponds to ἰοδόκη (sc. φαρέτρα) in Greek, and similarly is treated as feminine. Roman poets often use two words to express a Greek compound (e.g. 731). Euripides (fr. 530. 4–5) described Atalanta as κύνας / καὶ τόξ᾽ ἔχουσα.

322–3. Compare ix. 712–13 'cultus erat pueri, facies quam sive puellae / sive dares puero.' Here, however, 'cultu' is much sharper than the variant 'cultus'.

323. possis : involvement of the reader even in this small degree is an un-epic touch. But Ovid likes to interject 'scires' (i. 162), 'videres' (xi. 126), or the like (cf. last note). With 'posse' the MSS. often vary between 'possis' and 'posses'. The present subjunctive is better supported here, and more vivid and arresting.

324–5. hanc pariter vidit, pariter Calydonius heros / optavit: cf. *Il.* xiv. 294 ὡς δ᾽ ἴδεν, ὥς μιν ἔρως πυκινὰς φρένας ἀμφεκάλυψεν. For the different ways in which later poets understood ὡς here see Gow on Theocritus 2. 82. Ovid seems to take it as demonstrative,

'as he saw, so did he desire her', Virgil as exclamatory, 'ut vidi,
ut perii' (*Ecl.* 8. 41).

325. **renuente deo**: 'though Heaven was against him', as at Tibul-
lus i. 5. 20; no particular god is intended. A backward nod
(renuo, Greek ἀνανεύω) was the ancient gesture of refusal, while
a forward nod (annuo, 780) signified assent.

325–6. **flammasque latentes / hausit**: a phrase made difficult by
'latentes'. One might expect the idea to be of 'scooping up' (see
D. A. West, *CQ* N.S. [1965] 271) the flames of love from outside.
This would fit x. 252–3 'haurit / pectore Pygmalion simulati
corporis ignes'. Here one might translate 'latentes' as 'flames
which had to remain hidden'; but the word suggests that the
fire already existed deep down inside Meleager (cf. vii. 554). Per-
haps the form of the expression is influenced by the secret of
Meleager's life and death, prefiguring his destruction—particu-
larly 516–17 'caecis torreri viscera sentit / ignibus'. This pre-
figuring would be akin to Ovidian irony as at 51–2 or 98.

327. **virum**: 'as a husband'.

329–444. *The Hunt*

Of all the sections in the *Metamorphoses*, this following one is the
most strictly formal piece of epic writing. Very many of the
incidents and turns of phrase contain unmistakable echoes of
battle-scenes in the *Iliad*. We find not only the stock formulas
used to describe the shooting of an arrow (381) or a warrior's death
(399–402), but also, more generally, some typical Homeric descrip-
tive patterns (see on 347–9). Old Latin epic also makes its con-
tribution (see on 359, 376, 412).

Ovid's setting of the scene (329–44) is splendid and visually
brilliant as always. But, although there is much ingenuity in the
transference of Homeric motifs from a battle to a hunt, the actual
fighting loses its impetus. The poet is then reduced to wooing our
interest with almost comic accidents to Nestor (365–7) and to
Telamon (378–9). Ovid's failure here is not surprising. To breathe
new life into the old epic tradition of combat was a formidable
task, particularly when there was no scope for the interplay of
human emotions, which Virgil used so well. At least Ovid does not
strive for effect by describing wounds and death in gruesome
detail—a fault which afflicts Roman poets of all periods, and some-
times even our most urbane of poets himself.

329. **quam nulla ceciderat aetas**: cf. ii. 418. 'Aetas' comes to mean
'generation of men'.

330. **incipit a plano devexaque prospicit arva**: the wood, as I take
it, occupies level ground (planum) above the valley. From there
the fields stretch away (devexa) down to the marsh at the val-
ley's foot, where lurks the boar (334 ff.). After being disturbed,

he charges up hill through the fields, and first skirmishes with
hounds and hunters on the wood's edge (340–75), until he is
forced to take refuge in more thickly covered country (376–7).

Several commentators have imagined the slope as climbing
upwards from the wood, but this is a perverse way to interpret
'devexaque prospicit arva', and it would not then be clear how
the marsh at the foot of the valley (334 ff.) fits in. Perhaps the
misunderstanding arose through taking 'a plano' as 'from the
plain' instead of simply 'from level ground'.

331 ff. For general information on ancient methods of hunting the
boar see D. B. Hull, *Hounds and Hunting in Ancient Greece*
(Chicago University Press, 1964), *passim*; cf. also *Aen.* iv. 129 ff.

331–2. pars with a plural = 'some of them' is quite regular. As
a small point of style, notice that Ovid avoids the commonest
pattern of anaphora by postponing the second 'pars' from first
word in its limb, as, for example, ii. 107–8; cf. Call. *hymn*
3. 110–12 χρύσεα μέν τοι / ἔντεα καὶ ζώνη, χρύσεον δ' ἐζεύξαο δίφρον / ἐν
δ' ἐβάλευ χρύσεια, θεή, κεμάδεσσι χαλινά.

332. vincula pars adimunt canibus: the hounds are led to the
hunting-ground on a leash, and only then let loose. Ennius
(*Annals* 339–41 W.) has a simile from a 'vinclis venatica velox /
apta' which scents a wild animal.

334 ff. A fragment of Accius' *Meleager* seems to describe the boar
wallowing in a stream before being disturbed (431 W.): 'frigit
fricatque corpus atrum occulte abstruso in flumine', cf. the
similar picture at Ap. Rh. ii. 818–20 κεῖτο γὰρ εἰαμενῇ δονακώδεος ἐν
ποταμοῖο / ψυχόμενος λαγόνας τε καὶ ἄσπετον ἰλύι νηδὺν / κάπριος ἀργιόδων.

335. ima lacunae: phrases of this type with neuter plural of the
adjective and genitive of the noun are common from the time
of Lucretius—cf. Austin on *Aen.* ii. 332 'angusta viarum'. The
genitive is strictly partitive, and here the partitive sense is clear
and appropriate, as at 692.

339. excussis elisi nubibus ignes: Ovid combines two ideas: first the
lightning forced out (elisi) from clashing clouds—a common
opinion, e.g. at Seneca, *Q.N.* i. 1. 6, and secondly the clouds
themselves disturbed or 'shaken out' (excussi) by the light-
ning's passage. The latter picture is the more important, as it
represents the boar breaking through the undergrowth. In the
simile there is no word referring to sound; the poet leaves his
readers to supply this element for themselves.

The text is quite satisfactory here; later variants and conjec-
tures need not be considered.

340. propulsa fragorem: a hint of onomatopoeia to describe the
crack of branches as they bend and break before the boar's
onslaught; cf. 776 n.

342. lato ... ferro: the hunting-spear differed from the war-spear

in having a particularly wide metal head, as did the specialized
boar-spear (venabulum, see 404 n.), cf. x. 713 'pando venabula
rostro', *Aen.* iv. 131 'lato venabula ferro', Oppian, *Cyn.* i. 152
σιγύνην εὐρυκάρηνον.

vibrantia refers not just to the spears being brandished, but
to the play of sunlight on the metal heads. 'Vibrare' often
depicts tremulous light, cf. 375 and Silius' striking 'in tremulo
vibrant incendia ponto' (*Punica* ii. 664).

343–4. spargitque canes . . . / . . . et obliquo latrantes dissipat ictu:
Ovid repeats the idea with the addition of a vivid detail on each
side—the boar's side-long blow, and the dogs' barking. Such
reduplication is notably a Virgilian trick, e.g. *Aen.* ii. 230–1
'sacrum qui cuspide robur / laeserit, et tergo sceleratam intor-
serit hastam'; cf. 158 n. and 741–2.

344. latrantes: of course a true participle, not a 'kenning' as
at 412.

345. contorta: see 28 n.

347–9 echo a common Homeric pattern: 'and he would have . . .
had not . . .', expressed with καί νύ κεν . . . εἰ μὴ (ἀλλὰ) or the like.
In this, the most epic section of the whole poem, Ovid uses the
Homeric pattern four times, straightforwardly at 365–6 (see ad
loc.) and at 376–7, more obliquely here and at 409–10. Compare
also v. 36–7.

347. usa: quite often meaning to experience or to suffer from
a disadvantage.

348. visa est haesura makes the unfulfilled possibility seem particu-
larly vivid.

349. ĭt represents the uncontracted perfect 'iit'; hence the lengthen-
ing is quite regular. Ovid also likes to write 'abiĭt' before a vowel
(see 870 n.).

Pagasaeus: Pagasae was the port from which Argo set sail.

350 ff. The seer Mopsus (cf. 316) appeals to his patron. For his
'bargaining' approach compare Chryses' prayer to Apollo at *Il.*
i. 39–41, εἴ ποτέ τοι χαρίεντ᾽ ἐπὶ νηὸν ἔρεψα / . . . τόδε μοι κρήηνον ἐέλδωρ.

351. da mihi: a solemn formula, cf., for example, *Il.* v. 118 δὸς δέ τέ
μ᾽ ἄνδρα ἑλεῖν, and in Latin *Aen.* xi. 789 'da, pater, hoc nostris
aboleri dedecus armis.' *TGF*², fr. adesp. 188 ὦ Ζεῦ, γένοιτο κατα-
βαλεῖν τὸν σὺν ἐμέ may well come from Euripides' *Meleager.*

352–4. Since the boar executes vengeance for Artemis (272)
Apollo can only grant the letter of his prayer; the goddess
immediately frustrates its spirit. The underlying principle is
stated at iii. 326–7 'neque enim licet irrita cuiquam / facta dei
fecisse deo'. Compare *Aen.* xi. 794 ff., based on *Il.* xvi. 250 ff.,
for partial granting of a prayer.

353–4. ferrum Diana volanti / abstulerat iaculo: this kind of divine
intervention is also typical of Homer. In the *Iliad* a god may

snap a bow-string at the crucial moment (xv. 463–4), divert
a missile in flight (viii. 311, xx. 438–40, cf. *Aen.* ix. 745–6) or
weaken its force (xiii. 562–3). At the climax of the *Iliad* Athena
even returns Achilles' spear to him after an unsuccessful throw
(xxii. 276–7)!

354. **venit**: 'reached its mark'.

355. **ira feri mota est**: perhaps it was traditional in such an epic
narrative that the beast should first be hit lightly, so as to
become even more formidable. Compare the lion-hunt of Pan-
crates (see on 284–6), fr. 2. 6 ff. Heitsch (Page, *G.L.P.*, p. 518):
πρῶτος δ' Ἀδριανὸς προιεὶς χαλκήρεον ἔγχος / οὔτασεν, οὐδὲ δάμασσεν . . . /
θὴρ δὲ τυπεὶς ἔτι μᾶλλον ὀρίνετο, etc.

356. Cf. Accius, *Meleager* 432 W. (not necessarily from the same
context) '. . . frigit saetas rubore ex oculis fulgens flammeo'.

357–8. A remarkable simile from Roman siege-craft (the ballista)
which breaks the Greek heroic atmosphere. It is no doubt
inspired by Virgil (*Aen.* xi. 616, xii. 921–2) and perhaps also by
Lucretius vi. 328–9, where we find 'impete'; cf. *Met.* ix. 218,
xiv. 183. Homer's similes sometimes reflect a later period than
his narrative, introducing features, such as riding or the use of
iron, which are alien to the main body of the poems. Latin epic,
too, often has similes from Roman life of the poet's time, e.g.
Ennius, *Annals* 88 ff. W. (crowds at a race-meeting in the Cir-
cus), *Aen.* i. 148–53 (orator). When the main narrative is from
Greek mythology, as here and, e.g., Valerius Flaccus vi. 402
(legions), the contrast is sharper than ever in Homer. Yet the
simile may still be successful. A notable case is at *Met.* iii. 111–
14, where armed men springing up from the dragon's teeth are
compared to figures gradually appearing on a theatre curtain as
it is raised from the ground.

358. **milite**: collective, cf. 103 'remige', *Aen.* ii. 20 'armato
milite complent' with Austin ad loc. The collective seems par-
ticularly common for soldiers or specific kinds of soldier, e.g.
Ennius, *Annals* 493 W. 'incedit veles', Lucilius 423 W. 'stabat
rorarius velox'; it is basically colloquial (Austin, ibid.).

359. **in iuvenes certo sic impete vulnificus sus**: this line owes much
to old Latin epic.

impete: as if from a nominative 'impes'. The form appeared
in Laevius (fr. 9 Morel) and is a Lucretian speciality; of course
'impetu' will not fit hexameter verse without an intolerably
harsh elision.

vulnificus: cf. *Aen.* viii. 446. Compounds in -*ficus* are com-
mon in old Latin poetry; at ii. 504 Magnus printed the even
more archaic form 'volnificus', of which there is no trace in the
manuscripts here.

Finally, the monosyllabic ending occurs frequently in Ennius (and Lucilius), but progressively less often thereafter, unless for special effect or imitation of Ennius (cf. 603 n. and Introduction, p. xxviii). One naturally regards such endings in the early poets as due to crudity of technique. But we should remember that this particular rhythm had precedents both in Homer (οὐρανόθεν νύξ) and in Hellenistic verse (Hermesianax, fr. 1 Powell ἐφλέγετο γλήν, Callimachus, *hymn* 2. 100 δαιμόνιος θήρ, Euphorion, fr. 4. 2 ἐχθομένη κρέξ). Lucilius, without practising what he preached, apparently said that the final position should be reserved for smaller animals (Servius on *Aen.* viii. 83). Certainly the boar is no *ridiculus mus*; the effect is rather one of abruptness and violence.

360. Neither of these hunters has been mentioned in the Catalogue, nor are they known from other sources. The name of the first is quite uncertain. I follow Riese with 'Hippalmon', but the older favourite 'Eupalamon' (from Planudes) is equally plausible. Slater suggested 'Euphemon', comparing Hyginus, *fab.* 173.

360–1. For the rhyme at the end of successive hexameters see on 441–2.

dextra tuentes / cornua: here the military connections of this scene are very clear.

361. socii rapuere iacentes: again a Homeric motif. When a man is struck down in battle, his ἑταῖροι (retainers in Homer) will carry him off, either for medical treatment, or to save the corpse from being spoiled (e.g. *Il.* viii. 332–4). Compare *Ilias Latina* 676 'ast illum fidi rapiunt de caede sodales'. The two hunters here are only wounded, as the next line shows.

362. Enaesimus: see 314 n.

363–4. trepidantem et terga parantem / vertere: a Virgilian pattern, with the rhyming participles; cf. *Aen.* ii. 790–1 'lacrimantem et multa volentem / dicere' with Austin's note, *Aen.* iv. 390, and x. 554–5.

365 ff. This is the most obvious example of the Homeric formula mentioned on 347–9; compare *Il.* v. 311–12 καί νύ κεν ἔνθ' ἀπόλοιτο ἄναξ ἀνδρῶν Αἰνείας / εἰ μὴ ἄρ' ὀξὺ νόησε Διὸς θυγάτηρ Ἀφροδίτη, etc. Nestor's method of saving himself is a little undignified for a great hero—but not more so than the pole-vault with which Athena takes off for celestial regions (ii. 786)!

365. citra: from the point of view of the hunters rather than the poet.

366. conamine: a rare word, but found earlier in Lucretius. Ovid has a great liking for nouns in -men; see further on 729.

368–9. Attractive is the way in which we are made to follow Nestor's eye down the tree-trunk. Presumably 'querno stipite' refers to the tree which is harbouring him.

369. ferox, as often, implies exulting at a recent success. The boar

sharpening his tusks appears in Homeric similes (*Il.* xi. 416,
xiii. 474–5).

370. imminet exitio: 'is intent on destruction', cf. i. 146 'imminet
exitio vir coniugis'.

　　recentibus armis: his newly sharpened tusks.

371. Eurytidae: this would be Hippasus (313), but once more the
name is quite uncertain—most copyists had their mind on the
nymph Orithyia.

　　magni is a little surprising in any case; probably no more than
a conventional epithet.

　　femur hausit: cf. 439 and v. 126; for the basic sense of this
verb see on 326. Here the notion is of a curved slashing blow
(see D. A. West, loc. cit., pp. 275 ff.), particularly appropriate to
the boar's tusk. Compare Lucretius v. 1324 (tauri) 'et latera ac
ventris hauribant subter equorum', and earlier Claudius Quad-
rigarius, fr. 10b Peter 'pectus hausit'. The extended meaning is
paralleled to a certain degree in Greek by ἀφύσσω (cf. Stanford on
Od. xix. 450).

372. gemini . . . fratres: Castor and Pollux (301). For the inter-
woven word-order in apposition see on 226. Perhaps a sub-
conscious recollection of *Aen.* vi. 842–3 'geminos, duo fulmina
belli, / Scipiadas' suggested to Ovid the pattern of those *Aeneid*
lines.

373–4. ambo . . . ambo / . . . ambo: this kind of repetition, lyrical
or even bucolic, is common enough, e.g. Theocritus 8. 3–4
ἄμφω τώγ' ἤστην πυρροτρίχω, ἄμφω ἀνάβω, / ἄμφω συρίσδεν δεδαημένω,
ἄμφω ἀείδεν, cf. Virgil, *Ecl.* 7. 4. Yet there is a slight irregularity
in Ovid's structure. With the anaphora of 'ambo', presumably
one should not understand 'erant' after 'conspicui'; but then one
feels the lack of another nominative to follow in the next limb.
Notice the postponement of the second 'ambo' (cf. on 331–2).

373. nive candidioribus: cf. *Il.* x. 437, the horses of Rhesus λευκό-
τεροι χιόνος; the expression was also proverbial in Latin (see
Otto, *Sprichwörter*, s.v. *nix*). Pindar calls the Dioscuri λευκό-
πωλοι (*Pythian* 1. 126).

374. vectabantur : 'were carried about'. The frequentative force
remains, cf. *Aen.* vi. 391.

374–5. vibrata . . . / . . . tremulo . . . motu: again, these words sug-
gest the play of light on a metal spear-head; cf. 342 n.

376–7. See on 347–9. The word-order in apposition is basically that
discussed on 226, although here the phrase in apposition itself is
more elaborate, and is made to contain the verb 'isset'.

376. saetiger: 'the bristler', a so-called 'kenning' description which
in Latin suggests the style of archaic high-flown poetry, cf.
Ilias Latina 595 'non sic saetigeri exacuunt fervoribus iras'. In
the only other place where 'saetiger' is found as a substantive

(Martial xiii. 93. 1) the reference is again to the Calydonian Boar, and the tone obviously heroic.

The original purpose of such descriptions is unclear—perhaps to avoid mentioning a dangerous or ill-omened animal by name. But they belong properly to the simple style of a fable or folktale; thus we find in the earthier parts of Hesiod's *Works and Days* φερέοικος (571) 'the house-carrier', i.e. snail, and other examples. See Ingrid Waern, '*ΓΗΣ ΟΣΤΕΑ, the Kenning in pre-Christian poetry*' (Uppsala, 1951), for the Greek material, although her instances cover a wide range, and some are hardly significant.

In Early Latin, kennings take a step upwards to Epic and Tragedy. The reason for the shift might be the influence of Hellenistic poetry, e.g. the riddling style of Lycophron. But another possibility is that such expressions were once used in connection with Roman sacrificial rites. Nothing more colourful than 'bidens' can confidently be established as a ritual term. But poets often use kenning terms when speaking of sacrifice, e.g. *Aen.* vii. 93, Ovid, *Met.* vii. 312, Juvenal 8. 155-6 'lanatas . . . / more Numae caedit'; similar, though not true kennings, are *Fasti* i. 334, Juvenal 13. 232-3 'pecudem spondere sacello / balantem'. Such passages may be alluding just to a poetic style, but perhaps also to the language of ritual. In Greek one may compare κραταίπους, said by a Pindar scholiast (on *Ol.* 13. 81) to be a 'Delphic', and thus perhaps sacrificial, word for a bull.

We find sheep as 'balantes' (Ennius, *Annals* 180 W., Lucretius vi. 1132, etc.) or 'lanigeri' (Accius, *Brutus* 20, if one takes 'lanigerum' as gen. plur., cf. Bailey on Lucr. i. 162), oxen as 'cornuti' (Accius 510), horses as 'sonipedes' (Accius 657, cf. Lucilius 512 W.) or 'quadrupedantes' (*Aen.* xi. 614, cf. Accius 657); birds appear as 'altivolantes' (Ennius, *Annals* 85), 'volantes' (Lucretius vi. 742, *Aen.* vi. 239), or 'pennipotentes' (Lucr. ii. 878, v. 789), fish as 'squamigeri' (Lucr. i. 162, etc.). Later epic poets, such as Silius, continue the tradition; but it is interesting that the fables of Phaedrus preserve this feature in a simple style, offering 'laniger' (i. 1.6), 'sonipes' (iv. 4. 3), 'auritulus' (i. 11. 6), 'barbatus' (iv. 9. 10), and 'latrans' (v. 10. 7, see further on 412).

378-80. Two great heroes in an undignified incident. Statius speaks of the boar as felling Telamon more seriously, 'iam Telamona solo, iam stratum Ixiona linquens' (*Theb.* ii. 473).

378. studioque incautus eundi: probably link 'incautus eundi'—'careless of where he went', cf. Virgil's 'certus eundi' (*Aen.* iv. 554), also *Met.* xi. 440.

379. ab . . . radice: the tree-root is almost personified as an active malevolent force—cf. 514, 515.

380. Tegeaea: Atalanta, as at 317.

381. imposuit nervo represents the Homeric θῆκε δ' ἐπὶ νευρῇ at the
beginning of a line, cf. 19 n.

382. destrinxit: merely a superficial graze.

383. rubefecit: the verb is an Ovidian speciality, used otherwise
apparently only by Silius.

385. erat: perhaps to be taken with 'illa' (384) rather than
'Meleagros'.

   putatur: cf. 273, 278. Such appeal to tradition is notably Hel-
lenistic (see Fordyce on Catullus 64. 1 f.).

388–90. By now the boar has been driven from the thicker parts
of the wood (376–7) into country more open but still lightly
wooded (410).

390. et, quos petit, impedit ictus: probably an intentional play on
words. This trick is not very edifying, but typically Roman,
e.g. Ennius, *Annals* 247 W. 'alter *nare* cupit, alter pug*nare*
paratust'. Other examples are given by Norden on *Aen.* vi.
204.

391–402. *The death of Ancaeus*. Apollodorus (i. 8. 2) also makes
Ancaeus a misogynist, ashamed to hunt with a woman until
compelled by Meleager. This characterization probably derived
from Euripides' *Meleager*; the abuse of women in Euripidean
tragedies was notorious.

391. contra sua fata: 'against his destiny', the phrase to be taken
rather with 'dixit' (393) than with 'furens'. The idea is that
a man may be allotted a certain amount of suffering by fate, but
that he can through his own sin cause himself trouble beyond
what was inevitable. Thus *Od.* i. 33–4 of mankind, οἱ δὲ καὶ
αὐτοὶ / σφῆσιν ἀτασθαλίῃσιν ὑπὲρ μόρον ἄλγε' ἔχουσιν.

   bipennifer Arcas: all the poets lay stress on Ancaeus' axe
(Euripides, fr. 530. 5–6, Ap. Rh. i. 168–9, and the elegiac frag-
ment, Appendix I, lines 22–3). Apollonius explains quaintly
that, to prevent his grandson sailing in the Argo, Aleus had
hidden Ancaeus' normal weapons. If so, he could not have
located them yet!

392. tela: 'blows'. Ancaeus is surely not comparing Atalanta's bow,
which only inflicts a slight wound, with the axe or javelin.

394–5. To his arrogance and rashness Ancaeus adds a worse sin—
blasphemy. That the deity involved is female lends especial
irony in the present context. For a similar boast, which also
led to disaster, compare *Od.* iv. 504 (the lesser Ajax) φῆ ῥ'
ἀέκητι θεῶν φυγέειν μέγα λαῖτμα θαλάσσης; this may be Ovid's model.
The *Ilias Latina* (821–2) uses our lines for a speech of Hector
which is not in Homer. Much material for the *Ilias Latina* has
been quarried from this episode (cf. particularly 412 n.).

398. primos suspensus in artus amplifies the first half of the line
(cf. 158 n.). 'Primos' = the edge of, cf. *Ciris* 212 'tum suspensa

levans digitis vestigia primis'. As at 654 'artus' refers to legs
and, in particular, feet. There is no cause to suspect the text.

399. occupat audentem: 'the beast forestalled him, for all his
boldness'. Compare places like *Od.* xix. 449, where Odysseus
attacks a boar οὐτάμεναι μεμαώς· ὁ δέ μιν φθάμενος ἔλασεν σῦς.

quaque est via proxima leto: imitating Homeric formulas such
as ἵνα τε ψυχῆς ὤκιστος ὄλεθρος (*Il.* xxii. 325, of a different spot).

402. viscera lapsa fluunt: Ovid's one gruesome piece of realism in
this episode; elsewhere, particularly in the battles of Perseus
and Phineus (v. 1–235), and of the Lapiths and Centaurs (xii.
210–535), there are many horrific details. Here he does not go
beyond Homer, cf. *Il.* iv. 525–6 ἐκ δ' ἄρα πᾶσαι / χύντο χαμαὶ χολάδες.

madefacta est terra cruore: following Homer to the end, as, for
instance, *Il.* xiii. 655 ἐκ δ' αἷμα μέλαν ῥέε, δεῦε δὲ γαῖαν.

403 ff. Pirithous is always hasty and impetuous, as at 612 ff.

404. venabula: the plural is merely poetic. This was a specialized
boar-spear, not thrown with the 'amentum' (on 28–9), but for
use at close quarters; see also 342 n. Meleager, more prudent
than Pirithous, employs his *venabulum* only after wounding the
boar (418–19).

405. Such word-order at the start of direct speech is typical of
Ovid. Here the interweaving throws special emphasis on 'procul'.

405–6. The proverbial friendship of Theseus and Pirithous is
expressed by two commonplaces. For the first cf. Cicero, *Tusc.
Disp.* iii. 72, and for the second, for example, Horace, *Odes* 2.
17. 5 'te meae . . . partem animae' (Horace to Maecenas).

406–7. licet eminus esse / fortibus: this might mean 'men may be
brave when fighting at long range' (cf. on 554–5). But it is both
simpler and more pointed to translate 'the brave may keep their
distance'—those whose courage is unquestioned do not need
to justify themselves by rushing to close quarters. This latter
interpretation is also favoured by the line-break, which empha-
sizes 'fortibus'. But there is no sneer at the dead Ancaeus;
Theseus recognizes the 'virtus' of Ancaeus, complaining only
that it was 'temeraria'.

409. quo bene librato votique potente futuro: another example of
the Homeric pattern 'and it would have . . . had not', cf. on
347–9. Also Homeric is the way in which the spear itself is
credited with a desire to reach its target, as at *Il.* xxi. 168 λιλαι-
ομένη χροὸς ἆσαι.

I have returned to the text of older editors. Magnus printed
'*cui* bene librato votoque potente futuro'. Certainly 'cui' has
better authority than 'quo', and fits well with 'obstitit' (410), but
the difficulties outweigh this advantage. For surely impossibly
awkward is the ablative absolute so coupled with '-que' to
a phrase in the dative as to split that phrase and the verb on

which it depends (obstitit). Also the weight of manuscript authority definitely favours 'votique' rather than 'votoque', and 'votum potens' is a doubtful expression (at 745 I accept Heinsius's emendation), while 'voti potens' is quite regular (e.g. 80).

410. aesculea . . . ab arbore: to specify the tree is quite appropriate, cf. 346, 369. Magnus preferred 'abscisa' (J M S), 'lopped-off', comparing for the general sense Horace, *Odes* iv. 4. 57 ff., where the poet says that a tree when pruned can show still greater vigour. But, even if we grant that 'abscisus' could refer to the tree rather than to the branches cut off, the detail is both un-necessary and irrelevant. It might be pedantic to insist literally on 'quam nulla ceciderat aetas' (329), but 'abscisa' would weaken Ovid's picture of the wood as remote and untamed. A possible reading, with slight manuscript support, would be 'herculea . . . ab arbore', although the poplar, as a tall, slender tree, is rather less appropriate to this incident.

412. latrantis: 'a barker', another kenning description of the same type as 'saetiger' (376 n.); it was perhaps coined by Ovid on the analogy of 'balans' = sheep (Ennius, *Annals* 180 W., etc.), cf. μηκάς and βρωμήτωρ (donkey). In later poetry 'latrans' leads a characteristic double life in high epic and fable—*Ilias Latina* 4 'latrantumque dedit rostris volucrumque trahendos', and Phaedrus v. 10. 7. There 'cui senex contra lātrans' is metrically unsound, but one should probably adopt a trans-position of words rather than emend away 'latrans' ('Lacon' Bentley). Many kennings in early Latin poetry are of participial form, so 'latrans' has a certain extra dignity as against 'latra-tor' = dog (Martial).

There is some confusion in the manuscripts here, but no real doubt as to the correct reading. For one thing, *Ilias Latina* 4 (above) practically guarantees 'latrantis', since the *Ilias Latina* also has 'saetiger' (from 376) but no other kenning. Ehwald printed Heinsius's 'Celadontis', as the name of a hunter. But 'immeriti' suits very well the dog embroiled in a contest not due to itself (cf. Horace, *Sat.* ii. 3. 211, Prop. iv. 5. 16). And the creature's fate is more appropriate to a dog than to a man; Ovid may be thinking of *Il.* xi. 377–8, where Paris shoots Diomede through the *foot*, διὰ δ' ἀμπερὲς ἰὸς / ἐν γαίῃ κατέπηκτο. A wider Homeric model lies in situations where a fighter misses his intended target, but kills someone else instead (e.g. *Il.* viii. 302–3)—in Homer always another enemy, but cf. *Met.* v. 90–1 (killing a neutral).

414. variat more probably refers to the varying fortunes of Meleager's two throws than to the fact that he was more successful than Jason. The decisive blow is recounted very quietly, without a climax.

416. dum corpora versat in orbem: trying to get at the spear.

417. stridentem: the word can apply to the hissing of any frothy liquid; cf. 287 and, for example, *Amores* iii. 5. 13 (of newly given milk). Here alliteration aids the effect.

420–1. Accius, *Meleager* 433–4 depicts the hunters rejoicing at the boar's death and congratulating Meleager: 'gaudent currunt celebrant, herbam conferunt donant tenent, / pro se quisque cum corona clarum conestat caput.'

421. It is certainly surprising that, after 'coniungere', 'dextram' should not refer to the subject's own hand. Possibly 'victric*em-que*' has been influenced by 'imman*emque*' immediately below. One might emend to 'victricique', interchanging 'dextram' and 'dextrae' with two late MSS., to preserve the enclosing word-order: 'victricique petunt dextram coniungere dextrae.' But this oddness may well be intentionally provocative. For the phrase cf. Livy xxx. 12 'victricem attingere dextram'.

422. multa tellure iacentem: cf. Homer's κεῖτο μέγας μεγαλωστί (*Il.* xvi. 776, etc.). The boar is measured by the amount of ground that it can occupy, as *Od.* xi. 577 (Tityus) ἐπ' ἐννέα κεῖτο πέλεθρα.

425. The peak of Meleager's triumph. He seems to have overcome the instrument of Artemis' wrath. In Homer (*Il.* ix. 547–9) the goddess then arouses strife over the relics of the boar; here it is her human counterpart Atalanta who is the unwitting cause of trouble.

427. et in partem veniat mea gloria tecum: he is more chivalrous than in Accius (438–9) 'remanet gloria / apud me; exuvias dignavi Atalantae dare.' Perhaps even here Ovid adapts Homer, while adding the Roman notion of 'mei iuris' (426); at *Il.* xvii. 231–2 Hector promises to anyone who can secure the body of Patroclus half the spoils (ἐνάρων) τὸ δέ οἱ κλέος ἔσσεται ὅσσον ἐμοί περ.

428 ff. Homer, who does not mention Atalanta, makes the quarrel arise between the Aetolians of Calydon and the Curetes, and so Nicander (Ant. Lib. 2, from the *Heteroeumena*). For Ovid's tradition cf. Callimachus, *hymn* 3. 219–20 τὰ γὰρ σημήια νίκης / Ἀρκαδίην εἰσῆλθεν, ἔχει δ' ἔτι θηρὸς ὀδόντας.

In the second century A.D., visitors to the temple of Athena Alea in Tegea were still shown the animal's hide, by now rotten with age (Pausanias viii. 47. 2). Its tusks had been carried off by Augustus, to Pausanias' intense embarrassment (viii. 46. 1)!

430. So Atalanta is not unmoved by Meleager's admiration. Euripides described her as Κύπριδος ... μίσημα (fr. 530. 4), but fr. 525 depicts her as considering marriage, however unwillingly: εἰ δ' εἰς γάμους ἔλθοιμ', ὃ μὴ τύχοι ποτέ ...

433. pone age: 'come, put them down.' 'Age' with another imperative is found most frequently in the phrase 'dic age' (e.g. xii. 177).

nostros: probably 'of us men'; the Thestiadae have not done anything of note in the fighting. But in one version Meleager's uncles claim the spoils through kinship, if he should renounce them (Apollodorus i. 8. 2).

435. ne sit longe: 'lest he be unable to help you', literally 'be far away', cf. iv. 649–50 and, for example, Silius xvii. 79–80 'longe coniugia ac longe Tyrios hymenaeos / inter Dardanias acies fore'. Here the threat may be modelled on Homeric lines like μή νύ τοι οὐ χραίσμωσιν ὅσοι θεοί εἰσ' ἐν Ὀλύμπῳ (*Il.* i. 566). This reading is more sinister and forceful than 'longeque tuo sit captus amore' favoured by Heinsius—'and let your lover keep away'.

437. Mavortius: for the form see 7 n. Euripides also mentioned Meleager's divine parentage ([Plutarch], *Parall.* 26); contrast 414 'Oenidae'. When a hero is credited with both divine and human birth, the poet may pass freely from one patronymic to the other as it suits him; so with Theseus, 'Aegides' (174, 560), but 'Neptunius heros' (ix. 1). Here, when Meleager oversteps the mark in blind fury, 'Mavortius' is obviously the more appropriate.

439 ff. Again we have a typical Homeric situation: a great hero has killed a lesser one, whereupon the latter's brother attempts to gain his revenge, only to share the same fate. Compare *Il.* xi. 426 ff., *Aen.* ix. 735 ff., *Ilias Latina* 414 'germanique cupit fatorum existere vindex.'

439–40. hausit . . . / pectora: see 371 n.

441–2. volentem / . . . timentem: rhyme at the end of successive hexameters (cf. 360–1) is for Ovid a small embellishment, often associated with further rhyme (e.g. 633–4, a Hellenistic pattern, and 844–5). It also appears occasionally in Lucretius, most notably in the long fragment of Cicero's *De Consulatu Suo* (fr. 11 Morel), and in Virgil quite freely (cf. Austin, *CQ* xxiii [1929] 50 ff., and on *Aen.* ii. 457). Here Ovid probably wants to reinforce his verbal prestidigitation; note how he picks up the following words: 'dubium' (441)—'dubitare' (443), 'fratrem—fraterna' (442), 'calidum' (443)—'recalfecit' (444). There is also considerable alliteration in these lines, which adds to the highly-chiselled effect of the verse.

445–525. Meleager's mother Althaea is overwhelmed with grief at the news of her brothers' death, but her grief turns to fury when she hears who is their murderer (450). She brings out the magic brand on which Meleager's life depends (460), and in an agonized soliloquy weighs her maternal duty against the obligation to her brothers (478–511). After swaying from one opinion to the other, she finally thrusts the stick into the fire (511–14). Meleager is not present, but he feels the agony as the brand burns; then gradually the flames die down, and his life leaves him (515–25).

LINES 433-451

89

Ovid's narrative of the Boar-hunt itself has been written in the
high epic style, but the following passage is clearly inspired by
Tragedy. Preference for a brother over a son may be a primitive
feature in the Meleager-story (cf. Kakridis, *Homeric Researches*,
p. 37, and Appendix III), but a tormented monologue such as we
have here argues the more sophisticated influence of Euripides.
Miss A. M. Dale suggested that *P.Oxy.* 2436 might belong to
Euripides' *Meleager*; we seem to hear of a 'son of Ares' (cf. 437 n.),
and a 'brand'. But line 6 εἴ τις κατὰ στέγας πυρσὸς ἔτι λείπεται is not
appropriate, unless conceivably Althaea had burnt the single
brand, and were in a state of derangement. Many scholars doubt
whether this piece comes from Tragedy at all. But one fragment of
Accius' *Meleager*, probably modelled on Euripides, clearly formed
part of a monologue by Althaea—'nunc si me matrem mansues
misericordia / capsit' (446–7 W., perhaps also 443 and 448).

In spite of some fine psychological touches, this seems to me
the least satisfactory part of the book; to judge from the *Medea*,
Euripides surely must have done better. By the Augustan period
such a struggle between opposing duties, or (as more often)
between love and modesty, had become so hackneyed a theme,
that to bring it to life called for especial genius. Ovid, however,
lacks power and thence credibility; his smooth antitheses destroy
all illusion of a woman in agony of soul torn between conflicting
loyalties. It is true that the same objections can be brought
against much of the Scylla episode, but, to my mind at least,
Scylla has a redeeming spark which Althaea lacks. All the same,
it is worth recording a dissentient verdict in the 1826 Variorum
edition: 'sequitur locus praestantissimus, qui fluctuantem Al-
thaeae animum, et pugnam materni affectus cum sororio amore
egregie describit.' Dryden even preferred Ovid's Althaea and
other heroines to the Virgilian Dido (see Wilkinson, *Ovid Recalled*,
p. 227). Perhaps we are inclined to undervalue such a passage, just
as earlier generations valued it too highly.

448. **auratis mutavit vestibus atras**: better attested, this is the
superior reading. The accusative describes what is taken in
exchange, as, for example, at Horace, *Odes* i. 17. 1–2 'Velox
amoenum saepe Lucretilem / mutat Lycaeo Faunus.'

450. **poenae . . . amorem**: cf. iii. 705 'pugnae . . . amorem' (also
Horace, *Odes* iv. 4. 12). The poetic use of 'amor' in this sense of
'desire for' is perhaps influenced by Homer's ποσίος καὶ ἐδητύος . . .
ἔρον (*Il.* i. 469, etc.), cf. 'amor . . . edendi' at Lucretius iv. 869
etc. Yet the juxtaposition of these two words is paradoxical, and
implies Ovid's own criticism of Althaea.

451–60. **stipes erat . . . / . . . hunc**: for the ecphrasis pattern, see on
788. The brand appears for certain first in the *Pleuroniae* of

Phrynichus (see introduction to the episode) and then in
Aeschylus (*Choephoroe* 602 ff.), but it is probably a much older
element of the story—perhaps from the oldest version of all,
says Kakridis (*Homeric Researches*, p. 14). A magic life-token is
a common feature of folk-tale; Kakridis (Appendix I) gives
thirteen modern variants of this story, mostly from Greece and
Turkey. Of these, the Cypriot version is the closest to Ovid's
Meleager.

452. in flammam . . . posuere: the accusative is strongly supported
by *Rem. Am.* 719 'omnia pone feros (pones invitus) in ignes',
and should not be doubted here. When forward motion is
prominent, Ovid likes to use an accusative instead of the regular
ablative (cf. 145 n., 201).

triplices . . . sorores: the three Fates, Clotho, Lachesis, and
Atropos, who make their entrance at Hesiod, *Theogony* 905.

453. Cf. Tibullus i. 7. 1–2 'Parcae fatalia nentes / stamina'. The
spinning of a man's destiny at birth appears already in Homer:
ἄσσα οἱ αἶσα / γεινομένῳ ἐπένησε λίνῳ, ὅτε μιν τέκε μήτηρ (*Il.* xx. 127–8).
At *Od.* vii. 197 the Fates are called Κλῶθες, 'spinsters'.

454–5. Compare Ant. Lib. 2, paraphrasing Nicander, ἐπέκλωσαν
(probably the poet's word) ἐπὶ τοσοῦτον αὐτὸν ἔσεσθαι χρόνον, ἐφ᾽ ὅσον
ἂν ὁ δαλὸς διαμένοι; also Accius, *Meleager* 444–5 'eumpsum vitae
finem ac fati internecionem fore / Meleagro ubi torrus esset
interfectus flammeus'.

455. carmine: implying an utterance which possesses especial
dignity, whether through its form, language, content or oc-
casion. Cf. Livy i. 26. 6 'lex horrendi carminis erat' and Ogilvie's
note.

457. liquentibus undis: a high-flown expression, with a slightly
archaic ring; cf. 650 'ferventibus undis', where there is also
a special graphic significance, and *Georgics* iv. 442 'fluviumque
liquentem'.

458. In Bacchylides (5. 141) and Apollodorus (i. 8. 1) the stick is
hidden in a chest.

459. servatus . . . servaverat: cf. *Aen.* ii. 160–1 'servataque serves /
Troia fidem', Silius xiv. 172 'servas nondum servatus ab hoste',
Seneca, *Contr.* iv. 2. 2.

tuos, iuvenis: apart from metrical convenience, the apostrophe
adds a certain liveliness; see further on 731 ff.

460. fragmina: small sticks. The context makes the meaning clear.

462–77. These lines are clearly meant to describe Althaea's ges-
tures and facial expression during the monologue which follows,
so that we cover the same ground twice, first seeing and then
hearing, with two mentions of the start of the fire (461 and
477–8). This device is a remarkable one, for which I do not know
a parallel. At several points during the speech, we must imagine

Althaea as trying to throw the brand on the flames, and then shrinking back in horror; 490–1, 498–9, and 505–6 are obvious places, though one cannot quite distinguish four attempts (462).

462–3. tum, conata quater . . . / coepta quater tenuit: a variation on the most usual pattern, which involves three failures, e.g. Ap. Rh. iii. 654 τρὶς μὲν ἐπειρήθη, τρὶς δ᾽ ἔσχετο.

463. pugnat: there is little to choose between this and 'pugnant', but the singular is more vivid and arresting, as well as better supported. Contrast 790.

464. diversa: grammatically with 'nomina', but sense requires it to be taken with 'trahunt', as almost equivalent to 'diverse'— 'pull her in opposite directions'. Thus Terence, *And*. 260 'tot me impediunt curae quae meum animum divorsae trahunt'.

465 ff. Ovid has one advantage over the tragedians in that he can describe changes of expression, which would not be allowed by the tragic mask.

467. nescio quid . . . crudele: in imitation of the Greek τι with neuter adjective, as xi. 52 'flebile nescio quid'. For the shortened ŏ, cf. 60 'at, puto', and Platnauer, *Latin Elegiac Verse*, pp. 51–2.

similis . . . minanti: modelled on Greek poetic expressions such as *Od*. xi. 608 βαλέοντι ἐοικώς.

470–4. A finer simile than others resembling it. More often we hear of conflicting winds, as *Amores* ii. 10. 9–10 'erro velut ventis discordibus acta phaselos / dividuumque tenent alter et alter amor'; cf. Aristaenetus 2. 11, where a man torn between love for his wife and mistress is compared κυβερνήτῃ ὑπὸ δυοῖν πνευμάτων ἀπειλημμένῳ, τοῦ μὲν ἔνθεν, τοῦ δὲ ἔνθεν ἑστηκότος, καὶ περὶ τῆς νεὼς μαχομένων. Of course wind and tide regularly symbolize strong emotion.

475. incipit esse tamen melior germana parente: this summarizes the general tenor of her monologue which follows—see analysis below.

476. consanguineas . . . sanguine: a forced and almost pointless word-play.

477. impietate pia est: the oxymoron is characteristic of our poet even if not very pleasing, cf. vii. 340 'ne sit scelerata facit scelus', ix. 408 'facto pius et sceleratus eodem'.

nam: another indication that Ovid is going to recover the same ground, this time giving Althaea's words.

478–511. He handles her vacillations with a certain subtlety, though, as usual, with too much attention to purely verbal cleverness. For each change of heart one can, I think, find some explanation in the words immediately before; the following analysis is disputable in places, but worth attempting. Althaea starts with

the firm purpose of burning the brand; a thought which weighs
heavily with her is that Oeneus must not rejoice while her own
father Thestius is desolate (486–7). Then the cost of the sacrifice
('magnoque paratas') reminds Althaea of her bond as mother, and
she draws back (491–3). But Meleager's terrible deed (492–3) and
the contrast between his condition and that of her brothers re-
call her to the first intention (494–8). However, the prospect of
universal misery (498) brings the return of maternal instincts (499–
500). From the mention of her childbirth, she wishes that she had
allowed Meleager to die as a baby (501–2); he has twice owed his
life to her, and now deserves to forfeit it (502–5); line 505 contains
the first intimation of her own death. In 506–8 motherly feelings
are still present, but by now even these are mixed with thoughts of
her brothers. Finally the conflict is decided (509–11); she will kill
Meleager, but then follow him to the grave.

A woman's preference for her brother over her son is one of the
most primitive elements in the Meleager-legend. As Kakridis
explains (op. cit., p. 37), 'The brother stands higher than the child
since in his veins exactly the same blood flows as in hers, whereas
in the child's veins half the blood belongs to a stranger, the father.
We may accept without difficulty that such a particular attach-
ment of a woman to her tribe prevailed among the pre-Hellenic
people of Greece, and has left its traces in the Meleager-legend.'
There is also the idea that a son may be replaceable, while a
brother is not, unless both parents are alive. This reasoning ap-
pears in the tale of Intaphrenes' wife, who, when given the chance
of saving one of her family from death, argues ἀνὴρ μὲν ἄν μοι ἄλλος
γένοιτο, εἰ δαίμων ἐθέλοι, καὶ τέκνα ἄλλα, εἰ ταῦτα ἀποβάλοιμι· πατρὸς δὲ καὶ
μητρὸς οὐκέτι μευ ζωόντων ἀδελφεὸς ἂν ἄλλος οὐδενὶ τρόπῳ γένοιτο (Hero-
dotus iii. 119). There is a similar argument, though less appro-
priate, at Sophocles, *Antigone* 905–12 (the status of these famous
lines is of course disputed), and the motif is also known from
ancient Indian stories and modern Greek folk-tales (see Kakridis,
App. III). But to us the bond between mother and son seems
much the more important, as it would to Ovid as well; this is one
reason why the soliloquy does not quite come to life.

478. **rogus iste cremet mea viscera**: 'may that be a pyre to con-
     sume my own flesh'; the present scene is anticipated at *Rem.
     Am.* 719–22. According to Servius on *Aen.* xi. 185, 'rogus' is
     strictly a pyre in the process of burning: 'pyra est lignorum
     congeries, rogus cum iam ardere coeperit dicitur.'
480. **sepulcrales . . . aras**: the fire is an altar of death, on which
     Meleager must be sacrificed (cf. 482 'sacra', 511 n.). Several
     commentators have cited this line as a parallel to difficult
     phrases like *Aen.* vi. 177 'aramque sepulcri' (the pyre on which

Misenus' body will be burned), but I doubt the relevance of these passages to ours. After all, the circumstances here are unusual; the sacrifice is of Meleager, not to him. Perhaps more significantly, the Romans used to erect altars to the Di Manes, on which they made offerings; thus Althaea sends down 'inferiae' (490) to her dead brothers.

481–2. Althaea's appeal to the Furies is no doubt based on *Il.* ix. 567 ff., where she curses Meleager, τῆς δ᾽ ἠεροφοῖτις Ἐρινὺς / ἔκλυεν ἐξ Ἐρέβεσφιν ἀμείλιχον ἦτορ ἔχουσα (571–2). But in Homer there is no mention of a magic stick, so that the Fury is a more active avenger. Here the 'deae triplices' called to witness Meleager's death counterbalance the 'triplices . . . sorores' who are present after his birth (452).

485. domus impia: containing three impious members, Oeneus, Meleager, and prospectively Althaea herself.

486. Throughout she shows no consideration for her husband Oeneus, perhaps because she holds him ultimately responsible for all the disasters. But this lack of consideration forms part of the poet's criticism of Althaea.

490. pignora: a word used for children strictly as tokens of loyalty between husband and wife, the basic meaning of 'pignus' being a deposit, cf. 48.

494. Ergo, as often, introduces an indignant question.
impune feret: this is the regular phrase—see 279 n.

494–5. victor: one would expect this to refer to Meleager's defeat of the boar (cf. 445, 486). But the emphasis given by 'et ipso' and the coupling with 'regnum Calydonis habebit' suggest that Althaea has another thought at the back of her mind: Oeneus is old (520), and by the murder Meleager has conveniently removed possible rivals to the throne of Calydon. So perhaps 'victor' and 'successu' refer at least in part to the killing of his uncles.

496. There is often imprecision in language referring to death, burial, and the survival of a shade. Thus 'iacebitis' is not appropriate to 'umbrae', nor even wholly so to 'cinis', suggesting an inhumed body rather than cremated ash.

498. trahat: one need not understand the verb in a different sense with 'patriaeque ruinam'. This last word means here 'a ruin' rather than 'the ruin', and the phrase is practically equivalent to 'patriamque ruentem'. Compare in a literal sense *Aen.* ii. 465–6 'ea lapsa repente ruinam / cum sonitu trahit'.

499. iura: here obligations rather than privileges.

500. bis mensum quinque: Priscian (vii. 77) quotes this line for the genitive in -*um*, which is common enough in prose too (Neue–Wagener, *Formenlehre der lateinischen Sprache* i. 395–7). Of course -*ium* genitives often would necessitate an ugly elision in dactylic verse, and so the older -*um* is retained, notably in

present participle forms, e.g. 745 'potentum' (*ex coni.*), 798 'serpentum'.

502–3. There is a triple antithesis, 'vixisti—moriere', 'munere—merito', 'nostro—tuo', but this represents a surfeit of verbal trickery.

505. redde animam: the verb is common with phrases for 'to give up one's life'. But here the meaning 'give back' (to me) is strongly felt.

    vel me fraternis adde sepulcris: a masterly touch. This is of course an impossible thought; Meleager is absent and unaware of his danger (515). But, however confused and illogical, we have here the first mention of Althaea's own death, which suggests to her the final solution of suicide (510–11, 531–2).

508. pietas could be invoked on either side (cf. 477); Ovid weights the scales against Althaea in referring it only to her maternal duty.

509. Lines with no third-foot caesura may be even rarer in the *Metamorphoses* than in the early elegiacs (e.g. *Amores* iii. 9. 53). A repeated word helps the rhythm here.

510. quae dedero vobis solacia: i.e. Meleager himself, cf. 773 n.

511. aversa: in horror (cf. vii. 342), but two further ideas may be in the poet's mind. When sacrificing to spirits of the underworld (481–2), one should turn away; cf. *Fasti* v. 437 and vi. 164 with Frazer's note, Virgil, *Ecl.* 8. 102 'transque caput iace, nec respexeris.' Also it was customary to avert the eyes before a funeral pyre, cf. *Aen.* vi. 223–4 'subiectam more parentum / aversi tenuere facem.'

513. aut dedit aut visus . . . est . . . dedisse: cf. Ap. Rh. iv. 1480 ἢ ἴδεν ἢ ἐδόκησεν . . . ἰδέσθαι, *Aen.* vi. 454 'aut videt aut vidisse putat'. Here, however, the figure virtually apologizes for a frigid conceit.

514. invitis: one might have expected 'invitus' (ς). But Ovid keeps the balance of nouns and epithets (cf. 278 n.), and almost personifies the fire as well (cf. 379).

515–25. *The death of Meleager*

515. absens: according to the later Greek epic tradition and Bacchylides (5. 144 ff.) Meleager dies on the battlefield fighting the Curetes. That version is not appropriate here, but Ovid avoids unnecessary detail.

517 ff. We have been shown the flaws in Meleager's character—his incontinent love for Atalanta (325), and the blind fury which led to the killings (437). Now for the final scene Meleager must be rehabilitated, with stress on his courage (517) and devotion to his family, including his wife (521).

517. at is more pointed than 'ac', though not an essential change.

518. sine sanguine leto: the phrase functions as a Greek adjective

with a- privative, i.e. ἄναιμος (see also 789 n.). There is a remark-
ably audacious example of this device at i. 20 'mollia cum duris,
sine pondere habentia pondus', where 'sine pondere' represents
a Greek adjective in the dative plural with definite article.

519. For the death of Ancaeus see 391 ff.

520. grandaevum: a Virgilian word, as is 'longaevus'. Earlier we
find 'grandaevitas' in both Pacuvius and Accius.

Nicander credits Meleager with five brothers and four sisters
(Ant. Lib. 2); the latter show their devotion after his death
(535 ff.).

521. sociamque tori: Cleopatra or Alcyone (Il. ix. 556 ff.). Ata-
lanta is forgotten.

ore supremo: here 'os' has come to mean an individual utter-
ance, cf. Tristia iii. 3. 87–8 'accipe supremo dictum mihi for-
sitan ore / . . . "vale" .' Sophocles sometimes uses στόμα in the
same way (e.g. O.T. 426).

522. forsitan et matrem: he presumably does not know the secret
of his life, or at least who is responsible for its ending. 'Forsitan'
is effective, but an un-epic touch; the epic poet need not specu-
late on what his characters may have said. Compare x. 467–8.

522–5. These lines are excellent, particularly the quiet con-
clusion. I cannot believe 525 an interpolation (Heinsius), even
though it is missing from E U Plan. Quite apart from its excel-
lence, Ilias Latina 1062 'inque leves abiit tantus dux ille
favillas' looks to be based on a combined reminiscence of 524
and 525.

524–5. The repetition of 'paulatim' with change of stress is typical.
Meleager's spirit neither rejoices nor laments when leaving him;
it is just mercifully released from pain.

526–46. *The desolation of Calydon, and changing of Meleager's
sisters into birds*

We know that Sophocles mentioned the transformation of
Meleager's sisters (see introduction to the whole episode). But it is
clear that Ovid's main source for this final section was Nicander.
In the paraphrase (Ant. Lib. 2), καὶ πένθος ἐπὶ Μελεάγρῳ μέγιστον
ἐγένετο [παρὰ] Καλυδωνίοις· αἱ δὲ ἀδελφαὶ αὐτοῦ παρὰ τὸ σῆμα ἐθρήνουν
ἀδιαλείπτως ἄχρις αὐτὰς Ἄρτεμις ἁψαμένη ῥάβδῳ μετεμόρφωσεν εἰς ὄρνιθας
(see further on 543–6). It is quite a frequent procedure for Ovid to
graft a metamorphosis from some Alexandrian source on to an
episode which is mainly of quite a different character.

To catch the exact tone of ancient poetry is one of the most
difficult exercises. Yet surely these lines are meant to be comic;
the poet's use of a traditional epithet (526) and formula (533–4)
are only two of several indications. Could the humorous tone
have come from Nicander? This is just possible—we should not

consider only the dismal didactic poems—but even the few surviving *Heteroeumena* fragments are heavy (see Introduction, p. xxvi). More probably the whimsical, almost Callimachean humour is due to Ovid himself, and to be explained by the position of these lines in the whole episode. We have passed the climax of the story with Meleager's death; after that the transformation of his sisters can hardly arouse any great emotion. And so, to avoid competition with the earlier sections, Ovid makes a complete change in atmosphere, a change as big as that from the magniloquent portrayal of Erysicthon to the fairy-tale adventure of Mestra (847 ff.).

526. **alta iacet Calydon**: a mixture of literal and metaphorical which is made even more sportive by the traditional epithet, αἰπεινῇ Καλυδῶνι at *Il.* xiii. 217. Evelyn-White (*CQ* vii [1913] 219) wished to restore ὑψηλῷ . . . Καλυδῶνι in the Hesiodic *Catalogue* (*P.Berol.* 9777 recto, l. 7). But the first reading was apparently optimistic—contrast Merkelbach–West, fr. 25. 7!

527. **vulgusquē proceresque**: such lengthening, which imitates Greek patterns with repeated τε, belongs to the second foot, and occasionally the fifth foot, of a hexameter. It can even stand before one consonant, as *Aen.* iii. 91 'liminaquē laurusque dei' (see Williams, ad loc., and Austin on *Aen.* iv. 146).

528. **planguntur**: 'beat themselves', probably in imitation of the Greek middle κόπτεσθαι.
   Calydonides Eueninae: Greek influence is very noticeable hereabouts, and Ovid could have borrowed this rather precious spondaic ending (see 23 n.) straight from Nicander.
   Eueninae: daughters of (i.e. dwellers by) the river Euenus. Patronymics in -ίνη are much favoured by the Hellenistic poets, although this one occurred in Homer together with the spondaic fifth foot: κούρη Μαρπήσσης καλλισφύρου Εὐηνίνης (*Il.* ix. 557, of Cleopatra).

529–30. A conventional description of Oeneus' grief; cf. Catullus 64. 224, *Aen.* x. 844, xii. 611—perhaps derived ultimately from *Il.* xviii. 23–4, Achilles mourning for Patroclus.

530. **spatiosumque increpat aevum**: Oeneus has witnessed the funeral of his son, a reversal of the natural order which seemed particularly shocking to the ancients. If Nestor had been killed at Troy, 'non ille Antilochi vidisset corpus humari, / diceret aut "o mors, cur mihi sera venis?"' (Propertius ii. 13. 49–50). Later Oeneus is presented as an even more wretched old man in the *Periboea* of Pacuvius.

531. **nam**: perhaps we should understand some such words as '(I do not mention his mother among the mourners) *because* . . .'. One could also take 'nam' more simply as giving another reason for Oeneus' grief (above).

manus diri sibi conscia facti: her right hand had been the instrument of sin when it cast the brand into the fire (511); it must also be the instrument of her suicide. Although Althaea ended her monologue with a resolve to kill herself (510), we must assume that she came to her senses and saw the horrible deed in its true light.

532. Diodorus (iv. 34. 7) knows of a version in which Althaea hangs herself—a more usual way for a tragic heroine to commit suicide.

533–4. non mihi si centum deus ora sonantia linguis / ingeniumque capax totumque Helicona dedisset: this formula stems from *Il.* ii. 488–90 πληθὺν δ' οὐκ ἂν ἐγὼ μυθήσομαι οὐδ' ὀνομήνω / οὐδ' εἴ μοι δέκα μὲν γλῶσσαι δέκα δὲ στόματ' εἶεν, / φωνὴ δ' ἄρρηκτος χάλκεον δέ μοι ἦτορ ἐνείη. It had a long history in serious Latin poetry. First Ennius, *Annals* 547–8 W. 'non si, lingua loqui saperet quibus, ora decem sint, / innumerum, ferro cor sit pectusque revinctum'. Next came Hostius, who raised the number of voices to one hundred (fr. 3 Morel, *Bellum Histricum*, bk. ii) '. . . non si mihi linguae / centum atque ora sient totidem vocesque liquatae'. Hostius seems to have been an epic poet in the old Ennian tradition. He is conventionally dated soon after the Bellum Histricum of 129 B.C., and perhaps was an ancestor of Propertius' Cynthia (Hostia), cf. iii. 20. 8 'splendidaque a docto fama refulget avo'. From Hostius the formula passed to Virgil (*Georgics* ii. 43–4, *Aen.* vi. 625–6) and to Ovid. But the satirist Persius (5. 1–2) found it slightly ridiculous, and Ovid too seems to have his tongue in his cheek when he uses it for the present context.

533. sonantia linguis: an attractive detail, and seemingly Ovid's own.

534. totumque Helicona: 'all the inspiration of the Muses'. Homer and Virgil had complained of a lack of stamina for their task. Our poet seems to be saying that, even with all the Muses' gifts, an account of the sisters' lament would still be too tedious.

536. immemores decoris of course only emphasizes the undignified aspect of their grief.

　　liventia: proleptic.

537 ff. We are shown various stages of the funeral, first the body, then the bier on which it is laid out for cremation (538), next the gathering up of ashes into an urn ('haustos' 539), and finally the tomb with its inscription (540–1).

537. refoventque foventque: cf. 163 n.

538. oscula dant . . . dant oscula: repetition of more than one word, with a change of stress (as here) or of word-order (as here and 860) or of the part of a verb (860) is one of the poet's most typical devices. The emphasis on perpetual kissing is perhaps meant to be comic.

posito: placed on the pyre.

539. post cinerem: after the body had been reduced to ash. Such expressions more often contrast death with life, e.g. *ex Ponto* iv. 16. 3 'famaque post cineres maior venit'.

haustos: 'scooped up' into the urn, cf. 325–6 n., 371 n.

pressant: frequentative.

542 ff. According to Ant. Lib. 2, Artemis transformed the sisters ἁψαμένη ῥάβδῳ, which looks like a scrap of Nicander that has survived the paraphrase. I would be cautious about trying to disentangle any other fragments.

542–3. Parthaoniae . . . / . . . domus: cf. Statius, *Theb.* i. 670–1 'Parthaoniae . . . / . . . tibi iura domus'. Parthaon or Porthaon was the father of Oeneus. Artemis, whom Oeneus originally offended (273 ff.), now decides that the family has suffered enough.

543–4. The detail that these two sisters escaped transformation also comes from Nicander (Ant. Lib. 2); they were spared κατ' εὐμένειαν Διονύσου, a mythological curiosity. Ovid perhaps troubles to mention that Heracles' wife Deianira was not transformed because she will play an important part in *Met.* ix.

544–6. Nicander related more fully that the sisters were called Meleagrides, and transferred to the island of Leros, where they were said still to lament for their brother every year. Unlike κεῖρις, μελεαγρίς was in general use as the name of a real bird—the guinea-fowl. See further Pearson on the fragments of Sophocles' *Meleager* (vol. ii, p. 66).

545. longas per bracchia porrigit alas: in a characteristic way Ovid makes us watch the transformation happening stage by stage (cf. on 714 ff., 717).

547–610. *The Banquet of Achelous, and Origin of the Echinades*

Theseus, on his way back to Athens, is delayed by the river Achelous in spate, and the river-god offers the company his hospitality until the stream subsides (558–9). During the feast Achelous explains that the islands visible out to sea were once nymphs who offended him (577–89). Then he goes on to relate the transformation of his beloved Perimele (590–610).

In fact, the estuary of the Achelous lies westward of Calydon, so that Theseus would not have to cross it when returning to Athens. But Ovid neglects this point to gain a smooth transition to the next group of stories—the hunters remain talking with Achelous until the next dawn, when 'lux subit, et primo feriente cacumina sole / discedunt iuvenes, neque enim dum flumina pacem / et placidos habeant lapsus totaeque residant / opperiuntur aquae. vultus Achelous agrestes / et lacerum cornu mediis caput abdidit undis' (ix. 93–7, splendid lines).

We have no earlier source for the metamorphosis of the Echi-

LINES 538–550

nades, but there were Hellenistic works on Rivers and on Islands,
e.g. by Callimachus and Philostephanus (see on 183–259); perhaps
Ovid consulted one of these. Or he may have used a local history of
the area, such as the *Aetolica* of Nicander. For the less important
stories or parts of them Ovid probably sometimes drew on prose
works, but even these had a distinctly Hellenistic tinge (cf. the
inventions of Perdix, 244–9).

547. Interea: a flash-back to the end of the boar-hunt. Although
  Theseus has played a very small part in the hunt, this book is
  included within the framework of his exploits. So Ovid re-
  emphasizes his importance several times in the coming passage
  ('inclite' 550, 'hospite tanto' 570, 'maximus heros' 573).
548. Erectheas . . . arces: Athens. Homer describes Athena as
  entering the abode of Erectheus (*Od.* vii. 80–1). The classical
  Latin equivalent of Greek -χθ- is -*cth*- rather than -*chth*-; simi-
  larly we should write 'Erysicthon', not 'Erysichthon' (see W.
  Schulze, *Orthographica*, pp. lii ff.).

  Tritonidos: This title was usually referred to the goddess's
  birth by the Libyan lake Triton.
549 ff. Achelous, although somewhat uncouth, is portrayed as
  a kindly but pompous old gentleman. His pomposity is shown
  inter alia by the frequent Ennian ring of his language; see 550 n.,
  551 n., 603 n., ix. 43–5 with *Ann.* 507–8 W., and particularly ix.
  48–9 with *Ann.* 91–2. It is no coincidence that Achelous relates
  the high-flown Erysicthon, while the idyllic Baucis and Phile-
  mon is given to Lelex.

  When speaking of Achelous, Ovid constantly plays on dif-
  ferent levels of personification. Sometimes Achelous is no more
  than the river-water; sometimes we must think of him as almost
  human in form, but inhabiting the stream (cf. 162 n.), while at
  556 ff. he seems to be a detached spectator, unable to control the
  flood. For this alternation compare Callimachus, *hymn* 4. 77–8
  ὁ δ' εἵπετο πολλὸν ὄπισθεν / Ἀσωπὸς βαρύγουνος ἐπεὶ πεπάλακτο κεραυνῷ
  where βαρύγουνος suits the river-god, πεπάλακτο ('was sullied') the
  river-water. One may think such playing undignified, but Virgil
  did not disdain it in the *Aeneid* (iv. 246–51, Atlas, giant and
  mountain). Certainly there is a narrow division between the
  sublime and the ridiculous; some unattributed Augustan (?)
  lines stray over the mark—'te, Neptune pater, cui tempora cana
  crepanti / cincta salo resonant, magnus cui perpete mento / pro-
  fluit oceanus, et flumina crinibus errant' (Morel, *incert.*, fr. 34).
550. inclite: a dignified, archaic word, used by Ovid only in the
  Metamorphoses. It comes from early Epic, and sometimes sug-
  gests superhuman qualities; the older form 'inclutus' gives the
  connection with 'clueo'.

551. Cecropida: this form has strong manuscript support, and is stylistically appropriate with 'inclite'. It is high epic, modelled on Ennius' 'Aeacida' (*Annals* 174 W.), which is also at *Met.* vii. 798 and Silius xiii. 796; thus perhaps 'Dardanida' at Silius xvi. 191. We should probably take these vocatives as Doric, cf. forms like 'Scipiadas' in archaic Latin poetry. Many early Latin borrowings from Greek have a Doric tinge because of the Doric-speaking colonies in Southern Italy. Ovid usually has the patronymic vocative in -ē, reserving -ā for special names and special effects. Also at *Aen.* vi. 126 there is an interesting though late variant 'Tros Anchisiada' for 'Tros Anchisiade'.

552. obliquaque volvere: to be taken together, referring to the boulders' irregular course. Notice the alliteration of *s*, *x*, and *m* in this and the next line; 'magnum murmur' looks like a traditional alliterative phrase, cf. Lucretius v. 1193, *Aen.* iv. 160.

554. Cf. *Aen.* ii. 499 'cum stabulis armenta trahit'.

554–5. nec fortibus illic / profuit armentis nec equis velocibus esse: 'fortibus' and 'velocibus' are attracted into the dative after 'profuit'. Compare 690–1 with 'dabitur', but 406–7 are best interpreted otherwise.

557. turbineo . . . culmine: editors have rejected 'culmine', the clear manuscript choice. But, if the word can refer to the peak of a mountain (Catullus 63. 71, form 'columen'), why not to the crest of a wave? From the *Thesaurus* I accept with gratitude Cassiodorus on Psalm 96 (97): 1, fluctus 'undosis culminibus' (Migne, *Patrologia Latina* lxx, col. 683). With 'culmine', the unique 'turbineus' perhaps means 'cone-shaped', 'pointed' rather than 'whirling', 'raging'; compare the use of 'turbinatus'.
    iuvenalia: i.e. even men in the prime of life, as are the hunters.

559. suus alveus: 'its proper channel', cf. 35.

562 ff. *The cave of Achelous*. Ovid presents the *décor* as moist and sombre, appropriate to a river-god; jewelled wine-cups (573) provide the only flash of bright colour. Our poet owes something to the underwater dwelling of Cyrene (*Georgics* iv. 363 ff.). No doubt he had also seen artificial 'grottoes of the Muses' (musea) such as are mentioned by Pliny (*N.H.* xxxvi. 154).

562. multicavo: 'porous', a unique compound; Varro has 'multicavatus'.
    nec levibus = 'et asperis', cf. 634, 678.

564. The ceiling is studded with alternate rows of plain mussels and spiral murex-shells. Pliny says of the murex-shell 'color austerus . . . et irascenti similis mari' (*N.H.* ix. 127).
    lacunabant: the verb is a new Ovidian formation.

565. menso: from metior, 'when the sun had measured out two-thirds of the day'. We have now reached the time of the evening meal.

566. discubuere toris: cf. 660. Ovid attributes to the heroes the custom of reclining, which was a relatively late introduction to Rome; cf. Varro *ap*. Isid. *Orig*. xx. 11. 9.

567–8. Lelex originally came from Naryx in Opuntian Locris (362), but lived for some time in Troezen under the guidance of Pittheus (622). The manuscript variations here and at xv. 296 and 506 lend some support to the form 'Trozenius', which W. S. Barrett printed in his edition of the *Hippolytus*; see, however, W. M. Calder III, *CP* lx (1965) 279–80.

568. iam sparsus: rather than 'sparsus iam' (F). In the *Metamorphoses* Ovid happily leaves an isolated fourth-foot spondee thus, where he could invert words to avoid corresponding ictus and accent. Sometimes MSS. 'correct' to the poet's normal elegiac practice. The isolated spondee is much rarer when the third foot is a dactyl (see 858).

570. amnis Acarnanum: for part of its course Achelous forms the eastern boundary of Acarnania.

571. nudae vestigia: a true accusative of respect, to be distinguished from examples with 'middle' verbs such as 'exuvias indutus' (*Aen*. ii. 275).

573. in gemma posuere merum: 'they set down wine in jewelled cups' (or mixing-bowls) rather than 'they poured wine into jewelled cups'; cf. vi. 488–9 'Bacchus in auro / ponitur', *Georgics* ii. 506 'ut gemma bibat'.

maximus heros: Theseus, cf. 547 n.

574 ff. It is a favourite device of Ovid in the *Metamorphoses* to start a new episode from post-prandial conversation. This was a very natural convention; it is pleasant ἐν δαιτὶ καὶ εἰλαπίνῃ τεθαλυίῃ / τέρπεσθαι μύθοισιν ἐπὴν δαιτὸς κορέσωνται (pseudo-Hesiod, fr. 274 M.–W.). Ovid also had at least one Hellenistic precedent in the *Aetia* of Callimachus, who begins an Ician story from a dinner-table conversation with a visitor from that island (fr. 178). Probably there were other similar transitions in Callimachus.

575. nomen: direct object of 'doce' in the next line.

578. The Echinades (589) are islands out to sea, formed by alluvial deposit from the Achelous. Ancient estimates of their number vary; according to Herodotus (ii. 10) and Strabo (i. 59), the area was continually silting up, and the islands being joined to the mainland. Statius writes an attractive description of the scene 'flavo tollens ubi vertice pontum / turbidus obiectas Achelous Echinadas exit' (*Theb*. ii. 730–1).

spatium discrimina fallit: 'distance hides the space between them.' The idea of concealment in 'fallit' predominates over that of deception—cf. Propertius iv. 5. 14 'et sua nocturno fallere terga lupo' (see Shackleton Bailey ad loc.).

579 ff. He is modestly proud of this attempt at frightfulness, which parallels on a much smaller scale Diana's punishment of the Calydonians.

579–80. quoque minus ... mirere ... / naides hae fuerant: '(I tell you that) these were once Naiads.' A common Ovidian brachylogy, cf. 620.

580. bis quinque iuvencos: unable to afford a hecatomb.

581. Cf. 276.

582. festas duxere choreas: the invariable occupation of nymphs, cf. 746.

583. intumui: the play on two levels is very obvious (see on 549 ff.); the river bursts its banks, and the River-god bursts with indignation.

584. pariter as often in Ovid introduces a zeugma, cf. ii. 312–13 'pariterque animaque rotisque / expulit', here covering the real ('undis') and the personified ('animis').

587–9. This transformation is a curious one. The nymphs have been swept out to sea with the ground on which they stand; then the ground is split up by the current, and we must imagine that the nymphs are somehow combined with their islands. Ovid wishes not to rob Perimele's transformation (605 ff.) of any glamour, and so restrains himself here.

588. partesque resolvit: much the best reading, though poorly attested. Magnus followed the MSS. preference 'pariterque revellit'. He understood 'pariter' to mean 'at the same time'; that is just tolerable, but 'revellit' is hardly the right word here. Surely there has been a double intrusion: 'pariterque' partly from 584, partly from *-terque* immediately above, and 'revellit' from 585 where the verb is quite appropriate.

591. Perimelen navita dicit: the reference to passing sailors is a slightly Alexandrian touch (cf. ix. 228–9, xiv. 74, Call. *hymn* 4. 41–3, Nicander, *Ther.* 230), but also shows the speaker's pedantry. Achelous himself had better cause to know the girl's name than the sailors! This exact form of the legend does not recur (scholiast on Pindar, *Ol.* 3. 28 hardly helps). Apollodorus (i. 7. 3) speaks of Perimede (*sic*) as mother of Hippodamas (cf. 593) by Achelous. So Magnus suggested 'Perimeden' here, but it is unsafe to emend, since Ovid's relationships differ from those in Apollodorus.

593–4. [Probus] on *Georgics* i. 399 gives a similar tale of a father, enraged at his daughter's unchastity, throwing her into the sea —apparently from the *Metamorphoses* of Theodorus (cf. Ovid, *Met.* vii. 401).

594. periturae: an amusing variant is 'pariturae', which even won the approval of Heinsius; for 'corpora natae' see 236 n.

595 ff. There follow the two most interesting possible cases of double recension in this book. For a discussion of the whole

problem see Introduction, pp. x–xi; with Enk, whose arrange-
ment I adopt (from *Ovidiana*, pp. 333–8), I believe the present
instances to be genuine. Textual questions in these lines are
handled in the apparatus criticus and the commentary below.

A

595 excepi, nantemque ferens 'o
     proxima mundi
596 regna vagae' dixi 'sortite,
     tridentifer, undae,

601 adfer   opem,   mersaeque,
     precor, feritate paterna
602 da, Neptune, locum—vel sit
     locus ipsa licebit.'

609 dum loquor, amplexa est
     artus nova terra natantis,
610 et gravis increvit mutatis in-
     sula membris.
611 Amnis ab his tacuit . . .

B

595 excepi, nantemque ferens 'o
     proxima mundi
596 regna vagae' dixi 'sortite,
     tridentifer, undae,
597 in quo desinimus quot sacri
     currimus amnes,
598 huc ades atque audi placidus,
     Neptune, precantem.
599 huic ego, quam porto, nocui:
     si mitis et aequus,
600 si pater Hippodamas, aut si
     minus impius esset,
600ᵇ debuit illius misereri, igno-
     scere nobis.
601ᵃ cui quoniam tellus clausa est
     feritate paterna,
602 da, Neptune, locum—vel sit
     locus ipsa licebit:
603 hunc quoque complectar!'
     movit caput aequoreus rex,
604 concussitque suis omnes ad-
     sensibus undas.
605 extimuit nymphe, nabat
     tamen; ipse natantis
606 pectora tangebam trepido
     salientia motu,
607 dumque ea contrecto, totum
     durescere sensi
608 corpus, et inducta condi
     praecordia terra.

611 Amnis ab his tacuit . . .

597–601ᵃ and 603–8 are omitted by a E F L M N S U (added by a
later hand in E F N). N also omits 601–2. MSS. which give
version *B* also carry 609–10 and, in some cases, 601 after 601ᵃ.

Version *A* is certainly unimpeachable, if not very exciting; 601 follows smoothly after 596, and 609 after 602. It is the status of *B* which has been questioned. But, in spite of the fulminations of Magnus (*Hermes* xl [1905] 218–21), I agree with Enk and others (e.g. Brooks Otis) that the lines are completely Ovidian. The transformation at least is far more colourful in *B*. Presumably the longer version represents Ovid's second thoughts. If he had written *B* first, he need have had no reason for dissatisfaction, but, after writing *A*, the poet could have felt that he had missed a chance over the metamorphosis. And the witty prayer to Neptune underlines the somewhat ridiculous character of Achelous. These lines might be due to a gifted interpolator. But if so, perhaps he was the only interpolator of Latin poetry who could keep pace with such a consummate artist as P. Ovidius Naso.

595. excepi, nantemque ferens: one should not, as Magnus does, imagine Achelous in human form carrying Perimele upon his back. At this point Achelous is no more than the stream, though there is constant alternation between language appropriate to the stream and language appropriate to the anthropomorphic god (see on 549 ff.).

595–6. proxima mundi / regna: the sea is ranked as the second kingdom of the universe, below that of the sky, but above the rule of the underworld ('sortiti tertia regna dei' at [Tibullus] iii. 5. 22). Cf. *Il.* xv. 187 ff. for this drawing of lots between the three sons of Cronos. The originator of the variant 'terrae' might have taken 'proxima' spatially.

597. in quo desinimus: Magnus condemned 'in quo', holding that 'in quem' would be necessary. But since rivers come to rest in the sea, one can hardly quarrel with the ablative. In fact an accusative would suggest that the rivers end by turning into the sea, cf. 'desinit in piscem' (iv. 727, also Horace, *Ars Poetica* 4). A more fundamental objection of Magnus was that the idea of a river 'ending in the Trident-bearer' is barbarous and quite impossible. 'Tridentifer' should strictly be taken with 'Neptune' (598), though it could well stand alone, and virtually does so because of the wide separation. But it is typical of Ovid that 'tridentifer . . . Neptune' should refer at once to the sea and to the sea-god. Besides the treatment of Achelous, compare ii. 383 (Phoebus) 'lucemque odit seque ipse diemque', xi. 621 (Somnus) 'excussit . . . sibi se', also 819 n.

quot: I adopt Burman's elegant correction, although it is not absolutely necessary—for a possible defence of the second 'quo', see Enk in *Ovidiana*, pp. 334–5, citing xiii. 193–4.

sacri . . . amnes: bright, flowing water (Aeschylus, *Supplices* 23 λευκὸν ὕδωρ) was considered sacred. When first arriving in a new country, a stranger should pray to the rivers; so Aeneas 'adhuc ignota precatur / flumina' (*Aen.* vii. 137–8). Rivers also received honour as κουροτρόφοι (rearers of boys).

598. huc ades atque audi placidus, Neptune, precantem: correct invocation of a god, cf. *Aen.* iv. 578 'adsis o, placidusque iuves'. But this line does not contribute much, and might eventually have been cut out.

599. nocui: a reticent word which avoids cruder expressions. This is a nice point, and not to be attacked.

599–600. si mitis et aequus, / si pater Hippodamas, aut si minus impius esset: note the typical tricolon, with anaphora of 'si' and the limbs growing in length. As Enk says, there is a gradation in the three limbs: if Hippodamas had any generous feelings, if he were a true father—one would expect 'verus pater' in prose—or, finally, if he were less of a monster. Each successive clause demands less of Hippodamas. Misunderstanding through taking 'pater Hippodamas' together as 'father Hippodamas' has afflicted both scribes and modern scholars.

601ᵃ. quoniam: Bothe's easy and obvious correction of the manuscripts' 'quondam'. For the thought cf. 185–6 and Seneca, *Contr.* i. 6. 6 quoted there.

602. vel sit locus ipsa licebit: sc. 'per me', 'or I have no objection to her actually becoming a place', cf. Propertius ii. 11. 1 'scribant de te alii, vel sis ignota licebit'. Achelous is being helpful, and this second suggestion virtually supersedes the first, which is neglected in the next line. The transition to 603 may seem a trifle rough, but no more.

603. hunc quoque complectar !: a truly Ovidian touch, cf. i. 553 'hanc quoque Phoebus amat' (the transformed Daphne). Magnus complained that the river cannot be said to 'embrace' the island, since it lies out to sea. But Achelous is still carrying the nymph at this point, so he must still be able to touch her when she is transformed (thus Enk in *Ovidiana*, p. 336). It is easy to imagine Achelous stretching out beyond his mouth, cf. Statius, *Theb.* ii. 730–1, quoted on 578.

movit caput aequoreus rex: for the epic formula of assent see on 780–1. A monosyllabic line-ending (359 n.) in 'rex' has a faintly Ennian ring, from his 'divum pater atque hominum rex' (*Annals* 207 W.).

604. Neptune's nod shakes the sea as the god's own element, cf. 781. For the unemphatic 'suis' one might be tempted to conjecture 'suas', but cf., for example, 780, 849.

605. nymphe: Ovid uses the Greek nominative ten times in the *Metamorphoses*, seemingly just for metrical convenience. Others (Horace, for example), prefer the Greek forms for a more elevated style.

nabat tamen: 'but she went on swimming.' The transforma-
tion is splendidly handled, with a great concentration on move-
ment—the waves stirred by Neptune's nod, Perimele swimming,
her breasts heaving, and Achelous fondling the nymph. Sud-
denly all this movement is interrupted, as Perimele's body
begins to grow stiff and hard.

606–7. Notice once more the playing on Achelous' double nature.
   tangebam is a relatively colourless word, describing the stream
in contact with the nymph's body.
   contrecto: a more active verb, appropriate to the river-god's
fondling, cf. *Heroides* 20. 141 'contrectatque sinus'.

611–724. *Baucis and Philemon*

No extant authority earlier than Ovid tells this story, yet in an
important way we can trace it back to Homer's *Odyssey*. Our
theme is the reception of the great at a humble peasant dwelling;
its special fascination, to bring a god or a grand figure of the heroic
age into contact with mundane details of life among ordinary
country people. Such was the reception of Odysseus by the swine-
herd Eumaeus, and this was the pattern which Callimachus took
for his description of Theseus' visit to the old woman of Attica,
Hecale (see Pfeiffer on the vocabulary of fr. 239).

Callimachus covered much of the same ground in his Molorchus
(*Aetia*, frs. 54–9); this told how Heracles was entertained hospitably
at the old man's hut in Cleonae before going out to kill the
Nemean lion. Between them, the two stories clearly set a vogue in
Hellenistic poetry. We have an anonymous fragment in hexa-
meters (Powell, *Collectanea Alexandrina*, p. 78) in which an im-
poverished old woman tells of her miseries to someone whom she
addresses as 'child' in language clearly borrowed from the *Hecale*.

A successor in the tradition was Eratosthenes, a pupil of Calli-
machus. This great scientist had both the time and the ability to
write an elegiac poem highly praised by 'Longinus' (33. 5), his
Erigone. Erigone was the daughter of Icarus (or Icarius), who
received Dionysus when the god came to Attica, and in return was
taught how to plant the vine, hitherto unknown. The poem has
perished almost completely, but in the few surviving fragments we
seem to hear of Icarus lighting his fire (fr. 24 Powell) and putting
a poor man's meal before his guest (fr. 34, not certainly from the
Erigone). Another similar theoxeny was that of the Boeotian
Hyrieus, at least mentioned by Euphorion of Chalcis (fr. 101
Powell); the story also appears in Ovid's *Fasti* (v. 493 ff.), where
both in language and in approach it is a doublet of Baucis and
Philemon.

Roman poets found the theme no less attractive, and were fully
conscious of the tradition which they had inherited. Virgil, even in

the few lines with which he relates Aeneas' entry into Evander's house, sets the tone of the piece (*Aen.* viii. 364–5),

> aude, hospes, contemnere opes, et te quoque dignum
> finge deo, rebusque veni non asper egenis,

and sits the hero down (367–8),

> stratisque locavit
> effultum foliis, et pelle Libystidis ursae,

remembering how Eumaeus had received Odysseus (*Od.* xiv. 48–9).

Callimachus' *Hecale* has already served as a main source for one episode in the *Metamorphoses* (ii. 531 ff.), and perhaps contributed to another (vii. 404 ff.). Ovid's debt to this poem here is obvious even from the meagre fragments remaining. But it seems that Baucis and Philemon quickly became no less famous than its model. Our episode was much imitated by later Roman poets; an ugly consequence of this popularity is that the text has been interpolated at least once (696 ff.) and possibly more often, though I believe the variants at 651 ff. and 693 f. to be due to double recension.

Petronius' picture of the priestess Oenothea (chs. 135 ff.) owes much to Baucis and Philemon (cf. Garrido, *CR* xliv [1930] 10–11). In it he makes fun of the literary figure, well established by now, of the poor but hard-working old woman, 'mirabar equidem paupertatis ingenium'; the poem at the end of the chapter expressly compares Oenothea to Hecale:

> qualis in Actaea quondam fuit hospita terra
> digna sacris Hecale . . .

The aetiological account of the beginning of the Falernian vineyards in Silius Italicus (vii. 166–211) is particularly close to our episode (cf. Bruère in *Ovidiana*, pp. 491–5), and also interesting because it represents a link with the *Erigone* of Eratosthenes, an earlier member of the tradition (as first pointed out by G. Procacci, *Riv. Fil.* xlii [1914] 441–8). Juvenal, too, selects Baucis and Philemon as his source for some playful mockery of the good old days when

> . . . Curius parvo quae legerat horto
> ipse focis brevibus ponebat holuscula,

and there were

> sicci terga suis rara pendentia crate

(*Sat.* 11. 78–9 and 82, cf. Ovid, lines 646–8 and Thomas in *Ovidiana*, p. 513).

The hospitality-theme is well established in later Greek epic. I believe that the fragment of Dionysius (? third century A.D.) in Appendix II came from yet another similar episode, while the theoxeny of Brongus (Nonnus, *Dionysiaca* xvii. 37 ff.) is said to be based on that of Molorchus (ibid. 51–6). Finally we can see a Christian poet, Prudentius, expressing a Biblical story (Genesis 18: 2 ff.) in terms of the pagan literary tradition (*Psychomachia*, Intr. 45–6):

> mox et triformis angelorum trinitas
> senis revisit hospitis mapalia.

Elements of the Story

The scene of Baucis and Philemon is set in the Phrygian hills (621). Is the epithet merely picturesque, or should we look for genuine Near Eastern elements? The first attempt must be to find Greek parallels, and this, I think, can be done in every instance. For example, the gods come down to earth to watch how mortals are conducting themselves in the *Odyssey* (xvii. 485–7):

> καί τε θεοὶ ξείνοισιν ἐοικότες ἀλλοδαποῖσιν
> παντοῖοι τελέθοντες ἐπιστρωφῶσι πόληας
> ἀνθρώπων ὕβριν τε καὶ εὐνομίην ἐφορῶντες

(cf. L. Malten, *Hermes* lxxiv [1939] 179–82, J. Fontenrose, *Univ. of Cal. Publ. in Class. Phil.* xiii [1945] 98 ff.).

The flood as a punishment for men's wickedness (Ovid, 689 ff.) also appears in Homer, as a simile (*Il.* xvi. 384 ff., cf. Malten, ibid., p. 191), and was exemplified in the legend of Deucalion. Finally the sacred tree with a wall round it, claimed by W. M. Calder as a non-Greek feature, can be paralleled from Minoan gems (Nilsson, *The Minoan–Mycenean Religion*[2], pp. 266 ff.). Nilsson also refers to what may be a sacred tree surrounded by a wall from Pompeii (ibid., p. 270 n. 29).

Yet we should not conclude that there is nothing genuinely eastern in this story just because everything can be explained adequately in Greek terms. At least three points of agreement between Baucis and Philemon and Near Eastern traditions are remarkable, particularly the first one.

The Theophany

When Paul and Barnabas on their missionary travels arrived at Lystra in Phrygia Galatica, Barnabas was at first hailed as Zeus, and the more loquacious Paul as Hermes (Acts of the Apostles 14: 11 f., cf. Ovid, 626–7) οἵ τε ὄχλοι . . . ἐπῆραν τὴν φωνὴν αὐτῶν Λυκαονιστὶ λέγοντες· οἱ θεοὶ ὁμοιωθέντες ἀνθρώποις κατέβησαν πρὸς ἡμᾶς, ἐκάλουν τε τὸν

Βαρνάβαν Δία, τὸν δὲ Παῦλον Ἑρμῆν. The occasion was the healing of
a cripple in the city, and it shows local expectation of the ap-
pearance of these gods. Significantly the people spoke Λυκαονιστί
(verse 11); these were the native inhabitants and not Roman
colonists of Lystra. An inscription relating to the joint worship of
Zeus and Hermes was found by W. M. Calder in 1908 near the
shores of Lake Trogitis, a day's journey southward from Lystra
(published in *CR* xxiv [1910] 76 ff.; for a detailed map of the area
see W. M. Ramsay, *Historical Commentary on the Galatians*,
frontispiece). Since then more evidence has come to light of the
joint local worship of Zeus and Hermes (Malten, *Hermes* lxxv
[1940] 168-71). No doubt these were Anatolian gods masquerading
in Greek dress.

Sacred Trees in Asia Minor

We have seen that the sacred tree with a wall around it, and
hung with garlands (619-20, 722-3) can be accounted for in
a Greek and Roman context. But the reports of travellers in Asia
Minor from more recent times are remarkably similar. W. J.
Childs in the early years of this century so described a tree in the
Cilician Gates Pass which was covered over with pious rags and
surrounded by a rampart of small stones placed there one by one
by Moslem travellers (given by Calder, *Discovery* iii [1922] 207-11):

'These sacred trees are found wherever trees and bushes grow;
are decorated always by rags, and surrounded by an accumulation
of stones. The best explanation that I got was that these bushes
marked the haunt of some dead holy man, at which, as at a shrine,
offerings might produce lesser miracles, or at least be accounted as
good works.'

Ramsay tells a similar story of a place on the boundaries of
Lycaonia and Cappadocia (*Pauline Studies*, pp. 172 ff.). Malten,
however, thinks that if these sacred trees went back to ancient
times, they point rather to vegetation-worship (*Hermes* 1940, 174).

The Phrygian Flood-Tradition

This can be traced mainly through references to two cities,
Apamea and Iconium. It is worth mentioning from further west
a coin of Candyba in Lycia with the legend ΚΑΝΔΥΒΕΩΝ ΔΕΥ-
ΚΑΛΙΩΝ, published by L. Robert, *Hellenica* x (1955) 220-22 and
plate iii. 2. Apamea (Celaenae) in Roman imperial times had a
large Jewish community (Ramsay, *Cities and Bishoprics of Phrygia*,
ch. 15). For this reason the hill of Apamea was said to be Mount
Ararat, on which Noah's ark had come to rest (*Sibylline Books* i.
261 ff.). We even have Apamean coins of the time of Severus,
Macrinus, and Philip showing an ark or chest floating on water,

with two figures inside and the inscription ΝΩΕ (*Cities and Bishoprics*, plate ii. 1 and 2, cf. British Museum Catalogue, *Phrygia*, p. 101, 182). Most scholars (see Ramsay, ibid., pp. 671–2) believe that the Jewish version of the flood at Apamea was merely superimposed on a native myth of great antiquity. While considering Apamea, it is interesting to note that Nonnus has a story of a great flood in Phrygia (*Dionysiaca* xiii. 522 ff.) which includes the characteristic saving of one man for his piety (542–3). How he came by this remains a mystery, but, perhaps significantly, at xiii. 512 ff. Nonnus shows considerable and unexpected knowledge of the geography of Apamea (*Cities and Bishoprics*, p. 483 n., cf. Cook, *Zeus* iii. 527 ff.).

Our information about Iconium comes from Stephanus of Byzantium and Suidas on Nannacus. The latter was king of Iconium, and prophesied the flood which would overwhelm his people. 'To weep the tears of Nannacus' was a proverbial expression at least in the third century B.C. (Herodas 3. 10)—H. J. Rose suggested, with parallels, that originally Nannacus' tears may have caused the deluge—and this story is usually thought to be very much older. According to Calder, the myth of a local flood lingered on in the folk-lore of Iconium until modern times.

So it seems that Phrygia had a well-established flood tradition, in particular concentrated around Apamea, with its great concourse of rivers, and Iconium, near the Phrygian lakes. Connections with other flood-stories (e.g. Babylonian) are quite possible (cf. Fontenrose, loc. cit., pp. 93, 112). But obviously it would be rash to insist on any correspondence of details between Baucis and Philemon and other eastern flood traditions. Ovid's tale is likely to have been changed much from the original, and only the broadest outlines have probably remained constant—the wickedness of mankind, punishment by a flood, and the saving of one pious couple.

How could Ovid have known a local story from Phrygia? The answer of Calder (*Discovery* iii [1922], 207–11), based upon the joint ideas of himself and Ramsay, is highly ingenious. The lake at 624–5 is Trogitis, south of Lystra, which has a remarkable rise and fall and, for good measure, a local tale of a town at the bottom. This story was brought back by an officer of P. Sulpicius Quirinius, who fought a war against the Homonadeis in roughly this region possibly *c.* 4–3 B.C. (see now Barbara Levick, *Roman Colonies in Southern Asia Minor*, App. V). Some of Strabo's topography of the area (xii. 568–9) may well derive from Quirinius' campaigns, as Ramsay and Calder believed. Ramsay wished to fix the location even more closely by reading 'Tyrieius' or 'Tyriaius' for the ethnic at 719 (see n.) from Tyriaeum (Strabo xiv. 663), north and a little west of Iconium.

This scheme, or at least the location, has generally received cautious approval from later scholars, even if they criticize details; see Malten, *Hermes* (1940), 172 ff., Fontenrose, op. cit., p. 105. But, although the district of origin may be right, we can say confidently that either the poet does not have information of such a specific kind, or else he is deliberately misleading his audience. Our lake is said to be 'not far' from the kingdom of Pelops, which Lelex had visited in his youth (624). Now the rule of Pelops centred around Sipylus in Lydia. He and his family were called 'Phrygian' in literature only by a courtesy title, as explained by Strabo (xii. 571), and Ovid's readers would have known this. But Lake Trogitis is a very long way from Sipylus. Also the ethnic 'Thyneius', almost certainly the correct reading at 719, points to a place much further north. So it appears that Ovid's 'Phrygia' is not the Roman province, but a land of literary associations.

In my opinion this story quite probably originated either from the Phrygian lake district (including Trogitis) or from the region of Apamea. But Ovid's source cannot have been precise as to local details, or else the poet has blurred these intentionally so as to facilitate his Graeco-Roman colouring. Thus an officer of P. Sulpicius Quirinius is not a very likely informant for Ovid. He could well have drawn on a local writer of the Hellenistic age, and a possible candidate is Alexander Polyhistor. That encyclopedic scholar was born about the end of the second century B.C., probably at Miletus. He came to Rome as a prisoner of war, received his freedom from Sulla, and was tutor to a friend of Ovid, C. Julius Hyginus. Alexander's voluminous writings included a work περὶ Φρυγίας in at least three books. But Ovid equally well may have had a poetic source, and much the most likely one would be the *Heteroeumena* of Nicander. With his Attalid connections, Nicander was well placed to cull a story from the district of Trogitis or Apamea. Also there is a typical Nicandrean touch at lines 719–20.

So perhaps the lineage of Baucis and Philemon can be traced back to Callimachus and the *Odyssey* on one hand, on the other to a local Phrygian legend. These two elements are a strange mixture, and in combining them Ovid has overlaid yet a third. In many ways Philemon is a type of the traditional Italian peasant, with a cottage which he has lived in all his life (see on 632–3), his ideal marriage (see on 703 ff.) and the Italian meal which he lays before his guests (664 ff.); Juvenal was right to take Baucis and Philemon as his model for the good old days. Readers must have smiled to see all these Roman virtues attributed to a couple living 'in the Phrygian hills'. But the attribution takes on a new significance in Augustan Rome. There it was official policy to glorify the simple life of Italy's past—as viewed from a comfortable distance away. The picture is of course idealized; Baucis and

Philemon have none of the hardships of Hecale and her people
(cf. chiefly Call. frs. 252, 254, 275, 290, 329). Instead (633–4),

> paupertatemque fatendo
> effecere levem nec iniqua mente ferendo.

What better paradigm could there be for Horace's advice to the
Roman youth 'angustam amice pauperiem pati' (*Odes* iii. 2. 1)?
Although the propaganda value of Baucis and Philemon would be
small, the attitude is typical of Augustan poetry.

This episode has been much admired through the centuries. So
the dissentient verdict of Professor Brooks Otis (*Ovid as an Epic
Poet*, pp. 203–5) should stimulate us. But I feel that he under-
values both Baucis and Philemon and Erysicthon, mainly through
ascribing a false motive to the poet (he 'felt it necessary to make
some obeisance to Augustan morality and Virgilian seriousness',
p. 205). Although ideal simplicity was an Augustan political
theme, Ovid's treatment is lightly humorous (e.g. 659, 668–9) and
quite unpolitical. We may agree that the two following episodes
illustrate the reward of piety and the punishment of impiety, but
the contrast and effect should be explained by appropriateness in
the context rather than a desire to re-establish the gods' power
and morality impressively (Otis, p. 203). After all, Achelous, pro-
minent throughout, does not enhance the prestige of his fellow
gods.

To match his subject-matter, Ovid's telling of the story is
simple and straightforward. His language is hardly 'epic' at all,
and after the bridge-passage (611–25) we find very few Virgilian
echoes, compared with an abundance in the next episode.

611–25. *Transition to Baucis and Philemon*

611. ab his: 'after this', cf. Homer, *Il.* viii. 54 ἀπὸ δ' αὐτοῦ, Luci-
lius 683 W. 'ab eo'.

612–13. utque deorum / spretor erat: 'being, as he was, a despiser of
the gods'. Pirithous is 'spretor deorum', like Erysicthon (see
740 n.), probably because of his attempt, together with Theseus,
to carry off Persephone from Hades. This usually ended with
Theseus escaping, but Pirithous being chained there for ever (cf.
Frazer on Apollodorus ii. 5. 12). Ovid may follow the tradition of
Euripides' *Pirithous*, in which both are released through the
help of Heracles (Page, Loeb *G.L.P.* [Poetry], pp. 120 ff.).

613. Ixione natus: of course Ixion himself had also fallen foul of the
Olympians.

615. si dant adimuntque figuras: Pirithous is at least inconsiderate
to his divine host. The abrupt manner conceals, at several
removes, deep philosophical speculation about the limiting of

divine power through having to work in human material—'non
potest artifex mutare materiam' (Seneca, *Dial.* i. 5. 9). See Pease
on Cicero, *De Natura Deorum* ii. 86.

616. **obstipuere omnes**: a good epic phrase (see 765 n.). The variant
'obstrepuere' is attractive, but of negligible authority.

617. **animo maturus et aevo**: like Aletes 'annis gravis atque animi
maturus' (*Aen.* ix. 246). Lelex has imbibed the teaching of his
mentor, the righteous Pittheus (622–3).

619. **quidquid superi voluere, peractum est**: Trimalchio puts it
succinctly, 'cito fit, quod di volunt' (Petronius, ch. 76), a com-
mon proverb; see Otto, s.v. *deus* 2.

620. The linden, as the slenderer of the two trees ('levis' at *Georgics*
i. 173) would represent Baucis, and the oak Philemon (cf.
714 ff.).

621. **modico circumdata muro**: the best manuscripts give 'medio',
which Magnus retained, arguing that it meant the same as
'modicus'. It could indeed mean 'middling', of something like
intellect or age, but here would be confusing together with
'circumdata'. For this wall see introduction to the episode.

622–3. Pelops' father Tantalus was king of Sipylus in Lydia,
whence Pelops himself set out to give his name to the Pelopon-
nese. This reference would also remind readers of the passage of
time since vi. 418. Then Pelops' son Pittheus was not yet on the
throne of Troezen, 'neque adhuc Pittheia Troezen'. Now Lelex
himself, probably sent to Phrygia in early manhood, is 'animo
maturus et aevo' (617).

623. **arva . . . quondam regnata parenti**: cf. *Aen.* iii. 14 (terra)
'acri quondam regnata Lycurgo', *Aen.* vi. 793–4, Horace, *Odes*,
ii. 6. 11–12, all = 'reigned over' with dative of the agent.

624–5. The structure of these lines recalls *Aen.* ii. 21–3 'est in con-
spectu Tenedos, notissima fama / insula, dives opum, Priami
dum regna manebant, / nunc tantum sinus et statio male fida
carinis.' The similarity might account for an inferior variant
pointed to by Planudes 'nunc statio mergis fulicisque palustri-
bus uda'; or perhaps there was contamination from *Aen.* v. 128
'statio gratissima mergis'.

625. **celebres mergis**: cf. Callimachus' picture of Delos αἰθυίῃς καὶ
μᾶλλον ἐπίδρομος ἠέπερ ἵπποις (*hymn* 4. 12).

626. **specie mortali**: in these stories the gods must at first be
unrecognized, so that the behaviour and conversation (654)
of their host can be completely natural and uninhibited. Thus
Fasti v. 504, Silius vii. 176–7. In Eratosthenes' *Erigone*, too,
Dionysus may have revealed his true nature only by a miracle
similar to that in our episode (see on 679 ff.).

627. **Atlantiades**: papponymically. Hermes was son of Zeus and
Maia, and so grandson of Maia's father Atlas.

caducifer is treated as a fixed epithet here and at ii. 708 (cf. in Greek χρυσόρραπις). Clearly Hermes does not have his caduceus or herald's wand with him.

628–9. **mille domos adiere locum requiemque petentes, / mille domos clausere serae**: such repetition and symmetry with pronounced rhyme is typically Hellenistic, perhaps employed as an affectation of simplicity. Thus Call. *hymn* 4. 84–5 νύμφαι μὲν χαίρουσιν ὅτε δρύας ὄμβρος ἀέξει, / νύμφαι δ' αὖ κλαίουσιν ὅτε δρυσὶ μηκέτι φύλλα, Theocritus 11. 22–3 φοιτῇς δ' αὔθ' οὕτως ὅκκα γλυκὺς ὕπνος ἔχῃ με / οἴχῃ δ' εὐθὺς ἰοῖσ' ὅκκα γλυκὺς ὕπνος ἀνῇ με, Euphorion, fr. 2 Powell ἵκτο μὲν ἐς Δωδῶνα Διὸς φηγοῖο προφῆτιν / ἵκετο δ' ἐς Πυθῶνα καὶ ἐς γλαυκῶπα Προνοίην, and even more strikingly in Nonnus, e.g. v. 427–8 υἷα, πάτερ, γίνωσκε τὸν οὐκ ἐσάωσεν Ἀπόλλων / υἷα, πάτερ, στενάχιζε τὸν οὐκ ἐφύλαξε Κιθαιρών. The seed is perhaps contained in some four-line patterns from early epic, notably Hesiod, *Theogony* 722–5 (see West ad loc.). Similarly Virgil in bucolic mood (*Ecl.* 4. 58–9) 'Pan etiam Arcadia mecum si iudice certet / Pan etiam Arcadia dicet se iudice victum'. From Ovid cf. Norden's list on *Aeneid* vi, p. 383, with (for example) vi. 430–4.

Here Ovid has chosen to preserve the rhyme (-ōs and -ēre) at the expense of grammatical symmetry by changing the subject in 629. Not only this couplet but the succeeding lines also until 636 are conspicuous for rhyme: 'illa . . . illa' (632), 'consenuere . . . effecere' (633–4), 'fatendo . . . ferendo' (633–4), 'dominos . . . famulos' (635), 'parentque iubentque' (636). The result is a much lighter effect compared with the epic character of the bridge-passage.

630. Compare Lucan v. 516–17 'haud procul inde domus non ullo robore fulta / sed sterili iunco cannaque intexta palustri'. That echo lends some weight to the conjecture 'texta'. Similarly Silius (xvii. 88) writes 'castra levi calamo cannaque intecta palustri', where Heinsius conjectured 'intexta'.

631. Ehwald would punctuate heavily after 'sed pia'; this may well be right.

Baucis: a rare name, also held by Erinna's lamented friend (*New Chapters in Greek Literature*, Third Series, pp. 180 ff.), and perhaps to be connected with Hesychius' gloss βαυκά· ἡδέα. The 'pannucia Baucis' of Persius (4. 21) may be from Ovid, but the old woman there is of a very different character from our Baucis.

Malten (*Hermes* [1939], 196 n. 4) gives references for the name 'Philemon' in Asia Minor. But it is not especially common there, and appears also in fifth-century Athens; that the Philemon of Aristophanes *Birds* 763 is taunted with having Phrygian blood can hardly be more than a coincidence. Both names may be meant to stress the couple's mutual affection.

632-3. illa sunt . . . iuncti . . . illa / consenuere casa: Italy in the
good old days peeps through Ovid's narrative. Philemon is
a type of the hardy Italian peasant like Sp. Ligustinus the
Sabine (Livy xlii. 34, 171 B.C.) who says of himself 'pater mihi
iugerum agri reliquit, et parvum tugurium in quo natus educa-
tusque sum; hodieque ibi habito.' At the other end of the
Roman Empire, Claudian writes (*Carmina Minora* 20. 1-4):

> Felix qui patriis aevum transegit in arvis,
>   ipsa domus puerum quem videt, ipsa senem,
> qui baculo nitens in qua reptavit harena
>   unius numerat saecula longa casae.

633. casa: an evocative word for Ovid's readers, reminding them
of the thatched 'casa Romuli' (*Fasti* i. 199), preserved on the
Palatine Hill together with a duplicate on the Capitoline.
Propertius shows the nostalgic associations (ii. 16. 19-20, cf.
Enk ad loc.) 'atque utinam Romae nemo esset dives, et ipse /
straminea posset dux habitare casa!'

634. nec iniqua mente ferendo = et aequa mente ferendo. Only
M¹ S U give 'ferendo' rather than 'ferendam', but the former is
neater and preserves the rhyme (see on 628-9).

637. caelicolae: an Ennian compound (*Annals* 292 W.) which
stresses the dignity of the heavenly beings. Silius' Falernus is
very close to Ovid, and even lends support to 'parvos': 'nec
pigitum parvosque Lares humilisque subire / limina caelicolam
tecti' (vii. 173-4).

638. summisso . . . vertice: this touch further intensifies the con-
trast between the gods, even if unrecognized, and the country-
man. Compare *Aen.* viii. 366-7 (Evander and Aeneas) 'angusti
subter fastigia tecti / ingentem Aeneam duxit', *Fasti* v. 505, and
Silius quoted above.

639. We have a parallel fragment from Callimachus' *Hecale*. There
Theseus has slipped out from Athens unnoticed, making for
Marathon. But, in the late evening, a sudden and violent rain-
storm forces him to take refuge in the hut of an old woman,
living perhaps on the slopes of Mount Brilessos. He enters, and
throws off his wet cloak (fr. 239); she makes him sit down on the
couch, τὸν μὲν ἐπ' ἀσκάντην κάθισεν (fr. 240), cf. *Od.* xiv. 49, *Aen.*
viii. 367-8.

640. He is still following the *Hecale* closely (fr. 241): αὐτόθεν ἐξ εὐνῆς
ὀλίγον ῥάκος αἰθύξασα.

641 ff. Undoubtedly Callimachus mentioned the fire from which
Hecale heated her cauldron (cf. frs. 242-4). Eratosthenes, fr. 24
Powell may describe Icarus' fire from the *Erigone*; compare
Fasti v. 506, [Virgil], *Moretum* 8-9, Petronius, ch. 136.

Instead of lighting a new fire each day, the ancients kept a special kind of log smouldering on the hearth overnight, under a pile of wood-ash, which Baucis first brushes aside (641). See Headlam on Herodas 1. 38.

643. Cf. *Fasti* v. 507 (Hyrieus) 'ipse genu nixus flammas exsuscitat aura', and [Virgil], *Moretum* 12–14: 'excitat et crebris languentem flatibus ignem. / tandem concepto, sed vix, fulgore recedit / oppositaque manu lumen defendit ab aura.' The minutely detailed description, especially in the *Moretum* passage, is typical of Hellenistic-inspired poetry.

644–5. Cf. *Fasti* v. 508 'et promit quassas comminuitque faces'. These lines account for two *Hecale* fragments; fr. 242 παλαίθετα κᾶλα καθήρει, and fr. 243 δανὰ ξύλα . . . κεάσαι ('ramaliaque arida . . . / . . . minuit'). In the piece of Dionysius (App. II), line 7 κάγκανα κῆλα probably belonged to a similar description. The logs have been hung up among the rafters, and dried in the smoke (cf. *Georgics* i. 175, Hesiod, *Works and Days* 45).

646–8. This is the passage parodied by Juvenal (*Sat.* 11. 78–9, 82)—see introduction to the episode.

647. furca levat . . . bicorni: many scholars have noted the resemblance to Callimachus, *Aetia*, fr. 177. 2 δίκρον φιτρὸν ἀειραμένη; it is conceivable that the corrupt Call., fr. 785 (authorship not certain) may hide a like passage from the *Hecale*.

ille: a difficult problem. The original reading of M and N was apparently 'illa'. But Philemon would then be under-employed, after welcoming the guests (639) and collecting some vegetables (646); 'ille' (also well-attested) makes him lend a hand.

648. sordida terga suis: we enter the Roman world, in which the meal will be conducted from now on. Fraenkel (*Elementi Plautini in Plauto*, pp. 124–5, 408 ff.) points out that the basic Athenian poor man's diet was fish, the Roman's pork (cf. *Fasti* vi. 169 ff.). So pork appears often in similar contexts among Roman writers, e.g. *Moretum* 56–7, Petronius, ch. 135, Juvenal 11. 82.

nigro pendentia tigno: the pork is dried with salt, and then hung up on the wall to be smoked ('sordida'); Columella (xii. 55. 3) gives instructions. André, *L'Alimentation et la cuisine à Rome*, p. 32 shows a painting from Pompeii of a kitchen with part of a pig hanging up—see further André, pp. 139 ff.

649. servatoque diu: Oenothea's 'sinciput' is 'coaequale natalium suorum' (Petronius, ch. 136).

tergore: the rarer form 'tergus' is mainly poetic and only in the *Metamorphoses* of Ovid's undisputed works (also in the doubtful *Halieutica* fragment).

650. undis: a very good graphic word to describe water boiling in a pan, as at Virgil, *Georgics* i. 296 'undam trepidi . . . aeni'. See also 457 n.

651 ff. With slight divergences the MSS. offer two alternative schemes in the following passage. I arrange as Enk in *Ovidiana*, p. 339.

A	B
651 interea medias fallunt ser- monibus horas	651 interea medias fallunt ser- monibus horas
	652 sentirique moram prohibent. erat alveus illic
	653 fagineus, curva clavo sus- pensus ab ansa:
	654 is tepidis impletur aquis, ar- tusque fovendos
655 concutiuntque torum de molli fluminis ulva	655ª accipit. in medio torus est de mollibus ulvis
656 impositum lecto sponda pedi- busque salignis:	656ª impositus lecto sponda pedi- busque salignis:
657 vestibus hunc velant, ...	657 vestibus hunc velant, ...
Thus M N, except that in 655 N has 'conficiuntque'.	652–655ª are added in the margin of M N, and appear in the other MSS.

As with 595 ff. and 693 ff., we have several possibilities here; is version *A* genuine, *B* the work of an interpolator; or *B* original, and *A* due to attempts to patch a lacunose text; or might both versions be from the pen of Ovid? Just as in the other instances, we can never prove that both versions are genuine; at best we can only say that there is no reason to condemn either.

B is the work of an interpolator. Magnus argued this in *Hermes* xl (1905) 221 ff., and he clung steadfastly to the same opinion in his edition—see apparatus criticus there. Yet the objections which he brings against *B* are all very small ones, well answered by Enk, and, even cumulatively, carrying little weight. As extreme examples, one may cite first Magnus's complaint that the beginning of 652 says the same as 651. If the point is granted, what would be un-poetic about that—or even un-Ovidian (cf. 662–3)? Then he alleged that 'artus' in 654 must refer to the whole body, and so produce a ridiculous picture of total immersion. But 'artus' can refer to particular limbs, when made clear by the context. Of course here the word means legs and feet, as at 398 'primos suspensus in artus'. Not all of Magnus's objections are quite so misguided, and we may concede, with Enk, that the double ecphrasis-pattern at 652 ff. and 655ª ff. is a shade clumsy. But emphatically nothing in these lines requires their condemnation.

B must be genuine, because it imitates Callimachus' *Hecale*. Many scholars recently have held this position; as Eurycleia washes the feet of Odysseus, so Hecale performs the same office for Theseus, and Baucis and Philemon for Zeus and Hermes. The *Hecale*-fragments are a weak link in the chain, since, of the four originally assigned to the foot-washing by Pfeiffer (244–7), only fr. 246 stands a good chance of referring to this (*CR* N.S. xv [1965] 259–60). Even so, the argument provides extra support for version *B*.

One could argue that *A was not original*. Suppose that 652, 653, and 654 had by some mischance fallen out. A copyist would then be faced with a quite unintelligible 'accipit' at the beginning of 655ª. Differing attempts to patch the line could account for the variants 'concutiuntque' (M), 'conficiuntque' (N), 'constituuntque', 'consternuntque' (the last two in an extra line, akin to 655, added in MSS. which carry *B*). Yet one point in Magnus's discussion of *A* strikes home; 'concutiuntque' (655, M) is a vigorous and imaginative expression, unparalleled, but describing very well the action of somebody 'shaking up' a mattress for another person to sit on.

So again, the possibility must be left open that both versions go back to Ovid. Mendner asked why the poet should have omitted the foot-washing in his first recension, seeing that the model of Callimachus' *Hecale* was constantly before his mind. We cannot give a definite answer, but that is no cause for great concern. Perhaps Ovid had not yet decided just how closely he would follow the *Hecale*. Our poet's imitation is never slavish, and he might debate which elements to borrow from Callimachus, and which to reject.

652 ff. The double ecphrasis-pattern 'erat alveus . . . is' (654), 'torus est (655ª) . . . hunc' (657) may seem a little clumsy. But there is a partial parallel at 329 ff. and 334 ff., although in neither case is the ecphrasis quite typical. Critics have needlessly attacked the change from imperfect ('erat' 652) to present ('est' 655ª). With a double ecphrasis a variation of tense is quite welcome; compare 329 ff. and 334 ff.

653. fagineus: as Enk notes, this form somewhat favours the genuineness of *B*. It is used twice elsewhere by Ovid (*Heroides* 5. 87, *Fasti* iv. 656), but among other poets only by Ausonius. Tibullus, Virgil, Silius, and Martial prefer 'faginus'.

   curva: probably the right reading, though only given as a variant in the thirteenth-century *Barberinianus*. The 1727 Variorum edition ad loc. notes a similar variant (not mentioned by modern editors) of 'duro' for the correct 'curvo' at *Amores* iii. 10. 14.

   clavo suspensus ab ansa: hung by a hook from its handle—a reversal of the expected order not unlike 421. Enk compared *Il.* xxiii. 852–4 ἱστὸν δ᾽ ἔστησεν νηὸς κυανοπρώροιο / τηλοῦ ἐπὶ ψαμάθοις, ἐκ δὲ τρήρωνα πέλειαν / λεπτῇ μηρίνθῳ δῆσεν ποδός, where ποδός corresponds to 'ab ansa', one being part of the dove, the other part of the basin.

656ᵃ, 656. Whether MSS. read 'impositus' or 'impositum' is a matter of small significance. M N, which give 655, clearly ought to read 'impositum' (as they did originally, according to Magnus). Other MSS. having 655ᵃ require 'impositus'. The later hand in M, after writing 652–655ᵃ in the margin, has crossed out 655, and apparently changed 'impositum' to 'impositus'.

sponda: the framework of the couch.

659. lecto non indignanda saligno: 'at which the willow couch could not grumble', a slight pleasantry.

661–3. For such tiny details cf. 643 n. Ovid tells us three times that the table was made level—a good example of poetic redundancy which is at the same time elegant.

664 ff. Callimachus clearly describes in great detail the meal which Hecale set before Theseus. We have just a few fragments, nos. 248–52, also 244 and perhaps others listed by Pfeiffer in his note to fr. 240. The same may have been true of Eratosthenes' *Erigone* (see fr. 34 P.).

So in this respect too the *Hecale* was a direct ancestor of Baucis and Philemon. But Ovid has not just taken over Callimachus' description. With the help of the Roman agricultural writers, we can see that the meal described here was one such as a poor man might eat in the Italian countryside, and not an artificial concoction transplanted from the *Hecale*. In one place where Ovid echoes Callimachus (665) he has changed the subject-matter, and the Athenian olive gives way to the cornel, which, as Columella says (xii. 10. 3), was used as an olive by the Romans. It is worth recalling that Ovid had a precedent for his account of an Italian peasant's meal in the *Satires* of Lucilius (123–32 W.), although there is no clear proof of Lucilian influence on our poet.

Special mention may be made of one element here—a certain amount of 'Golden Age' phraseology, although, unlike Silius' Falernus, this is not a Golden Age story. The simple diet is taken as a sign of a blessed life. Of course the people's day-to-day existence was really like this, but its glorification belonged mainly to poets and philosophers. We find traces of such an attitude as early as Hesiod, *Works and Days* 41: the unjust rulers do not know ὅσον ἐν μαλάχῃ τε καὶ ἀσφοδέλῳ μέγ' ὄνειαρ. The diet involved is usually vegetarian, noted as a virtue in Plato's account of the two cities (*Republic* ii. 372 c ff.). The original city eats no meat; only in the τρυφῶσα πόλις must a flesh diet be introduced (373 c). Likewise in the *Phaenomena* of Aratus men begin to eat animals only in the Age of Bronze (132).

Ovid's meal is not wholly vegetarian, including salted pork
(648). As we have seen, that gives a greater sense of reality to
the Italian context. But in Silius' parallel story Falernus serves
no meat: 'nulloque cruore / polluta castus mensa' (vii. 182–3,
perhaps borrowing a phrase from *Met.* xv. 98). A similar detail
appears in the meal of Brongus, εἰλαπίνην ἐλάχειαν ἀναιμάκτοιο τραπέζης
(Nonnus, *Dionysiaca* xvii. 62) which could go back to Calli-
machus' Molorchus (*Aetia*, bk. iii). But a likely introducer of
vegetarianism into stories of this kind was Eratosthenes, with
his Platonic affiliations. The importunate goat which gnawed the
vines in the *Erigone* was presumably the first to be eaten (cf. fr.
22 P., *Met.* xv. 114–15, Porphyrius, *De Abstinentia* ii. 10).

The Romans conveniently adapted many Greek ideas about
the Golden Age, with its simple life and food, to the past of their
own country. Ovid's 'omnia fictilibus' (668) is a commonplace
of contemporary poetry. A lesser Augustan, Grattius, even
makes the topic of simple food for hunting dogs a pretext to
denounce luxurious fare (*Cynegetica* 312 ff.), and culminates in
'at qualis nostris, quam simplex mensa Camillis, / qui tibi cultus
erat post tot, Serrane, triumphos!' (321–2). Only Ovid's treat-
ment of the theme is quite unpolitical—between our poet and
Grattius there lies a considerable gulf.

664. The olive was of course distinctively Athenian, and so appro-
priate to the *Hecale* (fr. 248, see 665 n.). None the less, olives
also formed an important part of the poor man's diet in Italy—
among items to be distributed to a landowner's retainers (Cato,
Agr. 58).

bicolor: green and black, i.e. picked when not yet wholly
ripe.

sincerae: doing double duty, first as a transferred epithet
meaning 'fresh', without admixture of salt (contrast the olives in
Call., fr. 248 below). At the same time Ovid at least glances at
the meaning 'virgin Pallas'.

665. corna: cf. André, *L'Alimentation et la cuisine à Rome*, p. 83. The
preserving of fruit in a liquid was very common (André, p. 90
gives examples); for cornels Columella (xii. 10. 3) recommends
a mixture of must and vinegar. The wording of this line is
modelled on *Hecale*, fr. 248 (with a little added by *P.Oxy.* 2529,
verso, l. 3):

> οἶσε ('she brought') δ' ἐλαι[ῶν ?
> γεργέριμον πίτυρίν τε καὶ ἣν ἀπεθήκατο λευκὴν
> εἰν ἁλὶ νήχεσθαι φθινοπωρίδα.

666. intiba: cf. *Georgics* i. 120 'et amaris intiba fibris', probably the
endive. This is a salad plant hardier than the lettuce, and so of
especial value in winter (André, p. 27).

radix: the radish too was considered very useful in winter-time, and cultivated in Italy since the time of Cato (*Agr.* 6), cf. André, p. 16.

lactis massa coacti: the cheese to which Polyphemus compares Galatea (xiii. 796), cf. Theocritus 11. 20 with Gow's note.

667. Compare Martial xi. 52. 9 (ova) 'tenui versata favilla'. Eggs usually, as here, formed part of the *gustatio* or entrée (cf. André, pp. 152–3). Hence the proverb 'ab ovo ad mala', i.e. 'from beginning to end', cf. Cicero, *ad Fam.* ix. 20. 1, Horace, *Sat.* i. 3. 6–7 with Porph. ad loc. So Ovid preserves the regular order of a Roman meal—we have the apples in 675.

668. omnia fictilibus: a commonplace of Augustan poetry, as, e.g., Tibullus i. 1. 37 ff. 'adsitis, divi, nec vos e paupere mensa / dona, nec e puris spernite fictilibus. / fictilia antiquus primus sibi fecit agrestis / pocula, de facili composuitque luto.' Compare *Fasti* i. 202 with context and v. 522; for the reality Pliny, *N.H.* xxxv. 157–8 and Frazer on *Fasti* i. 208.

668–9. caelatus eodem / ... argento crater: made of silver equally as much as the rest, i.e. not at all. Ovid is probably pointing a contrast with the luxury of his own day; a commentator on *h* has written ' "terra" "argento" dicit, reprehendens superfluita-tem temporum.' Cazzaniga (*La Parola del Passato* xviii [1963] 30–1) thinks that the contrast is not with Ovid's own times, but with Homer, where mixing-bowls may be silver (*Od.* x. 356–7). That is rather less likely.

Daniel Heinsius suggested 'eadem / ... argilla' which has very slight manuscript support, but probably through a copyist's failure to understand the joke. There is no real doubt as to the text.

caelatus, normally used of embossed metal work (e.g. 702, v. 189–90), is left in a somewhat anomalous position. That does not matter greatly (Housman compared Manilius v. 276), but the verb is found of wood-carving (*Ecl.* 3. 37), and the noun 'caelatura' of clay statues (Pliny, *N.H.* xxxv. 158).

669–70. fabricataque fago / pocula, qua cava sunt, flaventibus illita ceris: the cups are coated with wax on the inside to make them impermeable, cf. Theocritus 1. 27 κεκλυσμένον ἀδέι κηρῷ and Gow's note. Virgil (*Ecl.* 3. 36 ff.), while clearly following Theocritus, also has a beech-wood cup instead of the latter's ivy-wood. So too *Fasti* v. 522 (Hyrieus) and Silius vii. 188 (Falernus).

671–3. 'Just as wine was served (668 ff.) after the *gustatio*, so, having been removed for the *cena* proper, it is served again after it. This ... was not fresh wine, but the same as had been served before. Then came dessert, and for this the wine was not taken away, but only put a little on one side' (W. C. Summers).

672. nec longae = 'et non longae'.

referuntur: the same wine again—a token of the couple's poverty.

673. mensis . . . secundis: the dessert course, cf. Horace, *Sat.* ii. 2. 121-2.

674. Nuts were a regular part of the Roman dessert, as in Horace, *Sat.* ii. 2. 122.

carica: originally from the East, as the name (Carian) implies, but successfully introduced into Italy (André, p. 75). In its preserved form this was the cheapest of all types of fig (ibid., p. 88).

palmis: see André, p. 84.

676. Grapes were popular as a table-fruit (André, pp. 77–8). Here they are eaten fresh, as opposed to the dried 'pensilis uva' of Horace, *Sat.* ii. 2. 121 (cf. André, p. 91).

677. The honeycomb also appears in Silius (vii. 181).

678. nec iners pauperque: 'neither slack nor niggardly', the whole phrase negatived by 'nec'.

679 ff. This recognition scene is more satisfactory than the parallel one in *Fasti* v. 513–14 (Neptune speaking): 'quae simul exhausit "da nunc bibat ordine" dixit / "Iuppiter"; audito palluit ille Iove.' Bacchus gives proof of his divinity to Falernus in just the same manner as here (Silius vii. 187 ff.). Since this is a more appropriate way for a wine-god than for Zeus to announce himself, it seems possible that Silius did not take the idea merely from Ovid, but both poets from the *Erigone* of Eratosthenes (thus Merkelbach, following G. Procacci, *Riv. Fil.* xlii [1914] 441–8).

681. manibusque supinis: with palms turned upwards—the normal attitude of prayer in antiquity, and a natural one.

684 ff. unicus anser erat . . .: very likely Ovid remembers Molorchus' intended sacrifice in Call. *Aetia*, bk. iii. [Probus] on *Georgics* iii. 19 tells the story: 'Molorchus fuit Herculis hospes, apud quem is diversatus est cum proficisceretur ad leonem Nemeum necandum. qui cum immolaturus esset unicum arietem, quem habebat, . . . impetravit ab eo Hercules ut eum servaret . . .' (see further Pfeiffer on Call., fr. 54). Nonnus' Brongus-episode (*Dionysiaca* xvii. 37 ff.) is said to be based on the story of Molorchus: οἷα Κλεωναίοιο φατίζεται ἀμφὶ Μολόρχου / κεῖνα, τά περ σπεύδοντι λεοντοφόνους ἐς ἀγῶνας / ὥπλισεν Ἡρακλῆι (ibid. 52–4) and line 56 Βρόγγος, ἔχων μίμημα φιλοστόργοιο νομῆος. Nonnan imitation of Callimachus probably explains a remarkable similarity to Ovid (688 n.).

684. minimae custodia villae: Columella writes (viii. 13. 1) 'anser . . . sollertiorem custodiam praebet quam canis. nam clangore prodit insidiantem'—he quotes the famous incident when geese saved the Capitol from the Gauls. Cf. xi. 599 'canibusve sagacior anser'.

685. dis hospitibus: although the guests have not yet formally revealed their identity, the miracle of the mixing-bowl has been enough to prove them more than human; witness the couple's immediate reaction (681 ff.).

686–8. Their vain attempts to catch the goose make a contrast with the unhurried and dignified gods, and also prevent the narrative from becoming too elevated.

688. superi vetuere necari: so with Brongus (Nonnus xvii. 46–8): καὶ μίαν εἰροπόκων ὀίων ἀνελύσατο μάνδρης / ὄφρα κε δαιτρεύσειε θυηπολίην Διονύσῳ / ἀλλὰ θεὸς κατέρυκε. The startling resemblance to Ovid is probably caused by a common source in Callimachus (see on 684 ff.), although Nonnus may well have read Ovid (cf. on 36–7). Molorchus himself was told to put off the sacrifice for a month (Apollodorus ii. 5. 1), while Hyrieus' ox was altogether less fortunate (*Fasti* v. 516).

690–1. immunibus . . . / esse . . . dabitur: cf. 554–5.

692. ardua montis: see on 335 'ima lacunae'.

693–4. Here again the manuscripts split into two streams, cf. Enk in *Ovidiana*, p. 343.

A	B
693 ite simul!" parent ambo, baculisque levati	693ᵃ ite simul!" parent, et dis praeeuntibus ambo
	693ᵇ membra levant baculis, tardique senilibus annis
694 nituntur longo vestigia ponere clivo.	694 nituntur longo vestigia ponere clivo.

693 appears in M alone, but was also in the lost S; the original reading of N has been erased. 693ᵃ and 693ᵇ appear in the other MSS., and were added by later copyists in M N S.

One of the greatest Ovidians, Heinsius, joined battle with version *B*, calling it 'nugatoris commentum', but, sadly, his arguments were not very strong. He objected that 'tardique senilibus annis' is quite superfluous, since the age of the couple has been mentioned so often before (e.g. 631, 661, 686), while 'dis praeeuntibus' is redundant because Ovid has already told us of the gods' command and the obedience of Baucis and Philemon. But a poet is allowed to repeat details, and, as Enk rightly observes, 'dis praeeuntibus' adds to the vividness of the picture. Also, is not 'tardique senilibus annis' particularly relevant at this point? It describes the slowness and labour of their efforts to escape from the all-engulfing flood, as do 'nituntur' and 'longo' (694). They have been told to make for the heights (692). Yet, when still an arrow's flight from the summit (695), Baucis and Philemon look back, and already the whole district is sub-merged. So 'tardiquesenilibusannis' causesamomentofanxiety—will they in fact be quick enough?

It is not possible to reject 693 (version A) merely by supposing that 693^b fell out, because 693^a followed by 694 would make good sense, and there would be no motive for changing 'et dis praeeuntibus ambo' (693^a) into 'ambo, baculisque levati' (693). So again both versions may be genuine. One cannot confidently assert a cause for re-writing, but perhaps the poet felt that 'baculisque levati' was by itself a less happy phrase than 'pennisque levati' (ii. 59, cf. 212), and so needed amplification.

695–6. **quantum semel ire sagitta / missa potest**: a nice adaptation of the Homeric formula ὅσον τ᾽ ἐπὶ δουρὸς ἐρωή / γίγνεται (*Il.* xv. 358–9), the bow being humbler than the spear. Notice that Ovid's phrase is almost a metrical equivalent of Homer's (cf. 18 n.).

696–8. Out of the remarkable diversity of manuscript readings (see apparatus) Helm tried to construct an alternative scheme (B) as below; cf. Enk in *Ovidiana*, p. 345.

A	B
696 . . . flexere oculos, et mersa palude	696 . . . flexere oculos, et mersa palude
697 cetera prospiciunt, tantum sua tecta manere.	697^a mersa vident, quaeruntque suae pia culmina villae.
698 dumque ea mirantur, dum deflent fata suorum	698^a sola loco stabant. dum deflent fata suorum
699 illa vetus . . .	699 illa vetus . . .

The most crushing objections to B as it stands are the point-less repetition of 'mersa' (quite unlike, for example, 882–3), and the lack of any noun for 'mersa' to qualify. Vollgraff's 'cuncta' in 697^a would be an improvement, if such patching were deemed worth while.

K. Dursteler (*Die Doppelfassungen in Ovids Metamorphosen* [Hamburg, 1940], pp. 45 ff.) brought in two lines (696^a, 697^b) written by a later hand in the margin of e, following them with 698^a as in a *Codex Berolinensis* (called 698^b by Dursteler), and then 698. The result is:

696^a . . . flexere oculos, et inhospita tecta
697^b mersa vident, quaeruntque ubi sint pia culmina villae.
698^b sola loco stabat quae dis fuit hospita magnis.
698 dumque ea mirantur . . .

Apart from the extreme tenuity of manuscript evidence, this compilation hardly repays such effort. In particular we want

a word for *their* house in 697ᵇ—of course one could borrow from
697ᵃ 'suae' for 'ubi sint'. Rather less convincing to me is Enk's
contention that 'pia culmina villae' could not stand for 'culmina
piae villae'.

It seems very unlikely that anything genuine could lie behind
all these variants. Magnus may have been right in thinking that
the extra lines were concocted from marginal glosses, together
with a reminiscence of i. 295 'mersae culmina villae'. But this
fact does not weigh too heavily against other possible cases of
double recension. The standing of *B* in the manuscript tradition
seems rather different here (cf. Magnus quoted in the apparatus);
also there is no clear alternative version, only a mass of variants
from which we can try to construct one. The presence of
doublets elsewhere in this book may have encouraged later
copyists to try their own hand at composing.

699 ff. The cottage turns miraculously into a temple of the utmost
magnificence, described for all the world as if it were Augustus'
new temple of Palatine Apollo.

699. parva: 'small for its two owners'. Presumably the cottage
grows in size while being transformed. Burman's 'plena' would
produce an image too sharp and almost ridiculous.

700. furcas: the fork-shaped gable-supports of the house.

subiere: 'took their place below', an imaginative use of the verb.

701–2. Manuscripts, as quite frequently in the *Metamorphoses*,
interchange the second halves of these lines; one would expect
'aurataque', etc., to succeed 'flavescunt'. In a characteristically
vivid way (cf. 368–9) we follow the couple's eye, seeing first
details of the roof and house, then the doors, and finally the
surrounding area.

701. stramina flavescunt: thatch into gilt, a clever touch designed
for Ovid's Roman audience. In the seventies or sixties B.C.
Catulus gilded the tiles of the Capitoline temple—public reac-
tion to this was mixed (Pliny, *N.H.* xxxiii. 57). The Palatine
Apollo probably had a gilded roof too (Propertius ii. 31. 1).

videntur: 'are seen', to be understood also with 'caelataeque'
(702); supply 'est' with 'adopertaque'.

702. caelataeque fores: presumably of metal or ivory with relief
work. The doors of Palatine Apollo were decorated with ivory
reliefs showing the repulse of Brennus and his Gauls from
Delphi, and the deaths of the children of Niobe (Propertius ii.
31. 12–14).

703. talia tum placido Saturnius edidit ore: a line with some of the
slow-moving dignity of early Latin epic. Both 'Saturnius' (cf.
Κρονίδης and Κρονίων) and 'edidit ore' have Ennian affiliations,
so that Norden (*Aen.* vi, p. 374) was right to speak of 'Ennian
colouring'.

704 ff. Several details in the next few lines reflect pictures of ideal married life on Italian epitaphs.

704–5. iuste senex et femina coniuge iusto / digna: equal merit on both sides is often stressed, e.g. Warmington, *Remains of Old Latin*, vol. iv, Epitaph no. 53 (*C.I.L.* i. 2. 1221, circa 80 B.C. or later) 'fido fida viro veixsit'; cf. R. Lattimore, *Themes in Greek and Latin Epitaphs*, p. 277.

707. esse sacerdotes: worth mentioning is an Attic theoxeny of Dionysus, which ends with the host's daughters becoming priestesses (Steph. Byz., s.v. Σημαχίδαι). Of this no poetic treatment is known.

708. concordes egimus annos: cf. Warmington, op. cit., no. 110. 5–6 (*C.I.L.* i. 2. 1732, c. 45 B.C. ?): 'coniuge sum Cadmo fructa Scrateio [an incomplete hexameter] / concordesque pari viximus ingenio', also Lattimore, p. 279.

709. auferat hora duos eadem: as Propertius predicts for himself and Cynthia (ii. 20. 18) 'ambos una fides auferet, una dies', cf. Horace, *Odes* ii. 17. 8–9.

711. templi tutela fuere: the office of Baucis and Philemon seems to be that of *aeditui, νεωκόροι*, whose duties included looking after the building, and instructing visitors on the history and ritual of the cult (713, cf. Headlam on Herodas 4. 41)—or were they just reminiscing about the old days to each other, like Cadmus and Harmonia (iv. 569–70) ?

712. donec vita data est: cf. Warmington, no. 65. 4 (*C.I.L.* i. 2. 1223) 'vixi dum licuit superis acceptior unus', Lattimore, p. 273 'qui, dum vita datast . . .' (*Carmina Latina Epigraphica* 1106. 1).

714 ff. This metamorphosis fulfils the second part of their wish (709–10). Gradual transformation, described in clinical detail, is a regular feature of our poem (see Introduction, pp. xx–xxi). Sixty years before, Lucretius was quite familiar with scenes like the present one; cf. *De Rerum Natura* ii. 702–3 (an impossibility) '. . . et altos / interdum ramos egigni corpore vivo'.

717. dum licuit: interrupting the action at a moment when Baucis and Philemon have partly turned into trees, but their mouths are still free to talk; cf. ix. 369–70.

719–20. To end a story by mentioning some local landmark or custom still observed by the ἐπιχώριοι (cf. 720 'incola') seems to have been a regular practice in Nicander's *Heteroeumena*, to judge from the paraphrases of Antoninus Liberalis; e.g. no. 26 Ὕλᾳ δὲ θύουσιν ἄχρι νῦν παρὰ τὴν κρήνην οἱ ἐπιχώριοι, no. 30 καλεῖται δὲ καὶ τὸ ῥέον ἐκ τῆς πέτρας ἐκείνης ἄχρι νῦν παρὰ τοῖς ἐπιχωρίοις δάκρυον Βυβλίδος. A certain instance of the transference of this motif from Nicander to Ovid was noted by Haupt on ii. 706.

A very similar transformation to the present one is given from Nicander by Ant. Lib. 31: καὶ οἱ παῖδες, ἵναπερ ἑστήκεσαν παρὰ τὸ ἱερὸν

τῶν νυμφῶν, ἐγένοντο δένδρη. καὶ ἔτι νῦν ἀκούεται φωνὴ ... These points
somewhat favour Nicander as an immediate source for Ovid's
Baucis and Philemon.

719. Thyneius: the reading clearly indicated by the best manu-
scripts. Older editors were sceptical—what has Bithynia to do
with Phrygia? But the text was restored by Ehwald, and rightly
defended by Malten (*Hermes* 1939, p. 178). Strabo (xii. 571)
explains that the name 'Phrygia' was applied both to Greater
Phrygia ruled over by Midas, that is southern Asia Minor
centring round Apamea–Celaenae, and to Lesser Phrygia which
stretched as far north as the Hellespont. The latter is relevant
here; Catullus conversely speaks of his Bithynian sojourn as in
the 'Phrygii ... campi' (46. 4). This ethnic is clearly damaging
to the contention of Calder and others that Ovid *consciously*
describes the region of Lake Trogitis, near Lystra (see introduc-
tion to the episode).

Other readings worth mentioning are 'Tyaneius', from Tyana
in Cappadocia (ς, accepted by early editors), and 'Tyrieius' (Polle)
favoured by Ramsay and Calder, from Tyriaeum, north and
slightly west of Iconium. But almost every city and river in
Phrygia (as well as some elsewhere) can boast its supporters.

**720–1. hoc mihi non vani ... / narravere senes ; equidem pendentia
vidi ... :** according to Calder (loc. cit.) 'it would be a blind critic
who would miss the significance of this feature in the story'; he
calls such a method of collecting information one of the most
characteristically Anatolian touches of all. But the formula was
a time-honoured one in classical literature. Its spiritual father
deserves to be Herodotus: μέχρι μὲν 'Ελεφαντίνης πόλιος αὐτόπτης
ἐλθών, τὸ δ' ἀπὸ τούτου ἀκοῇ ἤδη ἱστορέων (ii. 29). Thus Callimachus,
fr. 384. 47–8 τοῦτο μὲν ἐξ ἄλλων ἔκλυον ἱρὸν ἐγώ, / κεῖνό γε μὴν ἴδον αὐτός
... Lucian parodies pleasantly: γράφω τοίνυν περὶ ὦν μήτε εἶδον ...
μήτε παρ' ἄλλων ἐπυθόμην (*Vera Historia* i. 4).

724. cura deum di sint, et qui coluere colantur: strict parallelism
between the halves would require 'cura' to be active in sense (as
Heroides 1. 104 of Eumaeus 'cura fidelis harae'), and so Planudes
understood the line. But this story illustrates 619 'quidquid
superi voluere, peractum est', and therefore the meaning must
be that the gods can make divine those whom they love; cf.
Aen. iii. 476 'cura deum', *Amores* iii. 9. 17 'at sacri vates et
divum cura vocamur.' Heinsius emended neatly but unneces-
sarily to 'cura pii dis sunt'.

It should be remembered that Hecale too received honours
after her death (Call., fr. 264, cf. Petronius, ch. 135 'digna sacris
Hecale'). In Seneca's *Apocolocyntosis* (ch. 9) Diespiter is made
to say 'censeo ut Divus Claudius ex hac die deus sit ... eamque
rem ad Metamorphosis Ovidi adiciendam.' No doubt Seneca

was thinking primarily of Romulus (xiv. 816 ff.) and Caesar (xv. 746).

725–37. The river-god Achelous takes over the narrative from Lelex. A brief mention of Proteus serves to introduce the story of Mestra, daughter of Erysicthon; both of these could assume various different forms at will. Since the same is true of Achelous himself (880), Ovid has already ensured a smooth transition to the next story but one, in which the river-god will speak of his own experiences.

725. cunctos: even Pirithous is impressed (contrast 612 ff.).

727. innixus cubito: quite probably Ovid has in mind some colossal statue of a river-god reclining on one elbow—the usual posture.

729. renovamine: nouns in *-men* were favoured by Lucretius (see Bailey's edition, vol. i, pp. 134–5), and no doubt that was Ovid's precedent. But, besides words used by Lucretius (e.g. 'conamen' 366), our poet seems to have formed an astonishing number of new ones, viz. 'caelamen', 'curvamen' (194), 'firmamen', 'irritamen', 'moderamen', 'oblectamen', 'piamen', purgamen', 'renovamen', 're-'spiramen', 'simulamen', 'tentamen'. The vast majority of these words occur only in the *Metamorphoses*; 'piamen' alone appears elsewhere (*Fasti*) and not in the *Metamorphoses* at all. So clearly Ovid meant these forms to give his hexameter poem a distinct flavour.

731 ff. ut tibi . . . Proteu . . . : the apostrophe was a neoteric mannerism, equally common in the Greek and the Roman poets; for an early Latin example cf. Cicero, *Aratea*, fr. 37. 1–3 Buescu, where Cicero addresses the frogs although Aratus had not done so. But here the apostrophe seems pretentious and so half-comic—in keeping with Achelous' character.

731. complexi terram: equivalent to the Homeric γαιήοχος.

732–7. For the transformations of Proteus cf. *Od.* iv. 456 ff. πρώτιστα λέων γένετ' ἠυγένειος, / αὐτὰρ ἔπειτα δράκων, καὶ πάρδαλις ἠδὲ μέγας σῦς, / γίγνετο δ' ὑγρὸν ὕδωρ, καὶ δένδρεον ὑψιπέτηλον, also Virgil, *Georgics* iv. 409 ff. Proteus was a regular example of one who could assume many shapes, e.g. Euphorion, fr. 64 Powell (Periclymenus) ὅς ῥά τε πᾶσιν ἔικτο, θαλάσσιος ἠύτε Πρωτεύς.

732. videre: this unattached third plural, 'people saw you', is common enough, cf. Shackleton Bailey on Propertius ii. 6. 1.

737. interduin undis: The elision of more than a short vowel (e.g. 725) over the caesura is rare in the *Metamorphoses*.

738–878. *Erysicthon and his daughter Mestra*

This is primarily a Thessalian story with, as we shall see, strong Coan connections. Our earliest authority for it lies in pseudo-Hesiod; recently-published fragments of the *Catalogue of Women* tell much about Mestra. We hear how Poseidon took her to Cos, where she bore him a son, Eurypylus, later to become king of the island (fr. 43a. 55 ff. Merkelbach–West, cf. Ovid, line 851); also how her father was afflicted with insatiable hunger (fr. 43a. 5 ff.). Most important of all, Mestra already has her powers of transformation (fr. 43a. 31–3, cf. the testimonium of Philodemus given by M.–W. as fr. 43c). She is sold as in Ovid, though as a prospective wife and not a slave, then escapes by changing shape, and returns home, resuming her normal form (cf. West, *Gnomon* xxxv [1963] 754, Ovid 869 ff.). Other witnesses to the same tradition are the scholia on Lycophron, *Alexandra* 1393, and perhaps the rationalizing account of Palaephatus (*De Incredibilibus* 23, see 873 n.); cf. J. Schwartz, *Pseudo-Hesiodeia* (Leiden, Brill, 1960), pp. 265 ff., K. J. McKay, 'Erysichthon, a Callimachean Comedy', *Mnemosyne*, Supplementum Septimum (1962), pp. 19–33. The story thus revealed closely resembles that of Ovid. Only the motive for Mestra's sale differs (see above); also the Hesiodic chronology is not quite clear, and perhaps less neat than Ovid's (see 851 n.). Whether 'Hesiod' mentioned the marriage of Mestra to Autolycus (Ovid 738) remains uncertain because of the fragmentary condition of his text. McKay (op. cit., p. 44) expresses a common view when he writes 'there is no chance that Ovid draws directly on pseudo-Hesiod.' But the Hesiodic *Catalogue* contained much useful material for Ovid, and was written in an attractively direct and simple style. It seems quite probable to me that our poet draws on the *Catalogue* both here and elsewhere in the *Metamorphoses*; if he has read Boeus and Nicander, why not pseudo-Hesiod?

In the *Catalogue* Erysichthon himself is called 'Aethon' (fr. 43a. 5). Whether or not the latter started as an independent character (thus McKay, pp. 8 ff.), already in pseudo-Hesiod Aethon is a nick-name (ἐπώνυμον εἵνεκα λιμοῦ, fr. 43a. 5) which Erysicthon bears for his 'burning' hunger (αἴθων λιμός). Lycophron typically used Aethon as a recherché synonym for Erysicthon (*Alexandra* 1396), and Nicander may have done so too in the *Heteroeumena* (Ant. Lib. 17. 5, cf. McKay, pp. 28–9, and below). From the surviving Hesiodic fragments we cannot learn the cause of Erysicthon's hunger. The same is true of Hellanicus, who mentioned the story in the first book of his *Deucalioneia* (Athenaeus x. 416 b): Ἑλλάνικος . . . Ἐρυσίχθονά φησι τὸν Μυρμιδόνος, ὅτι ἦν ἄπληστος βορᾶς, Αἴθωνα κληθῆναι. In Callimachus (*hymn* 6), as in Ovid, Demeter condemns Erysicthon to perpetual hunger because he cut down trees in a grove sacred to her. But Lycophron (*Alexandra* 1396) implies that he violated the plough-land of the goddess, and this version may be as old as or older than ours (McKay, pp. 15–19).

Just as Ovid seems mainly to follow 'Hesiod' when describing Mestra's share in the action, so for his account of Erysichthon he is clearly indebted to Callimachus' *Hymn to Demeter*. Direct imitation occurs in at least three places (746, 835–6, 843); Ovid's account of the attack on the grove and the hunger of Erysicthon follows his predecessor quite closely. But the two versions disagree in many points, not all of them so trivial as, for instance, what exact species of tree was cut down. Callimachus leaves Erysicthon begging for food at the cross-roads, a social disgrace to his parents; Ovid follows the prince right down to his death by autophagy, and the *Etymologicum Magnum*, s.v. αἴθων suggests that he had a Greek precedent for this: . . . αἴθωνα λιμόν, τὸν μέγαν ἢ ἑαυτὸν φονεύοντα. Callimachus treats Erysicthon as a spoilt child; Ovid makes him a fully-fledged villain in his own right, with a grown-up daughter.

It would be helpful to discover further detailed treatments of this legend which Ovid might have used. And the words of Antoninus Liberalis (17. 5) in a chapter taken from Nicander look promising: Ὑπερμήστραν πιπρασκομένην ἐπὶ γυναικὶ μὲν ἄρασθαι τῖμον, ἄνδρα δὲ γενομένην Αἴθωνι τροφὴν ἀποφέρειν τῷ πατρί; a temporary change of sex also appears in Ovid (853–4). But Ant. Lib. has just a brief mention of this story together with three parallel ones, and the only reasonable conclusion is that Nicander too merely alluded to the transformation of Mestra or Hypermestra when telling of Leucippus (cf. McKay, pp. 28–9).

But here further possible evidence comes from a very unexpected quarter. At the end of the last century, an old woman of Asphendiou on the island of Cos told to Jacob Zarraftis a folk-story (Appendix III) which she herself called 'Myrmidonia and Pharaonia'. R M. Dawkins, who published it (*Forty-five Stories from the Dodekanese* [Cambridge, 1950], pp. 334 ff.), suggested as an alternative title 'The Fairy's Revenge'. 'Pharaonia' is obviously just a wonderland name, but, as McKay points out (p. 35), 'Myrmidonia' could be significant because the Erysicthon legend derives from Thessaly, and in Hellanicus (see above) Erysicthon's father is even called Myrmidon.

The early parts of this story have little relevance for us. The king of Myrmidonia falls in love with a beautiful girl called Dimitroula. But she will have none of him, because she already loves a ploughman. So the king challenges the latter to fight with one of his servants in a wood. Dimitroula herself hides in a hollow oak-tree to watch the contest; the king is there too, but in the course of the fight he falls down an old well, and dies. Finally the ploughman is killed, and so are all but one of the king's servants. This only survivor takes the news to the king's son, who swears in his rage to cut down the grove, believing that the wood-spirits have caused his father's death.

From the arrival of the prince, the resemblance between the folk-tale and Ovid's Erysicthon is quite startling. In both the prince arrogantly urges on his servants to cut down an oak; in

both there is hesitation on the part of one. Blood flows, the oak
groans, and there is a dying curse, in the folk-tale uttered by
Dimitroula still hiding inside the tree-trunk, in Ovid by the
Dryad. Then follows a dream whereby the prince is given a fore-
taste of his future punishment. In both accounts he is attacked by
Hunger, personified as a hideous old woman; the two descriptions
are very close to each other. After vain attempts to satisfy his
appetite have been exhausted, the poor man adopts the same final
resource—attempted sale of his children. At the last, he turns to
autophagy, and that is the end of him.

Direct survivals of stories from antiquity are said to be very
rare. But scholars expert in this field have hailed 'The Fairy's
Revenge' as such (see McKay, p. 35), and in that case Ovid might
have known it through the mediation of some local chronicler. It is
particularly interesting that the tale should have been found on
Cos, while being otherwise unrecorded (Dawkins, p. 348), for in
pseudo-Hesiod (fr. 43a. 57–8 M.–W.) Mestra bore Eurypylus on Cos.
We know several other links between the mythology of Thessaly
and Cos (see W. R. Paton and E. L. Hicks, *The Inscriptions of Cos*,
pp. xiv–xv and 344–8); also near-by Cnidus was connected with
the family of Erysicthon (Call. *hymn* 6. 24, cf. Theocritus 17. 68).
Dawkins points out that Cos has been continuously inhabited by
Greeks since antiquity, and preserved from any great shift of
population, so that an ancient story might hope to survive on
Cos, if anywhere.

We can find elements of the Ovid–Fairy's Revenge version else-
where in the ancient tradition. That should not surprise; whether
the folk-tale is older than Ovid or not, our poet hardly invented
details like the autophagy of Erysicthon (cf. the *Etymologicum
Magnum* quoted above), which are not in Callimachus. The only
sure proof of the folk-tale's antiquity would be to demonstrate
elements of the folk-tale which do appear in the ancient tradition of
Erysicthon, but not in Ovid, since a double literary contact can
hardly be imagined (Dawkins, p. 348). Dawkins himself held that
the folk-tale had details from both Ovid and Callimachus, but
only two parallels between Callimachus and the Fairy's Revenge
seem at all cogent. First (D., p. 348), when the prince tries to
strike Dimitroula within the tree-trunk, his sword sticks and
remains there; similarly in Callimachus the servants flee ἐνὶ δρυσὶ
χαλκὸν ἀφέντες (*hymn* 6. 60)—for the importance of this point see
McKay, p. 53. Secondly (M., ibid.), when Hunger in the folk-tale
'raises herself to her full height and becomes three times as tall and
three as big', she recalls Demeter revealing her true nature in
Callimachus: Δαμάτηρ δ᾽ ἄφατόν τι κοτέσσατο, γείνατο δ᾽ ἁ θεύς· / ἴθματα
μὲν χέρσω, κεφαλὰ δέ οἱ ἅψατ᾽ Ὀλύμπω (*hymn* 6. 57–8).

If we accept that the folk-tale can have influenced Ovid, it

follows that some typically Ovidian details may not have been his
own invention, but may have come to him ready-made (McKay,
p. 58). This applies particularly to the personification of Hunger
(801 ff.), which is characteristic of our poet, and has a well-defined
literary history (see ad loc.). Yet such ideas also occur in folk-tale,
cf. K. Chrysanthis, 'The Personification of Plague and Cholera
according to the Cypriots', *Folk-Lore* lvi (1945) 259–66, quoted by
Dawkins. Ovid's own scope for invention is thus diminished, but
we should worry less about what details Ovid has invented than
about his reason for choosing the story, and his treatment of it as
a whole.

There is an alternative to believing this folk-tale a survival from
antiquity. E. J. Kenney (*Mnemosyne* xvi. 1 [1963] 57) suggests
that it might be derived from the Greek translation of Ovid by
Maximus Planudes, a Byzantine monk and diplomat born in the
second half of the thirteenth century (cf. Palmer's *Heroides*, Intro-
duction, pp. xlvi ff.). The idea is ingenious and certainly credible.
It may seem unlikely that this story should have survived for two
thousand years by oral tradition, and still be so close to a literary
account in matters of detail. Derivation from a fixed literary
source and a shorter period in the oral tradition would more easily
explain the folk-tale's striking resemblance to our version. So
Kenney's suggestion may be right. But the credentials of the
Fairy's Revenge remain impressive. Even if we discount the pos-
sible contacts with non-Ovidian ancient tradition, it would be
a remarkable coincidence that this particular tale should be found
on Cos, of all places. On balance it seems rather more plausible to
accept the folk-tale's antiquity.

Ovid's Treatment

Quite in contrast to Baucis and Philemon, Ovid's Erysicthon is
written in the high epic style. Such a simile as the Bull before the
Altar (761–3) would be instantly recognized as belonging to the
most elevated type of poetry. Another standard epic situation is
when a great tree falls headlong (774–6), usually appearing as
a simile, here in the main stream of the narrative. The highly-
coloured personification first of the spirits of barrenness, then of
Hunger herself (801 ff.), recall seventh-century Greek epic, but are
considerably expanded by Ovid. Above all, there are many
reminiscences of Virgil. The impious Erysicthon, despiser of the
gods (739–40), is a type of Mezentius in the *Aeneid*; his daughter
Mestra, deserving only to have a better father (847), corresponds
to Mezentius' noble son Lausus. Erysicthon's attack upon the
sacred oak of Demeter is described in language reminding us of
Laocoon hurling his spear at the Wooden Horse.

There is much exaggeration and overdrawing in these passages,

as the poet no doubt intended. Erysichthon's sole motive force is
a dominating impiety, and Ovid's lack of realism contrasts with
the delicate social comedy in Callimachus. Some typical pieces of
cleverness (e.g. 785–6, 811–12, 841–2) go oddly with the high epic
style. Yet this is not simply an 'absurd pastiche of Virgil' (Brooks
Otis, *Ovid as an Epic Poet*, p. 68). Such exaggeration, particularly
in the portrayal of Erysichthon, goes back in spirit to an earlier
Latin writer, the tragedian Lucius Accius. Accius specialized in
princes of extraordinary wickedness and arrogance—Atreus, Thyes-
tes, Tereus; the famous 'oderint dum metuant' (*Atreus* 168 W.) is
typical. Ovid was struck by Accius' rhetorical fervour ('animosique
Accius oris', *Am.* i. 15. 19), but equally by the ferocity of his
characters (*Tristia* ii. 359, if one could judge a poet's nature from
his work 'Accius esset atrox'). Of course a literary treatment cannot
escape criticism just because it belongs to a tradition; as a whole
the influence of Accius on our poet was scarcely happy (see further,
Introduction, p. xxviii). But at least in the picture of Erysichthon,
Ovid was not merely producing an overblown version of Virgil.
His combination of ferocity with flippancy, of verbal cleverness
with high epic technique, leaves a final impression which is quite
un-Virgilian.

A special mention must be made of the Mestra-passage (848 ff.),
which has an utterly different atmosphere. The girl is changed into
the shape of a fisherman to avoid capture, and her late owner
arrives to find footprints in the sand leading nowhere, and the
only human being in sight one man intent upon his fishing. The
resulting conversation, conducted with admirable courtesy on
both sides, is delightful, and shows Ovid at his very best.

738. Autolyci coniunx, Erysicthone nata: Mestra is never actually
named; this periphrastic method of description is regular in epic
poetry (cf. 317).

Autolycus (xi. 313 ff.) was a son of Hermes, and himself a
remarkably tricky character; his father gave him the power
ὥστε τοὺς ἀνθρώπους ὅτε κλέπτοι τι λανθάνειν, καὶ τὰ θρέμματα τῆς λείας
ἀλλοιοῦν εἰς ὃ θέλοι μορφῆς (Scholiast on *Od.* xix. 432). His mar-
riage to Mestra, mentioned by no other extant authority—new
Hesiodic fragments might help—is best thought of as subse-
quent to the death of Erysicthon (see next note).

739. habet: a true present. Mestra should certainly still be alive at
the time of narration; her father is dead (cf. 'erat'), and she has
settled down to respectable matrimony and a single shape. In
his prologue to the *Metamorphoses* (i. 3–4) the poet sets himself
to writing a 'perpetuum carmen' from the beginning of the world
to his own time. So quite often, with small touches like this, he
brings stories into chronological relationship with one another,

or reminds his readers of the passage of time since an earlier
situation (cf. on 622–3). Of course Ovid also has chronological
difficulties because of varying traditions in many myths and the
need to link his stories.

739–40. Erysicthon's impiety is repeatedly stressed (761, 765–70,
792, 817). He is the counterpart of Mezentius 'contemptor
divum' (*Aen.* vii. 648, viii. 7), as Mestra (847) is of Lausus
'dignus patriis qui laetior esset / imperiis, et cui pater haud
Mezentius esset' (*Aen.* vii. 653–4).

740. adoleret: literally 'to magnify' ('votis ac supplicationibus
numen auctius facere', Nonius Marcellus); by a transferred
usage, the verb applies to the offering made to a god, and carries
the meaning 'to burn'.

    odores: preferable to 'honores' (perhaps from *Aeneid* iii. 547).
The former is the *difficilior lectio*, and Virgil's 'verbenasque adole
pinguis et mascula tura' (*Ecl.* 8. 65) shows that 'adolere' could be
followed by such a word as 'odores'. For the MSS. variation cf.
also [Virgil], *Ciris* 439.

**741–2. Cereale nemus violasse securi / . . . et lucos ferro temerasse
vetustos:** the second clause adds only one detail, that the grove
was ancient. Ovid keeps such Virgilian repetition (see on 343–4)
for his most epic passages.

    Of the gross impiety of this invasion one can not doubt; cf.
Horace, *Epist.* i. 6. 31–2 'virtutem verba putas, et / lucum ligna
. . .'. When P. Turullius was murdered on Cos by order of
Augustus (Dio li. 8), the general opinion was that he had brought
it on himself by cutting down the grove of Asclepius for building
boats. We have an old Roman inscription from the middle or
late third century B.C. which forbids the cutting down of trees
in a grove (*I.L.S.* 4911, Warmington, *Remains of Old Latin* iv.
154); see also Frazer on *Fasti* iv. 751.

743. Cf. *Aen.* iv. 441 'annoso validam . . . robore quercum'.
Ovid's oak is also in the Fairy's Revenge; Callimachus (*hymn* 6.
37) has a poplar.

744. una nemus: 'by itself a grove'. This neat, epigrammatic
phrase was imitated, more diffusely, by Silius (v. 482–3) of an
aesculus 'instar, aperto / si staret campo, nemoris', and perhaps
even by Pliny, *N.H.* xvi. 242 (ilex) 'silvamque sola faciens'.

    vittae: (στέμματα), properly made of wool, symbolize the gods'
binding power, and show the sanctity of the place (Dodds on
Euripides, *Bacchae* 350, cf. Headlam on Herodas 8. 11). They
were used, for example, at the re-dedication of the Capitoline
temple under Vespasian (Tacitus, *Histories* iv. 53).

    tabellae: tablets placed in the shrine of a god, recording
a granted prayer or discharged vow, especially after escape from
illness (Tibullus i. 3. 27–8) or shipwreck (Cicero, *D.N.D.* iii. 89).

They often carried a painted representation of the god's benefit, and were really hung up on trees in the grove of Diana at Aricia (*Fasti* iii. 268), of which Ovid may be thinking. See further Headlam on Herodas 4. 19, and Mayor on Juvenal 10. 55.

745. voti argumenta potentum: 'proofs of men who had gained their desire', with 'voti' as an objective genitive, cf. 80, 409 with n., *Fasti* iii. 269. I print Heinsius's conjecture, which accords with Ovidian usage, and produces a more forceful sense than 'voti … potentis', 'a powerful prayer'. One might retain 'potentis', but the emendation is undeniably an improvement.

746. Ovid follows Callimachus (*hymn* 6. 38) τῷ ἔπι ταὶ νύμφαι ποτὶ τῶνδιον ἐψιόωντο.

748. The 'ell' may here be reckoned as about eighteen inches, from elbow to finger-tip, so that the oak would have a circumference of some twenty-two and a half feet.

749–50. nec non et cetera tantum / silva sub hac, silva quantum fuit herba sub omni: Magnus printed in 750 'silva sub hac omnis, quantum fuit herba sub omni'. In spite of the manuscripts' favour, that leaves 'silva' overburdened with both 'cetera' and 'omnis', while 'omni' at the end of the line hangs uneasily. The text, a conjecture of Heinsius adopted by most editors, is very much crisper and more Ovidian. Confusion perhaps arose because scribes punctuated mentally after 'silvā' instead of after 'hac', and, being left with nonsense, tried to emend.

The interlocking word-order gives both chiasmus, 'silva … hac, silvā … herba' and a balancing structure 'silva sub hac … herba sub omni'. Ovid perhaps echoes Hesiod, *Theogony* 720, where Tartarus is τόσσον ἔνερθ᾽ ὑπὸ γῆς, ὅσον οὐρανός ἐστ᾽ ἀπὸ γαίης; cf. *Aen*. iv. 445–6 for a similar idea applied to a tree.

749. nec non et: strictly a near solecism, this phrase occurred in Varro. Virgil made it poetically respectable.

751. Dryopeius: 'the Thessalian', a recherché synonym. We have 'Thessalus' in 768, 'Haemoniam' in 813, and Ovid likes to vary his geographical names (cf. 40 n.). Pliny writes (*N.H.* iv. 28) 'sequitur mutatis saepe nominibus Haemonia, eadem Pelasgis et Pelasgicon Argos, Hellas, eadem Thessalia et *Dryopis*, semper a regibus cognominata.' The epithet also has a special significance at this point in the story, describing the climax of Erysichthon's sacrilege, since the Dryopes were themselves a byword for violent and barbarous behaviour (e.g. Ap. Rh. i. 1219 and scholia).

Modern editors have printed 'Triopeius', 'son of Triopas', which seems to have no better authority than one minor MS. and a late correction in U. This may possibly be right, but the MSS., with a rare degree of unanimity for a proper name, point to 'Dryopeius'; similarly at 872.

753–4. Take together 'ab uno . . . rapta . . . securi'. Again we have interwoven word-order, typical of the poet; for similar but not quite identical patterns cf. J. Marouzeau in *Ovidiana*,   -5. At *Aen.* vii. 510 'rapta . . . securi' occupies the same position in the line.

755–6. Cf. the blasphemy of Ancaeus (394–5). Erysicthon's words are nearer to the truth than he realizes.

757–8. The description is reminiscent of Laocoon's attack upon the Wooden Horse (*Aen.* ii. 50–3): 'sic fatus, validis i   viri- bus hastam / in latus inque feri curvam compagibus alvum / contorsit; stetit illa tremens, uteroque recusso / insonuere cavae gemitumque dedere cavernae.'

758 ff. There follow two portents of increasing menace (758–60, 761–3). Only after Erysicthon disregards these is he cursed (771–3).

758. Deoia: Vivianus s secure correction of the chaotic manuscript readings, from Δηώ a by-form of Demeter, first at Homeric Hymn, *Dem.* 47.

760. Wholly spondaic lines are rare enough in the *Metamorphoses* to provoke attention; in the present case Ovid is clearly aiming at a weighty effect.

   longi pallorem ducere rami: cf. iii. 484–5 'ut variis solet uva racemis / ducere purpureum nondum matura colorem', also Virgil, *Ecl.* 9. 49. Here at least the verb may be more pictorial than just = 'to take on'; paleness extends the whole length of the branches (cf. 881 n.).

761–2. haud aliter . . . / quam: a consciously epic way to introduce the simile, as, for example *Aen.* iv. 669 'non aliter   cf. 'haud (non) secus'.

762. discusso cortice sanguis: of the bewildering number   er- mutations which the MSS. offer, this balances best with 'abr. ta cruor e cervice' (764). But also possible is 'discussus sanguine cortex', approved by Heinsius from his *Quartus Mediceus* and conjectured independently by Magnus, which would harmonize with Ovid's use of 'fluo' at ix. 57.

763–4. ingens ubi victima taurus / concidit: cf. *Georgics* ii. 146–7 'et maxima taurus / victima'. Here, however, I would take 'ingens' with 'taurus' (as at *Aen.* ii. 202), 'victima' being in apposition. We thus have a rare departure from the usual Ovidian word-pattern discussed on 226. Compare, with the phrase in apposition enclosing, xiv. 833 'praecipuum, matrona, decus', which corre-sponds to the Virgilian order 'ignavum, fucos, pecus' (*Georgics* iv. 168).

   The bull before the altar was a favourite epic simile, cf. *Il.* xx. 403–5, *Aen.* ii. 223–4.

765. obstipuere omnes, aliquisque . . . : -*ēre*+(e.g.) *omnes,*+-*que* is

a Virgilian pattern, e.g. *Aen.* ii. 1 'conticuere omnes, intentique ora tenebant'.

Hesitation on the part of one of the prince's servants also occurs in the Fairy's Revenge: 'one alone hesitated, for the blood was running in front of him.' There it is Dimitroula, hiding in the hollow tree-trunk, who is being wounded.

767. aspicit hunc: as Erysicthon glares at the disguised Demeter, τὰν δ' ἄρ' ὑποβλέψας χαλεπώτερον ἠὲ κυναγὸν /ὤρεσιν ἐν Τμαρίοισιν ὑποβλέπει ἄνδρα λέαινα (Call. *hymn* 6. 50–1).

770. The correct reading is not quite clear. 'Redditus' may be marginally more attractive than 'editus'. Many editors print 'redditus et medio sonus est de robore'. 'Et' can often mean 'and then' (e.g. 'dixit et'); here, however, there have been four -*que*s since 767, so that the 'et' would lose all power. Appropriate might seem 'redditus at . . . de robore', but Ovid apparently does not postpone 'at'.

771. The ancients were uncertain as to the exact relationship between nymphs and trees. Did the two have equal life-span (H.H., *Aphrodite* 257–72, cf. Call. *hymn* 4. 82–3) Were the nymphs enclosed within the tree-trunk, or confi to the neighbourhood (cf. McKay, pp. 86–7)? Or did they ely take a warm personal interest in the fortunes of their e (Call. *hymn* 4. 84–5)? A similar story to ours is told by bllonius Rhodius (ii. 476 ff.) of the father of Peraebius:

> ὁ γὰρ οἶος ἐν οὔρεσι δένδρεα τέμνων
> δή ποθ' ἁμαδρυάδος νύμφης ἀθέριξε λιτάων,
> ἥ μιν ὀδυρομένη ἀδινῷ μειλίσσετο μύθῳ
> μὴ ταμέειν πρέμνον δρυὸς ἥλικος, ᾗ ἔπι πουλὺν
> αἰῶνα τρίβεσκε διηνεκές, αὐτὰρ ὁ τήνγε
> ἀφραδέως ἔτμηξεν ἀγηνορίῃ νεότητος.
> τῷ δ' ἄρα νηκερδῆ νύμφη πόρεν οἶτον ὀπίσσω
> αὐτῷ καὶ τεκέεσσιν.

772. Augustan poets generally avoided such an -*orum* . . . -*orum* rhyme. Possibly Ovid thought it fitting here to a prophetic curse, as to a magic spell at Theocritus 2. 21, 62, and Virgil, *Ecl.* 8. 80. Dimitroula, dying in the tree-trunk, curses the prince with 'Even as God punished your wicked father, even so and three times worse will He punish you.'

773. solacia: almost in the jurists' technical sense of 'compensation'.

775–6. The description of a great tree being felled, here occurring directly in the narrative, was a time-honoured simile in epic poetry. Compare the fine passages at *Il.* iv. 482 ff., xiii. 389 ff., Ap. Rh. iv. 1682 ff., Virgil, *Aen.* ii. 626 ff. See also Bruère in *Ovidiana*, pp. 485–9 for a Silian imitation of our passage (v. 475–516 *passim*).

776. Note the onomatopoeia achieved mainly by an impressive accumulation of consonants in 'prostravit', with the letters *p, d, t,* and especially the repeated *r.* This and similar passages (e.g. *Aen.* vi. 179 ff., xi. 135 ff., Statius, *Theb.* vi. 90 ff.) gives at least a faint echo of Ennius' lines in *Annals,* bk. vi, particularly 183–5 W.:

> fraxinus frangitur atque abies consternitur alta,
> pinus proceras pervortunt; omne sonabat
> arbustum fremitu silvai frondosai.

Observe the *f*s, and, as in our passage, the *p*s and *r*s. Of course none of the later poets can compete with Ennius for fury of sound.

778. omnes germanae : perhaps a shade weak after 'dryades'. Slater (Prolegomena, p. 35) commends the variant 'et nece germanae', cf. xii. 240. For 'nece' in this position of the line see x. 233, xiii. 62, also *A.A.* i. 336 'et nece natorum'. The variant could be right, even though the dryad's death is adequately covered by 'suoque'.

780–1. Ceres shakes the fields with her nod, because they are the element appropriate to her, just as Neptune shakes the sea (603–4). The nod of Zeus will shake Olympus (*Il.* i. 528–30) ἦ καὶ κυανέῃσιν ἐπ' ὀφρύσι νεῦσε Κρονίων / . . . μέγαν δ' ἐλέλιξεν Ὄλυμπον, cf. *Aen.* ix. 106, or even the whole universe (*Met.* i. 179–80). Several scholars (e.g. McKay, p. 177) have thought of the corn as Ceres' hair, which moves when the goddess nods her head. Such figures certainly occur, but here the emphasis is on the fields, not the corn.

784. lacerare fame: 'to torture him with hunger', cf. Pacuvius 131–2 W. 'nam te in tenebrica saepe lacerabo fame / clausam' (which W. understands differently). A capital letter for 'fame' is not apposite here (nor at 812). As with Achelous (see on 549 ff.), Ovid alternates between hunger and personified Hunger, cf. 819.

785–6. At ii. 760 ff. Pallas goes personally to enlist the services of the equally repulsive Invidia, 'quamvis . . . oderat illam' (782). Here, for good reason, the Fates forbid.

The following incident in which Ceres employs the aid of Hunger is based ultimately on *Il.* xiv. 225 ff., where Hera persuades Ὕπνος to send Zeus to sleep. A closer parallel to the present scene occurs in Euripides' *Heracles,* where Λύσσα (Madness) is ordered to attack the hero; Ovid probably also had in mind the Allecto episode in *Aen.* vii (323 ff.). Again, in Nonnus, *Dionysiaca* xlviii. 370 ff. Nemesis is sent from the heights of Taurus to punish Aura for an insult to Artemis; she fulfils her task, and then returns home. This last narrative has some points of close resemblance to Ovid, and so perhaps such

LINES 776–790

139

scenes were to be found in Hellenistic poetry. But our poet makes them peculiarly his own; the visit of Iris to Somnus at xi. 583 ff. is particularly notable.

786. montani numinis: collective.

787. talibus . . . compellat . . . dictis : cf. Ennius, *Annals* 41–2 W. 'exin conpellare pater me voce videtur / his verbis.' The opening and closure of direct speech provide a fruitful field for Ennian reminiscence (cf. 703 n.). Sometimes the Great Man's comfortable redundancy verged on the comic; Lucilius 18 W.'haec ubi dicta dedit, pausam ⟨dedit⟩ ore loquendi' looks a playful parody.

788–90. Est locus . . . / . . . illic: a most elevated way to introduce the epic device of ecphrasis. This involves first portraying a scene, and then fitting into it the events related. So we regularly find patterns like ἔστι πόλις ᾿Εφύρη μυχῷ Ἄργεος ἱπποβότοιο / ἔνθα δὲ Σίσυφος ἔσκεν, etc. (*Il.* vi. 152–3). In Latin a parallel technique, with 'est locus', may have been employed already by Ennius. A single line of the *Annals* has survived (24 W.), 'est locus Hesperiam quam mortales perhibebant', which seems to have been Virgil's model for *Aen.* i. 530–4. See further Austin on *Aen.* iv. 480 and 483.

788. Scythia represented to the poets all that was cold, barren, and deserted (e.g. Aeschylus, *P.V.* 2), and thus is a most fitting dwelling-place for Hunger and her entourage. R. Martin, *R.E.L.* xliv (1966) 286–304 'Virgile et la "Scythie"', gives material concerning the fabled Scythia, and argues that some of Virgil's description refers to a real land known to the Romans—Moesia.

With Ovid's vivid portrayal here compare the abode of Invidia (ii. 760 ff.), of Somnus (xi. 592 ff.), and of Fama (xii. 39 ff.); see also 801 n.

789. sine fruge, sine arbore tellus: these phrases correspond to Greek adjectives with α-privative, ἄκαρπος, ἄδενδρος (cf. 518 n.). Ovid echoed these words when writing of his place of exile 'nudos sine fronde sine arbore campos' (*Tristia* iii. 10. 75).

790. Frigus . . . Pallorque Tremorque: the last two reminiscent of Δεῖμός τε Φόβος τε (*Il.* xi. 37, etc.), though strictly speaking the latter pair are war-spirits, represented in Ovid by Pavor and Terror (iv. 485). Compare the children of Night at Hesiod, *Theogony* 211 ff., those of Strife (ibid. 226 ff.) and the spirits on the *Shield of Heracles* (154 ff.). Virgil enrolls a host of equally unpleasant characters into the *Aeneid* (vi. 274 ff.). See also on 801 ff.

habitant: plural by anticipation, a so-called 'schema Alcmanicum' of which the stock ancient example was Alcman, fr. 2 Page Κάστωρ τε πώλων ὠκέων δματῆρες ἱππόται σοφοὶ / καὶ Πωλυδεύκης κυδρός (see further P. Maas, *Maia* N.S. ix [1957] 157). Compare, with a dual verb, *Il.* v. 774 ἧχι ῥοὰς Σιμόεις συμβάλλετον ἠδὲ Σκάμανδρος.

791. See 16 n. for Ovid's use of 'is'; 'ea' here and 'eam' in 793 have a slightly contemptuous ring.

793. superetque meas certamine vires: in a paradoxical way Ceres also fights against Hunger on the side of Erysichthon, cf. 814–15.

794–5. Demeter's dragon-chariot (cf. v. 642 ff., Nonnus vi. 109 ff.), drawn by snakes sometimes with wings, sometimes without, is a common subject for artistic representation; cf. Daremberg and Saglio, s.v. *Ceres*, p. 1054 and n. 1039.

798. Caucason appellant: as well as the real Caucasus, we can trace in ancient writers another Caucasus, seemingly to be equated with the Rhipaean mountains (J. D. P. Bolton, *Aristeas of Proconnesus*, pp. 39 ff.), from which the North Wind rises. The latter fits the fabulous context here (cf. 788).

    serpentum colla levavit: adapting a phrase which has survived only in the *Certamen Homeri et Hesiodi* (107–8 Allen) αὐχένας ἵππων / ἔκλυον, but no doubt was elsewhere in the epic tradition (cf. Aristophanes, *Peace* 1282–3, Call. *hymn* 5. 9–10).

800. raras: I follow Heinsius, who compared Lucan ix. 438 'hoc tam segne solum raras tamen exerit herbas'. The clear manuscript preference is for 'raris', which may be right; cf., for instance, Pliny, *N.H.* xi. 274, Suetonius, *Div. Aug.* 79 'dentes raros et exiguos et scabros'.

    'Raris' has generally been rejected on the ground that Ovid is not yet describing Hunger herself, only her habitat. That argument is not decisive, but 'raras' still seems preferable to me. The word-order 'unguibus et . . . dentibus' is characteristic of our poet.

801 ff. *The Personification of Hunger*

Personifications appear first in the *Theogony* of Hesiod; thence Ovid could have learnt that Hunger was a child of Strife (227). Also in the latest parts of the *Iliad* we find personification, chiefly of war-spirits. For example, at *Il.* xi. 36–7 a Gorgoneion surrounded by figures of Δεῖμος and Φόβος has been inserted into a much older description of Agamemnon's shield, with the result that the whole picture is thrown into confusion (see Leaf ad loc. and on v. 739–42, Miss Lorimer, *Homer and the Monuments*, pp. 190–1). If we are to judge from contemporary art, then these lines should be ascribed to the seventh century B.C.

In the later epic period abstractions come to be described in greater detail, sometimes allegorically (e.g. the Λιταί at *Il.* ix. 502 ff., see Leaf ad loc.). Ovid's picture of the hideous old woman is distinctly reminiscent of Ἀχλύς in the pseudo-Hesiodic *Shield of Heracles* 264–70 (? first third of sixth cent., R. M. Cook, *CQ* xxxi [1937] 213):

πὰρ δ' Ἀχλὺς εἱστήκει ἐπισμυγερή τε καὶ αἰνή
χλωρὴ αὐσταλέη λιμῷ καταπεπτηυῖα
γουνοπαχής, μακροὶ δ' ὄνυχες χείρεσσιν ὑπῆσαν.
τῆς ἐκ μὲν ῥινῶν μύξαι ῥέον, ἐκ δὲ παρειῶν
αἷμ' ἀπελείβετ' ἔραζ'· ἦ δ' ἄπλητον σεσαρυῖα
εἱστήκει, πολλὴ δὲ κόνις κατενήνοθεν ὤμους,
δάκρυσι μυδαλέη.

The author of the *Shield* specializes in such horrors.

Personifications were also quite familiar to the Romans. Many abstractions were officially deified and had temples in the city (Cicero, *D.N.D.* ii. 79); besides Mens, Fides, Virtus, and Concordia mentioned there, even Febris had altars on the Palatine and Esquiline (Cicero, *De Legibus* ii. 28). But one can hardly prove that personifications are found in Rome before the growth of Greek influence; the cult of Fides, for example, was attributed to Numa, but R. M. Ogilvie doubts whether it can have been so old.

Ovid's description of Hunger is close to that of Invidia at ii. 760 ff. Bearing in mind also the pictures of Somnus (xi. 592 ff.) and Fama (xii. 39 ff.), we can say that Ovid outdoes his fellow poets in detail and vividness—although this passage is hardly so notable as the other three. Yet what is typical of Ovid was not necessarily invented by him; the portrayal of Hunger in the Fairy's Revenge (App. III) is astonishingly close to that of our poet, who may have known the folk-tale through an intermediary source (cf. introduction to the episode).

802. scabrae rubigine fauces: particularly appropriate because 'rubigo' can mean a blight which attacks the crops. In the picture of Invidia 'livent rubigine dentes' (ii. 776) exploits another association of 'rubigo' with backbiting, cf. Martial, bk. xii, Preface 'municipalium rubigo dentium'. Petronius combines the two Ovidian passages for Eumolpus' description of Discord: 'stabant aerati scabra rubigine dentes' (ch. 124, l. 274).

807. Some older editors read 'rigebat' with Heinsius, but 'tumebat' is appropriate; compare the epithet γουνοπαχής in the description of Ἀχλύς at pseudo-Hesiod, *Shield of Heracles* 266, quoted on 801 ff.

808. et immodico prodibant tubere tali: cf. Hesiod, *Works and Days* 497 παχὺν πόδα. Proclus ad loc. quotes an Ephesian law μὴ ἐξεῖναι πατρὶ παῖδας ἀποθέσθαι ἕως ἂν διὰ λιμὸν παχυνθῇ τοὺς πόδας—also [Virgil], *Catal.* 13. 40 'pedes inedia turgidos'.

812. visa tamen sensisse famem est: similarly at xi. 630–1 Iris hastens to leave the dwelling of Sleep 'neque enim ulterius tolerare soporis / vim poterat'.

815 ff. Both Ovid and the Fairy's Revenge make Hunger operate during the prince's sleep. But the dream motif, which also

appears in both, plays a more important part in the folk-tale.
There the prince is taken to the scene of his crime, and, as in
Ovid, given a foretaste of his future sufferings, but the seeds of
hunger are implanted in him by his own sword, left sticking in
the oak (App. III).

815. vento: Hunger is so insubstantial that she floats on the breeze.
On grounds of both sense and metre (avoidance of $\smile\smile\ \smile\smile$ -*a* -*a* at
the line-ending) 'vento' is much superior to 'vecta' (? due to
intrusion from 796).

819. seque viro inspirat: i.e. hunger as opposed to the personified
Hunger. Ovid once more is playing on the two levels, as at ii. 383
(Phoebus) 'lucemque odit, seque ipse diemque', xi. 621 (the god
Somnus) 'excussit . . . sibi se'.

820. spargit: M N here give 'peragit'. But, in spite of Magnus's
defence, the latter has probably intruded from 815. For 'spar-
git' cf. the analogous procedure of Envy (ii. 800–1) 'inspiratque
nocens virus, piceumque per ossa / dissipat et medio *spargit*
pulmone venenum'.

822. antra: the best-supported reading, though, according to
Magnus, from xiii. 777 'sub opaca revertitur antra'. Most editors
have adopted the variant 'arva'. But with 'domos' 'antra' is the
more appropriate; Hunger actually lives in a cave.

823 ff. This dream appears in rather a different form in the Fairy's
Revenge: 'In the night, when the prince lay there asleep, he saw
a dream; a Fairy came to him, and caught him by the hand, as
tight as a vice: she brought him out of his palace, and took him
to the place where the trees had been cut down.' There he is
tortured by heat and cold, and finally attacked by ravening
Hunger (App. III).

823. Winged Sleep is found in literature not before Callimachus
(*hymn* 4. 234 ληθαῖον ἐπὶ πτερὸν ὕπνος ἐρείσει), but earlier in art.

826. delusum: only a fanatical devotion to M can justify 'desue-
tum'—? from 822. Note the piling-up of words to express
Erysicthon's delusion: 'sub imagine—vana—fatigat—delusum
—inani—tenues—nequiquam.'

   inani: 'unreal'. Silius writes of Hannibal in his sleep 'inania
bella gerentem' (i. 69).

827. devorat: 'gulps down'.

828. ardor edendi: stronger than 'amor edendi' (450 n.), cf. the
phrase αἴθων λιμός (no doubt in pseudo-Hesiod, Call. *hymn* 6. 67).
In the Fairy's Revenge: 'As soon as he woke up, his first word
was "I am hungry."'

829. incensaque: Heinsius's conjecture, which gives excellent sense
(cf. 'ardor edendi' 828, 'flamma gulae' 846), and harmonizes
well with 'avidas'. It is not, however, strictly necessary; the

MSS. reading 'immensaque' may be right, stressing the monstrous and superhuman scale of Erysicthon's appetite (cf. 832–3, 843).

830 ff. Attempts at feeding the prince are described in greater detail by Callimachus (*hymn* 6. 68 ff.) and the Fairy's Revenge, where shepherds, butchers, poulterers, hunters, fishermen, and fruiterers all play their part to no avail.

832. inque epulis epulas quaerit: an adaptation of the proverb 'quaerere aquas in aquis', for someone who will not recognize when he is well off (cf. Enk on Propertius i. 9. 16).

835–9. Double (or even triple) similes descend from Homer. The poets will often strive for some artistic contrast between each one—here the simple opposition of fire and water (cf. *Aen.* xii. 521–5, *Il.* xiv. 394–9, *Georgics* iv. 261–3). Sometimes the contrast is more sophisticated, e.g. between a conventional Nature simile and one taken from Roman life (xi. 24–7, Catullus 68. 119–28).

835–6. The first simile may be suggested by Callimachus (*hymn* 6. 89–90) τὰ δ' ἐς βυθὸν οἷα θαλάσσας / ἀλεμάτως ἀχάριστα κατέρρεεν εἴδατα πάντα. Ovid seems to contrast rivers from a far-away land ('peregrinos') with those from a whole country ('de tota . . . terra') bordering on the sea. That is a little odd, and the lines have been suspected (by Zielinski), but unjustly. Claudian expands the comparison with some verbosity: 'ac velut innumeros amnes accedere Nereus / nescit et undantem quamvis hinc hauriat Histrum, / hinc bibat aestivum septeno gurgite Nilum, / par semper similisque manet: sic fluctibus auri expleri calor ille nequit' (*in Rufinum* i. 183–7).

838. faces: preferable might seem 'trabes' (M, by correction according to Magnus), as denoting a wider conflagration. But the vital point is that the fire should, like Erysicthon, be fed intentionally.

839. turbaque voracior ipsa est: 'and is made all the more greedy by abundance'.

841–2. A paradoxical *sententia*, which owes more than a little to commonplace utterances about wealth and misers, e.g. Stobaeus iv. 31. 84 (πλοῦτος) καὶ ὥσπερ ἡ τῶν ὑδεριώντων νόσος (cf. Horace, *Odes* ii. 2. 13) αὔξεται πρὸς τὸ μᾶλλον ποθεῖν ἀφ' ὧν πίμπλαται. See Otto, *Sprichwörter*, s.v. *avarus*.

843–4. Cf. Callimachus, *hymn* 6. 113 ἀλλ' ὅκα τὸν βαθὺν οἶκον ἀνεξήραναν ὀδόντες . . . ; and in the Fairy's Revenge: 'But his insatiability had no bounds, and so in a few years he had consumed all his possessions, and was left in poverty, always hungry.'

844. The attempt of some MSS. to apostrophize Hunger with 'tu quoque', and 'manebas' in 843, is diverting but can hardly be taken seriously. 'Inattenuata' is an Ovidian coinage.

845. implacatae: a Virgilian formation (*Aen.* iii. 420 'implacata Charybdis') equivalent to 'implacabilis', as, for example, 'inaccessus' may mean 'inaccessible'.

846. demisso in viscera censu: this, I think, would strike Roman readers as an intentionally comic phrase, since 'census' had an everyday technical use to describe a man's property-rating, with special reference to the amounts necessary for senatorial or equestrian status; e.g. *Fasti* i. 217–18 'dat census honores / census amicitias.' Juvenal 11. 39–40 'aere paterno / ac rebus mersis in ventrem' seems to echo Ovid. Briefly we glimpse a noble wasting his *patrimonium* (e.g. Cicero, *Phil.* ii. 67).

847. non illo digna parente: cf. *Aen.* vii. 653–4 quoted on 739–40.

848. hanc quoque vendit inops: 'He had nothing more to sell to buy food to eat, nothing but one daughter and one son . . .' (The Fairy's Revenge). The selling of Mestra is in the tradition from pseudo-Hesiod onwards (fr. 43a. 10, cf. 43b); there, however, she is sold not as a slave, but as a prospective wife, in return for the bride-price customary in heroic times (see further 870 n., 873 n.). In Plautus' *Persa* (329 ff.) Saturio the parasite proposes to sell his daughter to alleviate his hunger.

 dominum generosa recusat: Mestra is not a willing accomplice in her father's trickery—indeed, that would spoil the point of the story. Erysicthon sells her through his *patria potestas*, and each time she escapes because of her noble spirit. We may admire as typical in the next few lines the economy with which Ovid gives the essentials of a situation.

850. eripe . . . domino balance **raptae . . . nobis.**

851. Mestra was the mother of Eurypylus by Poseidon. Ovid's chronology, by which this had happened already, is much the neatest. In the Hesiodic *Catalogue* Mestra be snatched away to Cos during her attempts to feed Erysicthon, unless fr. 43a. 68–9 is supplemented so that she was '*not yet* tending her ill-fated father' (cf. McKay, p. 27).

853–4. vultumque virilem / induit: possibly a trace of the form of this legend as given by Ant. Lib. (17. 5): ἄνδρα δὲ γενομένην Αἴθωνι τροφὴν ἀποφέρειν τῷ πατρί, from Nicander's *Heteroeumena* (attempts to torture these words into metre are unwise). Nicander seems not to have treated the story at any length (see introduction to the episode and McKay, pp. 28 f.); it is not clear whether in pseudo-Hesiod Mestra changes first to a man or to an animal.

854. piscem: better than 'pisces'. For the collective cf. 857, xv. 101, Plautus, *Captivi* 184 'venare leporem', 'hunt the hare', *Georgics* iii. 410.

855 ff. This fishing interview which follows (surely invented by Ovid) is quite delightful. The effect is achieved brilliantly by contrasting elevated language with everyday subject-matter. We have the stately periphrasis 'moderator harundinis', 'wielder of the rod', and the complicated syntax with 'sic . . . sic', taken up in turn by Mestra (866–7), all set against this minutely detailed and highly practical prayer. One would like to know why 'Lactantius' changes Mestra 'in piscatorem . . . *processioris aetatis*'; perhaps because of the admirable courtesy with which the two address each other?

857. sic . . .: 'may you prosper *on condition that* you help me'—a very common formula in wishes at all levels of Latin; on epitaphs see Lattimore, *Themes in Greek and Latin Epitaphs*, § 23; among the rhetoricians Seneca, *Suasoriae* 7. 14; in ordinary speech Petronius, chs. 61 and 69. The wish is normally followed by an imperative, as here (861); rather different is 866–7 below, where the *ut*-clause asserts a fact on which Mestra stakes her own profit, cf. Prop. i. 18. 11–12 'sic mihi te referas, levis, ut non altera nostro / limine formosos intulit ulla pedes.'

858. et nullos, nisi fixus, sentiat hamos: he knows all about the one that was hooked but got away. Much better attested than 'nullos' is 'nullus'. But Ovid likes to preserve a balance of nouns and epithets (cf. 278 n., 514 n.); also 'nullus' would not harmonize with the collective 'piscis' (857), since a colloquial strong negative = 'not at all' is hardly conceivable in the *Metamorphoses*.

860. litore in hoc steterat (nam stantem in litore vidi): Ovid's parentheses (usually with some repetition of words) never fail to be witty and elegant. They perform many functions—e.g. a quick story-teller's aside at 851 (emphasis on 'Neptunus'), while here (emphasis on 'vidi') the poor man is utterly bewildered, but will not abandon his one solid fact.

862. illa dei munus bene cedere sensit: these words suggest, without necessarily implying so, that Mestra had previously been offered a gift by Neptune, and now is as delighted as Theseus (Eur. *Hipp.* 1169–70) to find that it really works. The gift would no doubt have been in compensation for her rape (cf. xii. 197 ff., Caenis), and be either a promise to grant prayers, or, more specifically, an offer to change her shape. Periclymenus received a gift of transformation from the sea-god (pseudo-Hesiod, fr. 33a. 12–18, partly quoted at Introduction, p. xx).

862–3. et a se / se quaeri gaudens: cf. ii. 430 of Jupiter in disguise with Callisto 'et sibi praeferri se gaudet'.

863. his est resecuta rogantem: a phrase found only in Ovid, cf. vi. 36, xiii. 749.

865. gurgite: commonly used by the poets for an expanse of sea. **operatus:** so two Heinsian MSS., cf. vii. 746 'studiis operata Dianae'. But 'oneratus' could still be right, 'burdened by my toil', explaining more clearly why she had paid no attention to her surroundings.

866. quoque minus dubites: on the contrary, Mestra's double-banked argument should greatly increase his suspicion. She has been wholly concentrating on the fish, and yet is prepared to swear that in fact no one has passed her way. The man's acceptance of such an argument heightens the atmosphere of pure fantasy.

866–7. sic has deus aequoris artes / adiuvet: a *double entendre*. The fisherman's craft is an 'ars' (τέχνη), and he quite naturally swears by Neptune. At the same time, 'has . . . artes' refers to Mestra's powers of transformation, for which the sea-god is responsible (850–4); at *Od.* iv. 455 Proteus' ability to change himself is called a τέχνη.

Since Mestra swears by Neptune, one would like her to tell the truth at least according to the letter. But no playing with use of words seems to achieve this end; perhaps we should rather concern ourselves with the foolishness of her late owner. McKay (p. 54 n. 3) cites an interesting parallel for the whole scene in a Russian folk-tale.

870. abiit: the final syllable of the perfect in such a case was originally long, and Ovid often reverts to the older scansion. Indeed he seems to delight in placing 'abiit' and similar forms before a vowel (cf. Platnauer, *Latin Elegiac Verse*, pp. 60–1).

illi sua reddita forma est: the proposed restoration at pseudo-Hesiod, fr. 43a. 31–3 runs: . . . ἣ δὲ λυθεῖσα φίλου μετὰ δώματα πατρὸς / ᾤχετ' ἀπαΐξασα, γυνὴ δ' ἄφαρ αὖτις ἔγεντο / πατρὸς ἐνὶ μεγάροισι (see also West on fr. 45). Compare Tzetzes on Lycophron, *Alexandra* 1393: ἣ δὲ πάλιν ἀμείβουσα τὸ εἶδος φεύγουσα πρὸς τὸν πατέρα ἤρχετο (fr. 43b).

In pseudo-Hesiod Erysicthon takes it upon himself to swindle Sisyphus—he could hardly have made a worse choice of victim. Mestra is bought as a bride for Glaucus, then changes shape and returns home. By fr. 43a. 34 Sisyphus has caught up with her, whereupon 'there arose strife and contention between Sisyphus and Aethon over the long-ankled maiden' (lines 36–7). The case was eventually referred to Athena for arbitration, and Erysicthon seems to have come off much the worse (West, *Gnomon* xxxv [1963] 755).

871. transformia corpora: an unusual phrase, which utterly defeated Planudes. Probably the plural is poetic, and the meaning 'a body which could be transformed' rather than 'shapes into which she could turn'. The adjective 'transformis' occurs elsewhere only at *Fasti* i. 373.

872. Dryopeida: 'the Thessalian girl'. Editors have printed 'Triopeida', which again has the slenderest manuscript support (see 751 n.).

tradit: a slightly colloquial word for to sell, cf. Marx on Lucilius 668 M.

873. **nunc equa, nunc ales, modo bos, modo cervus abibat**: the repeated 'nunc... nunc... modo... modo' suggests ἄλλοτε μὲν ... ἄλλοτε δέ, regular in Greek epic for such descriptions (see 862 n.). We suffer here from a lack of detailed sources. Of course Mestra is not being sold as an animal, and the purpose of the transformations is hardly clear; were they for concealment, or for speed to avoid recapture? Also we cannot tell whether the masculine gender of 'cervus' has any significance. Ovid may be influenced by a noun common in Greek, viz. ἔλαφος (McKay, p. 30).

The rationalizing account of Palaephatus (*de Incredibilibus* 23 [24]) is obviously based on the same (? Hesiodic) tradition: ἐδίδοσαν δὲ (sc. Mestra's suitors) οἱ μὲν ἵππους, οἱ δὲ βοῦς, τινὲς δὲ πρόβατα..., cf. Tzetzes on Lycophron, *Alexandra* 1393.

875 ff. Scholars have wondered why the selling of Mestra could no longer support Erysicthon (cf. McKay, pp. 44–5). For Ovid at least, the answer is plain enough—Erysicthon's hunger becomes progressively more violent (793, 834, 838–9).

876. **dederatque gravi nova pabula morbo**: a typical paradox. In the sense of adding fuel to the flames and making something worse, 'dare pabula morbo' is quite a familiar idea, e.g. Propertius iii. 7. 3 (Pecunia) 'tu vitiis hominum crudelia pabula praebes', cf. *Fasti* i. 214 'atque ipsae vitiis sunt alimenta vices.' But here the metaphor of feeding is also literally appropriate (cf. 135 for a similar mixture); hence the paradoxical effect. Close translation is difficult, but A. E. Watts caught the essence well: 'When all was gone that could his pangs appease, / And nought was nourished save the dread disease'. Burman's 'deerantque' deserves a mention, and has pleased some scholars. But we should try to explain such difficulties rather than emending them away.

McKay (p. 51) considers taking 'nova pabula' as 'strange, untoward food', with a suggestion of cannibalism. Agathias (*Anth. Pal.* xi. 379) is not very strong evidence for a cannibal Erysicthon, but this element appears in the Fairy's Revenge, 'He flings himself on his daughter to devour her.' Even so, Ovid's words are better explained as in the last paragraph.

877–8. With a certain reticence, Achelous stops before the point of death. The prince in the Fairy's Revenge comes to a similar end: 'Then he began to tear at his own flesh, and to eat, insomuch that he died, his very nails actually in his mouth.'

878. **et infelix minuendo corpus alebat**: the elder Seneca (*Controversiae* iii.7) tells of a speaker who said 'ipse sui et alimentum erat et damnum', and was immediately accused of copying Ovid—

148 COMMENTARY

a reminder that the traffic between Roman poetry and rhetoric
went both ways.

879–84. In these lines Ovid prepares a transition to the first
episode of bk. ix, in which Achelous recounts how he fought
with Heracles for the hand of Deianira, and, in spite of being
able to change shape, was defeated and lost one of his horns.
Transitional passages, bridging two books like this, help to give
the whole poem a greater sense of continuity.

879. nempe: thus Polle. It is hard to extract any sense from the
manuscripts' 'saepe'. The latter could not well refer to Achelous'
number of possible shapes, for they are just three (881–2) and,
in any case, covered by 'numero finita' (880). Nor is there point
in saying that Achelous 'often' has the power to transform him-
self. On the other hand, Ovid uses 'nempe' freely, and the em-
phasis is quite welcome here.

881–2. At Sophocles, *Trachiniae* 11–13 Deianira herself describes
how Achelous came to woo her φοιτῶν ἐναργὴς ταῦρος, ἄλλοτ' αἰόλος /
δράκων ἑλικτός, ἄλλοτ' ἀνδρείῳ κύτει / βούπρῳρος. River-gods were often
represented as human in shape, but wearing horns (cf. Farnell,
Cults of the Greek States v. 422–3). And although Achelous is
clearly not in bull form at the moment, by a certain licence
the missing horn is still obvious (884). We find an interesting
reflection of this incident among the exploits of Theseus (cf.
268 n.). The hero is said to have broken off a horn while fighting
the Marathonian bull; M. L. West's restoration of οἰόκερως at
Callimachus fr. 260. 1 (*Harvard Studies in Class. Phil.* lxxii
[1968] 130) illustrates the story.

881. qui nunc sum: older editors read 'quod nunc sum'. Either
would be equally good Latin (cf. Shackleton Bailey on Proper-
tius i. 12. 11), but 'qui' is better attested.

flector in anguem: 'I twist myself into a snake', an enter-
prising and successful phrase which suggests sinuous movement.
The poet may allude to a simpler meaning, by which 'flecti'
becomes a mere synonym for 'mutari' (Lucretius iii. 516, 755).
But the more picturesque rendering is quite justified, cf. 760 n.

882. armenti ... dux: cf. 'dux gregis' = 'aries' (vii. 311, etc.). Such
phrases suggest an Alexandrian refinement of the Hesiodic
'kenning' (see 376 n.); one may compare Aratus' πατέρες ... γυρίνων
(*Phaen.* 947), 'fathers of the tadpoles' i.e. frogs, imitated by
Nicander (*Ther.* 620, *Alex.* 563).

vires in cornua sumo: the accusative has the idea of concen-
trating all his strength in his horns. Perhaps Ovid remembers
Virgil's 'irasci in cornua' (*Georgics* iii. 232).

883. cornua, dum potui!: he can no longer use the plural. The
repetition is half-pathetic, half-humorous, and very nice. These
are among the most effective positions for a repeated word, as,

for example, *Aen.* ii. 405–6 'ad caelum tendens ardentia *lumina* frustra, / *lumina*, nam teneras arcebant vincula palmas.'

884. The finish is well contrived, to make a satisfactory ending, and yet to provoke curiosity, so that Ovid can begin bk. ix with 'Quae gemitus truncaeque deo Neptunius heros / causa rogat frontis'.

APPENDIX I

THE CALYDONIAN BOAR-HUNT IN AN ELEGIAC FRAGMENT

THIS piece appeared first in vol. ii of the *Recherches de Papyrologie* (1962), pp. 99–111, edited by M. Papathomopoulos. A new text was produced in *Studi Italiani di Filologia Classica* xxxv (1963), pp. 205–27 by J. W. B. Barns and Hugh Lloyd-Jones, to both of whom I am grateful for permission to reprint the following extract.

The style of this fragment suggests the early third century B.C., before the influence of Callimachus became so strong. Its authorship is quite uncertain. The mediocre quality may inhibit attribution to a better-known figure such as Alexander of Aetolia, Hermesianax, or Phanocles.

14   . . . σῦν ἀργιόδοντα

15   ὅς τε δι' Αἰτωλ]ῶν ἐρχόμενος καμάτους

χήλῃσιν μα]λερῇσι—τὸ γὰρ φίλον ἔπλετο κούρῃ—

σίνετο μὲν σῖτ]ον σίνετο δὲ σταφυλάς,

μῆλα δὲ καὶ σκύλ]ακας θηρήτορας ἐξενάριξεν,

μέσφ' ὅτε οἱ μ]ελίην πῆξεν ὑπὸ λαπάρην

20   Οἰνείδης Με]λέαγρος· ὁ γὰρ θηρέστατος ἦεν

ἡρώων πάντ]ων σὺν τότ' ἀθροισαμένων.

ἦλθ' ἀπὸ γῆς Θη]σεὺς Πιτθηίδος, ἦλυθε δ' αἴθων

κοίρανος Ἀγκ]αῖος σὺν μεγάλῳ πελέκει,

24   ἦλθον καὶ Λή]δης κοῦροι καὶ Ζηνὸς ἄνακτος . . .

The supplements, some of which can be little more than *exempli gratia*, are as follows: 15 Ll.-J. 16 Ll.-J. 17 Ll.-J. 18 ed. pr. 19 Ll.-J. 20 ed. pr. 21 Ll.-J. 22 W. S. Barrett. 23 Ll.-J. 24 ed. pr.

'. . . a white-tusked boar, which, coming through the tilled fields of the Aetolians, despoiled corn and grapes with its violent hooves—for such was the Maiden's pleasure—and ravaged flocks and hunting-dogs, until Meleager son of Oeneus stuck his ash-spear under its flank, for he was the best hunter of all the heroes then gathered together. Theseus came from the land of Pittheus, burning prince Ancaeus came with his great axe; there came too the sons of Leda and lord Zeus . . .'

APPENDIX II

IN THE TRADITION OF BAUCIS AND PHILEMON

A FRAGMENT OF THE EPIC POET DIONYSIUS

THE date of this Dionysius (hardly to be equated with D. Periegetes, who wrote under Hadrian) remains obscure—the third century A.D. may be as likely an estimate as any. He is credited with two epics, entitled *Bassarica* and *Gigantias*; the fragment below (*Archiv für Papyrusforschung* vii, p. 7, fr. 5 verso) had been attributed to the *Bassarica* by most scholars, but Heitsch prefers the *Gigantias* (fr. 26 in his *Die griechischen Dichterfragmente der römischen Kaiserzeit*). My interpretation, if correct, would favour the *Bassarica*, because Dionysus is a regular guest on such occasions. I am grateful to Mr. P. J. Parsons for re-examining the papyrus, and to Dr. M. L. West for comments.

> τοῖς ἐνὶ μὲν κύαμοι ζ[
> οἴκυλά τε ζειαί τε περ[
> αὐτὰρ ἐπὴν χαλκὸς μ[
> τινθαλέος ζείῃσι τα [
> 5 δὴ τότ' ἐγὼ θάλαμόνδ[ε
> ερχομαι ὄφρα κε δαῖτα [
> ....]ι κάγκανα κῆλα [
> ....]ν ὕδω[ρ

Text Line 6 Wilamowitz's ἔρχομαι is acceptable (P. J. P.).

7 Previous editors have given ...]ν. φῆ κα]ὶ (A. S. H.) 'seems to suit space and trace. The trace is a single vertical. ... I think that a vertical fibre has come off just before the vertical, and obliterated any trace immediately preceding' (P. J. P.).

8 Previous editors have given ...]ϵθ'.

Commentary

1–2. Cf. *Od.* iv. 603–4 (horse-fodder produced by the plain of Sparta) ... ᾧ ἔνι μὲν λωτὸς πολύς, ἐν δὲ κύπειρον / πυροί τε ζειαί τε ἰδ' εὐρυφυὲς κρῖ λευκόν. Here τοῖς may refer to some kind of receptacle, but there is no indication whether the food is being stored

152 APPENDIX II

or cooked—for the latter possibility cf. *Fasti* v. 509 'stant calices; minor inde fabas, holus alter habebat.'

1. M. L. W. suggests κύαμοι ζ[οφοειδέες, comparing *Il.* xiii. 589 κύαμοι μελανόχροες. The fact that ζοφοειδής is a Nicandrean word (*Theriaca* 256) favours this; similarities of language between Dionysius and Nicander have been noted before.

2. οἴκυλα: a very rare word = 'pulse' (LSJ, *Supplement*, p. 107). M. L. W. adds, for example, περ[ιθλαστοί τ' ἐρέβινθοι.

3–5. Cf. *Il.* xviii. 349–50 (the washing of Patroclus' body) αὐτὰρ ἐπεὶ δὴ ζέσσεν ὕδωρ ἐνὶ ἤνοπι χαλκῷ / καὶ τότε δὴ λοῦσαν, etc.

4. τινθαλέος: again rare. It was perhaps an Attic word, which Callimachus used for local colour in his *Hecale* (see Pf. on fr. 247); also at Nicander, *Alex.* 445, 463.

5. θάλαμόνδε suggests itself, but is not the only possibility. When Penelope goes θάλαμόνδε (*Od.* xxi. 8), she goes to the store-room. Here the significance is not obvious.

7. φῆ κα]ί: D.'s variant on the Homeric ἦ καί, cf. fr. 9 verso 26 Heitsch φῆ καὶ μέσσον ὄρουσεν ἀνὰ στρατόν. Of course the reading is not certain, but the closure of direct speech after line 6 seems to fit the context; it explains why the dry sticks and water (7–8) are mentioned after the boiling of the cauldron (3–4). Note also the effective alliteration.

κάγκανα κῆλα: H.H., *Hermes* 112 offers κάγκανα κᾶλα; κῆλα is a hyper-Ionic form.

The style of this fragment agrees with that of the better-preserved passages (especially fr. 9 verso Heitsch, *A.P.F.* vii, pp. 3–5, Page, Loeb *Greek Literary Papyri* [Poetry], pp. 538–40). We find the same tinge of Homeric colouring in the syntax and individual phrases; the general style is closer to Homer than to Callimachus, and certainly quite unlike Nonnus. But the influence of learned Hellenistic poetry shows both in subject-matter and in the use of rare words (οἴκυλα, τινθαλέος) and forms (κῆλα).

Since the structure of this passage is apparent even from the half-lines, a tentative reconstruction may be worth while. The speaker describes preparations for a meal. Although the food seems undistinguished (1–2), it is presumably being offered to those present: ' ". . . in which there are [? dark] beans, . . ., pulse, wheat [? and . . .]. But when the cauldron . . . becomes hot and boils . . ., then will I go to the chamber, so that [? you may eat] the meal." So he (she) spake, and, [? taking] dry sticks [? from . . .], [? poured] water [? into . . .].' Details are of course arguable, but it is tempting to see here another domestic episode in the Hecale–Baucis and Philemon tradition.

In its subject-matter, Dionysius' *Bassarica* prefigured Nonnus' *Dionysiaca*, describing the god's eastern conquests. Now an epic on this theme would need contrasting digressions to avoid unbearable monotony; so perhaps here someone is unwittingly entertaining Bacchus, and Nonnus was not the first poet to include such an episode in a Dionysus epic.

APPENDIX III

THE FAIRY'S REVENGE, OR *MYRMIDONIA AND PHARAONIA*

THIS folk-story was told to Jacob Zarraftis by an old woman
from Asphendiou on Cos near the end of the last century. I repro-
duce part of R. M. Dawkins's translation (*Forty-five Stories from
the Dodekanese*, pp. 334 ff.) by kind permission of the Cambridge
University Press. For a discussion of the tale's origin and a sum-
mary of the earlier parts see introduction to Erysicthon, pp. 130 ff.

. . . He buried the king his father with great parade and honour
and also the others, and afterwards he takes some young men with
sharp axes, and goes and lays the chopper to the poor silent trees,
which stood there like beautiful maidens, children of the heroes of
old. Some chopped here and some there and some further on, and
ten fine youths with the king's son were chopping at a great oak-
tree, the strokes of their axes making a terrible din. In a little
while they had half cut through it, all the way round; then each of
them gave it yet once more a powerful stroke with his axe. Then
there was heard a cry of 'Ah!' from the midst of the oak, and so the
youths stood there trembling. But the cruel prince shouts to them:
'Smite; pay no heed to Spirits, to their lying murmurs and groans.'
The youths with their axes deal still stronger blows, and the
blood spurted out from a place where the axe of one of them had
struck: it jetted straight out, and, lo, from where it fell a reek
arose. 'Oh, ye who fear not God!' was then heard, again a voice
from the midst of the blood, and the youths in a moment cast their
axes on the ground and looked into one another's eyes trembling
with fear. The cruel prince looked at them furiously, shouting out
savagely: 'Smite, you dogs; do not stay.' And because they were
afraid of him they all began again. One alone hesitated, for the
blood was running in front of him. But the oak began to rustle,
groaning like a human creature, and after a few more strokes
from the men it swayed and fell. In that terrible fall much small
wood was broken and crushed beneath it with a noise as if it were
a palace crashing to destruction. The youths drew to one side,
looking and listening as the whole tree fell in terrible ruin. The
blood did not cease to run, and when the thundering noise of the
fall was over, the voice was again heard coming from the severed
trunk close to the roots of the tree, and it said: 'Even as God

punished your wicked father, even so and three times worse will
He punish you.' They all then turned towards the voice, and they
saw a girl's head covered with blood and round it her hair all
dishevelled, there in the very place where the blood was dripping.
The youths were filled with terror; the hair on their skin stood on
end and their hearts failed. And the cruel son of the king turned
pale with fear and anger together, and cried out like a madman:
'Whoever you may be of the female spirits, run howling like a dog
and eat your own ravening tongue.' He draws his sword, raises it
on high and rushes upon her like a madman, and with all his
strength brings his sword down on her. Then he tries to draw
back his sword and he cannot. This he could not, because in his
great mad fury he had brought his sword down, not on the body
of the girl, but without knowing it on the trunk of the tree, and in
it the sword was wedged. Then fear came upon him; trembling he
leaves his sword and runs off like a madman to his palace. When
they saw their king go the youths too went off after him, full of
terror. And when the rest saw them they laid their axes on their
shoulders in great haste and went away after them.
   . . . In the night, when the prince lay there asleep, he saw a dream:
a fairy came to him and caught him by the hand as tight as a vice;
she brought him out of his palace and took him to the place where
the trees had been cut down. She says to him: 'Stay and behold
what you did when you cut down the trees.' He looks and sees that
from all the trees that had been cut down there was going up
a fire as from a furious burning, and the fires were all around him,
a thing truly terrifying. And then all the fires gradually joined
almost in one, and the prince trembled at the brightness and the
fierce heat which from time to time singed his hair. Later all the
fires unite and become one great conflagration beyond the powers
of vision, and full in the midst the prince was burning and friz-
zling. Cries as if bewitched, leapings and contortions! But how
could the prince escape? Wherever he ran he was burning and on
fire, and the more he ran the more his flame was kindled. The
tongues of the unheard-of conflagration ascended to mid-heaven,
and above him far up in the sky, shot through with light there
appeared the fairy with outstretched hand shaking her finger at
him threateningly and saying: 'This and very much worse is the
lot of those who cut my beautiful trees.'
   In a little while the fires were quenched entirely, and from the
sores where the prince had been burned there flowed a dropsical
humour, and he cried out in great agony from the pain. Im-
mediately then there set in an unendurable cold from the moun-
tains; every north wind in the world with its harshness was there
in that fire-ravaged place. The prince began to shiver and his
lower jaw to shake up and down and his teeth to chatter like the

bones in a skeleton. His wounds at once broke in dry cracks right down to his bones, and with the shaking of his body they stretched and slackened; he suffered such pain that he could not speak. Wherever he turned his eyes all that he could see was the fairy, and she was shaking her dreadful finger at him threateningly, and he heard her saying: 'This and very much worse is the lot of those who cut my beautiful trees.'

Then suddenly he sees something afar off moving very slowly and coming towards him. Presently it came near him, and what does he see? It was an old woman, hunchbacked as a hook, and her hair in its filth hung disordered on her scabby head; her forehead was all wrinkled, covered with a scaly rust; her eyebrows had half fallen out and were hardly to be seen for pimples and pustules; her eyes were sunken deep as though in basins; her nose was eaten away—far and away may this be from us!—by gnawing ulcers; her mug was as yellow as a sulphur candle; her lips were white and black, covered with slaver; her teeth were like axes hung up in a row, dirty black and all rotted into holes; her body was skin and bone; her ribs you could count, so lean was she; inside her you could see her entrails; the bones of her hips in broken array stuck out like dugs; where the joints should fit they were coming apart, she was so decrepit; the cap-bones of her knees seemed to stand out like the pulleys in wells; she was altogether a terrible old maumet.

In the plight the prince then was he could not stir to escape from her coming, and so she came right up close to him. By his side was his sword, still wedged in the trunk of the oak-tree. She reached out her disjointed hand, and just as if it had been set on springs she stretched it out to the sword. She snatches it away in her hand; raises herself to her full height and becomes three times as tall and three times as big. Then, like a priest in the ritual, three times she breathes on the sword, filling every part of it with seeds like the knots in measly pork. Then like a virago she raises the sword high above him, and with her terrible voice says to him: 'I am the Ravening Hunger.' Then the prince was so much frightened that he opened his mouth a full span and cried out: 'Oh, oh, oh!' As he cried out thus, she plunged the sword right down from his mouth into his belly; then she drew it out, and all the seeds of the ravening hunger remained there in his entrails.

At once he was aware of hunger, and with his tongue he licked the bloody sword as it was being withdrawn. And when he had licked it, he began to feel thirst unquenchable and hunger insatiable. Then he engulfs everything before him, and so abides in rivers, in wells, and in cisterns where there is water. But satiety his thirst could never attain. All the victuals of the world were set before him, and still he wanted more to appease his hunger. And so great was the lust of his thirst and of his hunger that it woke him up from his dream.

As soon as he woke up his first word was: 'I am hungry.' And at once they made ready for him various foods, and he would eat them all and still ask for more. The palace servants did nothing else at that time but cook him different dishes, but yet he could never have enough. His shepherds every day used to bring milk, curds, butter, lambs, cream cheeses and cheeses of all sorts; his butchers every day of his herds of oxen slaughtered the best and sent them to him; the poulterers sent fowls, the hunters game of various kinds, the fishermen fish in abundance, the fruiterers fruit of all sorts, and whatever he fancied was at once brought and set before him. But his insatiability had no bounds, and so in a few years he had consumed all his possessions and was left in poverty, always hungry.

He had nothing more to sell to buy food to eat, nothing but one daughter and one son. His son he at last thought fit to sell, and so he managed for yet some days. Then he tried to sell his daughter, but he could find no one to buy her. Then in his furious hunger he flings himself on his daughter to devour her. But by her good fortune her brother happened to be there; he snatched her away from him and they ran off, and so the poor girl escaped. Then he began to tear at his own flesh and to eat it, insomuch that he died, his very nails actually in his mouth.

APPENDIX IV

SELECT BIBLIOGRAPHY

BOISSONADE J. F., *Opera*, vol. v of Lemaire's edition, containing the translation of Planudes. Paris, 1822.

BURMAN P., *Opera*, vol. ii, *Metamorphoses*. With notes of N. Heinsius and others. Amsterdam, 1727.

COLLINS A. J. F. and HAYES B. J., *Metamorphoses viii*. With notes. University Tutorial Press, 1925.

CRUMP M. M., *The Epyllion from Theocritus to Ovid*. Oxford, 1931.

DEFERRARI R. J., BARRY M. I., and McGUIRE M. R. P., *A Concordance of Ovid*. Washington, The Catholic University of America Press, 1939.

DURSTELER K., *Die Doppelfassungen in Ovids Metamorphosen*. Hamburg, 1940.

EHWALD R., *Opera*, vol. ii, *Metamorphoses*. Editio Maior, Leipzig, 1915. Based on the second edition of R. Merkel (Leipzig, 1881).

—— Fourth edition (1916) of vol. ii (bks. viii–xv) of the Haupt–Korn *Metamorphoses* commentary. Fifth edition, with corrections and added bibliography by M. von Albrecht. Weidmann, Zürich/Dublin, 1966.

FRÄNKEL H., *Ovid, a poet between two worlds*. Univ. of California Press, 1945.

HERESCU N. I., editor, *Ovidiana, Recherches sur Ovide*. Paris, 1958. With the review by Brooks Otis, *AJP* lxxxi (1960) 82–9.

KAKRIDIS J. TH., *Homeric researches* (including a study of the Meleager legend). Lund, 1949.

LAFAYE G., *Les Métamorphoses d'Ovide et leurs modèles grecs*. Paris, 1904.

—— *Metamorphoses*, vol. ii (bks. vi–x). Third edition, Paris, 1960.

LEE A. G., *Metamorphoses i*, with commentary. Cambridge, 1953.

LENZ F. W., *Ovid's Metamorphoses*.[1] Prolegomena to a revision of Hugo Magnus's edition. Weidmann, Zürich/Dublin, 1967.

---

[1] I regret not having seen this work before my own was complete.

LUDWIG W., *Struktur und Einheit der Metamorphosen Ovids*. de Gruyter, Berlin, 1965.

McKAY K. J., 'Erysichthon, a Callimachean Comedy', *Mnemosyne*, Supplementum septimum. Leiden, E. J. Brill, 1962.

MAGNUS H., *Metamorphoses*, including *narrationes* of 'Lactantius'. Berlin, 1914. With a review by E. K. Rand, *CP* xi (1916) 46–60.

OTIS B., *Ovid as an epic poet*. Cambridge, 1966. With a review by J. P. Sullivan, *The Oxford Review* 4 (Hilary 1967) 72–80.

SLATER D. A., *Towards a text of the Metamorphosis of Ovid*. Apparatus Criticus, including *narrationes* of 'Lactantius'. Oxford, 1927. Based on the second edition of Riese (Leipzig, 1889).

SUMMERS W. C., *Metamorphoses viii*. With notes. Cambridge, 1901.

VARIORUM, *Opera*, vol. iv, *Metamorphoses viii–xv*. With notes of Bentley and others. Oxford, 1826.

WILKINSON L. P., *Ovid recalled*. Cambridge, 1955.

Additional Bibliography (1983)

VON ALBRECHT, M., *Die Parenthese in Ovids Metamorphosen, und ihre dichterische Funktion*, Würzburg, 1963.

ANDERSON, W. S., *Metamorphoses vi–x*, with Commentary, Univ. of Oklahoma, 1972.

—— *Metamorphoses*, Bibliotheca Teubneriana, 1977.

BÖMER, F., Commentary on *Metamorphoses viii–ix*, Heidelberg, 1977.

COLEMAN, R., 'Structure and Intention in the Metamorphoses', *CQ* NS 21 (1971), 461–72.

CURRIE, H. MacL., 'Ovid and the Roman Stage', in *Aufstieg und Niedergang der Römischen Welt*, II (*edd*. Temporini and Haase, 1981), pp. 2701–42.

GALINSKY, K., *Ovid's Metamorphoses: an introduction to the basic aspects*, Oxford, 1975.

KENNEY, E. J. 'The Style of the Metamorphoses', in *Ovid* (*ed*. J. W. Binns [Routledge and Kegan Paul]), pp. 116–53.

LYNE, R. O. A. M., *Ciris, a poem attributed to Vergil*, Cambridge, 1978.

ADDENDA TO INTRODUCTION AND COMMENTARY (1983)

p. xix. I now feel that the transformation of Rome into the World's capital is just an incidental piece of cleverness.

line 98. *tellusque tibi pontusque negetur*: cf. Euripides, *Hippolytus* 1030.

156. *monstri . . . biformis* (cf. 133 and 169): The Minotaur was called σίμορφος in Euripides, *Meleager* (*Lustrum* 1981–2, p. 188 fr. 692), whence no doubt 'biformis' in Virgil (*Aen.* vi 25) and Ovid.

298–328. *The Catalogue.* In Euripides' *Meleager* 'nuntius inducitur describens quo quisque habitu fuerit ex ducibus qui ad aprum capiendum convenerant' (Macrobius, *Sat.* v. 18. 17, quoting Eur. fr. 530 *TGF*²).

317 ff. Atlanta's appearance at the end of the Catalogue recalls the similar placing of Camilla at *Aen.* vii. 803 ff.

322–3. *dicere . . possis*: not un-epic, but derived from Homer's φαίης, 'you would say' (*e.g. Il.* iii. 220, 392, cf. *Aen.* viii. 676 'videres').

421. Without doubt the text is sound.

549 ff. (playing on different levels of personification). R. G. Austin compares the treatment of the river-god Vulturnus in Statius, *Silvae* iv. 3. 67 ff.

611–724 (p. 106). We now know more about Callimachus' Molorchus (P. J. Parsons, *ZPE* 25 [1977], 1–50). Call. fr. 177 about the poor man and the mousetrap, may also belong to the same *aetion* (E. Livrea, *ZPE* 34 [1979], 37 ff.).

741 ff. and **751 ff.** A curious adaptation in Lucan iii. 399 ff. and 426 ff. with Julius Caesar taking the part of Erysicthon!

757 ff. The series of portents which occur as Erysicthon attacks the tree (groans, blood and a voice) may be partly modelled on Aeneas' experience at the tomb of Polydorus (*Aen.* iii. 26 ff.).

835–6. David West would interpret as follows: the sea receives tributary rivers from the whole earth ('de tota . . terra'), but remains unsatisfied: 'peregrinos' may mean that in hot countries (not in Italy) rivers go dry in the summer, with an implied conceit that the sea drinks them up ('ebibit').

855 ff. The fishing interview almost certainly comes from Plautus, *Rudens* 306–24 (Currie, [see Bibliography] pp. 2736–7). This is particularly interesting, because it shows Ovid drawing yet another genre, Comedy, into the *Metamorphoses* (see Introduction, pp. xxiv–xxv). For comic colouring in the *Aeneid*, see Austin on *Aen.* i. 321.

INDEX OF ANCIENT AUTHORS AND PASSAGES CITED

Figures denote page numbers. Only the more important references from an Ovidian viewpoint are given here. In many cases further cross-references will be found at the indicated places in the Commentary or Introduction.

GENERAL INDEX